S0-ADT-698

BOOK PLACE
6122 Lake Murray Blvd.
La Mesa, CA 91942
(619) 462-4200

*Beautiful María
of My Soul*

ALSO BY

Oscar Hijuelos

The Mambo Kings Play Songs of Love

Our House in the Last World

The Fourteen Sisters of Emilio Montez O'Brien

Mr. Ives' Christmas

Empress of the Splendid Season

A Simple Habana Melody

Dark Dude

Beautiful María of My Soul

Or the *True* Story of
María García y Cifuentes,
the Lady Behind a Famous Song

A NOVEL

OSCAR HIJUELOS

HYPERION
New York

This is a work of fiction. Any references to real people, events, establishments, organizations, or locales are intended only to give the fiction a sense of reality and authenticity, and are used fictitiously. All other names, characters, and places, and all dialogue and incidents portrayed in this book are the product of the author's imagination.

Library of Congress Cataloging-in-Publication Data

Hijuelos, Oscar.
  Beautiful María of my soul / Oscar Hijuelos. — 1st ed.
    p. cm.
  ISBN: 978-1-4013-2334-9
  1. Musicians—Fiction. 2. Brothers—Fiction. 3. Cuba—Fiction.
4. Musical fiction. I. Title.
  PS3558.I376B43 2010
  813'.54—dc22
      2009035386

Hyperion books are available for special promotions and premiums. For details contact the HarperCollins Special Markets Department in the New York office at 212-207-7528, fax 212-207-7222, or email spsales@harpercollins.com.

Book design by Shubhani Sarkar

FIRST EDITION

10 9 8 7 6 5 4 3 2 1

TO THE MEMORY OF
AUGUST WILSON AND GUILLERMO CABRERA INFANTE

ACKNOWLEDGMENTS

I would like to thank Will Balliett, my editor at Hyperion, and his colleagues Ellen Archer and Gretchen Young, as well as Jennifer Lyons, Karen Levinson, and Lori Marie Carlson for their invaluable support during the writing of this book.

Beautiful María
of My Soul

PART I

Cuba, 1947

ONE

Over forty years before, when Nestor Castillo's future love, one María García y Cifuentes, left her beloved *valle* in the far west of Cuba, she could have gone to the provincial capital of Pinar del Río, where her prospects for finding work might be as good—or bad—as in any place; but because the truck driver who'd picked her up one late morning, his gargoyle face hidden under the lowered brim of a lacquered cane hat, wasn't going that way and because she'd heard so many things—both wonderful and sad—about Havana, María decided to accompany him, that cab stinking to high heaven from the animals in the back and from the thousands of hours he must have driven that truck with its loud diesel engine and manure-stained floor without a proper cleaning. He couldn't have been more *simpático,* and at first he seemed to take pains not to stare at her glorious figure, though he couldn't help but smile at the way her youthful beauty certainly cheered things up. Okay, he was missing half his teeth, looked like he swallowed shadows when he opened his mouth, and had a bulbous, knobbed face, the sort of ugly man, somewhere in his forties or fifties—she couldn't tell—who could never have been good looking, even as a boy. Once he got around to tipping up his brim, however, she could see that his eyes were spilling over with kindness, and despite his filthy fingernails she liked him for the thin crucifix he wore around his neck—a sure sign, in her opinion, that he had to be a good fellow—*un hombre decente.*

Heading northeast along dirt roads, the Cuban countryside with its stretches of farms and pastures, dense forests and flatlands gradually rising, they brought up clouds of red dust: along some tracks it was so hard

3

to breathe that María had to cover her face with a kerchief. Still, to be racing along at such bewildering speeds, of some twenty or thirty miles an hour, overwhelmed her. She'd never even ridden in a truck before, let alone anything faster than a horse and carriage, and the thrill of traveling so quickly for the first time in her life seemed worth the queasiness in her stomach, it was so exciting and frightening at the same time. Naturally, they got to talking.

"So, why you wanna go to Havana?" the fellow—his name was Sixto—asked her. "You got some problems at home?"

"No." She shook her head.

"What are you gonna do there, anyway? You know anyone?"

"I might have some cousins there, from my *mamá*'s side of the family"—she made a sign of the cross in her late mother's memory. "But I don't know. I think they live in a place called Los Humos. Have you heard of it?"

"Los Humos?" He considered the matter. "Nope, but then there are so many hole-in-the-wall neighborhoods in that city. I'm sure there'll be somebody to show you how to find it." Then, picking at a tooth with his pinkie: "You have any work? A job?"

"No, *señor*—not yet."

"What are you going to do, then?"

She shrugged.

"I know how to sew," she told him. "And how to roll tobacco—my *papito* taught me."

He nodded, scratched his chin. She was looking at herself in the rearview mirror, off which dangled a rosary. As she did, he couldn't resist asking her, "Well, how old are you anyway, *mi vida*?"

"Seventeen."

"Seventeen! And you have nobody there?" He shook his head. "You better be careful. That's a rough place, if you don't know anyone."

That worried her; travelers coming through her *valle* sometimes called it a city of liars and criminals, of people who take advantage. Still, she preferred to think of what her *papito* once told her about Havana, where he'd lived for a time back in the 1920s when he was a traveling musician. Claimed it was as beautiful as any town he'd ever seen, with lovely parks and ornate stone buildings that would make her eyes pop out of her head. He would have stayed there if anybody had cared about the kind of country music his trio played—performing in those sidewalk cafés and for the tourists in the hotels was hard enough, but once that terrible thing happened—not just when sugar prices collapsed, but when the depression came along and not even the American tourists showed up as much as they used to—there had been no point to his staying there. And so it was back to the *guajiro*'s life for him.

That epoch of unfulfilled ambitions had made her *papito* sad and sometimes a little careless in his treatment of his family, even his lovely daughter, María, on whom, as the years had passed, he sometimes took out the shortcomings of his youth. That's why, whenever that driver Sixto abruptly reached over to crank the hand clutch forward, or swatted at a pesty fly buzzing the air, she'd flinch, as if she half expected him to slap her for no reason. He hardly noticed, however, no more than her *papito* did in the days of her own melancholy.

"But I heard it's a nice city," she told Sixto.

"*Coño, sí,* if you have a good place to live and a good job, but—" And he waved the thought off. "Ah, I'm sure you'll be all right. In fact," he went on, smiling, "I can help you maybe, huh?"

He scratched his chin, smiled again.

"How so?"

"I'm taking these pigs over to this slaughterhouse, it's run by a family called the Gallegos, and I'm friendly enough with the son that he might agree to meet you . . ."

And so it went: once Sixto had dropped off the pigs, he could bring her into their office and then who knew what might happen. She had told him, after all, that she'd grown up in the countryside, and what girl from the countryside didn't know about skinning animals, and all the rest? But when

María made a face, not managing as much as a smile the way she had over just about everything else he said, he suggested that maybe she'd find a job in the front office doing whatever people in those offices do.

"Do you know how to read and write?"

The question embarrassed her.

"Only a few words," she finally told him. "I can write my name, though."

Seeing that he had made her uncomfortable, he rapped her on the knee and said, "Well, don't feel bad, I can barely read and write myself. But whatever you do, don't worry—your new friend Sixto will help you out, I promise you that!"

She never became nervous riding with him, even when they had passed those stretches of the road where the workers stopped their labors in the fields to wave their hats at them, after which they didn't see a soul for miles, just acres of tobacco or sugarcane going on forever into the distance. It would have been so easy for him to pull over and take advantage of her; fortunately this Sixto wasn't that sort, even if María had spotted him glancing at her figure when he thought she wasn't looking. *Bueno,* what was she to do if even the plainest and most tattered of dresses still showed her off?

Thank goodness that Sixto remained a considerate fellow. A few times he pulled over to a roadside stand so that she could have a *tacita* of coffee and a sweet honey-drenched bun, which he paid for, and when she used the outhouse, he made a point of getting lost. Once when they were finally on the Central Highway, which stretched from one end of the island to the other, he just had to stop at one of the Standard Oil gas stations along the way, to buy some cigarettes for himself and to let that lovely *guajira* see one of their sparkling clean modern toilets. He even put a nickel into a vending machine to buy her a bottle of Canada Dry ginger ale, and when she belched delicately from all the *burbujas*—the bubbles—Sixto couldn't help but slap his legs as if it was the funniest thing he had ever seen.

He was so nice that she almost became fond of him despite his ugliness, fond of him in the way beautiful women, even at so young an age, do of plain and unattractive—hideous—men, as if taking pity on an injured dog. As they started their approach towards one of the coastal roads—that air so wonderful with the scent of the gulf sea—and he suggested that if she got hungry he could take her out to a special little restaurant in Havana, for *obreros* like himself—workers who earn their living honestly, with the sweat of their brow—María had to tell him that she couldn't. She had just caught him staring at her in a certain way, and she didn't want to take the chance that he might not turn out to be so saintly, even if it might hurt his feelings. Of course, he started talking about his family—his faithful wife, his eight children, his simple house in a small town way over in Cienfuegos,—and of his love of pigs even when he knew they were going to end up slaughtered—all to amuse his lovely passenger.

One thing did happen: the closer they got to Havana the more they saw roadside billboards—"Smoke Camels!" "Coca-Cola Refreshes!" "Drink Bacardi Rum!"—and alongside beautiful estates with royal-palm-lined entranceways and swimming pools were sprawling shantytowns, slums with muddy roads and naked children roaming about, and then maybe another gas station, followed by a few miles of bucolic farmland, those campesinos plowing the field with oxen, and then another wonderful estate and a roadside stand selling fresh chopped melons and fruit, followed by yet one more shantytown, each seeming more run-down and decrepit than the next. Of course the prettiest stretch snaked by the northern coastline, which absolutely enchanted María, who sighed and sighed away over the hypnotic and calming effects of the ocean—that salt and fish scent in the air, the sunlight breaking up into rippling shards on the water—everything seeming so pure and clean until they'd pass by a massive garbage dump, the hills covered with bilious clouds of acrid fumes and half crumbling sheds made of every kind of junk imaginable rising on terraces but tottering, as if on the brink of collapsing in a mud slide caused by the ash-filled rain, and, giving off the worst smell possible, a mountain of tires burning in a hellish bonfire; to think that people, *los pobrecitos*, lived there!

They'd come to another gas station, then a fritter place, with donkeys and horses tied up to a railing (sighing, she was already a little homesick). She saw her first fire engine that day, a crew of *bomberos* hosing down a smoldering shed, made of crates and thatch, near a causeway to a beach; a cement mixing truck turned over on its side in a sugarcane field, a coiling flow of concrete spewing like *mierda* from its bottom; then more billboards, advertising soap and toothpaste, radio shows, and, among others, a movie starring Humphrey Bogart and Lauren Bacall, whose faces were well known to even the *guajiros* of Cuba! (Another featured the enchanting visage of the buxom Mexican actress Sarita Montiel; another, the comedian Cantinflas.) Along the way, she just had to ask her new friend Sixto the ugly to stop again—a few miles or so west of Marianao, where they had come across a roadside market, just like the sort one might find in a town plaza, with stalls and long tables boasting everything from pots and pans to used clothes and shoes. Half suffocating from the swinish gases wafting into his cab, Sixto didn't mind at all. What most caught her eye were the racks of dresses over which hung a sign.

"What's that say, *señor*?" she asked, and Sixto, rubbing his eyes and pulling up on the brake, told her: "It says, *rebaja*"—which meant there was a sale going on. A group of women, *negritas* all, were perusing the racks, and so María, needing a new dress to wear in Havana, stepped from the truck and pulled her life savings, some few dollars, which she kept in a sock, out from where she had stuffed it down her dress or, to put it more precisely, from between her breasts.

Most happily and with the innocence of a farm girl, María examined the fabric and stitching of dress after dress, pleased to find that the vendors were very kind and not at all what she had expected. For a half an hour she looked around, the women working those stalls and tables complimenting her on the pristine nature of her *mulatta* skin, nary a pimple or blemish to mar her face (the kind of skin which had its own inner glow, like in the cosmetic ads, except she didn't use any makeup, not back then, a glow that inspired in the male species the desire to kiss and touch her), the men giving her the up and down, the children running like scamps tugging at her skirt—

You see, my daughter; if I was incredibly good looking in my twenties, you can't imagine what I looked like in my prime, as a girl of sixteen and seventeen—I was something out of a man's dream, with honey skin so glowing and a face so pure and perfect that men couldn't help wanting to possess me. . . . But being so young and innocent, I was hardly aware of such things, only that— well, how can I put it my love?—that I was somehow different from your typical cubanita.

That afternoon, she bought, at quite reasonable prices, certain dainty undergarments, they were so inexpensive, as well as a blouse, a pair of polka-dotted high heels, which she would have to grow accustomed to, and finally, after haggling with the vendor, she decided upon a pink dress of a florid design, said to have been styled after the Parisian fashion, with ruffles cascading over the shoulders and hips; a dress which she, being frugal, would keep for some ten years. With such items in hand and after she and her benefactor, the half toothless Sixto, had eaten a little something from a stand, they proceeded east into Havana, the city of both torments and love.

Chapter
TWO

Years later, listening to her stories, her daughter, Teresa, long accustomed to a city like Miami, where she and her mother had lived for most of her life, and with her own fleeting remembrances of Havana from infancy, could only think that her mother, arriving from the bucolic countryside, must have found its very enormity overwhelming. Some twenty *guajiro* families had lived in her *valle,* in Pinar del Río, perhaps some one hundred and fifty souls at most, while Havana had a population of (roughly) 2.4 million people (in the "greater metropolitan area," so an antiquated atlas, put out by a steamship line, circa 1946, said). Surely she must have been dumbstruck to see so many people and buildings, and probably trembled at the prospect of spending time there, as if that city would swallow her up.

And Sixto? Once they had made it to Havana's famous Malecón Drive, and were rumbling along that crescent-shaped harbor, waves, at high tide, bursting over the seawall and onto the Avenida de Maceo in exploding plumes, Sixto, wanting to keep her around for as long as possible, decided to take María for a little tour of the center. The slaughterhouse district, way east of the harbor, could wait: *Those oinking and grunting, pissing and defecating pigs be damned, I've got a real queen with me!*

Soon enough María entered a honeycomb, a labyrinth as challenging as the depths of any forest, for Havana, with its salt-eaten walls, was monumental: a myriad of structures, that city had more than thirty thousand buildings, warehouses, hotels, and hovels, a bodega on practically every corner, a bar or saloon or barbershop or haberdashery or shoeshine stand next to it, and an endless array of alleys, courtyards, *plaẑuelas,* and more columned arcades and edifices than María could have ever imagined. With its streets of cobblestone, asphalt, and dirt (roosters and goats and hens in cages in the marketplaces, the smell of blood and flowers everywhere), that city of pillars and ornate façades, of winding alleys and cul-de-sac gardens and statuary—that fellow Sixto had told her Havana's nickname was Paris of the Caribbean—bustled with people and life. So many people, from tourists to policemen to merchants on the street, to crowds of ordinary citizens just going about their business, left María feeling as dizzy as if she had drunk down a cup or two of rum, a bottle of which, incidentally, Sixto had kept in a paper bag under the shredded leather seat of his cab. This he swigged from while showing her the sights—just getting from one end of Obispo Street to the other, in a glut of carts and taxis and lorries, took a half an hour. Driving for so many years, Sixto thought there was nothing to it, so why not a little sip of rum to ease things when the day's work was practically over?—just like her *papito*'s philosophy of life.

And so, as they headed over to the slaughterhouse district, which was at the far end of the harbor, beyond the last of the Ward Line warehouses, Sixto's manner changed somewhat, though not in a terrible way. He didn't start rubbing himself or make burning noises, nor for that matter did he try anything with María—she was just a young girl after all, a *guajira* with the kind of face and figure that make men do and say things that they probably wouldn't otherwise, and, in Sixto's case, certainly not back home with the wife, *nosireee*. He just started looking as if the world was about to end, kept gulping and licking his lower lips, and staring at her like a starved man with a terrible secret. Finally, not able to take it anymore, before turning in to the chain-link-fenced entry to the Gallegos slaughterhouse, he had to pull over; and once he had, he began to cry, tears the color of amber dripping from his eyes and over the ridges of his gargoyle's face.

María didn't have the slightest idea what the hell was going on— wondering if she was at fault for his sudden sadness. In his gruff and rustic manner, the poor man was so much like the *guajiros* back home that one part of her felt like doing something to please him. Back in her *valle* that had come down to letting some of the men, so weary from their days in the field, roam their callused hands over her face, so they could feel the softness of her skin; and all she had to do was just smile, and that was sometimes enough to make them happier. (Oh, but then there were the others, who, as she got older and filled out, wanted a little more from her, and, looking at her in the same way as Sixto, begged her to embrace them, or to lift her skirt just high enough so that they could see the shapeliness of her legs, which some, so good-naturedly, as if examining a foal, wanted to touch. . . .)

"Sixto, are you okay?" she asked. "Sixto, is there something wrong?"

"Nothing, nothing at all. . . . It's just that I wish," he said, his head lowered, "I wish I could go back in time, and get to know you better in a way that would make you happy, that's all."

"But, Sixto, I don't know what you mean."

"You're so precious, you make a nobody like me wish he could start over again in life."

And he seemed lost to the world, not just because of the rum or the fact he knew that he probably smelled bad to others, but because he had reached inside of himself and taken hold of his own heart, squeezing it until there was nothing left but his own pain, just like her *papito* used to.

Or at least that's what María thought, being such a softhearted girl in those days.

"I know I'm an ugly man and I smell of animals," he went on. "But, please, can you do me one little favor?"

"What kind of favor?"

"Just give me one little *besito*—that's all, doesn't have to be on my mouth, but here," he said, tapping his cheek. "Even one on the side of my face would make me feel content."

He seemed like an animal in pain, an aging one, like those old hounds she'd see on the farm who, no longer able to roam wildly across the fields, would just lie down on their sides, waiting for someone to caress their heaving bellies. She always did.

And because María was grateful for that lift into the city, and even if it turned her stomach to do it, she gave that Sixto a cautious nip on the side of his face, saw the bristles in his nostrils, the spiderwebs in his ears, smelled the rawness of his breath, and felt sad for the man; but wouldn't you know it, at the same time he couldn't help but take her hand and move it towards his right leg, where something had crept forward, uncoiling gradually, a stony gargoyle's erection, like a piece of tubing expanding inside his trousers—was it filled with tears or blood? (Of suffering, or of lust?) At the sight—and touch—of it, her knuckles having grazed that protuberance, María turned away, pulled back her hand, pretending that nothing had happened.

They both pretended, Sixto, with a deep breath, starting the truck again and driving it over to a delivery pen. There he had some kind of discussion with a foreman and, letting drop the rear gate, rousted his swine, some forty or so, into their own little compound, where they were to be counted, weighed, and, depending on that, kept to be further fattened up on *palmiche* or else led immediately to the slaughter. María, it should be said, for all the animals she had (reluctantly) killed herself on the farm, had never experienced such an overwhelming scent of blood and entrails in the air before. Or maybe it was all their suffering that she was feeling—squeals and blurting cattle cries resounded from the long stock houses inside. Somewhere nearby, and much worse, however, was a tannery, which filled the air with a viscous smell like lacquered rotting flesh, so foul as to turn her stomach. She had to get out. Stepping down from the cab, and feeling ashamed of herself, beautiful María, in her first act in Havana, stumbled over to a corner where she emptied her guts into a puddle of stagnant water—her lovely reflection, with her startling eyes, staring back up at her through the muck, her expression bewildered, as if to ask, Chica, *what on earth are you doing here?*

Oh, but the workers were nice to her. She cleaned up in one of their washrooms, its flush toilets and spigot taps delighting her. Someone gave María a bottle of Coca-Cola, someone else, a package of chewing gum, and a third offered her a cigarette, which she declined. Then, for an hour or so, she just sat waiting in an office thumbing through magazines that she couldn't read, though the pictures of Hollywood stars always engaged her. Johnny Weissmuller, still making those Tarzan movies, was the sort of man that always made her wonder just what men in loincloths thought about as they swung through the trees. And Tyrone Power, a dazzlingly good-looking fellow whose teeth were so white she wondered if they were real *(though, according to María, as she would tell her daughter a million times, he was not as handsome as her* músico.) Once Sixto had settled up, he introduced María to the boss, who, taking one look and caring little about what she could do, offered her a job "cleaning," as he put it, for a peso a day in the slaughterhouse. She turned him down—it was just too much for her, too much blood and stink, the torrents of flies alone enough to make her sick again.

Afterwards, Sixto drove her to a cheap hotel near the old quarter. And while she had pretended that everything was fine about staying there, she didn't feel too good about the way Sixto, with a happy look in his eyes, kept promising to visit her whenever he came back to the city, about three or four times a month, he said. So for the sake of avoiding any hurt feelings, she thanked him for all his help and stood by the doorway of that hotel waving farewell and smiling as if she really hadn't been offended and frightened by what she had seen in his trousers—men saying one thing, but meaning another. Once his truck had disappeared down a street of whose name she had no inkling, María, with her little cloth sack and her new purchases, excused herself and left the dingy lobby of that hotel. She had nothing against the sunken-eyed proprietor—he seemed nice enough in his forlorn way—she just didn't want to take a chance of Sixto getting any ideas about coming back to find her.

Chapter

THREE

Having gone from hotel to hotel and boardinghouse to boardinghouse for most of that afternoon, she found the cheapest place possible. It was off Virtudes, or perhaps San Isidro, or maybe along one of those narrow winding cobblestone streets near the harbor—a place of such squalor that she'd one day get the shivers just thinking about it. A kindly *anciana, la señora* Matilda Díaz, of portly dimensions, was one of those *gallegas* whose skin had a yellow pallor from smoking cigarettes from dawn to dusk. With a mustiness that no amount of nicotine could cover, she took a liking to the young woman, an innocent from the countryside with obviously no experience of what living in a city like Havana was about. The men around there, *muy suave,* or real slick, were not to be believed or trusted.

"You should be careful," she told María. "I was once as pretty as you, believe it or not. But, as you can see"—and she shrugged—"the passing of the years will wilt even the finest bloom." Shortly, she took María to a room on the third floor which cost about a peseta a night, or a quarter, a rent that, even in 1947, would have been considered inexpensive (as opposed to two hundred and fifty dollars a night for a suite in the Italian port town of Portofino, where María and her daughter, by then a doctor, were to stay many years later). There wasn't much to it, just a cot, a lamp, a chair, a washbasin, a speckled doorway mirror, with a toilet and shower down the hall—"Sometimes it works, and sometimes it doesn't"—but, though far from being comfortable, at least it had a high doorway with shutters and a little balcony that looked out onto an inner courtyard and over to other similar rooms.

Used to the countryside, where everyone knew your business, María made nothing of the fact that right across the way she could see one of her neighbors, a lanky dissipated fellow with a wild pompadour and pronounced gut, standing on his balcony in only a pair of *calzoncillos*. Frying some *bacalao* over a hot plate, he whistled as soon as their eyes met. From another direction, a woman, obviously a whore, closing her shutters, sent María a kiss off the upturned palm of her hand before going inside to do whatever whores did. (María knew but didn't let on, while the *señora*, well aware of the quality and livelihood of her tenants, simply shrugged again.)

Still, María took comfort in having neighbors and in the fact that she could at least open her windows to get a breath of air at night. But María, out on her own for the first time, and feeling frightened by the prospect of having to get along in a city she hardly knew, where she'd have to depend on strangers to help her get around—she was an *analfabeta*, an illiterate, after all—could barely work up the nerve to go out that evening. Just too much was going on—trolley cars clanging, cars honking horns, horses clip-clopping along, distant sirens blaring, radios sounding from a half dozen windows, voices chattering, a river of life out on the street. Coming from the sticks, she found herself feeling far more clueless than she, without knowing anyone, could have predicted. *Por Dios,* she even started missing that damned *campo,* where not much ever really happened, and her *papito,* who could be a pain in the *culo,* as well as the farmers and their animals; and she missed her younger sister, Teresita, and her *mamá,* who were both dead.

Lordy, it was a lonely place.

With her stomach queasy from hunger and her gum chewed down to nothing, all she could do was to go downstairs and ask the *señora* for something to eat. *La señora* Matilda was not a stingy woman, and cooked her a tortilla of potatoes and chorizo, but once María followed her into her little suite of rooms, the sight of the absolute filth of her kitchen did not do much for María's appetite—no wonder, as she later learned, the tenants of that residence had nicknamed it the Hotel Cucaracha. Nevertheless, María thanked her for the meal, devouring it quickly, and, once upstairs, finally unpacked her few possessions: a precious hand mirror, a photograph, cracked and fading, of her *mamá y papito* on their wedding day years and years ago, a remnant of Teresita's hair, which she kept in an envelope, along with a picture of them as girls, posed in a photography shop in San Jacinto, the town nearest to their valley, their faces pressed together, María beaming and Teresita showing not an inkling of the afflictions that would take her life. Among the superstitious charms and amulets that really don't make any difference to the world, she had brought along the rosary that had been her mother's. Of course, out of old habit, María, before turning in to bed, got down on her knees to pray, her whispers slipping out into the courtyard, from which she could hear many of her neighbors. They were either drunk and shouting or else singing, their voices rising into the night, up towards the sky, with its sprinkling of stars, towards the indifference of heaven.

FINDING A JOB AS A DANCER WAS NOTHING THAT SHE HAD GIVEN thought to, even if her *papito* had always told María that she was a natural *rumbera*. At first, it hadn't entered her mind, but after a month in that city, as a resident of her splendid hotel, with all its *chinches* and cockroaches, all María had to show for her daily excursions, when she had knocked on every factory and warehouse door, were sore feet and a fanny whose *nalgitas* had been worn thin by the staring of men. Those *habaneros*, as she would tell her daughter one day, knew a good thing when they saw it, and being more overtly prone than the *guajiros* of the countryside, made no bones about letting on to María that she was nothing less than spectacular, as far as the female species goes. In fact, she spent several days toiling at a tobacco factory off Comerciales, another few as a seamstress in a clothing concern, and had found occasional work cleaning up after customers in a café three doors over from the hotel. Now, if she had been hired at all, in a city filled with illiterates looking for work—or else begging, *pidiendo limosna*—it was because, in the first two instances, those establishments were managed by men who wanted something more than her labors. At the end of the second day's work, she ran out of the tobacco factory after the floor manager asked her to stay behind once the others had gone and, while pretending to teach her a special technique, pushed himself up against María and reached over to fondle her breast, the pig! The other boss, at the sewing factory, pinched her bottom every time he could, and, because she had her pride, María refused to take much more of that either. (That such a nice-looking man, who wore a medallion bearing an image of la Virgen de la Caridad, could do such a thing!) Her third job, in that little café, el Paraíso, really wasn't bad. Its gangly, hound-faced proprietor, an older man with a hopelessly immense scrotum, hired María for a few hours a day simply because he recognized her look of hunger; for her troubles, he paid her a couple of reales and, as well, occasionally fried her a thin oxen steak with onions with some *papas fritas,* which she happily devoured despite that dish's slightly rancid taste.

But as much as she appreciated his kindness, the dinginess of that café made her feel even more hopelessly lost and sadder than she had before. Something about standing in the doorway of such an establishment, a rag in hand, and peering down the narrow street, half lit by sunlight, with passersby, mostly men, slipping in and out of the shadows and brick or stucco walls in every direction she looked, made her feel wistful and heartsick for the more verdant spaces of her *valle.* And all the signage—hanging in shop windows, on banners slung across the street on wires, posters and pamphlets stuck on the walls—bewildered María, a sense of stupidity and ignorance churning in her belly. Having no idea of what that café owner wrote in chalk on a slate board behind his counter, left María wishing that all such words would go away. For all her gorgeous looks—Sí, mamá, *you've told me so a million times before*—she envied the brilliant winged birds of the forest back home, who, flying so happily through life, seemed free from such confusions. There in Havana, where every written word seemed a mystery, María's illiteracy hit her in ways it never had in the countryside.

At least the proprietor of that hole-in-the-wall café never tried anything, but with so little money in her pocket, and having used up the remainder of her paltry savings, she'd head back to la Cucaracha fearful that, because she was falling behind on the rent, her landlady might evict her. After a while she started to pay for her room by cleaning up the place— mopping the halls, scrubbing its toilets, and sweeping out its musty entranceway. Watching life in that hotel unfolding around her, she became aware of all the comings and goings of la Cucaracha's tenants, especially the professional women who took men up the stairs in the late hours of the afternoon into the night. One of them, a redheaded whore, always winked at María sweetly. On those evenings, terrified to go out by herself—even in the countryside in Pinar del Río nights always made her a little fearful—she'd pass the time sitting on a bench in the reception area, listening to radio melodramas with *la señora*, and nice music, by way of live concerts broadcast by CMQ. A musty bladed fan turning overhead, and moths dissolving into dust in the buzzing ceiling lights, they'd converse, Matilda, a widow, recalling the promise of her youth when she fell in love with the man she eventually married, a simple shoemaker from a town called Cárdenas, who died in her arms at the very foot of the staircase after a fall.

"And what is it that you'd like to do?" she asked María, and because María never gave an answer, *la señora* shook her head disapprovingly. "You should make up your mind, or else find a good man to marry."

Languishing there in boredom, María was in her room one evening, examining her naked body, smooth and stately and curvaceous in a full-length mirror, something which she'd never had the opportunity to do in the countryside, where the only *espejo* they had, hanging off a post outside their *bohío,* was the broken one, the size of a man's palm, before which her *papito* shaved himself every third morning. But there she stood, a gorgeous apparition of cinnamon-colored flesh, with breasts so perfectly shaped that even she found their symmetry startling, her nipples dark as raspberries, a shock of black hair, dense as a crow's nest, shooting out from between her long legs. Surprised by her own grace and voluptuousness, and stepping one way and the other, María had to admit that she looked pretty good, better than she could have imagined. And the mirror? If that mirror were a man, it would have been salivating; if it were a carpet it would have taken flight; if it had been a pile of wood it would have burst into flame, so lovely was María. Of course, she forgot that people could look inside—and, turning, glimpsed her across-the-courtyard neighbor, the fellow with the pompadour, out on his *balcón*, doing something to himself frantically, a cigarette burning between his lips, his face wincing in ecstasy as she hurriedly closed the shutters.

She came to a decision: seeing that men wanted certain things from a woman like her and that she hadn't had much luck with finding jobs of a normal sort, María became resigned to taking another route, as so many young girls had before her. And that was to entangle herself in the labyrinthine nightlife of Havana, for which the city was famous.

Oh, if she'd only known just how seedy that could be.

Pero, Mami, *didn't you always tell me how terrible you felt about being alive when your beloved sister, my aunt Teresa, was dead? Didn't you tell me, after you'd been drinking those Cuba Libres, that you really didn't give much of a damn about yourself? That even the way you looked seemed a curse to you sometimes, as much as you ride me about my own?* . . .

E ven those jobs didn't come easily. Warned by her matronly *dueña*, María had to be careful about getting mixed up with the wrong sorts. "And believe me, *querida*," Matilda told her, "Havana is full of them."

Nevertheless, for days María went to just about every club and saloon she could find, usually in the late afternoons. And while she overwhelmed most everyone she met with her beauty, there was just something about her too precious for even the most jaded of proprietors to despoil, though there were exceptions, some club managers looking her over so lustfully that they made her nervous. That she had never danced anywhere except in a *cervecería*—beer joint—in the countryside, the sort of place where the men pissed off a back porch, or had any professional training, did not help matters. Most, taking her for a rustic bumpkin or a child of the slums—they just knew from the wide openness of her expression, the gaudiness of her clothes—advised her to go back home, before she wasted any more of her time or, worse, ruined her life. But she had to eat.

You don't know what that's like, Teresita, unless you've had to go through it yourself, sabes?

At first the establishments she approached were, so it seemed to her, of the better sort, but she had no luck. And so, instead of going to those nicer clubs along the Prado, or out in Vedado, near Calle 21, she started lowering her sights.

. . .

AT ABOUT ELEVEN THIRTY ONE EVENING, SHE FOUND HERSELF knocking on an alleyway door in la Marina, the brothel district, not far from the harbor. A squat and corpulent Catalán, with a melted wax face and Xavier Cugat mustache, needed only one look at María before inviting her into his establishment. He called it a "gentleman's club," but it was just a sad-seeming place, filled with smoke and darkness and lots of drunken men. His office, at the end of a dingy and rank-smelling hallway, was just as bleak, cases of liquor piled against the walls, a haphazard collection of showgirl photographs pinned to a board behind his desk and, alongside it, a sofa, which emanated its own history of grief. There, as he looked her over, he couldn't have been more blunt: The job, if she really wanted it, would involve showing herself off, he said. There'd be no stage to perform on, just several tables that had been pushed together in a nearly lightless barroom, over which, in her new high heels and with her new dress off, she was to stride before that crowd, enticingly. He would pay her five dollars, just for that.

It wasn't the kind of thing she'd ever be proud of, but she would do it out of hunger, her stomach prevailing over her pride, may God please forgive her.

Of course, he wanted to see what she had to offer. When María, trembling, disrobed, at first just down to her slip and undies—she wore no brassiere, didn't own one—the Catalán, having watched her carefully, told María, "Now off with the slip." And when only one stitch of clothing remained, that was too much as well—"*Quítalo, todo,*" he demanded. Sighing, she did as he had asked and was soon standing naked before him, one hand placed over her breasts, the other over what *cubanos* euphemistically called the *papayún*. Tilting her head back, in shame, she closed her eyes, as if to pray. "Don't be afraid, *mi guapita,*" he said. "It's perfectly natural to feel a little shy the first time—but just remember, you have to start somewhere, after all." Courteously and with an almost avuncular manner, he handed her a black silk robe, reeking of perfume, its fabric covered with falling purple blossoms, and told her, "Now, come with me."

Why she somehow trusted him was beyond her future understanding; perhaps she felt protected by God—she had *"la fe"* then, and strongly so. Or, as she often also thought, she just wasn't thinking too clearly: being young and alone and hoping naïvely for the best, as if people were naturally good, will do that to you, *sabes?* Sighing, her stomach twisted into knots, she followed him into that bar, which, in the style of Spanish taverns, lacked windows, its interior hazy with shifting plains of smoke. Some big band *danzóns* blared from a jukebox. The room itself (in memory) smelled vaguely of urine and spilled beer, sawdust, stale fritters, and flatulence (perhaps), and was so dimly lit that its darkness almost came as a relief to her. Patiently (and out of hunger) she waited beside the Catalán, who, banging on a pot to gain his patrons' attention, made a quick introduction in what she took as English—"What's your name anyway?" he asked her. And then, without further adieu, once she had climbed atop the long table, he yanked off her robe, and María, tottering in high heels, revealed her naked graces before a room filled with men, mainly Americans, who, in their cups, whistled and hooted at her.

How did she feel? Slightly humiliated, and certainly ashamed; as María would confess to a priest a few days later, she had never sunk so low in her life. But as she strode unsteadily across that long table, from one end of the room to the other, she didn't falter, thinking of those men as no better than animals, whose desires and anonymous expressions would, at least, put a few dollars in her pocket. *And so forgive me,* she told herself, *for I have no one to look after me and I am hungry, amen.*

What happened? After those strangers had gotten their fill of what no man had ever seen so closely before, María, covering herself with that robe, sat off in a corner daydreaming about what she would do with her pay. (She'd buy a plate of fried *chuletas*—pork chops—and rice and beans for twenty-five cents, along with some plantain fritters from a stand near the hotel, a new blouse from one of the corner stores, and perhaps take in a Barbara Stanwyck movie in the center for another quarter, and *still* have enough left to give her *señora* some rent money, so that she wouldn't have to keep on scrubbing floors.) That's when the Catalán, who had gone from table to table speaking with his patrons, came over to María and, in a rather pleasant tone of voice, told her to come back into his office so that they might discuss some matters of business.

What followed, she never cared to talk about—she'd never tell her daughter, not even during their most earnest talks about her rough beginnings in Havana—only that, once upon a time, it had been her misfortune to have stumbled, and stupidly so, for the sake of earning a few dollars, into a shadowy place. What was it that she'd remember? Back in his office, the Catalán offered her a drink, but she didn't like her rum in those days—*"I was an innocent"*—and then he sat her down and told María about how everyone in the club had been much taken by her little performance and that, if she so wanted to, there would be other ways that she, a most beautiful young woman, could earn money. How so? she asked.

"By being nice to those fellows, that's all," he told her.

"Señor," she said, without much deliberation. "All I want is my pay. I've done what you wanted me to do."

But he just smiled and, stepping towards her, his expression changing, grabbed hold of her hair in his fist and, tightening his grip, asked her: "And who the hell do you think you are?" Then he slapped María's face with the back of his hand and threw her down on the settee near his desk. To her horror, as she looked up to heaven for assistance, he undid his belt. At first she thought he was going to beat her, the way her *papito* sometimes did—she wasn't always a well-behaved daughter—but, no, he wanted something else. Letting drop his linen trousers and his (rank-smelling) undershorts below his knees, he stood before her with his somewhat dense but not particularly long ardor in hand; truth be told, it seemed dwarfish, compared with the immensity of his belly. He then proceeded to do his best to deflower her, his enormous corpulence slamming achingly against her hip bones, his body sweating, his breathing labored—he was one of those grossly overweight men who, because of heft, thought himself a Hercules when it was far from the truth. She'd also recall that he wore a lilac aftershave.

But did he succeed? Screaming—surely, they heard her in the club— she fought him until her body was covered in bruises, his face and back with scratches. She prayed for her life, prayed to El Señor, who watches over the forlorn, until, in an instant, she was reprieved. Or to put it differently, until, in the throes of extreme physical exertion, some horrible and paralyzing pain seized the right side of the Catalán's body—she was, without knowing it, a *morena fatal* after all. Unable to breathe, or even to lift his arms, he slumped over, beside María. When he asked her desperately for a glass of water, *suspirando mucho, mucho,* María, may God forgive her, told him to go to hell. And when he asked her again, as she gathered her clothes, María, a practical *guajira,* answered, "Okay, but tell me, where are my five dollars?"

"*En los bolsillos de mis pantalones,*" he told her, gasping. So she rifled through his trousers pockets, encountering a stiletto, several condoms, some cards for his club—if she had been able to read she would have known that his establishment was called "El Savoy, a place for gentlemans [*sic*]"—and then she came to a clump of bills: from this she removed five American dollar bills. And then, because she'd been struggling lately, she availed herself of the rest, in both Cuban and American currency, which were equal in value, may God forgive her. Then, dressing, she made her way out.

LEAVING THAT ESTABLISHMENT, MARÍA HEARD NEITHER SONO-rous violins nor longing melodies echoing around her; nor any tremulous baritone voice, with its saintly inflections, confessing the greatest passion for her beauty, as if she were the object of devotion in a song of love. What she heard instead was Havana, circa 1947, at 2 a.m., a general din of restaurants, clubs, and distant voices coming from every direction and punctuated by the barking of dogs. Firecrackers—or shots heard in the distance; the caw-caws of seagulls alighting upon the slop barges in the harbor, or else swooping low to pick through the offal left in the trails of yachts. From a nearby edifice, a woman shouted at someone, *"Eres un pendejo!"* at the top of her lungs. Her high-heel shoes clacking along the flagstones of a *placita*. A cavalcade of partiers, honking their horns and whistling, in a postwedding procession of automobiles passed along the Malecón. The moon itself, a medallion, with a melancholic face looked down from the northwest, like a sanguine god without a word to say. From some alley, deep in the recesses of la Marina—or was it *el barrio* Colón?—a half dozen *batá* and *quinto* drums were beating. She heard police sirens: then, as the casino boats and cruise ships came into port, buoys and deck bells ringing, smatterings of music here and there from behind the closed doors of the all-night cabarets and bordellos; the skittering of cats and other scavengers foraging through the gutters in search of food. If she could have listened through the walls of some of the less respectable edifices she was passing, a thousand moans of drunken pleasure would have assailed her. If she could have eavesdropped into the cells of the central police command, where, unbeknownst to her, political agitators—the *socialistas*, the *comunistas*, the union organizers—were held, half dead from torture and beatings, in dingy lightless rooms, she would have heard them cursing, weeping, and moaning, not from pleasure but from agony.

Still reeling from her experience at the Catalán's, she walked and walked though the streets of a city she had yet to know better. In an arcade, María bought herself a half-stale *lechón* sandwich from an all-night stand. Its owner, with his one milky eye and tattered flat boater cane hat, left over from the days when he was a 1930s dandy, tried to act as if she wasn't the most ravishing young woman he had ever seen (even if she seemed a little sad). He checked her out just the same, as María, half starved to death, scoffed down the sandwich and then, meekly smiling, set off again. After roaming in the darkness of an arcade, and hearing the whistles of passing strangers, María, with her irresistible body, her high and firm buttocks jostling the fabric of her ruffled cotton dress, finally got back to her hotel, with its fifth-rate amenities. Stretching across her bed, she spent the night half feverishly, visited by nightmares and missing the countryside she'd left behind.

Oh, but her story to that point: Just leaving her tranquil valley, midway between the mountains and the sea, would have been enough to rip any heart into pieces; but she hadn't really been given much choice about the matter. For one thing, in the wake of her beloved *mami*'s death, her *papito*, Manolo, had taken up with the most horrible woman imaginable, a hard case from a town along the gulf coast whom he, still an occasional *músico*, had met while moonlighting with some of his *sonero* friends at a wedding dance. Her name was Olivia, and he must have been crazy or desperately lonely to fall for her, or maybe she had bewitched him, because she was neither pretty nor softly feminine nor even funny. If she had any virtues, as far as María could figure, it was that she could really cook and Manolo liked to eat, but, even then, poor María, for the life of her, couldn't begin to find anything else nice to say about the woman.

And Olivia must have known it from the moment they first laid eyes on each other, on the very day she moved in, with her horse-drawn cart filled with chairs and what few dresses she owned. After just a short few weeks, Olivia gave up on all her phony smiles and seemed to take a special delight in ordering María around and establishing herself as the new *dueña* of that household.

It was the worst for María at night, when she had to listen to them going at it from behind a hanging blanket that separated their sleeping space from the rest of that room, no more than ten feet across. With its floor of pounded down dirt, and its few paltry chairs, its kerosene lamp, and, among their sparse adornments, an altar to the Holy Virgin in a corner, which her *mamá* had kept, the interior of their *bohío* did not afford much privacy. María's cot, built of plywood and canvas, with straw-stuffed pillows, the same she had once shared with her younger sister, was near a back door, open to the *selva*, that dense forest around them, where insects buzzed all night against the mosquito netting. It was bad enough that her *papito* snored like a beast, and she was used to hearing his every movement, sigh, his dreamer's mumblings, the capricious workings of his digestive system, but once Olivia had settled in as his woman, those arrangements became a torment. Whereas her *mamá*, as far as María could remember, hardly ever made any noise at all, just letting out sighs and sometimes crying, *"Por Dios, por Dios!"* that horrid *bruja* Olivia, with her groans and yelps and filthy language, could have awakened the dead. That alone was enough to turn María's stomach, and it killed her to think that her *mamá*, off in paradise and watching them in life the way people watched actors in movies, could take in every bit of that hag's lascivious grunting.

What her dear departed mother looking down from the stars in heaven and shaking her head must have thought!

Well, at least poor *papito*, drunk half the time or under a spell, seemed not to weep as much as he did before that horrendous creature came along. Just hearing his cries of release and beastly snoring afterwards convinced María that giving one's body over to a man wasn't much different from a mother suckling a crying baby at her breasts. Besides, because Olivia seemed to satisfy her *papito* in that way—he was much calmer in the mornings and sometimes even whistled happily— María couldn't hate her completely, even if it was obvious that Olivia hated her.

Yet, it was hard to forgive her *papito* for taking up with such a woman, so shortly after Mamá had left the world. Not a year had passed since her *mamá*, at the ripe old age of forty-five, had died, slowly, slowly of a cancer that left her blind but still stubbornly whispering about the goodness of the Lord, a rosary burning in her hands (she claimed that the beads of her *avemarías, nuestro padres,* and those of the mysteries, heated up like embers between her fingers as she prayed). It had been a terrible time for María. She had spent countless hours beside her mother, attending to the messy business of looking after her, and, no matter how much she had prayed, María had watched her mother's body slowly shrivel up. Before that, Concha had been one of those sturdy no-nonsense *mulattas,* built low to the ground, her hands strong and fingers thick from sewing and plucking feathers and from holding the necks of chickens and the ears of pigs as she slaughtered them in their yard and made the sign of the cross in contrition afterwards. The sort of woman to throw open the door to their shack each and every morning, as if to invite in the grace of God, she believed that her faith would get her through anything. But in her illness, she had practically evaporated, her limp body, in her daughter's arms, nearly weightless, her hair falling out in clumps. Dutifully, María fed her *mamá* soup, changed her clothes, and attended to the white *palangana* that served as her bedpan.

The most difficult thing for Concha herself, aside from all that waiting, was to have watched the stars slowly fading from the horizon. Even before María's *papito* had finally gotten around to bringing in a doctor from the sugar mill, she had been complaining about having trouble seeing things, especially her lovely, lovely daughter María's face. But once the sky itself had started to fade, Concha, so quiet a woman, and demanding little for herself, had begun to sob wistfully over the passing of light from her life. By the time that doctor looked her over, when she had finally piped up, there wasn't much that could be done. She went slowly, with lots of their *guajiro* neighbors gathering daily around her bed, women mainly, joining hands to say prayers in the old-school there-are-angels-and-saints-and-tongues-of-fire way; and while her *mamá* had been blessed and given her final holy-oiled send-off by their circuit priest, Father Alonso, who would ride into their hamlet on a donkey, clanging a bell, her eyes, which had turned into pearls, sometimes welled over with fear. Nobody, not even the most religious *cubana,* wanted to die.

And she would clutch her daughter's hand as tightly as she could manage, begging María to hold her close so she wouldn't feel so alone when the final moment came and she joined her other children in heaven.

Along the way, Concha, despite her unending drowsiness, often reminded her daughter to look after her *papito,* even if he had been a *sinvergüenza* to her sometimes, to never forget what she had been taught about God and sins and the promise of salvation; above all, as she was such a beautiful young woman, never to allow any man to use her like a common whore—*"No eres una puta, me oyes?"*

María, nodding, always swore that she would keep those promises, no matter how many times Concha, having become forgetful, mentioned them all over again. There were other things that repeated: Concha's trembling and weeping in her arms, Concha's long hours of complete silence, Concha's milky eyes seemingly looking off into a distance when there was really nothing to see, her dried lips slightly parted as if in wonderment, Concha, forgetting that her daughter was sitting beside her, calling out, "María, María, where did you go?" Looking in at all this from time to time, her *papito,* Manolo, shook his head disbelievingly. Barely able to muster the courage to step into the room, he'd ask María, as if it were the most natural thing in the world, to leave her mother alone and cook him some food. "And you let me know when you think her time is coming, huh?" her *papito* added.

María obeyed, day after day, ever so grateful whenever her *papito* managed to pull himself together and, sitting down beside her *mamá,* did something to show his tenderness towards her—brushing back Concha's thinning hair with his hands, or planting a few kisses on her forehead, but never staying long. He just couldn't take the sight of Concha suffering so and preferred to sit on a crate outside their doorway, strumming some chords on his guitar and sharing a bottle of rum or paint-thinner-strength *aguardiente* with one of his *guajiro* pals, anything better than owning up to some of the things he had done to Concha over the years, things that involved other women and that used to leave her quietly weeping at night or that left her eyes reddened while feeding the pigs and sobbing when she thought no one was looking. "Just let me know, *niña*," he'd tell María again, as if his wife's passing was akin to waiting for a train to come by, that *guajiro* not having the slightest idea of just how monumentally hard he would take the whole business when her moment finally came.

One day, just as the cocks had started to crow, María had been sleeping beside her *mamá*—well, really dozing, because it's nearly impossible to sleep next to someone like that—when, all at once, she smelled something like strawberries or perfumed water in the air instead of the rot of her mother's illness, and then she felt a hand passing gently over her face, the butt of a palm moving over her cheekbone, a thumb pushing upwards against her thick mane of hair—that's when María opened her eyes, to see that her *mamá* had stopped breathing. Pressing her ear to her mother's withered chest, as she had seen the farmers doing with their animals, and hearing nothing, María cried out, *"Ven! Ven! Papito! Papito!"*

Manolo had taken to sleeping in a hammock under a banyan alongside their *bohío*, mosquito netting draped over his body, and when he didn't stir, María went outside to rouse him—it was early morning and thousands and thousands of birds, from woodpeckers to thrushes to silver-winged vireos were singing in the forests round them—but because her *papito* had, in his misery the night before, gone off to the local *cervecería*, at a crossroads far beyond the fields,—a place where María sometimes used to dance for pennies—and had come back home only a few hours earlier, he may as well have been dead. Shaking his arms and shouting at him to get up, María nearly started to weep herself. Out of nowhere, as crows began gathering in the sky over their house, he awakened and, hearing the sad news, for reasons she would never understand, got to his feet and, with his mouth twisted into a wince, slapped her so hard that the right side of her beautiful face, already covering in shadows, darkened with black and blue bruises. Her *papito*, his arms shaking, hit her a dozen times more, his face contorted with anger, as if María were somehow to blame for Concha's death. Then, coming to his senses and seeing that his daughter, the most precious thing remaining in his life, couldn't bear to look at him, he fell onto his knees begging her forgiveness. With her eyes swollen by sadness and shock, her jaw aching, María, as a good *cubana* daughter, grabbed him by the crook of his arm and led her *papito* to her mother's bedside.

There, at the sight of her *mamá*'s corpse, still as a saint's, her *papito* carried on with such sudden misery that María couldn't help but wonder where he had really been all those months before, the man crying out that he was worthless and undeserving of having married so wonderful a woman and saying many other things that left María feeling even more sorry for him, María repeating, while caressing his tightened shoulders and back, *"Ay, pero, Papito, Papito . . ."*

Naturally, after Mamá's funeral, a procession of their *guajiro* neighbors, and even some from farther away, beating drums and chanting, accompanied her pine coffin to the local *campo santo*, at the far end of the fields. María took to wearing a black dress and her *papito*, a black armband, and for weeks, out of respect, he did not once pick up his guitar and sing—nor did any of his neighbors. And, as might happen in any number of rustic enclaves all over Cuba, so obscure as to lack a proper name, where not a single electric light was to be found, once three days had gone by, people began to claim they had seen Concha's spirit materializing as a floating will-o'-the-wisp in the cane fields at night; and a few of their neighbors, out of pure sympathy and missing Concha, claimed to have seen her translucent spirit drifting through the moonlit hollows of the forest amongst the lianas and star blossoms (those *guajiros*, sobbing and drunk, were always seeing such things). But María herself never saw Concha again, except in her dreams, and in her loneliness and grieving, like any respectable *cubana* daughter, she turned her attentions to her *papito* in his time of distress. Which is to say that María, having made certain promises to her mother on her deathbed, and believing her *papito* when he swore to anyone who listened that he would live out the rest of his days honoring the memory of his late wife, forgave him for every beating he'd ever given her for no good reason and for every single moment when he had made María feel ashamed of being his daughter: as when she had once watched him, like any other who-could-give-a-shit *guajiro,* dropping his trousers, crouching down, and relieving himself amidst the oxen in a field, or for the way he used to linger in their *retrete,* their squalid outhouse in the back, without bothering to close the door, and thought nothing of calling for her to fetch him a Lucifer match, a thin black cheroot between his lips, while he emptied his guts noisily beneath him.

She had other reasons for detesting and loving him at the same time, but now, with her *mamá* gone, and no one else left in that house—she once had two older brothers, Luis and Miguel, who'd died of typhus and tuberculosis when she was little, and a younger sister, Teresita, gone just a few years before, whose death she blamed herself for—her *papito* constituted her only family, that of her flesh and blood, even though there were other more distant relatives here and there around the island. Just that fact alone made María put up with all kinds of things, mainly her *papito*'s rants that women, even young and beautiful ones like herself, weren't much use to the world except as adornments, and even then they were destined to grow old and rot (he was a little drunk, his eyes twisted, when he said that). Then her *papito* would say that, as much as he loved her, he would have loved her more had she been born a male. (They would be sitting on crates in front of their *bohío,* her *papi*'s best friends, Apollo and Francisco, poor farmers who sang improvised *décima* lyrics like no one else around there, their already drawn faces further dipped in lacquer after days of drinking the lowest grade of rums, in commiseration with Manolo in his widowed state, just waving off whatever cruel things he said to María and making crazy signs with their big knuckled hands so that María wouldn't take his cruel ramblings to heart.)

As long as he didn't hit her, María could care less about what her *papito* said—she just figured he was drunk, and even if he'd insulted her that made no difference to María, because, no matter what, his eyes were always contrite the next day—they told the truth about how he really felt. And, in any case, as his beloved daughter, the only daughter he had, she believed that he'd fall apart without her. Who else could he sing to in the evenings, out in front of their *bohío*, when his friends weren't around? After a night's restless sleep, who else could cheer him so in the mornings, her *papito* often declaring, at the sight of her: "When I look at you, María, I forget the misery of my days." He'd smile, in the same way he once did during their slumbers by the stream behind their hut, or in his hammock (sometimes with Teresita joining them) when she was a little girl, her arms wrapped around him and their limbs all entangled, happily, happily, nothing in the world able to harm them and life itself, poor as they might have been, filled with so many simple pleasures.

. . . And when he smiled, the journeys they'd made when María was a girl of seven and eight would come back to her. These were daylong excursions to different pueblos in the province, some with barely a road leading to them, and even some big towns like Los Palacios or Esperanza, where he'd find a columned plazuela *or shaded arcade in which to perform, Manolo singing and playing his guitar while his daughters, just little girls then, enchanted the passersby, danced to his music, and afterwards collected reales with their* papito's *hat. Sometimes, with Manolo riding a horse and pulling along his young daughters in a cart, they'd even go as far north as the foothills of the Órgano mountains, to timber country, and while those trips, taking a day or more in each direction, were intended just as visits with some old musician friends of his, neither María nor her* papito *could ever forget their tranquil passages through some of the most wonderful tracts of forests and valleys in Cuba. No matter that the going was rugged and sometimes frightening, as when they'd have to sidle along a narrow dirt trail at the edge of a ravine, or it suddenly began to rain torrentially and rivers of mud and stone came sliding towards them from the higher ground, once they reached safety and had entered yet another forest, thick with orchids and air plants, whose luscious scents alone would put them in mind of being inside a dream—they may as well have*

entered a paradise. And not just of one's childhood, for their papito *himself, with his guitar slung over his back, crossing a meadow of wildflowers, had never seemed so happy as when he was on his horse and in the company of his daughters, his precious loved ones, who, in those days, he introduced to anyone he happened upon as his "little angels."*

This María remembered on her lonely evenings in Havana.

SIX

After that night at the Catalán's place, her body felt dirty for weeks, her thoughts filled with disgust for such establishments, the sorts of places María swore she'd never step inside again. But after a few more attempts to find work—she even went down to the harbor, where the only women to be found seemed to be either saloon girls or *putas*—she began to miss the feeling of having a few dollars in her pocket, no matter how she had earned them. Despising the Catalán while cherishing the prospect of money, María tried to find her nerve again, but she was too timid to knock on any club doors. Still, she had a bit of luck, if it could be called so: it came down to the kindness of a prostitute, living in the hotel, who knew a photographer with a shop on Obispo Street, the friend of a club owner, an entrepreneur typical of that city.

This is what happened: At a certain hour of the day, around four thirty, if you wandered into the Residencia Cubana, you'd find María, having grown close to *la señora* Matilda, seated by her side in the hallway, fanning herself and sipping from a bottle of Polar beer, while the landlady, half stewed and always with darning needle in hand, proceeded to regale the young *guajira* with tales of her own youth (born in Vigo, Spain, a transatlantic journey to Havana at the age of five, love, desperation, faith, and despair), ever so grateful that the poor bewildered beauty from the sticks didn't mind providing company for such a Cuban relic as herself. In the background hummed the radio, and a calendar of Jesus holding his heart, at the center of the wall, soothed María's soul, but in any event, the two, like turtles in the sun, didn't really have to say much to each other to feel companionable.

After seven, however, as the shadows elongated in the streets, the prostitutes started to wander in with their fellows, earnest *cubanos* for the most part, trying to get in a leisurely romp before heading home, as well as some lower-end *turistas,* who couldn't help but smile at the young beauty sitting by the old biddy. Of those prostitutes, the oldest and most regal, a certain Violeta, whose mouth seemed fixed in a perpetual scornful smile, had taken a liking to María—"If you ever want to come work beside me, let me know. Men would like you very much"—and on occasion, when she wasn't breaking wind on the stairs, this Violeta—*"Ay, Teresita, she was a whore, but a sweet one"*—brought María (and *la señora*) a bag of greasy meat pastries from a cart on the street and sometimes a cup of fruit-syrup-drenched ice, succulent, chilling, and cleansing. On her way up, she always pinched María's chin, as if she were an older sister, and sometimes, for the hell of it, she'd slap her bottom, whistling and, often enough, reminding her: "I'm telling you, *querida,* men would pay to have a taste of this."

Then came another day when Violeta walked into the lobby with a thin gent, sad faced as José Martí, apostle of Cuba, that fellow, with one dormant eye—made of glass—pulling along a clattering black trunk on wheels, which, as it happened, carried the tools of his trade: a large box camera and various lights. Nearly falling over at the sight of María, who had been filing her nails in the stairwell shadows as they came in, he consulted with the prostitute.

His name was Enrique.

"My friend here," said Violeta, "would like to take your photograph, María, to display in his shop window. . . . He'll pay you a few dollars for your trouble, and who knows what other pictures he'll want to make. . . ."

Knowing the score, Violeta winked, as if it would be easy—every few months or so she herself posed for this fellow in her room upstairs, at a time of day when the windows flooded with light. Violeta sprawling naked on a bed, Violeta spreading wide her legs, her hairy bush and glinting Venus mound laid bare for the world to see, such shots to be sold as "artistic" photographs out of the back of his shop or by old lottery vendors on the street. Violeta was already mildly famous among the brothel set for an accordion collection of such postcard-size photographs, circa 1933, which she had posed for as a ravishing fourteen-year-old girl, new to Havana and willing to do most anything for money. And so why wouldn't María? The pay would be helpful, and she simply hadn't had many photographs taken of her back in her *valle;* but there was also something about the photographer's somewhat shattered, world-weary manner that immediately put María at ease. He seemed a harmless sort, one of those *habaneros,* as Violeta would say, who had fallen through the cracks of life but managed to survive anyway, without hurting a soul.

And so a few days later, María, having agreed to sit for the photographer in his studio, over at 17A Obispo, set out in the late morning, the ladies of the hotel, Violeta among them, having fussed over her. It was the first time she'd ever had her hair set in curlers, or worn makeup—not that she needed it—and though the face powders and lipstick seemed oddly confining, as she sauntered along those streets, the perfection of her features, along with the grandeur of her figure, stopped more than one *habanero* in his tracks: at the sight of her, grandly dressed Negroes, dapper in white from head to toe, bowed, smiled, and tipped their hats her way, as if, in fact, they felt blessed to see the most beautiful woman in Havana passing before their eyes.

At first as she sat before him, in her only good dress, María's formal side took over. Not a *jamoncita*—a ham—at all, when he asked her to smile, she could barely manage. For his part, he didn't really care but put on a show of fumbling about with his camera, making absurd faces, and, with every phrase, praising María's natural gifts. He, with his one dead eye, allowed the other to swim in hers—dark as opals, almost feline, and mysteriously alluring. "My God," he kept saying, "the more I look at you the more beautiful you become." It took him a while, but, as he went about the tedious process of making shot after shot—he used plates—all the while telling her the story of his life—no wife, no family, and never as much as a *novia* to care for him—his sad and tender manner touched her. No wonder Violeta trusted him. And suddenly she did too, for after an hour or so, María, who'd always mourned the carcasses of dead birds in the countryside, felt that she wanted to make that poor soul happy; and then, finally relaxed, she smiled in a way that seemed beatific.

After a while she began to enjoy the whole business, and got to the point that she didn't mind it when Enrique, thinking about a sale to a magazine, asked her to put on a bathing suit—he had racks of all kinds of dressing items in the back. Going behind a Chinese screen she squeezed herself into a blue one-piece and then posed, under the heat of those lights, stretched out like Goya's *Maja* on a settee. No comment about her lusciousness would suffice, but it should be said that Enrique, long accustomed to photographing the women of Havana, in various modes of dress and undress, would have gladly dallied that whole afternoon, luxuriating in the viscous femininity that, in the heat of that room—and it was ridiculously hot—escaped like perfume from her skin.

That, however, was not the photograph he would choose to put in his window. That same afternoon, he posed her in a virginal white lace wedding dress, María clutching a bouquet of roses to her breast, and supposedly dreaming about love. That black-and-white image, of María, her dark eyes looking imploringly out at the world through a lacy veil, soon graced the second tier of the photographer's window, and, wouldn't you know it, as María would tell her daughter one day, men gathered before that display just to get a second and third look of her daily.

"There are women who think they are beautiful," she once told her daughter, "and while they may be pleasant in some ways, real beauty doesn't come along too often." She'd laugh. "That real beauty was me, even if I didn't know it, back then."

With so many men stopping into the shop to inquire about the "pretty girl," it wasn't long before that face caught the attention of one Rudy Morales, the photographer's friend, who happened to own a cabaret on one of the side streets off the Prado, the Monte Carlo. It was Rudy who gave María her first dancing job, her audition held in the Lysol-scrubbed reception area of the hotel. Matilda turned up the radio, and to the music of el Trío Matamoros, María performed in the rumba style of her childhood, so fluid, so Congolese, so rapturously sensual—and sexual—her hips swaying so convincingly and her skin giving off a feminine scent so profound that, how to put it, Mr. Morales, the sort to wear dark glasses in the middle of the night, breaking into a sweat, decided to hire her on the spot. "I would have given you a job just because of the way you look," he told María. "But I'm happy to see that you can actually dance, and beautifully."

Within a few days she had joined a chorus of seven dancers, the stage shows dominated by the fabulous Rosalita Rivera (from whom María would borrow her stage surname), an affable third-tier star on her way down from a not too glorious height, with thighs and belly far too fleshly to be appearing in the spare costumes those shows required (she was, of course, the owner's mistress, bedding him at his convenience in the small flat he kept upstairs). The club itself, like so many María would work in, was a dump, selling water booze to a clientele of mischievous-minded tourists and servicemen, out for a night of oblivion and tarty entertainment. Its amenities were not elegant—its toilet was a disgrace, and their dressing area, with its speckled mirrors and pungent odors, of leaking pipes and kitchen grease, saw as much traffic as a street corner, the house band's musicians, waiters, and busboys drifting by their tables casually, as if, in fact, the ladies were wearing something more than just panties and brassieres, sometimes less. ("Get used to it," Susannah, one of the nicer dancers, told her as María scrambled to cover up her breasts when one of the musicians, a fellow named Rodrigo, happened by and, getting an eyeful of her nicely taut nipples, winked.)

She did not enjoy the cockroaches that sometimes crawled across the mirror, or the rats that skittered in through the stage door and in the early hours of the morning delighted in eating the cotton balls and pomades that the dancers left out, and it was disgusting to find their droppings inside their shoes and makeup kits. (It struck her as a gloomy and claustrophobic way to live: To be indoors at night, separated from nature by walls and passageways and doors, left María missing the country-side and the woods—the very air that seemed as delicious as anything in the world.) And it didn't make her happy to learn that she had to pay for her own costumes, for every flimsy sequined top with its gossamer meshing, for those bottoms that were two sizes too small and exposed her goose-pimpled *nalgitas* to the air-conditioned, smoke-filled chill; for the high heels that lifted her stately rump higher and left her feet sore for weeks, her toes growing horns and her soles covering over with scales like a lizard's. (Thank God that *la señora* Matilda, having become her friend, allowed María to soak in her bathtub with Epsom salts; that pleasure was a pure luxury, and the kind that she never knew back in Pinar del Río.)

The other dancers, who were all about María's age—Rosalita, at thirty, was practically an ancient by cabaret standards—were nice enough, happy to show María the ropes, but their choreographer, Gaspar, was of a different order altogether. A little fellow, he was one of those *fulanos* who, working so closely with women, seemed to have acquired some of their coquettish mannerisms; at the same time he liked to lord over them like a tyrant. With his tiny frame, muscular arms, and dyed blond hair, wavy as the sea, he was either constantly clapping his hands, to speed up their pace (flamenco-inspired numbers were the worst) or else putting on a show by tapping at the ladies' heads with his dense forefinger if they made any mistakes. He worked on their pos-tures, constantly lifting chins higher with his knuckles, and, while holding their bellies flat with one hand, ran the other up from the nubs of their spines to the bottoms of their necks; along the way, he held, brushed, pressed, and touched parts of their bodies with the kind of casualness that they would have objected to were he a more manly, and therefore lascivious, sort. (If he was acting, by pretending to show no interest in them, then he was a good actor.) Sometimes he'd fire someone on the spot for flubbing her steps, send her out into the street in tears, run after her, then bring her back, without as much as an apology about the matter.

He didn't mince words. "You are the worst dancer I've ever worked with—a disaster of the first order. You should go back to the sticks," he once told María, who would have slapped his face had she not needed the job. "You put my stomach in knots, *entiendes?* Now, do it over again!"

Not that María disliked him—he was the first to let you know if your work was good, but, God, just getting to that point amounted to a daily trial. For one thing, she learned that there was quite a difference between the limberness of an amateur and that of a professional: the stretches alone were a misery that she never quite got used to. Constantly scolding them about one thing or the other, Gaspar would tell the chorus that they were useless unless, in the midst of a dance, they could raise their insteps to touch their foreheads, because then, as he'd bluntly put it, the gawking tourists might have their dreams come true and catch a glimpse of their young and succulent Cuban vaginas through the glittering fabric of their garments. Such a display of feminine charms, he reminded them again and again, was the backbone of their business. "Now, never forget that, *señoritas!*"

So for several afternoons a week, María became a reluctant ballerina in training, her long legs rising slowly and her body contorting as she tried to touch her forehead with the high arch of her shapely foot. All that work, which she hated at the time, she'd remember with fondness—given the distance of years, even the moody Gaspar would seem a most *simpático* teacher—and while it may have been true that María, a sight to see in a skimpy bodice and leotard, could have wrung a chicken's neck and still drawn applause from the audience, a certain fact remained. During her seven months' apprenticeship at the Monte Carlo, she, in fact, proved herself an exceptional dancer and probably could have been the star of that show, except for the fact that, as such things went—*It is very true, Teresita, that men will take advantage when you are so very attractive*—she didn't want to put Rosalita out on the street, the boss having gotten in the habit of removing his dark glasses and looking at María in a way that disturbed her during those shows. Or, to put it differently, she couldn't see herself spreading her legs for him just for the sake of becoming a headliner, and so, feeling his eyes drilling into her backside each time she crossed the stage, María simply stopped showing up, even if she would miss those dancers, some of whom were to remain her friends.

Doting on her and knowing just how special she looked, her *papito*, Manolo, always made a certain joke: "Where'd you come from, *chiquita?*" It was a mystery. While Concha had been a pleasant-looking woman with a broad African nose and deeply soft dark eyes, there had never been anything particularly remarkable about her looks, save for a certain gentle piety—you've seen that on the faces of those sweet churchgoing *negritas* on Sundays. As for her *papito*, with his sagging *gallego* face, his droop-lidded eyes, he was no prize either (even when María thought that he would have been a handsome man if he hadn't liked his rum so much). Somehow, between the two of them, they had produced this masterpiece, the sort of little girl who, romping through the high grasses, lifted even the lowest and most forlorn of spirits up. Whenever Manolo took her around, guitar in hand, to neighboring farms and *valles*, she was as good as currency when it came to getting him free drinks and a little food. And, during the glory of her childhood, when she became aware of just how thickly and deliberately sunlight moved across a field, and just the scent of flowers sent her to heaven, there was no escaping the fact that, in a *valle* with lots of other Marías, and pretty ones at that, she and her younger sister, Teresita, for whom she would have cut off her right hand, surely stood out.

She was so pretty that whenever she was spotted from the fields tending to her chores in their yard—feeding their livestock from pails of slop mainly—even the most exhausted of those *guajiro* farmers, faces gnarled, bodies thin as bone, their skin leathery from the sun, would halt their oxen and call out to her, *"Oye, princesa!"*—"Hello, princess!"—or *"Hola, mi vida!"*—"Hey there, my life!" all in the effort to get her attention, as if for the first time, even if she had been tagging along with their plows and oxen for as long as she could remember. Well, things had just changed, that's all. First had come the blood, then the bloating, the terrible lecture about becoming filthy and having to wear a rag so she wouldn't drip blood everywhere. Then her body had filled out. It had seemed to take only a few months. Her angelic girl's figure, turning so voluptuous that Concha, fearful a drunkard might try to take advantage of her one night, made María wear a homemade corset tight around her chest, but, with María hating the thing, that lasted only a while, proving too painful and impractical for her to endure.

In those days, a toothless old *guajiro,* Macedonio, who slurped through his every saliva-driven utterance, once told her, "Looking at you, I can remember when I could chew." And when she, Teresa, and her *papito* went to the nearest town, San Jacinto, some ten miles away, to bring their livestock to market, María suddenly found herself being followed by one or another of the brasher young men, fellows who whistled after her, promised to buy her an ice cream cone if she would only tell them her name, and who, while her *papito* negotiated with a butcher, asked her out to see a movie in that town's little theater, El Chaplin. If she refused them all, or hardly seemed to care about hurting anyone's feelings, it was because María tried to forget about her own bodily changes: which is to say that she didn't want to let her childhood go.

They had no schools—not a single one of those *guajiros* being educated—and their *papito* just didn't think it worthwhile to make the two-hour journey back and forth each day to town just so that his daughters might learn to read and write. The best things for them to acquire would be more practical skills—like cooking, skinning animals, and sewing—just what a husband would want. Besides, they had enough work to keep them busy. With one day much like the next, once they finished looking after their livestock—so many pigs, chickens, and randy goats (who stank to high heaven)—María and Teresita, smelling of animals and dung, and with feather remnants in their hair, would make their way down through the woods behind their house, along a twisting path, enormous trees swallowing the light, to a gully and waterfall where rainbows often appeared in the mists. They were so happy then, for everything around them was so beautiful: the lianas and birds of paradise grew densely in that *jungla,* the fecundity of its earth sending up an endless variety of blossoms, all manner of starflowers and wild orchids sprouting alongside bottle palms, whose thorny fronds cascaded to the ground in clusters, hooded violets dangling like bells off vines around them. (The variety was endless: crimson begonias, red-bulbed *flor de euphorbias, flor de majagua,* purple jacarandas, hibiscus, *radiantes,* and tiny violets, as well as other peculiarly named blossoms—scratch bellies, burst horses, and chicken-dung blooms, not a one deserving such a homely appellation. Perhaps that's why, years later, María had so many silk flowers in her home, and why certain scents from the little garden she kept outside her house always made her cry, or come close to it, because such natural perfumes made her think about Teresa, Cuba, and her own youth. No matter how jaded she otherwise had become, María still missed the wonderment she had felt as a girl when each morning seemed to bring even more of those incredible flowers into the world, and gushingly so, as if God, peeking out from his religious stillness, had pointed a finger and made their pistils, tendrils, and petals suddenly ooze from the ground and up the moss-covered trunks of trees, all effortlessly coming into existence in the same mysterious manner that her own body had changed.)

That *cascada* flowed out of a massive cave, its roof dripping with stalactites, bats flitting in and out of the darkness. While stony drafts of cool air, redolent of guano and clay, came wafting out its entrance—so wonderful on a hot afternoon—they'd slip off their dresses and, down to their breeches, lie on the granite ledge, luxuriating in the torrents, as delicious as any *aguacero* or tremendous storm. A sheath of water pelting their bodies, the sisters held on to each other the way they did at night while sharing a bed, all the while whispering about how, as little old *viejitas,* they would remain close forever and forever like angels, amen.

They must have gone there hundreds of times since they were children, with very little changing in their routine, but on one of those afternoons, as they were walking home, Teresita, then twelve years old, in the midst of a smile and midstride while sidestepping some jasmine blooms—*"¡Qué bonitos son!"*—stopped suddenly as if she had hit a wall. Her eyes rolling up into their sockets, she bit her tongue, her teeth chattered, and her limbs began shaking so violently she bloodied the knuckles of her right hand while striking it against a rocky ledge—all that even before she dropped like a stone to the ground. And with that María fell to her knees, smothering her younger sister's body with her own, as if to protect her from *los castigos de Dios*—the castigations of God, as her *mamá* used to call such visitations of unexpected misery. But they still came floating down from heaven like the black ashes of a cane field fire, no sweetness in the air, María holding her sister as tightly as she could without hurting her, her right hand cushioning Teresita's head as it whipped from side to side, María's own knuckles soon bleeding from smacking against the ground in the effort to keep her sister still, a weeping mist settling around them.

LATER, WHEN TERESA'S TREMBLING HAD PASSED, AND MARÍA HAD gotten her *papito,* who had been strumming on his guitar with a friend, they carried that *inocente* back through the forest to the shack, where they laid her down on her *papito*'s cot. Finally coming around, Teresa hadn't the slightest idea of what had happened—and yet her cuts and bruises and aching teeth and bit up tongue told her otherwise—she just knew. One moment by the grotto, the next in that *bohío.* The first face she saw, so beautiful and sad and concerned, was María's, then her *papito*'s and Mamá's, a rosary in hand. One of their neighbors—maybe it was Apollo—peered in from the doorway and sipped from a tin cup of whatever her *papi* had poured to settle his nerves. He smiled broadly, being the rare *guajiro* with fantastic teeth, as if that would somehow make things better.

Just then that room, where their older brothers had died, seemed the saddest place on earth. Nevertheless, Teresita, always a sweet-natured soul, managed to sit up and ask: "Why's everyone looking so sad?"

And that made them laugh, even if her sudden illness was yet another of those tragedies they'd have to accustom themselves to. With pure affection, María wiped away her little sister's tears; and with tenderness kissed her pretty face a dozen times over, telling her, as they later sat out watching the stars, "You see, Teresa, everything's going to be all right, because I love you, and Papi and Mami love you, and nothing bad is going to happen to you while we're around." That's what they all wanted to believe. Local healers, examining her the next day, provided Teresita with some natural *calmantes* by means of a specially brewed tea containing equal parts of jute, ginger, and cannabis, among other local herbs, and suggested they sacrifice an animal to San Lázaro, but this advice was ignored. Papito told her to drink a cup of rum, whose taste she found burning and metallic, but, even after she had been administered a *santera's* cleansing, by means of burning roots and tobacco, as an added precaution, when she began trembling again a few days later, there remained no doubt that Manolo would have to fetch a doctor from San Jacinto or, failing that, from the sugar mill, a day's ride away.

He'd do anything for his daughters, of course, and though it made him sad to pay the fee—what was it, a dollar?—he truly believed that the doctor, a certain Bruno Ponce, so sanguine of manner, and slightly jaundiced with sunken eyes behind wire glasses, would find a cure. Her *papito's* hopefulness, however, didn't quite work out. Apprised of her symptoms and examining her, the doctor determined that Teresita had suffered from a grand mal seizure *(a tonic-clonic episode or status epilepticus, as her namesake, Doctor Teresita, would identify it, from her mother's descriptions, decades later)*, a condition related either to epilepsy or to a tumor within her skull. As treatment, he prescribed a twice daily dose of phenobarbital, a sedative they could find at the *farmacia* in town. Its proprietor, whom María would never forget for his homely but kind face, Pepito *el alto*, as he was known to everyone, never even charged them for their monthly amber bottles of the stuff, so sorry did he feel for those *guajiros* with the lovely daughters.

(In fact, that wonderful man, a widower, formed an attachment to María and actually took Manolo aside one afternoon to discuss the possibility of a marriage between them, even if he was in his fifties. While such arranged marriages weren't unheard of, and it would have made their lives easier, her *papito* just couldn't bring himself to subject his thirteen-year-old daughter to life with an old man. To the pharmacist's credit, he never held anything against them; though, whenever María entered his shop to get Teresa's pills, he became solemn in his demeanor, and, more often than not, while stepping back into the shadows, he'd let out with a sigh. Years later, with a wistfulness about *la Cuba que fue,* she'd wonder whatever happened to him.)

For a while several of those bitter pills daily seemed to do the trick. Still, with their foul taste, Teresita dreaded the very idea of having to take any medicine, and whether she took those pills or not as instructed, she seemed just fine.

A few months later, several days before the Christmas of 1943, they were out at the bodega by the crossroads, where trucks from distant cities sometimes stopped, dancing for a crowd of rum-soaked *guajiros,* who were whooping it up on one of those nights when the poorest of the poor pretended to be rich, the tables covered with all kinds of victuals—succulent *lechón* and pit-roasted chickens and doves, rivers of *aguardiente* and beer flowing like the Nile, their roosters and hounds meandering about, droppings left everywhere, as if anyone, some dancing barefooted on those sagging pine floors—covered in sawdust in the corners—gave a damn. On that night with their *papito* in good voice and on a little makeshift stage with a few of his musician friends from around—what were their names?—oh yes, Alvaro and Domingo, and a third fellow, the one-eared Tomaso, who played a *gaita* that he'd made from a pig's belly, his terrible wailings on that primitive bagpipe appreciated just the same, those *guajiros* were having so much fun.

Among the females were those charming *jamoncitas* in their best flower-patterned dresses: María and Teresita, displaying their youthful rumbas, white blossoms tucked into their hair, and laughing as they turned, spinning in circles like flowers fallen from a tree. In the midst of all that, with the musicians playing, their *papito* proudly beaming at them, and with the oldest of the old clapping along, and the other beautiful young women of their *valle*, usually pregnant or on their way to becoming so, nodding at *las muchachitas*—with all that going on, Teresita, in the midst of a dance, had the second of her serious attacks, falling stiffly into her older sister's arms and then, after appearing as if she were dead, trembling so violently on the floor that her limbs were soon black and blue. But, *la pobre*, even that wasn't the worst of it—the pretty thing lost control of her bowels, *coño*, a shame of all shames. That fiesta still went on, though with more restraint in respect to Manolo and his daughter, the pretty one, with the wistful spoon-shaped face, who had nearly died and then come back before their very eyes.

After that, it was María who kept after Teresa to take her medicine, whether she wanted to or not, but even so, those fits returned, her body contorting in frightening ways, her eyes becoming blank as stone. Looking after her, María preferred to think those seizures, lasting only a few minutes, would soon vanish altogether because of the medicines (and their *mamá*'s constant prayers). But they didn't. Out in the yard one morning, jumping rope with some of the local girls, Teresita, gleefully yelping as she took her turn, their hounds Blanco and Negro barking at her, died again, her eyes rolling up in her head. On another day, they were feeding the pigs and crying out with delight (and disgust) at the way the sows sniffed their feet and prodded their ankles with their moist and bristled snouts, when Teresita, in the midst of a laugh, suddenly turned to stone and fell right down into the swill, but this time, instead of violently shaking, she simply seemed to stop breathing, her lips and face becoming slightly blue. María, frightened to death, smothered her younger sister's face with kisses until, by some sleight of God's hand, she came around again, with a terrible belch that forced open the passageway to her lungs.

When it happened yet another time, while the sisters were accompanying their *papito* to town, it didn't take María long to figure out that

Teresita, detesting the bitter taste of those pills, only pretended to be taking them. From then on, María made sure Teresita actually swallowed them down, even if she had to force her mouth open by twisting her hair back before shoving one of those *píldoras* in herself. It wasn't easy. Just slapping Teresa in the face for her own good, in the same way that her *papito* had sometimes slapped hers, nearly brought María to tears—of anger and grief. She came to hate the way Teresita spat that phenobarbital at her face or doubled over, clutching her belly and sinking to the ground, trembling—not from bad nerves but from the very thought that María, who had always loved her so, had started making her life a misery. Every time Teresita told her *"Tú no me quieres"*—"You don't love me,"—or *"Te odio, hermana"*—"I hate you, sister," her voice cracking and eyes blistering from the strain of crying, María's heart broke a little more. *(Long after Teresita was gone, those memories pecked at María like crows.)*

Guajira sisters were never supposed to be at odds, but no matter how much Teresita abhorred those pills, María remained determined about fulfilling her duties—Teresita was her only sister, after all. And when her sister's condition seemed to improve and she didn't suffer any attacks for months, María, despite Teresita's misery and weeping, felt more than a little justified in her actions. Too bad that her younger sister seemed to become nervous and gloomy around her, as if she, *la bella* María, would ever lift a finger to hurt her. It took María a while to understand some other things: that such a medicine affected the *mente,* the heart and soul, in short, that phenobarbital had started to change her younger sister's sweet nature.

Indeed, that medicine had a bad effect on her younger sister; Teresita's moods were never the same from day to day. Sometimes she became so timid and afraid of people, trembling not from epilepsy but from the belief, without any reason, that even the most gentle of farmers wanted to hurt her. Her fears followed her to bed: Teresita couldn't sleep, spending half the night turning from side to side and sighing (and despairing over the aftertaste of that medicine, which lingered in the throat for hours even if she had consumed it with a sweet mango or papaya or mamey or *guineo*). To feel her sister's heart beating as quickly as a hummingbird's against her chest in the middle of the night, as she held her tenderly, to hear her breathing, but painfully so, while gasping for air—all that was almost more than María could bear, to the point that on certain days she would have welcomed one of her sister's fits again—possessed by the devil as Teresita seemed to be—instead of having to watch her turn into someone she didn't know.

One day Teresita was saintly, the next all she wanted to do was to stick her tongue out at passersby, or torment the animals, tying cords around their necks and pulling them cruelly across the yard. Whereas she used to show appreciation for even the smallest kindness—*"¡Ay, qué bonito!"*— "How pretty!" or *"¡Qué sabroso!"*—"How tasty!"—and never hesitated about saying nice things—*"Te aprecio mucho, hermana"*—"I love you, sister!"—days now passed when she wouldn't say a word to anyone. Her facial expressions were affected as well: it was as if she refused to smile and took to crying over nothing; and when she wasn't crying, she withdrew into herself, as if no one else in the world existed, and never lifted a finger to help around the house or yard, not even when her *mamá*, with her slowly failing eyesight, begged Teresita to help her thread a needle.

("I'll do it, Mami," María offered.)

As for prayers? Whenever their *mamá*, in her God-welcoming way, got them down on their knees to give thanks for the salvation that was sure to come, Teresita would refuse, shaking her head and running away— why should she? Neither her mother nor her father lifted a finger against her in punishment. *("Niña," as María once asked her daughter, "how on earth can you force someone to believe?")* Still, there came the day when things got out of hand. Teresita, with her own kind of beauty, also entered into puberty—and quickly so—but whereas María had been cautious and could care less about having a *novio*, or any of those birds-and-bees romances, Teresita became obsessed with the idea and started to do anything she could to avoid María's company, their excursions to the cascades long since behind them.

Well, María couldn't keep track of her sister every minute of the day, and she got used to tending to her chores alone. Where could Teresita go anyway, aside from the bodega, where they knew the owner and asked him to keep an eye on her? Most of the young men in their *valle*, respecting her *papito*, just didn't want to get on his bad side, and so María didn't think much of it when Teresita took off in her bare feet in the afternoons—to where and what, no one knew. María imagined her sitting in some lonely spot with her knees tucked up under her chin, fretting—as María, her body in its changes baffling her, once used to do herself. And while she often wanted to go after her, she left Teresita, so troubled by that medicine, alone.

One evening as María crossed the fields on her way to Macedonio's— where her *papito* had gone to borrow a hammer and a handful of nails— something, a blur of entangled figures, bending and weaving inside the forest, caught her attention. At first she assumed it was one of the local *putas* with a farmer—when they weren't working the bodega, they went wandering from *valle* to *valle*, looking for takers. María's eyes might be put out by *Dios*, but she moved closer anyway. From behind a bottle palm she saw a stringy *guajiro* standing behind a woman whose skirt had been hitched up above her waist. María wasn't stupid. She knew about fornication from the animals, the billy goats being the most insatiable, the males mounting the females at will; she'd seen mammoth horses dallying with their mares, and just about every other creature, from hens and roosters to lustrous dragonflies in midair, performing their duties as nature intended. And there they were, the woman holding on to the trunk of a banyan tree, raising her haunches higher, while the man pumped furiously at her from behind, the way María had seen the animals doing.

Desgraciados, she remembered thinking.

Oh, there was something agonizing and stomach turning about watching it. But she could not look away. She eased closer and, wouldn't you know it, nearly fainted when, getting a better glimpse of them, as the *guajiro*, in some kind of frenzy, started yanking that woman's head back to kiss her neck, and even as a gentle white-winged butterfly alighted upon María's arm, there was no doubt about it, she saw that the shapely woman was none other than her beloved sister, Teresita.

Two things happened afterwards:

Finding out about that whole business from María, her *papito* nearly beat that big-boned *guajiro* to death with a shovel. And because her mother was too *humilde* and mild, and her *papito* told her to do so, María, dragging Teresa by the hair out of the forest where she had gone to hide, and loving her so, to make a point, had to beat her too—with the branch of a tree, a beating that left her body covered, once again, with bruises.

They didn't speak to each other ever again, no matter how often María, feeling badly for her sister, followed her around, asking to be forgiven for her severity, even if she had been in the right. Teresa would not say a word, never recanting, nor for that matter did she ease the burden on María's heart. One of those evenings, when terraces of violet light went spreading across the horizon at dusk, as her *papito*, Manolo, sitting out on a crate in front of their house, picked up his guitar again and while María settled her head against Concha's lap, and as her mother peeled a few potatoes, the beads of her rosary, dark as black beans, which Concha always kept wrapped around her right hand, dangling down and touching María's face—while such simple things were going on, Teresa, who had gone off to use the *retrete*, stumbled into the forest and, following that trail to the waterfall, where they had often lingered as children, weighed down the skirt of her dress with stones and leapt off that moss-covered ledge into the depths of beautiful María's memory and soul.

All of the above occured to her while María had been on her way home to the Hotel Cucaracha one might, with fellows calling out, "Hey, gorgeous, why the long face?"

55

PART II

The Glory That
Entered Her Life

During María's first year in Havana, she had gotten jobs in places like the Club Pygmalion, the Knock-Knock, the Broadway, some of those stints lasting months, some just weeks. Along the way she had been a Hawaiian hula dancer, a sultry Cleopatra, and, during the Christmas holidays, one of Santa's Very Wonderful Cuban Ladies. She never earned too much in those days; dancers, however beautiful, were in plentiful supply in that city of music. She didn't like stripping for the auditions and took offense at any act requiring that she take off her pasties; mainly, she tended to put off some of her bosses by refusing their advances. One manager, a certain Orlando, at the Knock-Knock, off Zayas, fired her when she wouldn't become his woman—*"mi mujer"*—but as shabbily as he had treated her, having her thrown out on the street, at least he hadn't pulled out a knife like that hoodlum who ran a joint—was it the Club Paree?—by Ramparts Street; he cut off the buttons of her dress one by one and would have raped her on his office table had not María fallen to the floor feigning another epileptic fit—*forgive me, Sister*—her head twisting, teeth chattering, body shaking, as if she were possessed. Or she sometimes broke down crying, pleading that she was religious, and became so disconsolate that even the most heartless and goatish of men gave up their harassments, often thinking, as a trance burned in her beautiful eyes, *That woman is crazy.*

But there was something about a sad man that always tempted her. In that instance, such *tristeza* was found in a certain *Señor* Aponte, proud proprietor of the Versailles in the Vedado, with its Folies-Bergère floor show. A quite rotund fellow and a destroyer of chairs, he always sweated profusely, a kerchief pressed to his damp brow. His dark eyes seemed anxious, as if, in his burly, struggling, short-breathing manner, he might drop dead at any moment. While the other girls made jokes about what an ordeal it would be to go to bed with him, María, liking the man, found his loneliness touching—he kept a cage of parakeets in his office and would be often overheard through his door speaking endearingly with them as if they were children.

Still, it came down to the same thing. Called into his office to discuss a featured spot in the chorus, María had listened to him sing her praises as a dancer when, out of the blue, he pulled from a drawer a pair of elbow-length white satin gloves and then, with boyish reticence, asked her to put those gloves on and fondle him. "Please, I beg you." Then he made a confession, declaring that it was very hard to go through life loving one of his dancers the way he loved her; that with his days in the world so short—he just knew it—he could go to his grave happily if only she would perform that little act. She almost did—not for a better job, or because of the way he had set aside a twenty-dollar bill on the ink blotter of his desk for her, but because he seemed to be telling the truth—he certainly looked like he was not long for this world. That evening she almost gave in to the inner argument that, far from being a lowly act, it would be one of decency and grace—his sadness cutting into her. In the end, however, even when she had gone so far as to slip those gloves on, the words *puta* and *lowlife* flashing through her mind, her kindlier inclinations lost out to her virtuous resolve, and, with tears in her eyes, she fled that room.

A few weeks later, when she heard that *Señor* Aponte had dropped dead from a heart attack while walking in the arcades of Galliano, she surely had felt bad. When she heard the rumor that a love note written to one of the chorus girls had been found in his pocket, she was certain that it had been intended for her, though she wouldn't have been able to read it. For days, she wished to God that she had honored that man's simple request—perhaps a last wish—the money would have been useful and he would have been happy. Who would it have hurt, and who would have known about it?

No, she was not about to become one of those young girls who happen to lie down for money with men. It would have been easy enough to find takers, for she had already been stirring the male juices for a long time in that city, and the expression on María's nearly ecstatic face as she danced left men seriously fatigued with desire. She'd already received half a dozen marriage proposals from men on her street, a barber and a shoe repairman among them, and a few louts without jobs—maybe they were numbers runners for the races out at the dog track—with nothing more to offer her than the shirts on their backs. A few of her potential courters were wily neighbors at the Hotel Cucaracha who sometimes waited half the night for her to come traipsing up the stairs; but just walking along the streets of Havana, at any hour of the day, she attracted men who'd follow her for blocks and frighten her with the suggestive remarks they'd make. And some, most gentlemanly sorts, in their fine linen suits, adopting a more polite demeanor, doffed their hats at her and, with the utmost politeness, asked if they might accompany her for a while, and other questions followed, along the lines of where she lived and worked. She hardly ever told them the truth, even if she sometimes felt terribly alone.

She so stood out on the streets of Havana that, on many a night, while leaving one club or another at four in the morning, she'd drape a veil or a mantilla over her face, haunting the darkened arcades and alleys through which she passed like a spirit, her high heels clicking against the cobblestones beneath her. In the light of day, however, there was no way of concealing herself—if only she could be more like those carefree *cubanas* she saw, proudly swaying their big kiss-me *culos* as they sashayed down the street. But the truth is that María could have been wearing a crown of thorns and dragging a cross behind her and she still would have attracted amorous attention. Strolling along the Malecón in her simple ruffle-skirted dress, she'd slow traffic, the drivers of trucks and automobiles, and even the Havana Police in their cruisers, pumping on their brakes to get a better look at her shapely gait. Bootblacks scrambled to give her shoes a free buffing. Old men did double takes, for that desire's the last thing to go. So did the street sweepers, window washers, and those fellows who went from door to door with grindstones to sharpen household cutlery. Bicyclists tling-tlinged María. Fruit and produce vendors, selling their goods from carts and stands, refused to take her money or, when they did, never charged her the full amount, often sending María away with more mangoes, avocados, and garlic bulbs than she could possibly have use for. Florists gave her bouquets—chrysanthemums and roses and little bouquets of purple and white mariposas, the national flower of Cuba.

At the intersection of Compostela and O'Reilly, a blind beggar, Mercurio, standing by a newspaper kiosk, seemed to regain his sight whenever she happened to pass by, that sly *negrito* who sold pencils out of a jar and sang ballads for pennies breaking into a broad grin as if, indeed, through his pitch-black glasses he could see the shapeliness of María's body inside her dress. And in his goatish white-haired madness, el Caballero de París, as he was known in Havana, a locally famous eccentric of Bohemian habits, wearing a beret and a heavy frock even in the heat of the day, followed her around as well, expounding poetry in praise of María as he strode beside her. Even priests and monsignors, striding solemnly out from one or other of Havana's myriad churches, abandoned their vows of worldly indifference and, at the sight of María's *nalgitas* as they bobbed inside her dress, kissed their scapulars, thanking God for his handiwork.

"Eres una maravilla"—"You are a wonder"—was the kind of thing she heard over and over again.

Her face, in some ways, must have seemed saintly. During her church visits to pray and dream, Havana Cathedral with its musty and timeless interior being a favorite refuge, María received endless (useless) blessings from priests, supplicants, and beggars alike. Now and then, someone in the plaza would make her the gift of a rosary or a vial of holy water or a prayer card—even a relic sometimes. And while she could not have been more polite or gracious, or more thankful for their gifts, María had stopped believing that such religious objects made any difference in this world.

Street urchins, traveling in packs, followed her, tugged at her skirt hems, danced by her feet, and harassed anyone else who looked at her. From their second-floor windows, old women, Spanish fans in hand, smiled, admiring her as well (María, after all, was their own past). As she was cutting through a cul-de-sac alley between apartment buildings, there was always some fellow, bored to death or horny, on his balcony to call down to María, asking, with a sly expression on his face, if she would like to have a drink or go dancing. On the majestic Prado, managers offered her free meals just for sitting by a table in their outdoor cafés. (At least María knew she never had to go hungry.)

Among the suave and easygoing *cubanos* she encountered daily, who flirted as a matter of basic decorum, it often amounted to a pleasant enough game, the very fact that María, wearing a sphinxlike mask, might occasionally crack a *sonrisa,* a smile, was enough to send these dandies and caballeros dancing happily off into their futures. Crude sorts, however, also abounded. In a market off Lamparilla, there was a *carnicero*, a butcher, she tried to avoid. Whenever she passed by his stall, which smelled of fresh-killed meat, he always gave her body an up and down. It didn't matter if she was just trying to mind her own business. Winking, sucking air in through his teeth, he took delight in waving calves' tongues, bulls' testicles, and the biggest chorizos in his stall at her. And sometimes, if she were passing through a crowded marketplace, both disembodied hands and other parts pressed against her.

Worse, however, were the out-and-out obscene gestures that came her way, especially at night, as she went walking home. When the clubs had closed and even the bordellos of la Marina and Colón were winding down, there was always the chance that some *borrachero,* barely able to stand straight against an arcade column, might grab himself through his trousers, all the while boasting that he had a tremendous *malanga* awaiting her. (Some of those "caballeros" actually had a romantic gleam in their eyes—as if their ardor was akin to an expression of love, and as if María might actually fall to pieces and succumb to their masculine powers, the shits.) And you would be surprised by the number of times that such sorts of men, stepping towards María from the shadows, actually pulled their stiff *pingas* out to show her—oh, how María wished she had that butcher's cleaver with which to cut those chorizos off, may God forgive her for such unkindly thoughts.

On those occasions—twice with the same degenerate whose appendage, enhanced by the glowing penumbra cast by the arcade's light, seemed shockingly large—she spat and cursed such filthy-minded louses—the *chusmas*—for not leaving her alone; then she'd march stoically on. And each time she did, María felt her kindly *guajira* soul hardening a little more, her skin growing thicker, and her patience for the vicissitudes of men wearing thin.

Putting up with a lot, María could have used someone to look after her. And that feeling just grew stronger as time went on. Missing her *valle*, she sometimes spent her evenings off from the clubs in that hallway with *la señora*, with her slight urine smell, listening to anything on the radio, so long as she wouldn't have to sit in her room alone. She dreaded the prospect of sleep—she'd twist and turn thinking about her dead sister and the look of horror on her face when she gave her a beating, kept imagining her drowning in that pool beneath the cascades. She'd get down on her knees to beg Teresita's spirit for her forgiveness, but no matter what, no sooner did she finally get under the covers of her *chinche*-ridden bed, hoping for pleasant dreams, than she began to fill with a terrible apprehension that shot through her body like electricity; she'd sit up, trembling, and out of habit, and a feeble hope, she'd pray. And when that didn't work, though she knew it was a sin, she'd reach between her legs, her fingers dampened by her tongue, fondling herself until, writhing and churning her hips into her own hand's motion, she lifted out of her own history into the momentary oblivion of pleasure, breaking into pieces. And then, of course, she'd slip back into the gloom of guilt, even more deeply than before. But that was María.

In any event, she was working as a dancer in a new revue—that's what the professionals called it—at the Club Nocturne, in Vedado, where, one night, fed up with her loneliness, she first met the man who, years later, was to become her daughter, Teresa's, father.

Chapter
NINE

She'd noticed him coming into the club a few times before: he was older, somewhere on the far side of his thirties, had a pock-marked face, clear gray eyes, and a pencil-line mustache. He comported himself with authority, hardly ever looked up at anything, not even at the floor show, and always seemed involved with going over a ledger book, or some volume that he was reading. He always dressed nicely in a white silk suit, wore a lavender cologne, or was it lilac scented? The sort to drink only the best stuff, he ordered the same meal of fried pork chops with onions and *papas fritas* without fail, then smoked cigar after cigar until some late hour, when, as quietly as he'd come in, he would leave. A man of regular routines, without any interest in wasting his money in an adjoining casino room, where there were gaming tables and a roulette wheel, he seemed almost indifferent to that place—why he went there she didn't know, nor, in fact, did María particularly care.

That she met him at all was a matter of pure chance. Since part of María's job was to keep company with the club's patrons between shows—all the girls had to—she had the misfortune of finding herself at a table with a group of drunk Americans who were beside themselves over the fact that María happened to be wearing so little—just a glittery bandeau and a silvery, tasseled *pantalette* under a diaphanous chemise. And because the unspoken assumption, the myth (sometimes the truth) had it that such women were often very willing to moonlight as prostitutes, one of these men, a burly fellow, muttering all kinds of drivel she couldn't understand, had taken the liberty of reaching over to fondle María's leg under the table. As she, in a fit of pique, stood up to leave, the drunk took hold of her hand and pulled María onto his lap. Just then, before even the club bouncer, a bald black giant named Eliseo, could intercede, this man, Ignacio Fuentes, watching from his table, marched over and grabbed that drunkard's forearm, forcing it from around María's belly. Then, looking intently into the drunkard's eyes and saying a few words in English, and before his friends could make more of a commotion, Ignacio opened his jacket and showed him something that drained the fellow's ruddy face of color.

"Okay, okay," the man said, holding up his hands. "I get it."

"Good," Ignacio said firmly. "Now apologize to the lady."

The man mumbled his regrets—and Ignacio, in case María didn't get the drift, translated: "He says he's very sorry to have bothered you." Then, as if his contempt for the fellow had turned to air, and to smooth over the situation, perhaps for the sake of María's job, he called the waiter over, buying them a round of drinks: "Give those *sinvergüenzas* whatever they want." Bowing cordially, as if nothing out of the ordinary had happened, he headed back to his table, and María, who'd had that kind of thing happen to her before without anyone particularly caring, followed him.

They spoke for only a few minutes—she had another show to perform—but in that time, while thanking him, María had decided that this caballero, a gallant, wasn't the usual sort who came into the club. Despite his macho demeanor, there was something fiercely intelligent about his eyes, intimidating and somehow reassuring at the same time. Perhaps he was a teacher, maybe a university professor, and a very lonely one, a *soltero* with a preference for that kind of place. But obviously he couldn't be—how many *maestros* were so courageous, and for that matter carried inside their jackets the sort of *something* that so quickly quieted so unruly a man? What most intrigued her was what he wore on the thin gold chain around his neck: a crucifix, a medallion of the Virgin de Cobre, and a third symbol, which she supposed had something to do with *los judíos*: it was just like the Star of David hanging outside the synagogue on Santa Clara Street in the old city.

("Oh, these two," he would later tell her, *"are for my faith, and the third I wear in case* los judíos *were right all along.")*

He didn't really have too much to say to her: he seemed only obliquely aware of her lusciousness. It was as if her beauty meant nothing to him, which, in a way, she liked and despaired over at the same time. *(Was it that he didn't find her attractive?)* Just before going backstage to change into her costume for the second show, an elaborate dance routine staged to the music of Moisés Simóns' *"Cubanacan,"* she told him her name— "María . . . María García y Cifuentes"—and with that, he smiled for the first time. Though he had a few teeth missing, she found his appearance reassuring.

IT SHOULDN'T HAVE BEEN A SURPRISE TO FIND HIM WAITING FOR her on the street afterwards, at four in the morning, María in a raincoat and veil, Ignacio leaning against an alley wall across the way, casually smoking a cigar under the flickering glare of a misspelled neon sign— NIGTH CLUB. She'd come out with three other dancers, one of them, knowing María as a solitary sort (translation: a poor thing scared to death of the city), exhorting María to enjoy herself for a change. *(Pero con cuidado,* with caution.) So when he offered to accompany her for a while, she didn't mind. That night, without even attempting to hold her hand or to pull her off into the shadows for a kiss, he seemed a gentlemanly sort, a real caballero, as if he'd never push her up against a wall and take advantage. (Deep down, at the same time, she wanted him to.) Calmly, Ignacio told her about himself: he was a businessman, *un trabajador,* who'd gotten a little lucky with a going import and export concern, mostly in appliances, based in the harbor. His *negocio* required that he travel now and then, not just across the island but sometimes to the States—*"Tú sabes, pa' América, y los ciudades de Miami y Nueva York"*—but now that they were becoming acquainted, how could he look forward to leaving Havana?

"But, *señor* . . ."

"Call me Ignacio, please."

"You don't even know me."

"What should I know?" he asked. "To be honest, María, before tonight, I'd hardly noticed you—not that I haven't observed what a tremendous dancer you are—but I'm one of those fellows who believes there's a reason why things happen a certain way. You know that drunkard who was bothering you? I'm almost grateful to him for what happened tonight." He stopped on the corner of Calle 15 and began fingering the crucifix and the other medallions around his neck. "You see, María, *soy viudo*—I'm a widower, who once had a wife and *una muchachita*, a daughter. My wife's name was Carmen, and she had family up in Tampa, and so I would send them off every so often to visit." Then, a little sadly: "You remember the hurricane of 'forty-three?"

Of course she did, it was the same year that half their livestock drowned, the year that Teresita, so confused and lost, threw herself into the cascade's waters.

"Their plane went down in that storm, and since then, well, how may I explain myself—I've hardly cared less about normal things. I do my work, I sometimes go out, but little else. I can hardly sleep at night thinking of what happened to them. Do you know that feeling?"

"*Sí, señor*, I do," she said.

"That's the reason I'm always reading. It keeps my mind on other things. That's why I sit enjoying the company of others without really having to talk with anyone. I can do that in a club like the Nocturne, where the food is good, and, of course, the entertainment exceptional."

They were only a few blocks from the harbor walk, the Malecón, and because he could have cared less about going home and because María after a night of performances stayed up for hours, she didn't mind accompanying him there. It usually took her an hour to stroll back to la Cucaracha, and the moon, with a sad, pocked face that always seemed to be watching, had lit up the ocean, a tranquil sight to take in.

"So, María, some parts inside of me—how can I put it—have been asleep for a long time. Fundamentally"—Pero, carajo, he used big words—"I haven't had much interest in women. Not that I don't notice, but *mi deseo*, my desire . . . for love has vanished." And he tapped at his heart. "María, don't you understand? I've been a dead man inside."

Then he grew silent, a somberness overcoming him as if he had been embarrassed by his admission. On that night, automobile head beams flared along the grand curving roadway, a hundred residences and hotels, all aglow, their windows burning with light. It wasn't until they could see the Morro castle in the distance that he came around again, with a simple question: "Just where is it that you live?" And when she told him that she had been staying at the Residencia Cubana, he could only shake his head. "I know of that place—isn't it a disgrace?"

"Perhaps," she answered him, feeling vaguely offended. "But it's been my only home in Havana. I have my friends there, and the *señora* who runs it is very good to me."

"But surely you must know what goes on there?" And when she looked away, he quickly added, "I didn't mean to offend you."

Along the way, a police cruiser had slowed up and pulled alongside them. Usually when that happened to María at night, she'd feel terrified of being forced inside—who knew where she might end up? Or what might be expected of her?—the prostitutes were always telling her stories. So she felt relieved when Ignacio, approaching the cruiser, a green Oldsmobile, seemed to know the officer. As he bent by the window, he and the policeman spoke, about what she could not say. She had walked over to the seawall, looking out over the bay and wondering how the gulf waters, which appeared to be so majestic, could smell so bad; at the same time, while she was taking in the immensity of that horizon's expanse, which seemed to go on forever, a queasiness overwhelmed her, as if she feared that it would swallow her whole if she lingered too long. There was something else: as that cruiser took off, Ignacio rapping on its hood in a familiar manner, the policeman, with his visor cocked slyly down, smiled, nodded, and, as it happened, winked at María in an insinuating way that she found unnerving.

It simply offended her—*I am not one of them,* she thought—and now it was María who became sullen, so sullen that, once they reached the entrance to la Cucaracha, she could hardly wait to get upstairs. Though he mentioned an all-night cafeteria on Obispo where they could go for a while, she told him that if she didn't soak her feet soon in a pan of salts, she'd suffer the next day.

"*Bueno,* do as you like," he told her, though with a slightly wounded look on his face. And then, in a most courtly manner, he bowed. The last she saw of him that night, he was making his way into that quarter and had pulled out of his jacket pocket that book, that mysterious thing in which he took his solace.

Years later, while having lunch in one of those tacky South Beach sidewalk restaurants, all María had really told her daughter about the way she met this Ignacio—it could have been on one of many afternoons when mother and daughter, taking taxis, got slightly sloshed (Teresa, as usual, being a doctor, reminding María to go easy on those margaritas because of the salt) and María, with her own kind of dignity and pride, tended to give, depending on her mood, different versions of the same tale—was that she had first encountered Ignacio, "a very intelligent, hardworking man," in a club she had been dancing in; and that he was very kind to her at first, a gentleman through and through, at least until he changed into someone she didn't recognize. But before that they'd had a good enough time.

Weeks went by before María heard from him again, and though she had thought about Ignacio now and then, she could really have cared less. One evening, however, when she had arrived at work, there awaited María a bouquet of roses and, with them, a note. Since she couldn't understand it, and felt ashamed to admit her shortcomings to the girls in her troupe, she had to wait until she got home for *Señora* Matilda to read it aloud to her:

My dear María,
I haven't forgotten you and will see you soon at the club.
Ignacio.

That next night, swathed in gossamer, while vaulting across the stage in the midst of a solo, her hips in a deep swivel as if she were trying to wipe a table clean or wash a window with her *papaya—that's how she once explained the motion to her daughter, a wallflower when it came to dance—* María, spotting Ignacio sitting at a table, dedicated her performance only to him. He knew it, watching her every move onstage and standing during the applause.

Later, it was María, sitting by his table, who told him about herself: at the heart of it was this: she was just a country girl from Pinar del Río and wouldn't mind it all if she met a sincere man, honest and of good character, whom she could trust and be good to. And when he had heard her out, Ignacio, smiling, took hold of her hand, and told her, "It is my hope, María, to be everything for you."

And he seemed to mean what he said, for soon they were going out on María's nights off, heading here and there around Havana. She loved to take in a movie at the Payret theater, where between the shows singers and comedians entertained the crowds, and more than once they'd go into the kinds of hotels that she used to pass by and find so intimidating: like the Biltmore-Sevilla and the Astor-Havana, in whose fancy restaurants they dined, as well as his favorite bistro, Delmonico's. Everywhere they went waiters and concierges attended to them with the utmost politeness and respect—it seemed that this Ignacio was an important man— and because he liked the way she looked alongside him, they would sit in the outdoor cafés. Ignacio, in his largesse, set up an account for her at El Encanto, Havana's premier department store, so that she could buy whatever items of apparel she liked, and indeed, taking her around, he thought that a little jewelry would look nice on her, and soon enough that jewel of Havana went out into the streets wearing pearls around her neck, and gem earrings, for which she'd had her earlobes pierced. When she complained of a bothersome ache in her teeth, he paid for her to visit a dentist, who, falling in love with María, could barely bring himself to drill away the cavities that even the most beautiful of women suffer. Going off on trips, Ignacio saw to it that a florist deliver a weekly bouquet to the club—all the girls buzzing with excitement and jumping, quite easily, to the conclusion that she had become Ignacio's mistress.

Indeed, he took more than just a little interest in her. It was on a Sunday that he had turned up at la Cucaracha out of the blue—she thought he was away—and told her, taking a look around, that the place made him sick to his stomach, and that he would find her another. But did she really want to go? She had gotten attached to *la señora* and knew most of the shopkeepers along that street, and most of the other prostitutes besides Violeta, even the two she found out had pee-pees like men. And while she surely would have liked to live in a nicer place, she had made that forlorn room, her first home in Havana, comfortable enough and knew that she'd miss the daily life there, the way her neighbors cooked their meals on pans on their balconies, the caged birds, the barking dogs, the guitar players and drunken singers *(Ay, papito!),* the crying babies, and even the Peeping Tom across the way—they made her feel anything but alone.

But one day, she left.

Eventually, she allowed him to "make her into a woman," as they used to say, but it had not been an easy thing to accustom herself to. With her heart in her throat, she first bedded Ignacio down on a brand-new mattress with clean sheets in the bedroom of a sunny third-floor *solar* that he had gotten her in a better neighborhood, near a marketplace. On that afternoon she discovered the sorrowful history of a man whose body was covered with scars, his back in particular, a mess of claw-shaped welts, his cruel *papito*'s gift to him as a boy. The actual act of penetration made no great impression on her, it was more or less what she had imagined, a little painful and almost pleasurable, but she had learned from the whores of la Cucaracha that nothing pleased a man more than to hear a woman scream at the top of her lungs as if she were being torn to pieces by a horse.

The whole ritual of it, however, she found discomforting and wished she had covered over the crucifix above her bed with a black cloth.

The moment he had removed her dress and undergarments and stripped down himself, proudly displaying the brutish and tearful proof of his desire—"Go ahead, look and admire it," he told her proudly—she began to drift outside herself. Fondled, spread open, pulled at, bitten, and feeling the dampish and warm bundle of his inguinal sack—*sus huevos*—rolling over her taut belly and upwards over her rib cage as he, among first things, smothered his enraged *cosita* with her breasts, she couldn't help but think about Christ's last moments on the cross. As his blunt thrusts raised a wormy vein on his forehead, his eyes turning upwards inside their lids, she envisioned the journey Jesus Christ, upon his death and resurrection, had made, down to Purgatory and then Hell, before ascending to Heaven. And while he buried his head between her thighs, kissing the corona of her femininity, Mary Magdalene went kneeling before Him, to wash His feet with the tresses of her hair.

And so, even as she screamed, she kept praying that God forgive her, for however much she believed Ignacio when he muttered that she was the kind of woman he could really care for, María, dallying in the Holy Land, felt nothing for him beyond pity and a vague gratitude for the way he looked after her, and for his generosity, sentiments which she, being so young, had perhaps confused with the devotions of love.

Chapter

ELEVEN

After that afternoon, beautiful María got used to Ignacio's visits. Was she in love with him? She hardly thought so, but she slept with Ignacio often enough to make him happy. And while María preferred to keep those duties a secret, she found it comforting to know that such arrangements were common. Some of the girls in the troupe were always looking around for men with money, often gossiping about how nice it would be to have someone of means to look after them, no matter his callousness. Most of their would-be suitors weren't prizes, though they'd hear of dancers who had run off with an American, to places like Cincinnati and Arkansas. At least Ignacio was generous, and he wasn't ugly, or fat, and he was clean, dapper, and smelled good, even if María didn't care to believe the rumors that he was a gangster of some sort.

AH, BUT HOW THINGS CHANGE. LETTING IGNACIO DO WITH HER AS he wanted and drowning afterwards in guilt, she eased her conscience by going to church, not just to confess her sins but to feel purified by the sanctity of the altar and the oddly comforting gazes of the saintly statues. As often as she asked herself, while kneeling in prayer on a stony chapel floor, *Why Ignacio?* she concluded that El Señor, in his mysterious ways, had placed him in her life for a reason. And if she felt sometimes that Ignacio didn't really care about her—especially when they had gone out to a fancy place and he'd accuse her of chewing her food too loudly and eating like a goat, at least, while she was in his company, other men left her alone. As she'd tell her daughter one day, *she needed him.* Going anywhere in Havana by herself had become a nuisance, more so as she learned how to dress better and developed a taste for fancy clothes, as well as makeup and perfumes, which she had started using in the clubs. She could rarely go down the street without someone calling out or whistling at her, many a devouring stare attending María's every step. But when she took walks with Ignacio holding her by the arm, few dared even to glance her way. With his proprietary air, he just looked like the sort you didn't want to offend. (Men found ways of glimpsing her anyway—they'd look without seeming to look in the Cuban manner, a *mirar sin mirar.*) Whenever Ignacio happened to catch someone coveting María's bottom, he'd stop dead in his tracks, excuse himself, and march over to have some words with her admirer.

She appreciated this vigilance but wished he could relax; his severity was sometimes hard to take. He may have been courtly and suave, but, as time went on, he also became quick-tempered, especially in his efforts to teach her things: how to cut food, how she should dress, never to look a man straight in the eye. His moods were sometimes awful, however, and if there was anything María sorely missed, it was the sort of tenderness she had known with her *papito.* He may not have taught her much of anything about good manners, and his drinking had made her crazy, but he, at least, had a gentle soul. She just missed that *guajiro* warmth, the sentimentality of his songs, the way her *papito* sometimes touched her face, but oh so softly, as if she were a flower.

Not so with *el señor* Fuentes, who rarely smiled and never seemed to feel compassion or pity for anyone. Poor people disgusted him. If lepers or blind men or amputees held out their hands begging for coins, a scowl of contempt exploded across his face. Once, when they were walking along Neptuno to a ladies' haberdasher's and she asked him, "But, Ignacio, why are you so hard on those people? They can't help themselves, *los pobres,*" he laid out his philosophy of life:

"María, you may think me harsh, but when you've come up from nothing, the way we both did, you learn quickly that the only person worth looking out for is yourself, and maybe your family, if they actually give a damn for you." He turned a deep, frightening red. "And so what if I give those unfortunates a few centavos? How the hell is that going to change a thing for them in the long run?"

"But if you give them a little money, then at least they can have something to eat," María said, while thinking about the poor children she saw all over the city who begged for pennies. "Isn't that the right thing to do?"

"The right thing?" he said, laughing. "I'll tell you what, María." And he reached into his jacket pocket for his wallet, pulling a ten-dollar bill out. "This was going to pay for your hat, but, what the hell, let me just give it to that fellow over there, okay?"

Marching over to some unfortunate—*un infeliz*—sitting, one legged and grimy against a wall, Ignacio stuffed that bill into the tin can he held in his filthy hands.

"So there," he said, "are you satisfied? Now, look around you and tell me something: tell me if you're seeing this lousy world changing one bit."

"*Ay, pero* Ignacio, don't be so angry at me."

"All right then, but don't you ever preach to me again. Understand?"

FOR ALL HER MISGIVINGS ABOUT HIM, THEY HAD THEIR ENJOY-ments. On a Sunday, Ignacio drove her to a beach resort out in Varadero, where María, glorious in an Esther Williams swimsuit, the sort with fancy seashell pleats accentuating her breasts and midsection (translation, her smooth belly, her fabulous burst of hair, the fig of her heart-shaped pubic mound), parted those warm, clear waters before her. They journeyed to a pueblo by the sea, about three hours east of Havana, their route, along the northern coast, taking them past expanses of marshes, mangrove swamps, and beaches to Matanzas, where Ignacio had been born in utter poverty and received his first scars. He didn't know if his father was even alive, nor did he care, and his *mamacita* had died when he was a boy, which was how he ended up in Havana to fend for himself at an early age, he told her. Taking her around—what was there to see in a town that stretched only three or four blocks end to end along the coast?—Ignacio told María, with all sincerity, that it was his dream to construct a house in that place, so that he—and she—would have a wonderful retreat to escape to from Havana, maybe even live there one day as man and wife. Then they returned to the city, and, as he often liked to do, he pulled over to the side of the road and had María undo his white *pantalones* so that she might attend to him in a manner that he particularly enjoyed: the wonderful sun just beginning to set on the horizon.

On another occasion, he drove her out to Pinar del Río to see her *papito*, whom she had missed very much. Laden with gifts, and arriving in triumph in Ignacio's white 1947 Chevrolet, María had the pleasure not only of showing off her nice clothes and prosperous *"novio,"* whom her *papito* didn't particularly like, but also of letting him see just how well she had done for herself in Havana. Olivia, her *papito*'s haggish paramour, so gloomy in black, couldn't have been more solemn, or envious. For that alone, María felt thankful to Ignacio, who, for his part, could only feel contempt for the slop of pigs, the filth of an outhouse, and, after a while, even what he called the ignorance of the *guajiros*.

She was learning what men can be about, particularly when they like their drink. Her *papito* had sometimes been that way, that's why he used to beat her, and, as she got to know Ignacio better, she learned that he could be that way too. In the bedroom, the only place where he actually seemed happy, he could be quite unpredictable. She would almost enjoy it, as long as he wasn't being too rough with her, and rum sometimes made him that way. Once he had drunk too much, he'd start accusing her of denying him certain pleasures. She'd lock herself in the bathroom, and he'd smash in the door, throw her onto the bed, and take her from behind, all the while calling her nothing better than his little *mulatta* whore. And if she wept bitterly afterwards, he'd tell her, "Grow up and don't forget that, if it weren't for me, María, you'd still be sleeping in that shithole of a hotel and dressing like a tramp."

Drinking, he became a different man, who made her life a nightmare. Even when he behaved in a reasonable way, taking care of him with her mouth became a labor, not of love but of drudgery. Sober it didn't take much: just the sight of her lovely face in a posture of voluptuous submission, the proximity of her lips to that blood-engorged thing, and the merest licking of her tongue were often enough to make him gasp and cry out. But when Ignacio had been drinking heavily, because he had suffered a reversal in business or because he was simply getting bored with her, Mary Magdalene herself would have been hard put to make any progress at all. Still, she took care of him just the same, until her neck and jaws ached. And even then, he found ways to insult her: "You're too careful and look like you're about to throw up." And the worst? If he had been displeased with her lovemaking, or if she had even looked at him in a certain way—as if she'd rather leap from her window than spend another moment with him—she'd turn up at the club the next night covered with so many black and blue bruises that she couldn't go onstage without disguising them with heavy makeup. How the chorus gossiped and felt sorry for her.

It became the kind of situation that she would always remember in the manner of a bad dream. Started out good, ended up bad. A terrible mistake from which there seemed to be no escape. Sometimes after she had seen him and he had treated her poorly, María headed back to that filthy hotel la Cucaracha, which she had since come to regard with fondness, and, finding *la señora* Matilda at her usual place in the hall, wept on her urine-smelling lap. Recognizing her expression of regret and torment, something she had seen many times before, Violeta the prostitute would hold María in her arms and caress her hair. "Come back here, my love," she'd tell María. "Come back to your friends." Such little visits helped sustain her—*la señora* always told her that she could have her old *habitación* again—but when she looked around that place, with its click-clack of whores' heels on the steps, its dingy corners, and remembered the condition in which she sometimes found the toilet—an outhouse, a field was better than that—and of waking in the middle of the night jumping—*brincando, brincando*—from insect bites, María knew she'd never return. But then something would hit her: Short of going home to Pinar del Río, there would be no way of avoiding Ignacio, not in Havana at any rate. Where else could she go? Heading back to her *solar*, she'd imagine him lurking behind every arcade column; and once she'd climb the steps to her door, her greatest fear was that she'd find Ignacio, sprawled out on her bed naked, an electric fan turning by his side, waiting.

Not that Ignacio was always so harsh with her. Though she'd tend to remember him as a son of a bitch, *y como un abusador,* he ran so hot and cold that it always amazed María when they settled into a pleasant period. He might punch her arms and legs a half dozen times in a single afternoon, but within a few days flowers always arrived at the club in his name, so that while María, jamming a modesty pad into the front of her glittering undergarment, fatigued by sadness, softened towards him again. And sometimes he turned up at the Nocturne with a box full of lacy Parisian scarves, just to give away to the ladies of the chorus. And he'd tell anyone willing to listen that if he or she needed a good refrigerator, a nice radio console, or even an air conditioner, he was the man to talk to. And always at steeply discounted prices, given that they all—from the powder room ladies to the shoeshine boy in the back and the women of the chorus—were friends of María.

In a calm and decent mood, Ignacio, always dressed sportily and smelling nicely of cologne, could be incredible. He knew people like the advertising director at *El Diario de la Marina,* and other papers, who might have use for her as a model in their ads. And now and then, out of nowhere, Ignacio, stuffing a few twenty-dollar bills into a lipstick-stained coffee cup she kept by her makeup mirror, told her: "This is for your poor *papito* out in Pinar, if you want to give it to him." Cold with beggars on the street, he seemed to change his mind when it came to her little world. And that sometimes made her feel differently.

On some nights, at about four in the morning, when Ignacio was usually among the last to leave the Nocturne and the floors were already being swept around the tables, even while some patrons lingered, and he asked if he might "escort" her back to her place, María, whatever his recent transgressions, usually told him "Yes."

In the best of spirits, he even encouraged her about some things. When they were passing by the Palacio Theater along the Prado during a midafternoon Sunday stroll, and beautiful María saw that crowds were queuing in the entranceway for a performance of a ballet, *Giselle,* he didn't hesitate to buy tickets for the two o'clock show. The lead dancer of that troupe, one Alicia Alonso, a waifish half-blind brunette, moved so gracefully in the role that María's hip-swaying *rumbera* movements seemed crude by comparison. While watching the corps de ballet and feeling stunned by Alonso's elegance onstage, she could only think about what one of the dancers in her troupe, the aging Berta, had recently told her: "You're so good looking, it doesn't matter if you can dance at all." That remark had bothered her, and especially so after watching that ballet. It so nagged at María that she began to dream about becoming a ballerina.

In this, Ignacio, even while thinking it a bit of a joke, indulged her—paying for twice-weekly classes at an academy off Industria Street. And while she had begun to learn the fundamentals, and worked hard to perfect the placement of her feet, the various pliés, she lacked the classical grace of the others, who were, in most cases, adolescents if not children (and well off ones at that). At five seven and too voluptuous— she weighed one hundred and twenty-seven pounds—María, the oldest of them, seemed preposterously out of place. Still, she kept at it for a few months, until there came the day when she realized that it would take her years to become any good at all. By then, her feet had begun blistering all over again, to the point that they sometimes bled in her shoes while she was dancing in the floor shows at the club, and so, one day, María, putting that pipe dream aside, simply stopped taking those lessons.

At least those lessons helped her performances: she became somewhat more elegant in her stage movements, the nuances of those stances making a difference in her style. To the delight of her salivating audiences, it became easier for María to touch her forehead with her instep, and her contortions became much more fluid, not that she needed to improve on her routines. Having been exposed to her fellow, better off aspirants, who were picked up by chauffeurs and housemaids after classes and, almost to a one, attended a French lyceum (they were always practicing their French with each other during their rest periods), she, envious at first and then inspired by their air of refinement, began thinking about ways to improve herself.

Ignacio always laughed at the fact that she couldn't read worth much. He caught on right away, noticing that she really didn't know what she was looking at when handed a restaurant menu. Not once did she ever seem to know that among the books he'd carry around with him was a simple Spanish *diccionario*. (That's what he had been studying in the club the night they met.) He used to tell her that he would have written her love letters, but what was the point of bothering? In any case, there was no need to feel too bad, he'd say. Half of all rural Cubans, if not more, were illiterates anyway, he'd read in some newspaper. And what difference would it make to a woman whose *chocha*, in his opinion, was a national treasure?

But even when Ignacio knew that his jibes bothered her, and he was always talking about finding some brainy *fulano* to teach her, he just never got around to it: he was too ashamed of her in that way to approach anyone. Besides, he felt content to lord that superiority over her, and in any case, he really didn't care if María could even spell her name, as long as she had learned to comport herself like a lady in the classy restaurants they went to and took him to bed with abandon.

And María? Living in an incomprehensible world, she often wondered what the newspaper headlines said. Even when she recognized her stage name on a poster outside the club—M-A-R-Í-A R-I-V-E-R-A—she could only guess what the rest of such notices meant. Some words she understood, but not many, the gaps of lost meaning confounding, depressing her. Waking around noon each day and feeling that something was missing in her life—*forget love, that always turns to air, doesn't it?*—she resolved to find herself a teacher.

ow below her windows was a thriving market that started up at seven in the morning. Out of canvas-awning-covered stalls, in dense rows that faced each other on either side of the narrow cobblestone street, those vendors sold everything—live chickens, parrots in cages, cut-up sides of pig. There were stalls for household goods and plumbing tools, heaps of old radios and extension cords, books and outdated magazines—even American magazines such as *Look* and *Life,* which had been discarded in hotel bins and picked out like used rags for sale. A dozen cheap guitars and as many dented cornets and other instruments hung from wires strung along the canopy of one, and there was a stall that sold nothing but *tocadiscos*—record players—of every imaginable incarnation. From the old RCA windup Victrolas that played only 78s to the more modern GEs (always worn and used) that employed the speeds of $16\frac{1}{2}$ and $33\frac{1}{3}$ rpm, and around them, where they were stacked on the ground, piles and piles of brittle records. (Oh, if she could only have picked out one of them, during her leisurely strolls through the market, a 78 rpm *disco* by an *Oriente sonero* called los Hermanos Castillo, featuring two songs, recorded in 1944 in Santiago, one of which, entitled *"Mis sueños"*—"My Dreams"—was a plaintive bolero penned and sung by none other than Nestor Castillo, her future love.) There were stalls that sold shoes, men's apparel, racks of dresses, and much more.

Once María got up in the late morning, and Ignacio had not come around to carouse with her, it was one of her solaces to stroll through the market and say hello to the vendors who had become her friends. She even dallied by the bookseller's stall, a few steps from her door, picking up one volume or the other and pretending, in case anyone was watching, to read, flipping through their pages, pausing at some, and arching her lovely eyebrows at their supposed contents. The bookseller was such a friendly man that María often bought one or two just to be nice. Among them was an absurdly obtuse volume that contained biographies of the one hundred most prominent Cubans alive in 1902. This she liked for its genteel photographs. Another, more arcane, was a Theosophical Society tome, published in Barcelona in 1928. She picked that one for its cover, featuring a pair of celestial-looking beings flying disembodied, like shredding flames, towards a reddish pearl in the heavens. A third, of the twenty or so she would own and keep on a shelf like porcelain objects, happened to be a moldy edition of *Don Quijote*. (Its pen and ink illustrations enchanted her.) Otherwise, María sorted through the one- and two-day-old newspapers that the fellow sold for a penny apiece, all the while assuming expressions of interest. The vendor, Isidoro, hardly imagined that María was only going through the motions, but another man, a lanky old *negrito* with sunken eyes, sitting inside the shaded entranceway of her building, a cane in his large arthritic hands, had watched her going through her charade a hundred times, without saying a single word. All he ever did was smile and tip his hat at María, but one afternoon, he just couldn't resist and called out to her.

"You there," he said. And when she turned: "Yes, you my love! Come over here."

In a florid dress, and with a fan in hand, María approached him.

"I should talk to you," he told her. "I know what you're up to."

"What do you mean?" she asked, almost indignantly.

"Oh, come on now," he said. "I can tell by your eyes that you really don't know what you're looking at. *¿Tengo razón o no?*"—"Am I right or wrong?"

She had no response, just looked down at the ground.

"Well, there's no shame in it. Myself, I didn't learn to read until I was thirty, and believe you me, my love, that was a long, long time ago." He laughed, slapping his knee. "But the fact that you even pretend to tells me that you have the desire." Then he took hold of her right hand. "*Dime, mi bonita,* how old are you anyway?"

"Eighteen, but I will turn nineteen in October."

"Now that is young, *carajo!*" he told her. "You still have all the time in the world. And since I have nothing to do with myself"—he laughed again—"how about if I teach you the basics, you hear? You look like a bright young woman, even if you're a lousy actress, and like I said, I've got nothing else going on."

She didn't even hesitate, asking: "Do you want me to pay you?"

"Why, no, my love," he said, rapping his cane against the steps beneath his feet. "Just tell me your name, that's all."

"María," she said. "María García y Cifuentes."

"Well, María, I'm Lázaro Portillo, at your service, and a very happy *señor* I am, and grateful for all the times I've seen you lighting up this marketplace with your beauty."

Then, he moved aside and tapped the steps beside him. Unfurling a clean handkerchief from one of his pockets, he spread it out for her. "Wait here, and I will find some paper and a pencil, and then, my love, we can begin."

And so those lessons commenced in the midst of a busy market day, the first words he showed María, as she basked in his adoration and kindness, being *"Él"* for "him" and *"Yo"* for "I" and, as well, *"Ella"* for "her."

After that it became her daily routine to sit with Lázaro for a few hours each afternoon, and she made it a habit to bring along a notebook, in which she wrote everything he instructed her to copy down. In only a few months, this bony-limbed, knob-knuckled *negrito* angel had opened María's eyes, teaching her some things. At first, she could barely comprehend what she read, but she got better, bit by bit. And he, basking in the loveliness of her youth, wanted nothing for it, save for a few sandwiches now and then—he was the sort who looked hungry but didn't act it. In those months, words and their meanings, and the way the letters of the alphabet arranged themselves into words, began to follow her everywhere, along the streets of Havana, while she was soaking in a bath, and even as she danced, shaking her derriere onstage. They followed María like birds, or like those black notes that flew in clusters across a musician's arrangement charts at the club.

Chapter
FIFTEEN

One evening at the club a few months later—it was October—the house band had broken into a tropical jam. A jazzed up version of *"Rumba caliente"* began the show, and this, to much applause, was followed by a frenetic *"El cumbanchero."* But if she'd remember that particular evening of performances, it was because one of the dancers, fifteen-year-old Paulita, in the midst of an acrobatic routine, collapsed midstep, her right foot slipping off a bench as she leapt up to join María atop a piano, the poor thing falling head backwards to the floor. Even before the show, when Paulita, looking pale and drawn and sitting in front of her mirror, her hair in curlers, had complained that her belly ached, they knew what that was about. The girls in the chorus had raised money for the abortion she'd gotten a few days earlier—cost forty dollars, and with a real doctor, not some back-alley hack—but who among them imagined that it could have been botched so badly? For as she lay sprawled on the stage, the music stopping and the emcee, a suave crooner named Ricky Romero, coming out from behind the abruptly closed curtains to advise the muttering, drunken audience in both English and Spanish that all was well, and that momentarily the show would continue, out of the poor girl's tasseled bottom seeped a widening flower of blood. The boss had her carried off, and even gave one of the stagehands money to rush her to the hospital, *muy pronto*, the dancers, hysterical, crying, going on with their performance anyway and mostly finding their marks, but without much enthusiasm at all.

A dispiriting night, the kind of evening when María wouldn't have minded having Ignacio around, for sometimes she found his strength a

90

comfort, even if he beat her, but lately he hadn't been coming by the club as often as he used to.

As a matter of fact, she hadn't seen as much of him in general. He'd say that he had to go away, claiming he had business in Miami, or in the Yucatán, or in Santiago de Cuba. But she didn't know what to believe. Once when Ignacio had left a book on her table, by the window looking out over the street, María, driven by curiosity to see if she could decipher a few of its words, flipped through its pages to find, wedged deep into the spine, a small black-and-white, serrate-edge photograph of a sultry dancer known as the "fabulous Lola Sánchez," the back of it bearing the imprint of her burgundy-painted lips and an inscription; the only words María could pick out were *amor* and *besitos*. And by chance, she had gone to the harbor one afternoon to see one of her fellow dancers, Juanita Méndez, off as she boarded the Havana-Miami ferry to join the chorus of a traveling revue. If her intensely beautiful eyes weren't failing María, she had spotted Ignacio, on an upper deck, looking like a cat eating a canary, his arms wrapped around a quite stunning brunette who bore an amazing resemblance to the Lola Sánchez of the photograph. A few weeks later María had received a telephone call at the club from Ignacio, announcing that he wouldn't be coming to her place on Sunday afternoon because he had been detained in Holguín—one of his trucks, carrying a load of electric fans and refrigerators, had apparently been hijacked by thieves. Why then did she happen to come across him, later that same evening, walking in the arcades of Comercio with several men, and an unidentifiable woman, by his side? It wasn't long before María concluded that Ignacio, like most well-heeled men in Havana, had found someone new to amuse him, another woman whom he might treat well at first and then abuse later, a beauty onto whose body, stretched out on a bed, he might empty the contents of a bottle of rum, laughing at first and then later licking her up and down before concluding that she needed a slap or two across the face.

. . . your father was a liar!

María should have felt relieved to have Ignacio out of her life, or seemingly so, but, even if she wouldn't admit it, a bitterness and a kind of jealousy over Lola Sánchez, another queen of Havana nightlife and of shapely *culos*, overwhelmed her. It left María wondering if Ignacio, after all, had been correct in telling her that, despite her beauty, she was really worthless and stupid, and not worth much at all.

That was María's state of mind at three thirty in the morning, when she finally left the Club Nocturne the night of Paulita's incident and went roaming through the streets. Even at that hour Havana, circa 1949, still cooked and sizzled and popped even more than it had years before. Hordes of American servicemen flew headlong through its arcades, crowded its bars, stumbled down its steps, vomited behind its columns and against its flecked walls. In some purlieus, lining up before the brothel doorways, countless men jammed the narrow walkways and sidewalks. Musicians performed everywhere. Barkers tried to lure pass-ersby into their saloon doors, others into their casinos, slot machines glowing everywhere, *ching, ching, ching*; prostitutes, standing in door-ways or leaning over balconies, bared their breasts, nipples pointed out insinuatingly; drums and trumpets *(ay, Nestor)* blew open the night. One of the chorus—they all smoked and drank—passed María her first ciga-rette, a Royale, and though she coughed at first, having breathed the purest country air for most of her life, she thought it might turn into a glamorous habit—Joan Crawford always smoked cigarettes in her mov-ies after all. She wasn't a drinker, hated bars, because even in the most touristic of places, like Sloppy Joe's, men assumed she was a prostitute like Violeta, though sometimes they mistook her for either the Holly-wood actress Lena Horne or Ava Gardner or, in fact, one of her favor-ites, Sarita Montiel, none of whom, many years later, would mean much to her daughter Teresita's generation—María, so effortlessly enticing strangers with the radiance of her sculpted face, wouldn't have lasted as much as five minutes in most of those bars along Obispo, Trocadero, or O'Reilly without someone either propositioning her or making a fool of himself by assuming he had a chance on earth to seduce her. Ignacio, good or bad as he had been, who wasn't quite what met the eye, who loved to pull her jet-black hair back even while jamming himself into her shapely, quivering behind, that Ignacio, in meeting her, had surely been one of the luckiest men in Havana.

And so when she went along the Paseo del Prado, where many a young couple sat necking in the shadows of the park, María, in making her way over to the Malecón, a balmy breeze sweeping off the churning sea, had only wanted distraction, to take in from the spray-misted pavement the full moon, whose light, in those moments, seemed a river burning through the water. All along the Prado, people were still eating and drinking in the arcade cafés. Strolling about with guitars in hand, musicians, mainly *soneros* like her *papito,* serenaded anyone who would toss them a few coins, and, of course, aside from all the catcalls and whistles she heard coming from the side streets and alleys, there were children following behind her, tugging on her skirt and begging for pennies.

As María passed the haunted entranceway of the Centro Gallego and came to a café called El Paraíso (the Paradise), she saw, as might be inevitable in a bolero of dejection—not "Beautiful María of My Soul" but some other like *"Te odio"* ("I Hate You") by Félix Caignet—Ignacio sitting by a table beside a woman, and not just any woman, but the dancer Lola Sánchez. Ah yes, Lola, a light-skinned *mulatta* like María, her tar-baby black hair recently dyed platinum blond, her *tetas* half bursting out from the top of her dress, and whose skirt, slit up nearly to her hips, revealed thighs and legs that, in their musculature, María almost found herself admiring. And what else? Under the half-light of a Chinese lantern, Ignacio and this Lola Sánchez were locked in a fondling embrace, his mouth pressed against hers, his hand stuck deep inside her skirt. And in that instant, María, without knowing anything about Lola—other than that she sometimes gave interviews on the radio and headlined at the Sans Souci—suddenly despised her, and Ignacio as well. Who knows what possessed María, but when she marched over to their table, she couldn't help but call out, "Hey you, shit!" And when Ignacio looked up at her, without recognizing María at first, her face was so distorted by anger, he wondered why that very lovely but crazy-looking young woman, *esa encantadora loca,* had just kicked over their table, platters of *mariscos* and cocktails toppling onto the pavement. Then it came to him. "María, what are you doing?"

With that Ignacio stood up and took hold of her by the wrists and tried to calm her down, but she just wouldn't, María breaking from his grip, María cursing him with the kind of language her dead mother, in all her piety, would have found shocking. Which is to say, that beautiful María, sweet *guajira* from the sticks, dancer and head turner extraordinaire, had become angry at the sight of them in a way that even surprised herself.

Chapter

SIXTEEN

She spent the remainder of that night tossing in her bed, suffering from nightmares of sin and humiliation. Incredulous that Ignacio would betray her in so public a fashion, María wished that she could have shat him down the *retrete* behind their shack in Pinar del Río, so that he might swim among his brothers, wished that he had been swallowed up by the cavern's waters like her sister. Livid with pain and rage, María couldn't have cared less if she ever saw that *desgraciado* again. Yet, in the solitude of her *solar,* amidst all the furniture and an *armario* filled with the dresses he had paid for, she slipped into a state of superstitious forlornness. For to be alone made her think about her dead mother and sister, Teresita, and when she thought about them in another world of shadows, María felt more desolate than ever before, *tan solita, tan solita,* as if the city bustling around her were nothing more than a necropolis through which she wandered.

Still, with the light of day, such dark thoughts thankfully left her; and she had her dancing at the club and those pleasant lessons with Lázaro to occupy her.

About a week later, at dusk, however, she had been sitting by her window studying her notebooks—*ay, but so many words to learn*—when Ignacio, not wanting to let a good thing go, came knocking at her door. What could she do but allow him inside—he had his own key anyway. And though he had pleaded that she forgive him, María, having her pride, told him to simply take what clothes he had been keeping in that place and go. A slick caballero (the *pendejo*) by any standard, Ignacio claimed that he loved her, his mood suddenly calmer, contrite.

"I know I've done some things to offend you, but with all my heart

I'm asking you to forgive me. Please, María," he said, and he crossed himself. "I am sincere in telling you this. *Te juro.* I mean it."

"And that woman?"

"She's nothing next to you."

He tried to caress her, to kiss her lovely neck, but his breath reeked of rum, and the touch of that man, which at best she had found tolerable, seemed now repugnant. She threw open the door.

"Vete," she told him. "I'd rather die than take another day of your *joderías,* do you understand?"

"I don't believe you mean that."

"Just leave me, Ignacio," she told him. *"No soy puta."*

Then, all at once, what tenderness he possessed deserted him. His brows knotted fiercely. "Not my whore? Want to know something? You aren't even good at it." His face burned red. "You know why I went off with that other one? It's because she knows how to behave in the bedroom like a real woman. You may be beautiful and make a lot of noise, but you're stiff as a cadaver—"

"That's because you beat me, *hombre. . . .*"

And then it turned into something else. When he tried to throw her on the bed, she ran screaming into the hallway, Ignacio chasing after her and shouting insults, the two of them spilling down the stairways of her *edificio* and making so much of a commotion that passersby along that market street began to gather, curious about yet another familial Havana melodrama, drenched in sweat and contorted faces, unfolding before them. A miserable scene that María would probably have preferred to forget, and would have forgotten, if not for the *glory* that shortly entered her life.

ou see, it happened that a young musician with a most soulful expression and priestly demeanor had been walking home along that street. Wearing a white guayabera and linen slacks, and carrying a beat-up instrument case in hand, he had come upon the scene at the end of an afternoon of both music and dreams in a park on the western outskirts of the city, where along the banks of a river and under the shade of trees he, a trumpeter and singer, had played his heart out with the *batá* drummers and *congueros* of Marianao: his name was Nestor Castillo.

Fresh from a stirring *tumbao*, he could barely believe what he was seeing before him: not just a terrible squabble bursting out onto the street but a woman as beautiful as any he had ever encountered, her face contorted with pain and longing, a *cubanita*, her dress torn down the front, who instantly spoke to his soul. Just as Ignacio, his face twisted with anger, went lunging after María and chased her, sobbing, into the crowd, Nestor, perhaps possessed by a notion that music had a power of its own, or because he didn't know what else to do, took out his trumpet and began playing a melody so serene and consoling that even the indignant, foul-tempered Ignacio stopped in his tracks. His fist had been raised as if he was about to hit María when, all at once, like everyone gathered in front of that building, Ignacio seemed to forget for a moment why he was there at all, his attentions turned to the sonorous music echoing against the walls.

"*Caballero*," Nestor called out to him. "It's done. Why don't you leave the lady alone? Look, she's only a woman, huh?"

"And who are you to tell me what to do?"

"I'm just a *músico,* my friend."

With that Nestor lifted that trumpet to his lips again, another melody flowing forth, but this time, much as with love, the charm of it had worn off. Ignacio strode over to him and poked his trembling hand, his forefinger and index finger jamming into Nestor's chest.

"Let me tell you something: I would mind my own business if I were you." With that Ignacio, reeling around, turned his attention to María again.

By then the crowd, of neighbors and passersby, seeing clearly what was going on, became intent upon protecting her. And, as they formed a circle around María, and with shouts accused Ignacio of being a woman beater and a *cabrón*—a louse of the lowest sort—he, half drunk anyway and having better things to do, lost heart. In the meantime, a policeman, who had been eating a pork chop dinner in a café down the street, took a few last sips of his Hatuey beer and finally decided to see why so many people had gathered. He was approaching when Ignacio, his suit disheveled and feeling his guts twisting into knots, had taken off in another direction; along the way, every few yards, he'd turn around and curse María, then swear that he loved her, Ignacio's shadow elongating on the cobblestones behind him, Ignacio, in all his ferocity, gradually diminishing inside a forest of columns until, all at once, he disappeared into the recesses of an arcade.

"*¿ESTÁS BIEN?*" NESTOR CASTILLO ASKED MARÍA. EMBARRASSED from publicly weeping and twisted by shame over her recent troubles, she leaned up against her *edificio* entranceway, her arms covering her breasts, where the dress had torn. "Is there anything I can do to help you?"

"No, but thank you, *señor,*" she told him.

Just then, as María started up the stairs, he couldn't keep himself from following her. "If you would forgive my rudeness, I'm wondering if . . . if . . . you'd consider accompanying me out to a little place I know. . . . Perhaps it will make you feel better," he said.

"When?" she answered, wary but intrigued by this fellow's sincerity.

"Right now, if you can. Or tomorrow. Or anytime."

"Now? You must be joking."

María looked him over but with more clarity, amazed by how, in the heat of the moment, when she saw things with distortion, she'd hardly noticed his good looks. His dark eyes were liquid with mystery; and that mouth, almost too shapely and well formed to belong to a man, a *nariz* that would have looked perfectly at home on any movie star; even his teeth were pearly, and he had all of them to boot! His largish ears and crests of curly dark hair reminded her of a handsome postal courier she once knew back in Pinar del Río, this quiet fellow who'd come through their valley on a horse without anything to deliver, since nobody received mail, simply to pass the time and fill those *guajiros* in on what was going on in the outside world. (It was the courier who once told María about the dropping of an atomic bomb on the faraway island of Japan—who could have imagined that?) But there was also just something about this *guapito* that comforted her—a priestly air, perhaps, or something trustworthy if not beatific, and you know what else? He was so nervous around her and timid seeming, despite his killer looks, that she felt like taking care of him, as if he were one of those forlorn *guajiros* of her *papi*'s acquaintance, those salts of the earth who'd never hurt a soul and needed to be looked after by a woman of strength.

"It will make you feel better," he told her, trying again. "But I don't want to impose."

"All right," María told him finally. "But come upstairs with me. I'm filthy."

Closing the cast-iron gate behind them, as he followed her up the steps to her *solar*, dogs barking around them, María could almost feel his eyes alighting upon her rump. She needn't have been so suspicious; walking into her parlor, with shattered plates and turned-over chairs strewn about the floor, that *músico* couldn't have been more noble, more polite. He practically sat on his hands while María went into her bathroom to wash and put on a new dress, and passed his time looking around the place, probably wondering just who that miserable prick had been. All kinds of things would have hit that *pobrecito* just then. He noticed that she certainly had a lot of nice clothes in her closet; her appliances, including a Frigidaire, were new too, and he guessed that the pictures of the older folks in a frame on her dresser were her *mamá y papá*—or maybe *abuelos*—but, in any case, they looked like they'd had a hard time in life. The only thing he made a peep about was the beat-up guitar he saw leaning against a wall. She had gotten it for a few dollars in the market below from the fellow who sold instruments, so that she could practice the chords her *papito* once taught her.

"Say there, do you mind if I strum on your guitar?" he called to her.

"Do whatever you want, *pero es un tareco*—it's a piece of junk." Passing a sponge over her body, María felt grateful, but somehow sad at the same time, to have Ignacio so suddenly out of her life. She wondered if those little pains inside her heart meant that she'd always have a soft spot for that cruel man anyway. Once Nestor began singing, however, the intimations of his fine baritone, so sincere and somehow pained, got her all quivery inside and she wondered what was going on with her. Dressing quickly—a slip under a florid dress, no nylons, and a pair of low-heeled shoes—she soon joined him again in the room.

"You sing really nicely," she told him. And in that moment María began to wonder why she was already feeling affection, for a fellow she hardly knew.

Handsome as hell, Nestor Castillo made the oddest impressions on her. As they walked in Havana *vieja,* not once had he looked at any of the other women who passed by. He seemed so self-effacing, and beyond this tawdry world, it would not have surprised María if, while blinking her eyes, she had turned around to find him wearing a priest's vestments and holding one of those things that resemble ice cream scoops, an aspergillum, from which priests sprinkle holy water, Nestor blessing the narrow sidewalks and cobblestones before them. They'd hardly said a word to each other, but once they sat down in that café, up on a terrace, the horizon streaked with plains of conch pink in the sun's setting glow, and after a few glasses of hearty red Spanish wine, thick as blood, Nestor began to overcome his initial timidity. By their table, and for the first time that night, as he wasn't one for conversing easily, he broke into a big horsey grin and told her, "You know what? My mother's name is also María. Now isn't that something?"

Well, given that practically half of the females in Cuba were Marías, it shouldn't have seemed so amazing to anyone. But why shouldn't she smile back at that sweet fellow? While a squat but majestic jukebox glowed away in a corner of that café, playing some nice old romantic ditties—the kind Nestor aspired to write himself—María suddenly found that coincidence of their meeting on such a dismal day to be unimaginably significant, as if foretold by the stars.

Oh, it was all so very poetic, like something out of a bolero. And Nestor could have stepped out of a bolero as well. His outlandishly handsome features, his way of raising his eyebrows when something tasted particularly good, his dark eyes, which glanced at her from time to time, and the slightest of smiles that crossed his mouth now and then, but shyly, as if there was something unmanly about smiling, gave him a tragic air. She didn't know him well, but María liked his solemnity, as if he were a matador, and the shy manner with which he comported himself—such a pleasant change from how most men regarded her. She couldn't say he was easygoing or particularly talkative. But the way he looked into her eyes, as if he were seeing something wonderful in them, was more than enough to soothe her nerves.

It wasn't as if she didn't notice the way he struggled to look only at her face—surely he must have been aware of her body. And what was that hanging around his neck but a crucifix on a chain? Of course, she told him that she was a dancer at a cabaret, lately a featured performer, which was nice except that she only made a few dollars more a week than the others. She could have spoken about the problems she was having with the floor show manager, who, like most managers, unless they preferred men, eventually got around to expecting certain things from their dancers—how those bosses disgusted her. But she didn't. Nor did she share with him the tawdrier episodes of her experience, the sort that made a woman, however beautiful, feel cheap and used. In fact, María was sometimes ashamed of her profession, almost as ashamed of her ignorance. No, on that night, as she would remember, María preferred to hear about Nestor's own life and to take in the soulfulness of his expression, the tenderness of his voice.

AS THEY FEASTED ON A PLATTER OF *MARISCOS Y ARROZ*, WITH SOME chorizos—a paella—along with heaps of fried plantains, it was Nestor who did the talking at first. *"Soy un campesino de Oriente,"* he told her. "I'm a country boy from the east, from a quiet farm, *tú sabes,* near a little pueblo called Las Piñas, and I will tell you something, María. I was pretty happy growing up there amongst the oxen and pigs." He was chewing on a delicate morsel and looking straight into her eyes. "Not to say that I don't like Havana. I just miss my family *y mi campo*—my countryside. *El aire puro*—the pure air, *el perfume de la jungla*—the perfume of the woods."

Por Dios, it was as if María were hearing herself speaking.

"I should have been a farmer, like *mi papá*, but I was just too sickly as a child. I wasn't much good for anything when it came to the hard work in the fields. And because of *mi enfermedad*, I grew up holding on to my mother's skirt. It wasn't always easy, María. I practically never left that farm, and what learning I had, I owed to my older brother Cesar, who progressed as far as secondary school in Holguín. He taught me to read and write, and just about everything else I know."

He wiped his mouth with a napkin, refilled his glass with wine, took another bite, his expression uncertain.

"Cesar is everything to me, even if he can be a pain in the *culo*. If it wasn't for him, I wouldn't have gone anywhere. Surely not to Havana. He's always been much more adventurous than myself. He's a first-class *músico* and used to perform with many a *conjunto* out east, as a singer mainly, and because I was always the closest to him, the youngest—we are four—he took me under his wing and started me out playing different instruments and singing."

"And he is much older than you?" María, watching Nestor intently, asked.

"Yes, by ten years, but that didn't stop him from taking me around as a kid to all the pueblos and plantations where his *charangas* played. Sometimes we were away for days, and that created a problem with my *papito*, who didn't want me to waste my time." He shook his head. "He was always fighting with Cesar, and I was caught in the middle. But you know what? Once my *hermano* got me going with the music, well, what can I say? It gets in your blood, and there's no stopping the desire. Do you understand?"

"I do, *hombre*," María said. "My *papito* was a *músico* too."

"*No, me diga!*" said Nestor excitedly. Gulping his wine, he asked, "Is your *papito* someone I would have heard of?"

"No, just a nobody I'm afraid, *el pobre*. He was never able to make much of a living at it, and, well"—she shrugged—"*Papito* did what he had to do to support us, until he couldn't anymore."

She looked so sad then, he had to say something. "Is he still alive?" Nestor asked.

"Oh, yes—he lives out in Pinar del Río."

"*Y tu mamá?*"—"And your mother?"

She just shook her head.

Out of habit, at the very thought of her *mamá*, she made a sign of the cross, but quickly. And Nestor? Instead of rolling his eyes, the way Ignacio used to whenever she crossed herself while passing in front of a church entranceway, he sucked a slip of air through his beautiful lips and, shaking his head, said, "That life can be so sad is a tragedy, *verdad?*"

He went on, María listening. Mostly about how Cesar had first put him on a stage at the age of twelve, a skinny kid playing the trumpet with a band; how it was Cesar who persuaded him to come to Havana in the first place. "That was a few years back, and you know what, María? Since arriving, we've made four records, and not a single centavo; we've played in some clubs for a few pesos, but not much else. In fact, do you know how I make my money? As a waiter at a gentleman's club—the Explorers' Club—have you ever heard of it?"

"No."

"It's not far from the Capitolio. I spend my days there looking after its members, not a Cuban among them, bringing them drinks, their cigars, their meals, and tidying up after them. They are mainly Englishmen and Americans, some Germans too. I don't particularly like it, and I don't know what they're talking about most of the time, but it's a living, you know?"

"Oh, I do, *hombre*."

"Well, when I get home I'm always happy to leave that job behind. To be honest, it's a miracle that I'm even here sitting with you. See, if you haven't figured it out yet, I'm not your typical *fulano*."

Gracias a Dios *for that,* María thought, nodding.

"Take my brother Cesar. He likes to go here and there and have a good time whenever he has the chance, but me? No, I'm not that way at all. Most of the time I don't mind staying alone in our little *solar* at night, *tranquilito, tranquilito,* as long as it's not too hot. Then I'll stay out just to breathe. But," he said, and he shook his head, "I don't need the crowds, *la locura* of the clubs, not at all."

She just listened, unable to stop staring at Nestor's mouth and his elegant hands. "I don't know if there's something wrong with me, María, but I'm perfectly happy to sit at home with my guitar and trumpet, writing my little melodies and songs. Or sometimes, if there's a good boxing match on the radio, I'll listen to that; and if Cesar and me have a job, playing music somewhere, I'll certainly try my best to put on a show for the audience. But at heart, María, I've always been *un solitario,* a solitary sort, for whom getting to know someone has never been easy, or even worth fussing over."

He looked off just then, not at the fellow feeding coins into the jukebox, or at the other diners, happily eating their food, but towards the ocean, where the moon had risen, sighing, and the deepest melancholy suddenly emanated from his body like black threads that entangled themselves with María's heart, María's soul. To watch his expression in those moments was to witness an angel, fallen from heaven to earth, who, opening his eyes, saw mainly sadness around him.

"In fact, to be honest, María, sometimes when I'm alone and can't bear to write another note, or a single lyric—they seem so useless to me—I get so homesick that I feel like getting on a bus for Las Piñas. Just the thought of having one of my mother's *plátano* stews makes me happy, and then I start missing all the rest; the run of the farm, the harnessing of the oxen to the plow, hanging around with the *guajiros.* You know here in Havana I mostly play trumpet and sing, but out there, my favorite instrument is a guitar—it's so easy to carry—and, you know, you can have a pretty nice evening with a bunch of folks, just strumming some chords and singing a few songs. And then, when you get back home, you just lie down under the mosquito netting looking at the stars through your window dreaming, without a worry in the world." Then he sighed. *"¡Qué bueno fue!"*

He went on, telling María that he just didn't know what he was going to do with himself in life. Lately Cesar had been talking a lot about ditching Havana for New York, where they had some cousins living in a neighborhood called Harlem.

"My brother's been crazy about New York for as long as I can remember," Nestor told her. "He went there when he was sixteen, working on a ship, and since then it's been his dream to return, especially now. He thinks we'd have better luck as musicians up there."

"Do you want to go?" María asked him.

"Me? Hell no! Just the idea of living in a city like that frightens me—I mean, I can barely speak a few words of English, as it is. Uh-uh." He shook his head. "Here, we have our *guaguas* and trolleys, but you know what I've heard, María? They have trains, hundreds of them, that go from one point in the city to another in underground tunnels. I don't know if I would like that much—I just don't like the darkness at all, if I'm not in the right mood, and as I told you, María, I'm not a very adventurous sort at all; in fact, I sometimes feel like a coward, *un cobarde,* when it comes to life—"

"But you weren't a coward with Ignacio."

That almost made him smile.

"And this Ignacio? What's he to you?" he couldn't help but ask.

"Oh"—she shrugged, as if he meant nothing to her—"just someone who was once good to me."

LATER, WHEN THAT SWEET *MÚSICO* ESCORTED HER HOME AND María had climbed up the stairs and begun to undress, she heard his trumpet from down below: first the melody and Nestor's voice rising up into her window, Nestor improvising a song of love.

María, I don't know you well, but I feel that love is in our destiny.
(His trumpet's notes rising to the stars . . .)
Now I'm filled with the strongest desires.
(His trumpet's notes flying towards the sea . . .)
Even if we're practically strangers, I adore you already,
(His trumpet's notes echoing against the walls . . .)
beyond all reason and without any doubt.
(His trumpet's notes, so wonderful and filled with feeling, provoking,
   as well, a voice from another window: "Hey, you, Romeo!
   Cállate! *Quiet down!")*

María, charmed by his little serenade, leaned out her window. "Nestor, but are you crazy?" she called to him.

"With you I am," he called back, and he bowed like a gentleman. "When will I see you again?"

"Come back next Sunday, at noon," she told him. "Maybe we'll go to *la playa. Está bien?*"

"Okay!"

Then she sent him off into the world, Nestor, walking towards the arcades and turning every so often to see if she was still looking. While he headed home, in a state of pure joy, to the *solar* he shared with his older brother, María, examining herself as she rested in bed, touched her own dampness.

That next Sunday found them on a trolley heading out to an amusement park, west of the city, El Coney, which had been nicknamed by the locals after its famous Brooklyn counterpart to the far north. For the occasion María had put on a sundress and wore a wide-brimmed hat and white-framed sunglasses; she carried a one-piece bathing suit in a bag. Nestor had brought along his own swimsuit and a notebook, which he proudly showed her.

"I always carry this with me, in case I get an idea for lyrics," he said as they jostled along la Quinta Avenida towards *las afueras* of the city. "Because you never know when that might happen—you think you can remember a line the next day, but they're like little dreams that go away unless you write them down. I always use what I call my special pencils. You see, María"—and he pulled one from his pocket that was practically worn to the nub—"I use only pencils that I have found on the sidewalk or on the street and other places; it's as if I'm inheriting the ideas of the people who owned them. This one I picked up in front of the cathedral— probably belonged to a priest or a nun—and so when I'm writing with it, I feel that I'm getting a little help from Dios. But I also have a pencil that I found outside Ernesto Lecuona's house in Vedado. I can't prove that it fell out of his pocket, but just the idea of it gives me a different kind of inspiration. With that one, I write down my notes and the chords of songs." He smiled. "My older brother Cesar thinks I'm eccentric for believing such things, but I figure, what's the harm of it, if those notions help me make a beautiful song." Then smiling, he added: "María, *te parece una locura?* Do you think that's odd?"

"No," María said. "Not if it makes you happy."

But, my goodness, he was different from Ignacio.

"You think so?" And he flipped open his notebook, showing her a page filled with new lyrics. "I wrote this, thinking about seeing you again, just a few days ago. How do they read to you?"

She pretended to understand what he had written down. Though her lessons with Lázaro had slowly progressed, to the point that she had learned hundreds of words, she had yet to comprehend complete sentences, let alone the lyrics of a song; but it had to be about the majesty of love, though she couldn't say for sure.

"*Son bonitas,*" she told him. "*Muy, muy preciosas*"—"They're lovely and very, very fine."

"And the sentiments? Do you feel they are possible?"

"*Sí, cómo no,*" she told him.

"Oh, but María, if you only knew how happy that makes me feel!"

So perhaps he was already writing about her, María would think years later. Perhaps those lyrics, which she couldn't decipher, first opened his heart to the notion of their love. Perhaps, without intending to, she was already raising his hopes. What of it? She felt something for him, perhaps just gratitude for his kindness, and maybe a curiosity about his tender soul. What else could she have said without giving her ignorance away? In memory, that trolley floated along the laurel- and palm-lined streets of that avenue, the sea's air so clear and without any sense of passing time—she was just nineteen after all!—and just like that they were walking along the promenade, too mutually shy even to dare hold hands, but feeling like they wanted to.

The amusement park, just about three blocks long and nestled between the Miramar Yacht Club and the white sands and cabanas of la Playa de Concha, enchanted her, for as a *guajira* from the countryside, she'd never visited such a place before. She had loved the carousel, whose enameled horses went circling up and down, and left María laughing at the sheer foolishness of adults, among so many children, riding such things. Then they got on *La Montaña Rusa*—the Russian Mountain—a mousy roller coaster that whipped along its rickety, curved tracks with abandon, María screaming and Nestor holding her tight. (This they rode three times, Nestor feeling the weight of her breasts against his knuckles, María laughing in a way she never could with Ignacio, Nestor growing somewhat nauseated over the motion but not willing to let María go.) They played games of chance. They ate ice cream, sharing their cones like children. Later, as they were standing on the causeway, watching these adventurous and perhaps crazy fellows jumping off a diving board into the sea from atop a three-story-high replica of a Coca-Cola bottle of painted cement, Nestor first took hold of her hand, and she didn't resist.

Then, because it was such a beautiful day, they headed into the public restrooms, the floors covered with sand, to change. Shortly, out on the beach, María first saw the glory of Nestor's graceful physique—his broad shoulders and flat belly, the curling hair that flourished upwards from his navel like hands in prayer over his chest—while he, in turn, along with about every other man on the beach, felt like weeping at the sight of her spectacular dancer's body. In a green bathing suit, she had followed Nestor into the water, the two of them drifting out and splashing in the waves, oblivious to the people around them, when, out of nowhere, God threw them together. Or to put it differently, hit by a wave, she tumbled into Nestor's arms, and for a moment their warm bodies pressed together, and just like that Nestor lifted her up as if he were about to carry her across a threshold, and then, while holding her, his hand grazed the lower front of her bathing suit and then slipped back so that she could feel his palm against her right *nalgita*. When he dropped her into the water and she stood up, her dark and curly hair now slickened and falling straight and sparkling over her shoulders, through her bathing suit's modesty pad bubbles came seeping and popping out, and what surely made his heart beat faster, through the top of her suit jutted her stiffened nipples. Was she embarrassed or ashamed? No: what she felt was that she wanted more of that sweet man.

Soon they were embracing, and that was a mistake, or perhaps it was utterly natural, but once their bodies were touching, she started to feel within his trunks the kind of earthly response that made María gasp. And while part of her wanted to pull away, María, the same more or less pious *mujercita* who had been at Mass that very morning, let Nestor press even more deeply against her luscious center. The sensation was so pleasurable, and of an intensity she had never felt with Ignacio, that something unraveled inside of her. She forgot the nightclubs, the saintly gazes of church statuary, the very fact that they were only thirty yards or so from a crowded beach. Why she took hold of him through his suit, she could not say. *(Here's something else: sitting with her daughter and watching television, a rerun of* Zorro *with Tyrone Power playing the hero,* pero en español, *she'd recall to herself her first impressions of its weight and thickness and how it made her feel, if nothing else, that this* hombre, *Nestor Castillo, was* muy, muy virile y fuerte.*)* And, God forgive her, the sight of his excited *pene*, distorted by the amplifying effects of the water, so agitated María that she, floating out of herself, couldn't help but put her hand inside his trunks.

His face became a mask of pleasure and death at the same time, or, to put it differently, the tenderness in his eyes became overwhelmed by desire.

Okay, in retrospect, perhaps this was an exaggeration; it had happened so long ago that the pieces of that day came to her like snippets of vaguely remembered music; after so many years she couldn't even recall the timbre of his speaking voice, save that it was mild and gentle, a real tragedy because just hearing him somehow calmed her. One thing was certain: coming out of that water, they were in a state of mutual excitement. It would have been so easy for them to slip into one of the cabanas, which lots of young couples did in those days, to ease off their swimsuits and, in the confines of one of those narrow tents, make furious, hurried love. . . . But, as Maria believed, the heavens were watching—or someone was—maybe her late *mamá*, Concha, or poor Jesus himself, with the bloodied tears of *His* sacrifice dripping down his face instead of tears of pleasure, of sea salt and kisses and youthful love, and that thought so rattled María she had to fight herself, for as they, timidly holding hands, waded to shore through that tepid water—so clear she saw mollusks breathing through the bottom sand—all she wanted to do was to fall back into his arms so that Nestor could cover her body with kisses.

Later, after they'd showered and dressed, Nestor suggested they get a bite to eat at the dance club Panchín, which wasn't too far away. And because that wonderful singer Ignacio Villa, aka "Bola de Nieve," the raspy-voiced Maurice Chevalier of Cuban crooners, sometimes performed there, Nestor thought they might catch his act afterwards. María, however, just wasn't interested in visiting any cabaret, no matter how famous the singer. Her many nights in clubs were already enough to last her a lifetime. No, she preferred to sit out in the open air on the patio of a nearby fried seafood place, nothing special at all, taking in the sunset. As for music? It was relaxing to hear the boleros that played from a radio in the back, to drink enough beers to make her almost forget about Ignacio and lose herself in Nestor's tender eyes. The longer they sat and the more they drank—his side of the table had five empty bottles of beer already sitting there, while hers had two—the more Nestor drifted off into a mood of such sadness that, as he opened yet another bottle, she wanted to wrest it from his hands.

"Just last night I dreamed about you, María, and do you know what I saw?" he asked, taking her hand.

"Tell me."

"An evening just like the one we're having here and now. With you sitting across from me." He smiled tenderly. "I also saw something else: just down there," Nestor said and pointed towards a little pier where couples went strolling. "I saw us sitting there, on a bench looking out at the water, and we were embracing, *besando, besando,* with so much happiness, our kisses tasting of the sea, and your face so joyful that I knew that we were surely to fall in love." Then he crossed his heart and added: "*Te juro*—I swear—it's the truth, and, if you believe me, María, it will become the truth."

Maybe it was the beer she had been drinking, but when Nestor told her "Come on, let's see," she didn't mind going.

They passed the remainder of that evening sitting out on that pier necking, unable to let go of each other.

It's amazing what a single evening on a beautiful night by the sea will do. On their way back into Havana proper, as the trolley jostled along Fifth Avenue, they were holding each other, mostly in silence, as if, in fact, they were in love. Now and then, he would kiss her hand, and, more than once, she kissed his hand back. Their expressions must have been rapturous. Other passengers, especially the older ones, with their hound-dog jowls and memories of their own pasts, simply nodded their understanding: oh, to be that young again, to be in love, to feel the world expanding, and not diminishing around you. During that ride, Nestor sat beside María with a dumbstruck grin on his face, his notebook of lyrics, incidentally, set upon his lap, where his verses occasionally seemed to rise and fall in accord with Nestor's sighs and the ardent expansions of that upon which they rested.

OVER THE NEXT FEW MONTHS, THEY WOULD MEET AFTER HER last shows, late into the morning. She got used to finding Nestor waiting for her in the alley outside the backstage door (her fellow dancers, leaving after her, giggling about the *buenmoso,* the lady-killer, who had won María's heart). They always ended up embracing against an arcade wall, her right leg jammed between his knees, the pipe inside his trousers nearly bursting its seams every time and Nestor whispering the kind of poetry that made María let him sink his fingers inside her. Light-headed, they'd take a few steps, then begin to kiss and fondle each other against a column, to the point of madness. His eyes rolled up into his head, he'd tell her, *"Ay, María, mi María. Sabes que me estás matando?"*—"Don't you know that you're killing me?" Then he'd drop to his knees, lift up the hem of her skirt, press his face against the dead center of her panties, police sirens in the distance, the world ending—none of it mattering.

Still, she always stopped short with Nestor, fearing his *poder*, that she couldn't manage him, or that he would think her a *puta* in the end, that Ignacio would discover them.

But one night while unraveling a dancer's garter over her leg at the club, and realizing that the thought of Nestor made her feel like touching herself, her sheets at home covered with peacocks' eyes of her own moisture (or with outlines of the wound in Christ's side), María decided that she couldn't take waiting anymore.

A few days later, during the quieter hours of an afternoon, in a sun-soaked room near the harbor, in a *solar* that Nestor had borrowed from a friend, and on a mattress with springs so far gone that it took her back to la Cucaracha, Maria allowed Nestor to do whatever he pleased with her. The moment he removed her dress, he stripped down himself, proudly displaying his virility, and proceeded to fondle, bite, and spread Maria open in ways that she couldn't have imagined. She soon learned that romping with Nestor was like riding in her *papito*'s carriage up into the hills, and not just because of the way Nestor nearly burst her into pieces—the wider she spread and the more capacious she became the more he filled her—but because of his caresses, tender kisses, and endearments—*"Sabes que te quiero, María?"*—"Don't you know that I love you?" he'd say again and again, his long-fingered musician's hands brushing her hair from her eyes. As he'd take hold of a fistful of her hair, she'd raise her head, suckling him, but so differently than she had with Ignacio, who sometimes liked to slap her face or twist her nipple painfully while she was doing it. No, with Nestor she remembered the techniques the prostitutes at la Cucaracha had taught her while sitting around bored in the hallways: to bite and lick and then withdraw, to roll one's tongue in a certain way, all gently, then almost viciously, as if trying to draw out the last bit of sweetness from a piece of raw sugarcane—and soon enough her knuckles were soaked with him, and licking that off her hand, she tongue-kissed him with it until, just like that, he became excited again. Then, proving that a man's weeping member could be used like a stylus, he left traces of himself over every inch of her body, writing out the words *Amor* and *Te amo* with his seminal fluids on the small of her back and along the plumpness of her *nalgitas;* and when her upraised rump sent out that exquisite heat, like a woman softly breathing on a man's neck, Nestor, begging her forgiveness, had to go there too—he couldn't help himself, and María, despite that impertinence, found that it was a delicious pain and found that if she touched herself at the same time as she raised her haunches, she fell into pieces again. They went at it for hours, and no matter how many times they did, he wanted to go at her again, as if there would be no end of his desire for her. In fact, they hardly knew restraint and only finally stopped when her voice had gotten hoarse from screaming.

They could go hardly anyplace, not even church, without hounds following them in packs. At the Sunday movie matinees they attended, not a few hours after he accompanied her to Mass, they always sat in the darkest corner of the highest balcony, where the fewest people lingered, and in a row above everybody else. Even then they kissed so much and so loudly that there was always someone to snap at them. "Be quiet!" and "Where is your shame?" Once, during a Barbara Stanwyck film with Mexican actors overdubbing the lines (films with Spanish subtitles were more difficult for her to comprehend, but she generally got the drift of the dramatic formulas and, if anything, learned a little English along the way), Nestor, off in his own little world of passion, couldn't restrain himself any longer. Slumped down, with her eyes set on the screen, Maria, while luxuriating in the theater's *aire condicionado*, absently fondled Nestor through his trousers, and with that whatever remained of his sense of saintly behavior gave way. Just like that, with the fingers of one hand deep inside her dress, the priestly Nestor Castillo pulled his thing out with the other—she could hear its struggle against the fabric, its scraping against his zipper's teeth—and there it stood, silhouetted against the luminous on-screen visage of Stanwyck. Asking María for her forgiveness, as he always did, Nestor further begged her please, in the name of heaven, just to kiss him there, if only that one time. But in the balcony of the Payret? Sighing and hearing cries of *"puta"* and much worse coming from the

115

audience, she brought Nestor to climax, if only to watch the rest of the movie in peace.

Stupid, sinful, oh, what would Concha have thought? But she could not, for the life of her, get that músico *out of her head. She felt him inside her for days after they had parted, and even years and years later, María, sitting around with her daughter watching television, sometimes flashed on the magnificence of his* pene; *longer than her forearm, thick as her wrist, it was a work of art, which both terrified her and made her smile. But was it love—did she ever feel such wonderful emotions? One thing María knew was that she liked being with Nestor: The reverence with which he looked at her, the way his sex went down in one moment and came back up the next, the ecstatic passage of his tongue lapping at her* papaya, *licking her until kingdom come—her body quivering and doubling over onto herself, her head shaking—she felt herself the object of his earthly worship. In the end, he was genteel and humble about the whole business, as if there was nothing special about him; and, best of all, he was careful in his treatment of María.*

Chapter

TWENTY

With María working at night, save for when she had afternoon rehearsals, she never knew when Nestor might rush over from the Explorers' Club during his lunch hour, which was usually sometime after three, and call up into her window. At first, she didn't mind seeing him waiting below, among the market stalls, and introducing him as her new *novio* to her vendor friends. They'd go for walks, sometimes sit in the cool and dusty interior of the Mother of Mercy church, or in the cathedral, holding hands and praying. Sometimes they dallied in the Parque Central or visited the Havana zoo. He never had much money in his pockets, didn't even own an automobile, but still he bought her little things—ice cream cones from the popular Coppelia's parlor, mainly, or they'd sip rum and Cokes—Cuba Libres—in a bar, eat cheap meals in waterside fritter joints. As they passed by, men always checked her out, and fiercely so, but he didn't seem to notice, and if he did, he just wasn't like Ignacio, who'd never put up with that kind of thing. Nestor, *el pobre,* was just too good-natured for that. People liked him—old ladies, looking down from their balconies, with fans in their hands, were always nodding approvingly at the very nice looking young fellow with the dazzling *belleza* by his side. He seemed to know every street musician—*"Oye, Negro!"* he'd call out to some fellow playing his *tres* in a *placita,* "How are you doing?"And when he'd walk over to say hello, he'd introduce María as *"mi mujer,"* which always made her blush. He always did so with utter pride and, perhaps, disbelief that he could find himself with so glorious a beauty. Just to look at her, he'd say, filled his head with wonderful melodies.

On the weekends, they'd go to the beach and, after a nice swim, find a room for hire by the hour, Nestor never exceeding the limits of what he could afford. (But how delicious those hours were!) Monday nights, when her club closed, they'd sometimes roam the back alleys of the slums, where he'd seek out some of the finest street musicians in Havana, in the midst of drum and horn *descargas,* jam sessions. Those musicians were something else, and it was a joy for María to watch Nestor, blaring away rapturously on his trumpet, while those old-style *rumberos* in the crowd, some of the best dancers she'd ever see in her life, filled the alley with motion. The males, bone thin, jaunty, and dressed entirely in white, turned themselves into love-besotted roosters—the rumba was a courtship dance after all. They'd jerk their heads in and out as if wanting to peck the air before them, and flail their elbows behind them, like imaginary wings, their legs jutting up and down, and their steps taking all kinds of turns and backwards struts as if to scratch the dust behind them. The women emulated the movements of love-hectored hens, who didn't want to be bothered, backing off at one moment and yet, after another, coming forward, heads nipping at the air, hips swerving, then torturing the roosters with the fanning of their skirts, as if to give them their scent. They always ended up dancing as one, a rapturous embracing and twirling taking place; such displays always left beautiful María, standing in the crowd, breathless until, unable to take it, she'd cut loose and, slipping off her shoes, dance one hell of a rumba herself.

And sometimes, late at night, they'd linger by the Malecón, and she'd listen to Nestor, without a practical bone in his body, dreamily play his trumpet for the seagulls, ever so oblivious, as María thought years later, to the world that would eat him alive. He'd tell her that he loved her. They'd kiss, drive themselves into a frenzy, and feel desperate for each other. Yes, all that was so wonderful, but you know what? For all the things they did together, and despite her soft spot for musicians, they never really seemed to have much to talk about: maybe falling in love is just that way, she had thought in those days.

. . .

DURING ONE OF THEIR AFTERNOON STROLLS, ALONG THE PRADO, Nestor sat beside María on a bench and, under the shade of a laurel, took her gently by the hand.

"There's something I want to say to you, María." He was so timid he could barely bring himself to look into her eyes. "I . . . I . . . Nestor Castillo, want you to become my *prometida*." And he reached into his pocket, producing a thin gold band. "My fiancée . . . and then my wife."

He could barely breathe by then, she'd remember.

"*Pero,* Nestor." She was touching his face. "Do you mean it?"

"Yes, with all my heart."

"But why now, *mi querido?* Didn't you tell me that you're going to New York with your brother? What of that?"

He waved his hand in the air, as if being pestered by a bee.

"That is only a little bit true. It was true before I met you, María, but now, but now, I don't know. My brother Cesar has got all these crazy ideas about New York, like it's a paradise, where he thinks earning money will be easy, but the truth is, María, I really don't want to leave *mi país, mi Cuba.* And"—he kissed her hand—"you are everything I'd ever want here."

When María did not answer him, he went on. "We could go back east, to Oriente, to my family farm, to live there, away from all this. Or we could stay here in Havana. If I stay on at the Explorers' Club, who knows what kind of job I might end up with there—maybe as a waiter. The boss likes me."

That afternoon, María thought about everything Nestor had just said, every possible equation passing through her *guajira* mind. He had no real education, no reputation as a musician, and to live on a farm again was beyond her imaginings. She missed the simplicity of life in her *valle,* but not enough to return to the *campo.* That's when a veil fell over her emotions, and María, a practical soul, could only think that with Nestor, for all his handsomeness and the magnificence of his soul and body, she'd end up sharing a poor man's life.

And so, *por fin*, that afternoon, she told him, "*Te amo*, Nestor—please don't forget that—but you've asked me so suddenly that I need time to gather myself before giving you an answer."

Leaving him that day, she already knew.

STILL, SHE FELT TORMENTED ABOUT NESTOR, AND SOME PART OF her, the kindlier and less selfish María, wanted to stay with him. But hadn't she already had enough sadness in her life? These were thoughts that came most strongly to her during one of the few nights they had actually spent sleeping side by side, in his friend's *solar*, three in all. Nestor, after ravishing her, drifted off peacefully enough, María caressing his brow as if Nestor were an angel, until she too fell asleep. She was dreaming about seeing her sister, Teresita, in a field, picking flowers on a beautiful spring day, so happy that her sister seemed to be alive, the kind of dream that came to her as a pure joy, when Nestor awakened her, with yelps and cries. He sat up, his heart beating rapidly, his body trembling and covered in sweat, shadows, she would swear, swarming over his face. "What is it, Nestor?" she asked him, cradling him in her arms. "Tell me, Nestor." He opened his eyes, looked away, as if ashamed of himself over such a display of fear, as any man could be, as if no real Cuban *macho* should ever tremble so in front of a woman. "It's nothing," he swore to her. "Nothing, *te juro*."

But later that same night he awakened her again, and this time he told María about his dream, which always began as a pure memory: he was a boy again, of five, feverish and sick, on the brink of death, at his family's farm out in Oriente. A priest stood over him, muttering some gibberish in Latin and rubbing holy oil upon his forehead; his *mamá, una santa,* by his bedside, wept, her face ravaged by grief; from the yard he could hear his *papi* sawing wood, hammering nails, for his coffin. Outside, his older brother Cesar, in his stately adolescence, peered in from a window that faced his bed, smiling sadly. All those details, Nestor told María, were true. "You see, I was supposed to die, but I didn't." Of course, he was thankful for that, otherwise he would never have had the glorious pleasure of knowing her, of tasting her lips, of drowning in her body. . . . Still, he told her about other dreams. He'd find himself in a narrow and lightless tunnel, so confining that he could barely move, let alone breathe, and he would swear that if he as much swallowed a single gasp of air, he would die.

That's when he told María that he just didn't feel long for this world.

"I know it doesn't make sense, María, but since I cheated death as a boy, I sometimes think that it's following me, that something terrible is in the room and it's only a matter of time and that . . ." His chest was heaving, and he could barely catch his breath, his brow covered with sweat. ". . . if I just breathe I'll be swallowing poison and that poison is death—that's what wakes me up."

She covered his mouth with her hand, her naked body pressed against him.

"Please Nestor," she told him, "stop thinking about such things, or you'll make yourself sick."

But he went on and on, about the purgatorial sufferings of his past. She wanted to take care of him then, *el pobre*, as she'd always wanted to take care of her sister and her *papito*. But at the same time, as much as she felt for Nestor, she had to wonder, Who will take care of me?

One Sunday night she finally had the honor of meeting Cesar Castillo in one of those beachside dance bars in Marianao, a dingy, smoky, spilled-beer-and-lard-fried-fish-smelling place called El Oriente, its patrons, mostly black folks, tearing it up with rumbas. When she'd walked in, Nestor and his brother, in their linen slacks and guayaberas, were standing side by side on a narrow plywood stage with some five other musicians, playing, amongst them, double bass, a guitar, a *tres,* and several drums, in addition to Nestor's trumpet. If María had a puzzled expression on her face as she made her way through the crowd, the men whistling and sucking air through their teeth at the sight of her in a juicily tight pair of watermelon pink slacks and matching blouse, it was because she had spent most of that very afternoon with Ignacio, her former man.

Just how did this happen?

("Bueno, it was just one of those things," María would later think.)

He had been driving through downtown Havana in his white Chevrolet when he saw María, ever unmistakable, strolling along Neptuno on her way back from church. Slowing up, he beeped at her, and wouldn't you know it, Ignacio, one of those hard Cuban fellows willing to forgive and forget his own faults and transgressions, couldn't have been more friendly or charming, asking María if she wanted a lift anywhere. She didn't, but she got in beside him anyway, feeling a nostalgia—not for his abuses or even his money, but for his strength, as well as their "old times."

In fact, just to see Ignacio again had somehow made her feel happy.

That Sunday morning was gloriously defined by a perfect sky, the ocean looking pristine, and breezes, smelling cleanly of both salt and tropic spices, blowing languidly in. In fact, it was so nice a day that Ignacio suggested they take a drive to the beaches east of the city. At first María told him she wasn't interested, after all, she had *una cita* later in the evening—to finally see Nestor and his brother performing—but he promised they'd be away only a few hours.

Soon enough they were driving along the coast, the way they sometimes used to, and as they passed the marshes and mangrove swamps by the sea and came to an overlook, the gulf and sky brilliant before them, Ignacio, pulling over, heart in hand, made his confessions. Penitent, regretful, he told María that things between himself and the infamous Lola Sánchez were over.

"María, I don't know what happened to me," he said, "but whenever me and that woman were together, I was really thinking about you." As for the way he had treated her the last time they'd been together, he claimed that the pressures of business and too much drinking had made his temper get out of hand. That's why he had gone away from Havana for a time—to Miami and San Juan, where he had come to realize how much he missed her, "his little *guajira*." And so he swore that he was a changed man and wouldn't drink and treat her badly, if only she would come back to him.

"Because I want to be completely honest with you, María," he told her, "I'm going to tell you everything." It came down to this: "For years, I've made my living dishonestly. . . . There's not a warehouse in the harbor that I haven't broken into with my men, or a ship along the Ward Line and E & O wharves where I haven't found my merchandise. Or a policeman that I haven't taken care of," he went on and rubbed one of his medallions. "But I'm giving all that up, María. Not out of any guilt— I've always offered all kinds of goods for the people at very affordable prices—there's no shame in that, is there? God has obviously protected me. . . . Maybe he's even blessed me, for reasons that only he knows. . . . Along the way I've saved more than enough money, María, to open a legitimate *negocio*. . . . And so I have my plans. There's a commercial space over on Galiano that I'm going to rent, and I will fill it with the finest clothing from Europe and America. You, of course, can be a model in the photographs that I will put in that window."

She looked at him, smiling a little sadly.

"Why clothing? you are wondering," he said, driving on and turning the wheel of bright red leather. "Because Havana is booming these days, packed with tourists who have money in their pockets; the same ones who fill the clubs and brothels have wives they'll have to please. It'll be a fancy place. I'm planning to put a little bar in the back—so that my customers can have some drinks while they shop—and I think I'll put in a lipstick counter too. And that's just the beginning." He sounded a little crazy, but at least he wasn't pushing or slapping her around like he used to. "But above all, María, I want you to understand that I'm putting my life in proper order, and I want you to be a part of that order, *como mi mujer*—as my woman—if you will have me." He placed his hand over his heart. "I swear I'm telling you the truth."

María, in those moments, didn't know what to think. For all those months with Nestor, Ignacio had continued to pay her rent—but why? And while she had enjoyed Nestor's company, she had always wondered why Ignacio had not once contacted her at the club.

"Ignacio, I have someone, *un joven*, close to my own age," she finally told him. "He cares for me."

"Oh, the trumpet player, yes?" He hardly blinked. "His name is Nestor Castillo, and he's a two-bit musician who works in some nothing job as a lackey busboy at the Explorers' Club near the Capitolio, doesn't he? Lives with a relative in a flat off Solares Street near the harbor, number twenty-four, in fact. He leaves for his job about ten in the morning, and has his lunch break about three when he comes to see you, two or three times a week. Am I correct?"

"Ignacio, but how do you know?"

"I just know," he said, María's stomach going into knots. Then, before she could say a word, he added, "*Mi vida*, I wouldn't be sitting here if I didn't think that you deserved better." Then, "What you do with yourself and some nobody, who will give you nothing in life, is your own business. And so I'll leave that decision to you and hope that you will come to your senses."

That's when Ignacio took out a roll of twenty-dollar bills, thick as Nestor's *pinga,* and, unfurling a few, dropped them onto María's lap. "For your *papito,*" he told her. Then he pulled her close and gave her a nice kiss on her neck, and because she felt such gratitude that Ignacio hadn't yelled or insulted her, and it was such a fine day, María didn't mind when he undid the white felt buttons of her blue church dress, the very one he'd bought for her at El Fin de Siglo, and began to fondle, then suckle her breasts. *"Ay, María,"* he told her, "if you only knew how much I've missed you." She should have known better, but when he released the buckle of his belt, María, pulling back her hair, with resignation and detachment, took care of Ignacio the way she used to—why, she didn't know.

"If you give me another chance, María," he told her afterwards, "I promise that I will make you happy."

Altogether, it was as if Ignacio had stepped out of a bolero about the possible ruination of another's love.

That night, as she crossed the crowded dance floor to the bar, Nestor spotted María from the stage, his smile shooting across the room. By then several men had asked María to dance, and though she turned the first few away, this lanky *negrito,* who moved like a skulking burglar, pulled her out onto the floor, where, without even wanting to, she found herself putting on a show. That's when Nestor, up on the little stage, pointed her out to his brother, and Cesar, scraping a *güiro* and in the midst of a few dance steps himself, seeing her for the first time, nodded wildly in approval. "So that's your darling!"

From that moment on, Cesar and Nestor decided to put on a hell of a performance, the brothers harmonizing during the choruses, and then

Cesar stepping back and letting Nestor play his solos. They were a sight to see—each possessing deep-set and soulful, slightly melancholy eyes, the chiseled cheekbones, the cleft chins, the sensitive, well-formed mouths—two *buenmosos*, lady-killers—but with a difference. Whereas Nestor had a pristine handsomeness about him, an innocence and the pained expression of a saint, and moved modestly onstage, Cesar seemed to revel in a kind of sly majesty—his hair brilliantined to death, so that it crested like an ocean wave, his brow covered with sweat, a pencil-thin mustache in the manner of Gilbert Roland or Xavier Cugat (the fashion of the times) punctuating a visage that was anything but sincere—despite the way he poured his heart into his songs, whether *guaguancós, boleros,* or *rumba-tumbaos.*

And María? She'd seen his type before, swaggering cocks of the walk, from *guajiro* to government functionary, who considered themselves God's gifts to womankind, the sorts of men she encountered every day of her life, and did her best to avoid. But there Cesar stood, hamming it up on that little stage, while Nestor, occupied with the nuances of his mellifluous scales and melodies, could have not been more deferential, ever so happily allowing his brother the leading role, the way, María imagined, he did in life.

They performed a few of their own compositions; one of them was a lark of a song, no doubt written by Cesar, always at the edge of the stage between numbers sweet-talking any of the unattached women around. It was called "I Forgot It Was My Wedding Day!" and Nestor, strumming a guitar, launched into a romantic bolero that she was fairly certain he had written about her, even if he did not use her name. That song's title was a bit over her head; Nestor introduced it as *"¿Si la vida es sueño, qué es el amor?"* Or, "If Life Is a Dream, Then What Is Love?" The heart of the tune was about how some fellow with nothing particularly special going on in his life meets a woman who delights him so much that he is convinced he must be dreaming, or else so much in love he can't help but wonder if he is losing his common sense.

"Puede ser," the last lines went, *"este sueño es mi destino."*

"Could be that my dream is also my destiny."

"To love that which I cannot really see."

"A amar lo que no puedo ver."

By the time the brothers had gotten to that particular composition, sometime past ten, any sad, tear-jerking bolero—the music of romantic lives—would have pleased the crowd, who, in any case, would have slow-danced to it all night long. Up onstage, Nestor was so sincere in his sentiments that by the last verses of that song he was wiping his eyes and brow with a handkerchief. His expression seemed haunted, a darkness passing over his face.

They'd been onstage for two hours straight; now, leaving the jukebox to take over, the musicians headed to a table in the back. Joining them, María, somewhat shocked by Ignacio's sudden reappearance in her life, could not quite look Nestor in the eyes. But she greeted him with a kiss while Cesar, standing by his brother's side and checking her out with X-ray vision, smiled and waited for the introduction.

"So you're María?" then "Holy cow, Brother!" Cesar cried out, slapping Nestor's back. "Does she have a sister?" *(Oh, but how María wished she had.)* Then he sat right down next to her, saying, "So you are the one, huh?" And though Cesar was the sort who would have done anything to get her into bed if it weren't for the fact that she was with his brother, he behaved kindly towards her, as if he were her uncle, introducing the other musicians and making sure that she had anything she wanted to eat or drink. Then, while Nestor went off to the pestilential men's room, Cesar, sticking little knives in María's back, went on and on about how he had never seen his little brother so contented.

"Because you see, María, *mi hermanito* is a little too serious about life sometimes, and because of that he feels for all the *sufrimiento* in the world—which, as you know, there's plenty of it and always will be." His eyes were filled with nothing but pure appreciation. "But you have made him as happy as a little bird. I've never heard Nestor whistling so much in my life. You've turned him into a new man, and while there's still a lot of sadness in his heart—some *tipos* are just that way, and Nestor's one of them—he's now filled with more light, and if I may say so, *mi belleza*, that light has a name, and it's yours: María."

Oh, my lord, he was smooth.

Then he looked at her with the same expression that poor children get when they stare at people eating in fancy cafés. "I don't know how you feel about my brother, but I will tell you this," he said, pointing his finger at her, "be good to him, because that brother of mine is everything to me. Everything."

As María sat back, Cesar, noting her air of distraction, changed the subject: "So, are you enjoying the music?"

"Oh yes," she said, sincerely.

"Well, this group is something we put together just for tonight, this bar's owner is an old friend—he comes from Holguín after all—but, even if it's not a fancy place, you should know that we aren't slackers. We've sat in and performed with some of the best-known bands in Havana, like the Melody Boys! But I've got my own ideas for us." And he told her about the kinds of ambitions that left her feeling sad for that poor lost soul's dreams. Sooner or later, he believed, they were going to make their mark in Havana, a city already overrun with thousands of first-rate singers and musicians, where music hummed through the walls like water through pipes.

"And if not in Havana," he added, "then somewhere else!"

Of course, she already knew where that other place might be: New York City. Nestor, with a forlornness that was touching, had not so long before told her, while speaking about Cesar's ambitions, "If we ever do leave Cuba, María, I want you to accompany me. Because if you don't, I don't think I'll ever go."

Even then María knew that she never would. It was hard enough to have left the *campo* for Havana, but to leave Cuba was the last thing to enter her mind. She kept thinking about Nestor, however: if only he were a different sort—the sort to make her feel that she wouldn't end up living like a pauper.

Later, when Nestor had returned, Cesar ordered more drinks and, downing his rum with one swallow, slapped Nestor's shoulder. "Brother, why don't you take the rest of the night off? There are plenty of musicians around here to fill in for you." Then he winked at Nestor, traipsed off rather swaggeringly, and went back onstage.

Thereafter commenced their usual problems; María, alone with Nestor, really didn't have much to say to him. Not that she had much to say to anyone in those days, but with Nestor silence was more the rule, except when he would pull out his notebook and recite some of his newly composed verses, which she admittedly liked, despite the way they confounded her. In fact, sometimes at night, when she'd come home from the club, her feet blistered, and she had the peace of mind to think about her week's lessons with Lázaro, María found herself daring to think in verse herself. If only she could write them down . . . What those verses tended towards surprised her—her holy trinity: God, love, and death—even if they resided mainly inside her head, but she owed them to Nestor's inspiration.

With the bar's lights shining on the stage, Cesar Castillo said a few words into a pitifully sad, often muffled microphone—they had borrowed it from someone's tape recorder and plugged it into a little RCA amplifier. Then he launched, for Nestor and María's sake, into *"Juventud"* by Ernesto Lecuona, an old bolero about how youth is but a fleeting thing, which makes everyone, no matter his or her age, entangle in a tight embrace. Taking María by the hand, Nestor led her out onto the floor. She'd laugh (and curse) the fact one day, but it didn't take more than the touch of her body against his to excite him—excite them both. With Nestor leaning his handsome face against hers, whispering endearments, like clockwork, from deep inside his trousers rose, as surely as Christ, that which jostled her thighs in the darkness and kissed her belly button through the fabric. (*"Ay, pero María, María,"* he kept whispering.)

The sensation brought to mind the first verse she had ever composed in secret but did not know how to write down.

Pedazos de bambú tiesos . . .
Fragmentos de la cruz
Durísimos y llenitos de jugos dulces
Y sangres sagradas
Vosotros queman dentro mis interiores—
(Hard pieces of bamboo,
Fragments of the Cross,
Full of sweet juices and
Sacred blood . . .
You go burning inside of me . . .)

AFTERWARDS, STEALING AWAY, THEY SAT BY THE WATERSIDE, surrounded by an aureole of gnats, and as the moon, brilliant as God, looked down on them, Nestor told her about two new songs he had written: "One is called *'Danzón de los negros,'* the other *'Perla de mi corazón,'* which is really about you María . . ." As if it were the most natural thing in the world, he sang one of its lines: "Our love is a weeping ocean, whose tears become the loveliest of jewels."

"I haven't gotten it all worked out, María, but I know I will, in the same way I know that we are destined to be together." Happily he looked up at the sky. "That my brother Cesar likes you very much is really wonderful, María." Then: "Don't you know I can't wait for the day when we will be a family?" With that, taking hold of María's hand, he swore that he would do anything for her and broached the question he had been asking her for months each time they met: "María, have you considered your answer? Will you become my wife?"

She sighed, looked away, and as the lyrics to a song, a chorus part that went *"Y lo aprendí!"*—"And I found out!"—came from the club,

María, tears in her eyes, told him, "Nestor, please forgive me, but I can't, my love."

"But why?" His face was contorted with anguish.

"Nestor, I just don't want to be a poor woman all my life."

"And if I were to make something of myself?"

"Oh, but *hombre,* you dream too much."

And then, in the most kindly way, she kissed Nestor on his lips. "Forgive me, *amor,*" she asked him again, his head bowed, eyes filled with disbelief, on that night, long ago, by the sea.

O h, but it wasn't easy; she had grown fond of that *músico*. Out of pity, for every time she saw him, he seemed so forlorn, María continued to take Nestor to her bed, and, swearing to herself that it would be their last romp, each time they made love she gave herself to him as if there would be no tomorrow. Along the way, his creative side penetrated María almost as deeply as did his other parts.

In her moments alone, at the club or in her *solar* or while just finding some quiet spot in el Parque Central (well, for María there was really no such place in public, as she always attracted men to her), his words flowed into her head:

Bésame de nuevo, mi amor
Kiss me again, my love
Aquí, y allá.
Here and over there.
Déjame con el calor de tu lengua
Leave me the heat of your tongue
Cubriendo mi piel.
Covering my skin.
Dame unos besitos
Give me kisses
Hasta no suspiro más
Until I won't be able to breathe anymore
Y el sabor de tu leche, dulce y salada,
And the taste of your milk, so salted and sweet,

Me manda al cielo
Sends me to paradise
Pero contigo solamente
But only with you
Durante nuestro vuelo hasta el sol.
During our flight to the sun.
No habrá nadie más.
There will be no one else.

Still, it wasn't enough.

And in the meantime, Ignacio had started to look after her again.

THOUGH SHE HAD REMAINED TORN ABOUT NESTOR, IT ALL CAME down to Ignacio's automobile. One afternoon, a *camionero,* a truck driver, in from Pinar del Río, arrived at her *solar* with *noticias malas*—bad news— from that horrid woman Olivia, the only way she ever heard from her family in those days. Sweating and half out of breath, this truck driver was practically in tears, for he knew her *papito* from that crossroads place where he performed sometimes. *"Tu papá no está bien"*—"He isn't well," he told her. What had happened? During a sudden lightning storm a few days before, the horse her *papito* had been riding across a field had stumbled into a ditch, and he was thrown headfirst against a tree, so many of his bones and internal organs punctured or broken that it was likely he would die. Receiving that sad information on a Friday, just before she was to go into rehearsals for a new show, what else could María do but seek out Ignacio, who had an automobile, and beg him to drive her out to see her *papito* before it would be too late?

Ignacio, for his part, had his own plans, but, of course, when María called him later from the Nocturne, he dropped everything, and by eleven the next morning, he had picked María up for their drive into the countryside, hours away from the city. When they arrived at her beloved *valle,* the forests and fields were damp from rain, and as María, trudging through the mud, rushed to his bedside, her *papito* seemed, indeed, to be dying. A doctor from town had been attending to him. Stretched out on a cot and wrapped up with bandages, her poor *guajiro papito* could barely breathe. His internal organs too damaged to repair, he had fallen into the delirium of a fever. She did not leave his side that entire day, or the next; out of habit, she prayed over him, prayed until he finally heard her voice and opened his eyes. Smiling, as Manolo took hold of her hand and said, *"Ay, María, por favor pórtate bien,"* and then, *"Y ya está"*—"Now here it is," all María could think was this: *Once he's gone, everyone I have ever loved will have died.*

Then, while birds were chirping away outside the *bohío*, he drifted off into a sleep from which he would never awaken.

She was nineteen years old.

He'd passed away at ten in the morning, and, looking back, what she would be most grateful for was how Ignacio Fuentes had kept his head about the whole business. It was Ignacio who went to San Jacinto that same day to arrange for a proper funeral, Ignacio who paid for the coffin and organized the locals for the burial processional to the local campo santo, *that cemetery of soon to be forgotten souls; Ignacio who had paid for a funeral feast; Ignacio who had been a pillar of strength for María. And for that alone María felt a sincere gratitude toward him, no matter his faults, and swore that, whatever her desires for that* músico, *she would put Nestor Castillo from her mind.*

What would it matter? Her life had become a kind of a dancer's purgatory by then anyway.

Chapter
TWENTY-THREE

And Nestor? Unable to accept María's decision, he sent her notes nearly daily. Naturally they piled up beside her bed, unread, and when he turned up at her *solar*, whatever hour of the day, she was rarely at home. (By then, María had started to spend more and more time with Ignacio at a house he had bought just outside Havana, along the sea.) At her shows, Nestor became such a distraction that María had to ask Eliseo, the club bouncer, to turn him away at the door, and when she left through the backstage exit at four in the morning, María, head covered by a veil, came to dread the inevitable moment when she encountered Nestor on the street. He'd beg her to just sit with him for a few moments, to hear him out—there were so many things he had to tell her—but she couldn't because, deep down, she knew what it would lead to. It got to the point that Ignacio himself had to wait for her; failing that, he'd send along one or two of his men to accompany her.

Bodyguards.

By then, María, looking the other way, had come to accept the notion that Ignacio, as her fellow dancers had gossiped all along, happened to be a gangster. It made no difference to her; he had to earn a living after all, and since when had life been good to that man in the first place? Still, she drew lines. Once when Nestor started to get out of hand and Ignacio, as tenderly as possible, suggested that one or two of his colleagues have a "serious talk with the *músico*," María, not so entirely cold, told him: "Hurt that *joven*, and I will never let you touch me again." So they put up with a lot, especially at night, when Nestor followed behind her and played his trumpet, not dreaming melodies but mocking horse race

135

reveilles. And sometimes, having lost his mind, his voice echoing in the arcades, he'd scream that she was nothing more than some impotent's whore! All this Ignacio, with enormous patience, ignored; for María, however, it became too much, and she went through days when she wished that Nestor had never come into her life at all.

For months, Nestor continued to sweetly torment her (no, it wasn't easy) until there came the day when Ignacio, a bookish and, therefore, crafty fellow, seized upon a certain idea. From conversations with María, he had learned a central fact about the brothers' lives: that the older and vainer one, Cesar Castillo, had ambitions about going to New York, a city Ignacio knew well, having his own cousins there as well as friends in the nightclub and appliance businesses. So why wouldn't Ignacio have several of his colleagues, surveying the streets in their dark Oldsmobile, bring Cesar down to his office in the harbor, which was just a cluttered and stuffy windowless room off a loading dock, to discuss certain possibilities, the main one being that Ignacio, in his open-minded benevolence and wishing only the best for María, would pay Cesar five hundred dollars to get the hell out of Havana with his brother.

And not just out of Havana, but to a place they wanted to go to anyway: New York. What happened? As Ignacio, flavoring the tip of a cigar in a gimlet of Carlos V brandy, told María some days later: "Once I made the offer, that pretty boy *macho,* who had walked in wanting to knock my block off, became very friendly and grateful. We got a little drunk together, and, in fact, by the time he left, if we hadn't hated each other so much in the first place, we might have ended up good friends."

Nestor, however, never really wanted to leave and became so mournful about losing María that Cesar was sorely tempted to make the journey without him. But he dragged Nestor along, and his brother, that poor lost soul *(or, as María would put it one day, the darling sweet* pobrecito *who deserved every bit of her love)* stepped onto a Pan American Clipper to Miami only after being fortified by a night in the whorehouses, a quart of *añejo* rum, and the assurance that Cesar would beat him to death if he didn't.

In the meantime, as much as she had felt relieved to hear about

Nestor's departure, María, sitting with Ignacio in an outdoor café along the Prado, could barely wait for the moment when she might be alone again. Christ forgive her, Nestor was the one she thought about now when touching herself, her memories of his fevered masculinity staying with her no matter how cruelly she had treated him.

ON THEIR LAST AFTERNOON TOGETHER IN HAVANA, SPENT IN A dingy hotel room by the harbor, Nestor, sipping rum from a pint bottle, presented her with gifts. Stretched out on that bed, he had reached over to the end table for a box, his body damp with sweat.

"I have some things for you, María," he told her.

The first was a thin necklace, of fading gold, off which hung a little tarnished silver crucifix, the weight of a peseta.

"It's the same one I wore as a child, when I thought I was going to die. I feel it should be yours," he told her. "Wear it for me."

Gratefully, she put that crucifix and chain around her neck, and with that Nestor began fondling her. But no, she stopped him, pulling his hands away from her. *"No puedo,"* she said. "I can't." But what could she do that afternoon when, happy as a child, he got up and retrieved an envelope from his trousers pocket; it contained a dozen black-and-white photographs, the sort with serrated edges that had been taken here and there in Havana, by friends or passersby. Nestor and María posed by a table, surrounded by flowers in the back garden of a café called Ofelia's, Nestor and María holding hands in front of the marquee of the America movie house, after taking in a Humphrey Bogart double feature, a look of hopefulness and affection on each of their faces. She was truly touched, almost felt like bursting into tears over the decision she had already made but wasn't too good at carrying out.

"Son bonitos"—"They're pretty," she told him.

"But look at these. Remember the *playa* at Cojímar?"

They were fine photographs of them frolicking in the waves a few months before, the sorts one would always cherish, even if they were a little blurred: Nestor, eternally handsome with his penetrating gaze, and beautiful María in her clinging bathing suit rising out of the sea like a goddess.

"You see how happy we are, María? How much we are in love!"

"Oh, Nestor," she said to him. "Why are you so sentimental?"

"I just want to make you happy," he said, pulling her close. "There are so many things I want to do for you!"

This time, when the kisses started up again, she didn't resist—it was much easier to go along with that form of speaking than to say any actual words, especially when hers would only be so hurtful. Soon enough that crucifix, dangling from her neck, was pinching Nestor's thing as he, straddling María with his knees, availed himself of her breasts' plumpness. Oh, but what that crucifix witnessed! Perhaps because she thought that it might be their last time together, she dallied longer than usual, taking care of the man until she was blissfully sore in her deepest parts, until the harbor cannons began their 8 p.m. booming and night began to fall over the sad city of Havana. What was the last thing he told her?

"María, don't you know, I'd die without you."

THAT LAST AFTERNOON WAS HARD ENOUGH TO RECALL; BUT WHAT was harder came down to Maria's memories of tasting every bit of him, and thinking that Nestor's body, even his big *pinga,* was a part of her own. It was intoxicating: as much as she wanted to forget him, as she'd walk through the streets of Havana, everything she laid her eyes upon, even if only vaguely phallic, reminded her of Nestor. She could not put on a pair of soft slippers without recalling the joy with which she would unfurl, slowly and sweetly, a condom over him and the time it took, or glance at a quart bottle of milk or a sweating, tall Hatuey beer with its frosty exhalations and not think of his sweat, his passion, his gushing sperm.

PART III

Songs of Despair and Love
Havana, New York, 1953–1958

In the summer of 1953, some four years after her *papito* had passed from this world and Nestor Castillo and his brother had commenced a new life in America, María turned around to find that certain things were going on in Cuba that she hadn't noticed before. Not that she was unusual among her fellow dancers at the Lantern Cabaret, just off San Miguel, where María worked in those days—hardly any of them cared about anything other than pulling in good crowds nightly and keeping their jobs. But when certain events took place and military personnel began patrolling the streets of Havana at night, and foot traffic into the club fell off for a time, even those dancers became aware that an insurrection had broken out. According to the newspaper and radio reports of the day, it came down to the ire and moral indignation of one fellow, whose name María first heard while at the club: Fidel Castro.

> (Static) The government of the Republic of Cuba announces the capture of one . . . (static) . . . in the aftermath of a failed attack against the forces of our beloved president Fulgencio Batista . . . (static) . . . the rebellious corpses were laid out side by side in the courtyard of the Moncada Barracks, near Santiago, and their leader, one Fidel Castro Ruz . . . (static) . . . led away in chains, to await a charge of treason. . . .

She hadn't made much of that name, Fidel Castro, at the time, or of such events, which, in any case, hardly stirred much of an opinion, one way or the other, in the corridors and dressing rooms backstage.

In fact, the only person of María's acquaintance who even seemed to take special notice of politics was her faithful teacher Lázaro, whom María still visited at least twice weekly. It wasn't as easy as it used to be, when all she had to do was step down a few flights to find him sitting near the bookseller's stall. She and Ignacio had since moved into a nice sunny apartment in a new modern high-rise in Vedado overlooking the sea, and he'd even opened that clothing store along Galiano, a shopping street in Central Havana, an enterprise that had not turned out the way he had envisioned. Still dancing almost nightly, María sometimes worked there in the afternoons, looking breathtakingly exotic and photogenic by the dress racks, before heading off to the club. Occasionally, she took off early to see her friend Lázaro, the one who, in those years, had taught her so much.

As a matter of course, he'd have María read aloud from books and magazines, among them *Bohemia,* a national weekly, which had published letters from Castro and articles about the nobility of his cause. *"Tú verás,"* he'd say, tapping a sepia page showing Castro's photograph. "Sooner or later someone will come along who's not a crook. This young one, he'll probably rot in prison for the rest of his life, but there'll be others. If God is good to me, I will live to see the day."

She'd nod, she'd smile. Out in her *valle,* in Pinar del Río, she hadn't learned much about anything, except for the inevitability of death, and of music and dancing. Even the Second World War had been this distant calamity, which she'd had glimpses of in newsreels at the Chaplin, and what she had known of the goings-on in Havana, of that succession of presidents who came and went as she grew up, amounted to a few names, which those *guajiros* hardly mentioned. But if she knew anything about Cuban history in those days, she owed that to Lázaro. He'd seen it all. From the 1880s, when he was a boy and the Cuban rebels, fighting for independence, waged pitched battles with the Spaniards in the countryside, to when the Americans first occupied Havana at the turn of the century, the establishment of the Cuban republic in 1902, and life under a succession of presidents, the worst of them, in his youth, having been one Gerardo Machado, in the 1920s, who had been nicknamed a "second

Nero" for his suspension of civil liberties, his cruelties, and the ostentation of his greed. And Cuba's latest president, Batista, the one whom Castro, a lawyer, opposed? That previous March, of 1952, Batista had staged a military coup to gain his office, a violation of the constitution that had enraged a generation of idealists and muckrakers, among them that fellow Castro. And yet, she felt untouched by any of this; if Batista happened to be particularly corrupt, as rumor had it, she couldn't really care less. As far as she was concerned, her life would unfold in the same way no matter who happened to be in power. At heart, beautiful María's stance came down to a shrug that said, "Really, Lázaro, what does any of that matter to me?"

Her attitude always baffled Lázaro, who, knowing about María's *guajira* past, and the ignorance and poverty that came with it, forgave her anyway. Besides, he'd seen his beautiful protégée's demeanor changing before his very eyes. While in the midst of their lessons during those terrible months after her *papito*'s death, just the thought of his loss brought her quickly to tears. "There, there, *mi vida*, this pain will soon pass," Lázaro would tell her, and she would hope that it would be so. Yet, instead of that experience making María a little sweeter and more compassionate about life, the way it sometimes happened with people; instead of becoming more softhearted, María seemed to have gone in the opposite direction, her personality taking on a harsher edge, what María would describe to her daughter, years in the future, in a single sentence: *"Me puso muy, muy durita"*—"I became harder skinned."

It was as if María had walked into a room as a naïve nineteen-year-old beauty in need of some seasoning and education in one moment and, five minutes later, left through another door, not as the hopeful child, unrefined as an Ozark hillbilly, she had essentially been but as a woman aged, not in looks but in temperament, way beyond her years. By 1953, the graceful and ever so beautiful María had developed such a haughty and distanced manner around people that even Lázaro, who used to eat greasy chorizo sandwiches in front of her with abandon, now found that she had taken to looking at him disapprovingly the moment any of those delicious amber-red pork juices started dripping through their newspaper wrappings and down his chin. And heaven forbid if he smiled and actually wiped his mouth with his wrist (Lázaro, with his raspy voice always laughing and chortling, "My, my, but what's better than this!"), because then María, without intending to seem so severe, frowned, as if Lázaro were reminding her just where she had come from: the *campo*. Even if she'd once chewed her food like a goat, and had the manners of a field hand, loving to eat things with her fingers, and hadn't known what a flush toilet was until an afternoon in 1938, when she and her younger sister, Teresita—*ay, la pobre*—had seen their first show at the Chaplin movie house in San Jacinto (how many times they pulled on that overhead chain and jumped up and down at the sight of the vanishing waters!), she now comported herself with so much caution and formality that Lázaro hardly recognized her as the reticent girl he had known.

Or to put it differently: what was sweetest about María had been pulled so deeply into herself that she now seemed as haughty as she was beautiful. Still, Lázaro looked forward to their lessons and took pride in the way that their afternoons of study had paid off. María could read now, but slowly, and she had filled her notebooks with countless words that she had more or less memorized. And her handwriting, ever so careful, had been honed by the hours and hours she'd spent backstage between shows scribbling down rows of the alphabet's letters, the way schoolchildren did. Practice had gotten María to the point where she could write her name out with such elegant flourishes that it would have been hard for anyone to imagine that she'd come from a family whose father signed his name with a crudely rendered X, or that for years María had only pretended she could read signs while walking along the streets. As they'd sit in their usual spot, near the bookseller's stall, Lázaro had occasionally taken special joy in advising María what school grade she had graduated into. By the time Nestor had left for America, she had passed through to the second grade; a few years later, in 1951, she had slipped into secondary school, and now, in the days of Batista's presidency, she could read and write like a fourteen-year-old with certain bad habits—which is to say, she got some things right and some things wrong, spelling never being one of her strengths. Nevertheless, she'd reached a point where she really didn't need Lázaro any longer, and what more did he have to teach her?

Still, despite dressing as well as the El Encanto window mannequins (Ignacio wanted her always to look her best) and carrying herself as if she were the *dueña* of Havana, María loved returning to that market street and going from stall to stall to say hello to the merchants, who always joked about this fine uppity lady's resemblance to someone they once knew. It always pleased her to sort through the bookseller's selections. She had a weakness for romance novels by a certain Almacita Alvarez from Spain— and just recognizing the titles: *Bitter Love, Blood and Passion, Taught to Deceive*—filled her with pride. She also liked any books about spiritualism, for she often dreamed about her dead family and believed there had to be a way of contacting them. Though those books rarely cost more than eight or ten cents apiece, or the price of a trolley or bus ride, customers still haggled with the vendor, but never María, who believed each tome invaluable, whatever its tattered condition.

In fact, while María had kept working as a dancer, she didn't have too many expenses to worry about. Because she was Ignacio Fuentes's "woman," her rent and clothing were taken care of, but even if he had turned out to be a stingy man, she would have had sources of income beyond her twenty pesos a week as a dancer. Having caught the eye of more than one art director or advertising executive during her performances, María had started getting jobs as a model, posing beside kitchen appliances, soaking in bubble baths, leaning against the dimpled hood of a shiny Oldsmobile, usually in either a movie starlet's glistening gown or a tight bathing suit. In advertisements for Polar beer, her face adorned many a poster here and there in the city, and because the company also produced promotional coasters and waiters' trays, her mysterious and alluring expression was to be found peering up from the half-moon bottoms of frothy drinks and rum glasses at strangers in cafés and bars everywhere. If beautiful María had turned heads before just because of the way her *nalgitas* swayed inside her dress, and stopped traffic with her unmistakable looks, she now attracted attention for having become so familiar to the general public. She'd even appeared in a rum ad on a television show, broadcast from the CMQ building, but had disliked the sweltering lights, the way they made her diaphragm sweat under the tight binding of her dress, and the unearthly feeling that came from wearing what felt like pounds of makeup on her face. (*"Una miseria,"* she called that.)

In time, with more money than she needed, María put most of her wages into a savings account at a Chase National Bank on Brasil, her blue passbook something she liked to take out from under her mattress to "read" as if it were a novel. Never forgetting how her own *papi* never earned very much, she gave a few coins to nearly every beggar she encountered, and when she bumped into her friend El Caballero de París, she'd buy him lunch and a few glasses of first-class rum, sometimes even a Churchill cigar. When it came to Lázaro, who never wanted more payment than a sandwich or two, as well as a radiant smile, María began insisting that he accept a few dollars from her for those lessons.

Having taken to calling Lázaro *mi maestro*, a title that always made him wince with happiness as he'd spent most of his life as a bootblack, and then a Havana street sweeper, the brunt of that income derived from the largesse of local merchants along Obispo and O'Reilly streets—María had begun to look upon him with a fondness that made her fear for his well-being. He wasn't her *papito*, but she had grown attached enough to his laughter and kindly manner that, as surely as the sun began baking the rooftops of Havana in the mornings, she came to believe that he would go the way of everyone she had ever loved. It was the kind of thought that lingered in the back of María's mind each time he seemed a little tired or had trouble hoisting himself up from those steps, and especially so as he once tried to get to his feet and this old, lanky *negrito* nearly fell backwards into the hallway's shadows from whence he had come. (Those were Havana shadows, the temperature cooling with every foot of hallway you stepped into, like entering the recesses of a church baptistery, a scent of ashes, frying fish, and flowers, somehow musty, deepening.)

That was the only time María, accompanying Lázaro home, saw where he lived—inside an inner courtyard, under an awning set out over what must have been some old stone trough from when horses were kept in the alleys, all his possessions, mainly books and a mat, with only a single chair crammed into what amounted to a hole in the wall, his only luxury a solitary lightbulb, which hung off a bent wire, his toilet situated behind a rotted door that led into the back of a store. But did he complain? No; and when she, out of a generous impulse and knowing that *la Señora* Matilda would have looked after him, offered to put him up in la Cucaracha, he refused. "I'm just used to it here, that's all," he told her. "And at my age, I'm waiting for that *guagua* that goes to where it goes, anyway."

Pero, hombre, she thought. *No te mueras.*

She was already attached enough to Lázaro and his lessons that each time María turned up, she couldn't help but wonder if it would be her last, as if her affection for someone would surely spell his doom. Of course, María was imagining things, but having lost her family at so young an age, as she'd one day explain to her daughter, she became a "little *cucka en la cabeza*," without even realizing it . . . which was probably part of the reason why she had turned away from Nestor.

"And that nice fellow, the handsome one, I used to see you with—whatever happened to him?" Lázaro had once asked her.

"He went off to America, to New York."

"So, why didn't you go with him?" Lázaro shook his head. "I saw the way you looked at each other—yes, *señorita*, I certainly did!"

"I don't really know why," she told him, shrugging. "But he was a *músico*, and you know how musicians can be; they don't have much common sense."

Nodding agreeably, as if María were old enough to know what she was talking about, Lázaro punched out the inside of his lacquered cane hat on his lap and smiled. "You mean he didn't have much money, was that it?"

"No, it wasn't that at all. He just didn't seem proper in his thinking."

"Uh-huh," Lázaro conceded. "And that older fellow you're with now, the one who doesn't smile very much—is he your man?"

"He's good to me, Lázaro," she began, but then, not wanting to explain anything, she lost her patience. "Whatever happened between me and that *músico* is over with, and there's nothing left to be said or done."

"Oh, *amorcita,* don't you know there's more to life than money," Lázaro told her, turning to the next of the lessons. "The goodness in a man's heart, that's something else. But who am I to lecture you? I just hope you're happy."

She had to admit that the few times Ignacio had seen her with Lázaro, he hadn't reacted well, accusing her of consorting with a Negro as if that were the worst thing she could do with herself. "Next thing you know," Ignacio once told her, "you'll lose what few manners you have." The few times they met, when she was still living in that *edificio,* he never deigned to speak with Lázaro and always gave the kindly man, so politely singing her praises and doffing his hat in respect, a look that implied he was no better than riffraff, or the lowest of the low. It didn't help that Lázaro was black as a crow—Ignacio had no use for such men. In fact, he had filled María's head with all kinds of sentiments that would have been unthinkable to her back in Pinar del Río, sentiments that were insulting. As a light-skinned *mulatta,* she surely had black blood on her mother's side; nevertheless, María couldn't fault Ignacio for thinking that way; most white Cubans, *los blanquitos,* did.

"Oh, but that other one," Lázaro would say. "What was his name again?"

"Nestor—Nestor Castillo."

"You know, once when you weren't around, he came over to talk with me, played me a little tune, a sweet melody on his trumpet. Told me he was writing it for you, María. Did you know that?"

"Yes, he liked to write songs, but I suppose all *músicos* do."

"*Ay, pero, chiquita,* I could tell listening to it that the fellow was crazy about you. Pardon me for saying so, I took one look into his eyes and

I saw some wonderful things—like a poet's thoughts. Were I a lovely young woman, that for me would have been enough to throw all common sense out the window." Then: "Now, I won't say another word," though, forgetting, he always would.

She'd put up with his two cents, knowing that Lázaro only meant well, and there were times when she was tempted to explain how Nestor sometimes frightened her, not with his natural armature, a true wonder she'd never forget, but with a sadness that María, carrying enough of her own, found wearisome, as if there would never be any way of making him happy. That Nestor Castillo was such a high-strung *tipo* seemed a matter of bad luck, the sweet *músico* with a troubled soul and a doubtful future, the man, so much of a child, whom she'd had no choice but to turn away. He was, after all, a *campesino,* and like the *guajiros,* he didn't put up any barriers between his feelings and how he acted, or what he said— something which, in those days, María, being groomed as a proper lady by Ignacio, had come to forget.

Chapter

TWENTY-FIVE

A story: in 1953, the same year that Castro had started what would be known as the July 26th Movement, María, moonlighting, had posed for a four-color "Fly to Cuba" poster for Pan American airlines. This came about because an American executive with a New York advertising agency, Y & R, had caught her act one night at the Lantern and approached her after the show—which was how she got most of her modeling jobs. The ad itself, shot in the Torrens studio off Cuba Street, featured María, in a snug two-piece cream-colored bathing suit, her *nalgitas* prominently hanging out, and white-rimmed beach girl sunglasses, standing in juicy splendor before a towering royal palm. Sipping coconut juice from a gourd through a straw with one hand, she held a thick, fuming cigar in the other, its smoke rising into the air and resolving into the shape of a heart as a sleek four-engine Pan Am Clipper flew overhead through the bluest of Cuban skies. An afternoon's work that paid quite well—twenty-five dollars.

María could hardly have imagined that the finished product would have caught the eye of her former *amante*, Nestor Castillo, in distant New York. Or to be more precise, that poster, hanging in a travel agency window, had stopped Nestor dead in his tracks one autumn afternoon in 1953 as he passed through the cavernous lobby of the Hotel Biltmore on East Forty-fourth Street, on his way to visit a Cuban friend, José-Pascual, in the Men's Bar. Oh, poor, poor Nestorito, as she would come to think of him. He was that handsome dark-featured man, dapper in a linen jacket, peering dreamily at her image, his heart aching. Beside himself with rekindled memories of her lusciousness and the romance that had nearly

150

torn him apart, Nestor soon found himself by that agency counter, pleading, if not demanding, in his broken English that the clerk sell him the poster. He was trembling, his hands shaking wildly. To think that every Fred MacMurray–looking *fulano* passing by that window could see María holding between her elegant fingers that phallic cigar! Such was his agitation that he hardly noticed at first how the clerk, a transplant from Cuba himself, and a rather sympathetic one at that, had started speaking to him in Spanish.

It took him a while to calm Nestor down, and, in the end, he explained that, as much as he wanted to help him out, he just couldn't sell such things to everyone whose interest that poster had caught. "You see," he said, "with that one, someone always makes the same request, nearly every day." Instead, he advised Nestor to visit the local Pan Am office a few blocks north. "Go up to the fourth floor," he told him. "There's a customer relations office there, and they'll be happy to help you. Okay, *caballero?*" A little while later, in the bar, a few steps away from the hotel's Palm Court (in the Havana style), and not far from its famous clock and the young couples gathered there, Nestor, brooding over a fried steak with onions sandwich and enough rum to get him dreaming, confided to his friend, a fellow he had befriended at a party on La Salle Street, the mess this woman in Havana had left him in.

"She seemed to love me, and then she didn't, *carajo!*" he kept saying, his head shaking. "José-Pascual," he said, "if you only knew how I hate myself for letting her get away." Then, with José-Pascual, a good-natured *gallego* and a transplant from Jiguaní, pouring, mostly for free, he got good and drunk over the matter. By five, as Nestor, making his way a few blocks north, stumbled in through a Madison Avenue skyscraper's dizzily revolving doors, hundreds of office workers were swarming its lobby, and Nestor, put off by the crowd, and having to make a rehearsal in any case, lost heart and decided to head back uptown instead, sulking all the way. Later that night, tormented as always by the slightest reminder of María, he hardly slept—believing that María was mocking him from afar. And while he tried to forget her, for many a good reason that image of María, with that vaguely lip-shaped shadow dipping through the front cleft of her bathing suit like an orchid's fold, killed Nestor and distracted him for weeks. But then that was Nestor. On many a night after, he would sit on his living room couch with his guitar, whereupon, strumming chords, he would pour his musings and pained longings into yet another version of his song about her, a bolero he had decided to call "Beautiful María of My Soul."

She had known about that song for a long time. Thanks to Lázaro's lessons, María had slowly gained the ability to decipher the nearly weightless airmail letters Nestor had started sending her from New York, weekly at first, then twice monthly, then every other month. The first year, 1950—when María had accepted without regret her status as Ignacio's mistress and moved into their fourteenth-floor high-rise apartment, with its mirrored walls and sweeping view of the sea, the Hotel Nacional, and the Malecón—she had hardly ever thought about Nestor, except during her most lonely and longing (sexual) moods, his splendid physicality as deeply embedded in her skin's memory as a nagging melody in a musician's head.

On the other hand, once his letters started to arrive, at first with Nestor's musician friends from New York who'd come to Havana for work and would track her down, one way or the other, at the clubs, it was as if he were determined to enter her life again. (Finding María wasn't hard: on any given day, one was bound to come across a little ad tucked into the back pages of the *Havana Gazette* or *El Diario de la Marina* about the *"Phenomenally beautiful and enticing María Rivera—The Dancer You Must See!"* And many a photograph of María, in a heavy Aztec-looking plumed headdress and scanty costume, was replicated in the posters and half sheets pasted to the crumbling walls and lampposts of the old city.) At first, María couldn't have cared less about Nestor's missives. Aside from wanting to avoid the simple labor of deciphering them, she didn't care to deal with those pangs of guilt about him that occasionally arose to the surface of her dreams, already peopled enough by the ghosts of the *guajiro* family she had lost. (When she went back to her *campo* in her sleep, she always saw her *mamá* sitting on a rocking chair by the doorway to their *bohío,* her *papito* riding across the fields on a horse, the farmers and their oxen around him, and her late sister, Teresa, in the years before she fell ill, just ahead of her on that lovely trail through the forest as they headed toward their beloved *cascadas,* each of them seeming very much alive, a lovely dream until she'd remember that they were dead.)

Yet María couldn't help but keep those letters together, in a drawer in her dressing room table, beside a jar of Aphrodite pomade (as if she needed that), and the fact remained that she hadn't the heart to rip up any of the photographs of Nestor and herself that he had given her on their final day together. (On those nights when she grew bored with the routine, the repetitiousness of a show like "Queen Isabella's Dance with Columbus," or "A Peek at Marie Antoinette's Ladies in Waiting," or "A Cuban Tarzan with His Cuban Janes," she sometimes lingered over those photographs of Nestor and herself, taken during their excursions to the beach near Cojímar in the days when they could barely keep their hands off each other. In one of them, Nestor was carrying her out of the cresting gulf waters, María's arms wrapped around his neck, her breasts pressing, through her green bathing suit, against his happy face, his bathing trunks agitated and plump in the right places. In another, María and Nestor were captured necking in the surf, foam rising around them and their bodies so entangled, that their photographer, one of María's dancer acquaintances from the old days, Elenita Marquez, tagging along for the fun of it, wondered if they were going to do it right there and then. María had other such photographs, taken around Havana, and even if they were out of focus sometimes, they still commemorated their love and, jaded as she sometimes felt, she counted them, along with the crucifix Nestor had given her, among her most precious possessions.)

But the letters eventually provoked her curiosity, and by the summer of 1951, though she would have saved herself time by showing them to *la señora* Matilda, who often tortured her with the admonition that she should have gone off with Nestor, María made it a part of her studies to decipher them, slowly. By then, thanks to Lázaro, her abilities to read and write had improved greatly, to the point that she had finally begun to understand the myriad neon signs that glowed and blinked along the nightclub strips, and other things had become less of a mystery. Still, it had taken her the longest time to get through Nestor's letters. Once she did, María discovered that either she had a much longer way to go or Nestor's own command of the written language was that of a *campesino* who had been taught to read and write by a suave but barely educated older brother. Nestor's letters were always brief, however, as if he did not want to waste another page of that nearly weightless airmail paper. Some were written in pencil, others in smudged, light blue running ink, as if they'd been cried upon, sweated upon, or—who knows what men are capable of when they start to get carried away with their emotions and memories? Some were casual, others impassioned, heartbroken, but all of them were either riddled with words that María simply had not yet come to understand or confusing by virtue of Nestor's phonetic spellings—*'ablar* for *hablar* or *'rible* for *horrible*, among others. Nevertheless, through her own painstaking efforts, along with the occasional assistance of a certain ancient ladies' powder room attendant, Chi-chi, María came to get a general picture of Nestor's new life *en los Estados Unidos*.

Nueva York, he wrote, was deathly cold in the winters; from the skies came snow—*la nieve*, like something out of a dream; and people stared at you for speaking in Spanish, and some streets were unimaginably crowded. *"Imagine this, María, thousands of people rushing along on a single sidewalk! . . . And the people, of so many nationalities—Italians, Greeks, Germans, Chinese, Russians, and Poles, even* los judíos—*speaking in their own languages, a different world, a city much grander than Havana, but not as beautiful, and with rivers that stink of trash and chimneys that send up smoke and more automobiles and buses than you imagined possible. And the buildings,* por Dios! *Remember that giant* mono, *King Kong? That building he climbed really exists, it's called the Empires [sic] State!"* (That name he carefully wrote out in English.) *"Y* fíjate eso, *just looking up, you see more high buildings everywhere—so wonderful and horrible at the same time."* And with every mention of such things, Nestor told her how much he loved María and missed her terribly, that he didn't know why they had lost something so precious. *"But you understand, María, there's still time. . . . I'm waiting for you, and only you. . . ."*

Yes, even if she had treated him foolishly and badly, he knew that in her heart she really loved him. But at least he had ways of keeping himself busy, and not just by trying to learn English, which he called *un monstruoso idioma*—a monster of a language. He had a job, along with his brother Cesar—*"You remember him, don't you?"*—working in a meatpacking plant during the day and playing music with a little *conjunto* of musicians they'd found here and there in the city at night and on the weekends. They lived in an apartment in a neighborhood called Harlem with their cousins, "really kindly folks, *humildes y simpáticos*," up the hill on *el calle* La Salle from what's called an "El train" in New York—the rumbling of the tracks that shook their beds made him long for the quiet of the Cuban countryside. He told María he had days when he felt completely lost and ached with the desire to return to Cuba, to please just say the word—nothing was holding him there. (Cesar loved New York, he wrote, while he himself did not always understand what he was doing there, particularly when he still suffered so without her.) They had lively parties in that apartment, hosted by his brother Cesar, but they meant little to him, the *cubanas* and Puerto Rican women who turned up from all over the boroughs were nice enough, but they had nothing to offer him, simply because he could think only of her—*"Besides, they are too ugly compared to you. . . ."*

In concluding, he always promised to write her again, "faithfully," and would await her reply. *"Please answer me, even just a few words would make me happy. . . ."*

And when María, ashamed of herself, never answered him, he wrote this:

I don't understand your silence, María, and while my wounds have grown deeper and my love for you even stronger during these past few years, I've come to accept why you could not stay with me. And I don't blame you; in fact, I forgive you, because María, *mi vida, mi amor,* I know that you have only deserved the best, and what am I but some nobody *músico?* And that's why, María, I have vowed to make a success of myself, so that I will have something to give you besides my pure, pure love. Because of that I am writing so many wonderful songs, with hopes to sell them to orchestras. But the best of those songs I have saved for you, and I am only working harder to make it as perfect as you, and deserving of all your admiration. It comes from my heart, from deep inside, and it has a name that always makes me smile, because it makes me think of you. . . . *"Bellísima María de mi alma"*—*una canción* that I dedicate to you, my love. . . .

Chapter

TWENTY-SIX

Not that she ever got teary eyed over him, in the same way that Nestor did thinking about her—she was too practical minded for that kind of nonsense. There was no point to it—what had finally happened between them would remain in the irretrievable past after all. Besides, it would have been stupid to lose her head over something as ephemeral and useless as love. (*"Es como el aire,"* María would say. "It's like air.") Nevertheless, each night before her shows, while the band was warming up the audience with comic parodies of "Carmen" or with some old big band tunes, à la Tommy Dorsey (the crowds were mostly American), she still found herself thinking about him, as if, in some reversal of destiny, Nestor might come walking in through the stage door. Musicians, after all, were always traveling between New York, Miami, and Havana, wherever their work might take them. There were nights, in fact, when María wished that she had gone off with him; not for love, perhaps, but because her life with Ignacio had become so boring and, in its way, something of a prison.

Or, to put it differently, she found that going to bed with Ignacio had become a matter of duty. The truth be told, during those afternoon and late morning bouts of love, when Ignacio turned María on her side so that he, parting her *nalgitas* ever so slightly, could enter her from behind or, in the dress shop office, closed the door, took down his trousers, and stood before her with his hands on his hips so that she could take care of him with her mouth, or when he had María, her bathing suit dropped to her knees, lower herself onto him so that her bottom rested on his legs as he sat on a bench in one of those sandy-floored cabanas

157

out at Varadero—seven thrusts and then out, he came so quickly—she hardly felt anything at all, not even the guilt which used to send her on flights to purgatory. But was it his fault? Anatomically speaking, though he couldn't touch Nestor, he wasn't bad at all, and there were moments when, pulling back on her hair or suckling on her nipples, he seemed almost tender. And yet María, no matter what Ignacio did, had the misfortune of feeling simply too capacious for him. Besides, he couldn't really have cared less what she felt, as long as María carried on with the twisting of her head, the screams, her body trembling as if she were imitating poor Teresita's spells.

Afterwards Ignacio, having had his macho pride attended to, and most satisfactorily, always felt like the king cock of Havana and got into the habit of pinching María's cheeks as if she were a child. Now and then, if she were lying naked on her stomach on their bed, flipping through the pages of magazines like *Hoy* or *Gente,* with their articles about American movie stars, he might slide a few fingers inside her and out, for she always seemed so damp, María crying, *"Ay, ay, ay,"* as if ready to go at it again, and Ignacio, feeling like Tarzan, pulling up on the waistband of his trousers and checking himself out in the mirror, snorting pridefully, as if he were the greatest lover in Cuba, while she, of course, had been secretly thinking about Nestor.

PUBLICLY, IGNACIO HAD CONTINUED TO SHOW MARÍA OFF AROUND Havana, loving it when they entered a packed house at the Alhambra and caused a stir, even if they slipped in during the prelude of a Lecuona zarzuela, and she hadn't minded that until she noticed him reverting to his former ways, occasionally staring at other women, and in an obvious manner, as if it were his right to do whatever he pleased. She had long since concluded that he was a petty gangster, but one trying to reform himself, and while Ignacio had opened his clothing store for urban sophisticates and tourists, El Emporio, when it came down to it, he seemed to spend as much time as before attending to his other business at the harbor. (His colleagues were men whom María, in the few times she met them, neither disliked nor liked. Some she had only seen from a distance, usually meeting up with Ignacio on some street corner or in a bar, and on the rare occasion she had noticed a few of them acting like rowdy drunks in the clubs—otherwise she hardly knew them.) And while Ignacio sometimes dropped by the clothing store in the afternoon to check up on that business like a proper boss, she disliked his tendency to hire as salesclerks pretty young *habaneras* who didn't seem to know a thing about that trade. As before, for all his promises, he still went off on business trips all across Cuba and to the States, away for weeks at a time, turning into the disembodied voice of a man on the club's hallway telephone.

Which is to say that María, in those years, without any family of her own, and having sent away the one man who most probably truly loved her (why else would that Nestor Castillo keep writing her?), had begun to discover the castigations of loneliness. She had her friends and acquaintances, of course, particularly among the whores at la Cucaracha, who were always trying to persuade María to join their fold—"Don't forget, there are men who would pay a lot of money for a few hours of your time," she'd hear again and again from Violeta—and occasionally, backstage at the club, one or another of her fellow dancers cried on her lap about loves that had never worked out, studs who had gotten away, husbands who abused/cheated/lied, and worries (as always) about money and keeping their looks (no black and blue marks or broken noses, please). Still, some of those dancers took her private and quiet ways as snobbery (if only they could have seen her out in the countryside with the *guajiros,* or known the way she looked forward to her stolen hours of study with Lázaro and suffered through her lessons).

Walking along the streets of Havana, she continued to attract the attentions of many a *habanero,* dashing and downtrodden alike. One afternoon, the American movie star Errol Flynn, many a showgirl surely in his harem, had doffed his Panama hat and smiled as she passed by him on a street corner outside the Capitolio. (And, speaking of movie stars, one evening at the club, when the buxom actress Ava Gardner had turned up with some friends to take in the show and María had passed by their table, the famous brunette, who seemed to enjoy her rum and had a somewhat wicked air about her, had nodded approvingly at her, the way beautiful women do with other beautiful women.) But ultimately, for a woman so young and beautiful—possibly the most dazzling woman in Cuba in those years—María spent too much time alone in bed. On such mornings and afternoons, when she had said her prayers and let her mother's rosary fall from her hand, she'd finally put herself to sleep by touching herself, writhing, her hand covered in her own moisture (Nestor), the pain and solitude in her heart giving way to the condolences of pleasure.

(That was a vanity as well: though she had not yet reached the point when she began to go around with different men, that confusing impulse to find pleasure had been with María for a long time. No, it wasn't the kind of thing she would ever have talked about with her daughter, Teresita, but the fact remained that, for all the country-girl piety María had been raised with, in some ways she hadn't been that different from the farm animals she'd watched breeding day in and day out in the yards, in the fields, in the woods. A little history, then, about the habits, in that regard, of a beautiful woman. In the days when her sister, Teresita, first suffered her fits, and María, seeking an escape, found all kinds of ways in which to please herself, she discovered that even her papito's shattered shaving mirror could enhance her bodily joys. One afternoon, because she had so little privacy, and had never seen any of her parts in a mirror, she took her papito's espejo off its post into the woods behind their thatch-roofed house, and there, under the shadow of an acacia, María pulled her skirt up, and with her undies fallen to her knees, held that mirror at such an angle beneath her as to catch a reflection of that which she had never seen before: her second mouth, wearing a crown of bristly black pubic hair, curling and dense and new to the world, which upon the minutest inspection and spread slightly open resembled the interior of a conch shell; and when she expanded herself a little wider, the same folds and whorls rearranged themselves into the opened petals of an orchid. That's when she

discovered a mole on the left side, and that just a little distance away was the puckered eye of her bottom, the same nutlike color as her vagina. At the same time she discovered that, if she used the mirror to catch the sunlight through a break in the foliage above and directed it at herself from yet another angle, God's radiance, as if a beam from heaven—that's what it surely had to be—spread through her in such delicious waves of divine heat that with just the touch of her finger she started to have her own kinds of seizures, not of epilepsy, like those of her sister, but of pure and sinful bodily release. She ended that business by pressing the heated mirror's surface against the dead center of her body as if to swallow the sun and sky and, doubling over, in an agony of unspeakable pleasure, squirmed about as if possessed before falling backwards to the ground. After a few moments she became vaguely aware that a salamander had crawled onto her leg and that, perched atop the gnarled roots of that acacia, a large spider had seemed to be observing her; afterwards, she spent the longest time examining her face and could not help but lick the mirror's surface, as if to taste the outline of her dampness, which resembled an upturned eye or wound . . .)

In those days, when Nestor's presence in her life had been reduced to nothing more than those letters, and María could not put from her mind her memories of their lovemaking, which seemed to become more vivid with the passing of time, that bodily release, much like bathing, eating, and using the toilet, became a part of her daily regimen. Two versions of Nestor existed for her then. The first boiled down to a photograph she had of him—not from the ones of them together in and around Havana but a more recent black-and-white snapshot, circa the spring of 1952, for which he had posed sitting on a stoop in New York City (presumably at La Salle Street) wearing a simple guayabera, his notebook in hand, his expression of tenderness and longing, as if he were about to sing a mournful bolero, tearing into her heart. (The kind of face that trumpet notes were tucked into.) Just looking at him, in all his guileless innocence, made María sigh and think *"El pobrecito"—Oh, the sweet, dear man.* And: *"Sí. Es posible que lo amo"—Yes, it's possible that I love him.* The other involved a memory of Nestor on a bed in that sun-swept room by the harbor and María grasping his glorious *pinga* with both her hands, removing the hand nestled against his pubic bone and placing that hand above the other; even then it still went on, in a flourish of delicate veins, before finally ending grandly in a bell-shaped fleshly elegance, the size of a peach, from whose opening seeped the clearest of liquids, a dew-like fluid, which tasted both sweet and salty against the tip of María's tongue and stretched so easily when she pulled its translucence into the air with her finger. Memories of María tugging at him and feeling its strength; of his warmth, that thickness, wide as her wrist, pressed against the side of her face, almost burning against her ear; of just how terrifying and wonderful it seemed every time Nestor lowered himself onto her and, drowning her opening with kisses first, settled himself gradually and then frantically inside her, so deeply that, even those years later, she still felt some sensations lingering in the farthest reaches of her womb, in the vicinity of her heart. It was a sensation that surprised her, as she crossed a room or sat by a terrace restaurant table (salting a piece of crispy *plátano*), pulled a pair of dark mesh stockings over her thighs, or applied makeup before her mirror, her nipples growing taut inside her brassiere. It seemed akin to a *picazón,* a nagging spectral itch, a blossoming of desire, of bodily longing, that no man, certainly not Ignacio, had been able to satisfy since Nestor.

But she neither hated nor loved her life in those days, though there were times when María felt such sudden loneliness and misery that certain things made her nervous. She disliked lingering by the terrace railing of their fourteenth-floor *solar,* as if the magnificent views—Havana breaking up into a dazzling succession of sunlit rooftops and gardens, the ocean so radiant—would draw her over the side; and on those occasions when Ignacio took her out on a friend's schooner for a sail on the seas off Marianao, that railing, just off the buffeting waters, also tempted her, as if her departed family were awaiting her under the shimmering surface, among the marlins and medusas. Such inexplicable impulses sometimes came over her even while María went strolling in Havana, when just the sight of an oncoming trolley made her wary, and it was only the company of saints, in the churches she visited, that seemed to comfort her. She also found refuge in her bedroom performances for the bluntly prone Ignacio, even if it was a rare day when neither God nor one or another of the ghosts seemed to linger, watching.

Ay, por Dios, but it wasn't easy to have outlived the little family she once had. Her loneliness was such that one Sunday she even made her way to a little shantytown, near a municipal garbage dump east of the city called Los Humos, where María believed she had some distant cousins on her mother's side. But her search through that place of misery only made her feel lonelier than before. No sooner had she located the rundown shack in which dwelled a family of twelve who claimed they were her kin than did they overwhelm the well-dressed María with requests for money. And because the air was so bad, with fumes from the dump settling like a mist everywhere, she left Los Humos not only with the feeling that to befriend them further—who were they anyway, but cousins twice removed? And why had the men among them looked her over in an uncousinly manner?—would be more trouble than it could ever be worth, but also with her throat sore and a headache and runny stomach that lasted for days.

María first wanted to get pregnant back then, even when she knew it would probably mean the end of her dancer's career. She was twenty-three that year of the first insurrection, on the older side of a profession in which the majority were seventeen and eighteen, if not younger. But no matter how carelessly she comported herself with Ignacio, deliberately ripping open the heads of his condoms with her teeth or with her long fingernails during the agitated act of love, she did not become pregnant in those years, a mystery that she blamed on herself, and on God's castigations, all the while wondering if the more virile Nestor would have easily fathered her child. (That had to do with her *guajira* upbringing— the largest stud horses and oxen and donkeys, with their outlandishly sized appendages, coupling in the fields and easily siring offspring, had been a common sight.) Yet, despite her splendid, traffic-stopping body, María couldn't help but wonder if she were barren.

And so, for the sake of diversion, she put her energies into her studies with Lázaro, took up smoking, got herself a cage of feuding songbirds, filled her living room with silk flowers, and, the truth be told, despite her longings for maternity and love, began to find her dancer's life more agreeable than before. Not the hours, but the nightly applause and the release from the uncertainty that comes with knowing just what you're doing onstage. (And what they wanted to see in the shimmies and splits and turnrounds; that she had to smile constantly, no matter what else she happened to be thinking.)

But María also took pride in the fact that, bit by bit, she had begun to see her name appearing in magazines, a great honor for a *guajira* from the countryside who had been the daughter of a nobody *músico*. *Show,* an English-language publication out of Havana which most clubs and cabarets sold out of their hatcheck rooms, featured a photograph of María in just about every issue over a two-year period. *Life* (circa May 1954) showed a winking María in her dressing room hitching up a pair of dark nylons over her shapely legs; and a second one of her onstage at the Lantern in which, from a distance, it seemed as if she was hardly wearing anything but a dark mesh bodysuit, whose seams were dotted with fake gems, a titanic feathery arrangement tottering on her head. (Why had the tailor, she would complain, made the middle seam subdivide her body, her V, her pudendum?) The caption, in English, which her club owner, a fellow of Cuban descent from Boston, translated as they were standing by a newspaper kiosk off the Prado, proclaimed María as "one of the reasons we Americans want to come to Cuba."

In those years countless photographers went into María's dressing room to "shoot" her. María putting on one of those impossibly heavy plumed, rhinestone-beaded headdresses; María, in a skimpy outfit, described as "raven haired" with a "Spanish complexion" and "Ava Gardner build." (The complexion thing was a catchphrase, meaning tawny, swarthy, slightly dark or, let us say, a code for a light-skinned *mulatta* and therefore acceptably, even tantalizingly, dusky, like the actresses Dorothy Dandridge and Lena Horne.) In an issue of *Show* that featured profiles of famous or hoping to be famous dancers, there was a shot of María in a rather revealing and very tight leotard by her dressing table in the Club Tika Tika, eating, for some reason, a bowl of ice cream, the caption: "One Dish Enjoying Another." (Other copy? Here's a portion of one caption, which went along with a shot of María lunging across a stage, a mock-jungle backdrop behind her, in a tight leopard-spotted, one-piece bathing suit and four-inch-high heels, as she brandished a whip: "Refined in her features, there's something of the jungle, or most African and savage, about María Rivera. . . . With dance moves to make men crazy, this Cuban Salome vaults across a stage like an unleashed Tigress!")

Even *Bohemia*, otherwise engaged in sympathetic reportage about the imprisonment of that rebel leader Castro on the forested Isle of Pines, a penal colony south of the province in which she had lived, featured María in a one-piece black bathing suit on their *"belleza de Cuba"* pinup page, and one young fellow from *Carteles*, on the club beat, whose byline was Cain, fascinated that she had started out as a *guajira* and had seemed to achieve local stardom, had wanted to interview María "for the record," but she felt too inarticulate to go through with his request. (Nevertheless, this fellow took a photograph of María which ended up reinterpreted as a pastel cartoon on the margin of one of that magazine's end pages.)

If she happened to be locally well known, up and down the nightclub strip of la Rampa and in many a cul-de-sac establishment in the city, her renown did not come without the occasional annoyance. Whenever she went into the Lantern, it startled her to see the life-size plywood cutout of herself, in an enticingly revealing costume, set like a lure on the narrow curb by the club entrance: COCKTAILS AND CHA-CHA-CHA'S, TWO DOLLARS COVER PLEASE. Kids were always sticking wads of chewing gum over the top of her bodice, to make María's breasts and their nipples more prominent; these she'd scrape off with a nail file. After six years as a professional dancer in that city, she had developed an attitude about her image.

Though she had not started out in life as one prone to any sort of vanity, the nature of her profession required that María spend long periods of time before those mirrors, and once that habit formed, it seemed inevitable that her humility and tendency to self-deprecation gave way to self-admiration and, even in its most nascent state, grandiosity. *(Oh, but Lordy, what excesses of vanity her daughter would have to put up with one day.)* María simply began to believe that she had become someone special, even if she had mainly worked in second-tier clubs and had yet to hit the footlights of the more august venues in Havana, like the Tropicana, with its outdoor proscenium and gardens set out under the stars, in the suburb of Buenavista. She'd caught a few of the Tropicana's opulent stage revues with Ignacio, including an evening which starred a flamboyant fellow in a white mink coat by the name of Liberace, and had left breathlessly impressed by the sheer grandeur of the floor shows, which included twenty to thirty dancers and featured sets that looked as if they'd come from Hollywood movies. (One spectacular featured a high-society lady strolling in the jungle who, coming across a *santería* ceremony, is put under a magic spell and, losing her inhibitions, tears away half her clothes, dancing wildly with the *negrito rumberos.*)

Such spectacles far exceeded the more humble productions with which María had been associated, and toward those dancers she actually felt some pangs of envy, though she found the sheer size of the crowds intimidating. On her behalf, however, Ignacio had approached the owners—in a meeting that, despite María's beauty and real talents as a performer, never went anywhere: probably because the troupe's stars didn't want the competition, or because Ignacio demanded too much money for her, or, most likely, because Ignacio's reputation as a local tough guy (à la a Cuban George Raft) had preceded him and the owners wanted nothing to do with his sort. *(As María would tell her daughter: "They ran one of the few clubs in Havana that didn't have a connection with the mob; they believed that my* señor *was in that category—why I don't know; he was a perfect gentleman."* Sí, Mamá, *her daughter often thought. But we know what my* papi *did for a living, don't we?)*

At twelve noon in her Vedado apartment, María fondling herself until she breaks into pieces. Then María in her dressing room at the Lantern sitting beside a dancer named Gladys, covering her face with powder and pulling over her thighs the black mesh stockings that always make her legs and uppermost parts slightly uncomfortable. Then, turning her back to Gladys, María asking her to help out with the rear clasps of her sequined brassiere, which she has trouble unhooking. María reaching over to Gladys's ashtray to take a puff off her lipstick-smeared cigarette, and her brassiere slipping off, her engorged nipples, almost the size of wine corks, exposed. It was a bit drafty in there, but not that drafty. So, naturally, Gladys just had to ask in her nosy and singsongy way: "Noooo, Marrrría, who are you thinking about, you naughty girl?"

The truth remained that, for all her feelings about Nestor, María's life in Havana went on without him. Sometimes she agonized about his letters, whether she should attempt to answer him, a question she felt most greatly, for reasons she did not understand, while attending church. But mainly she had allowed Nestor to slip into the realm of memory, though there were times when María heard a sad strain of music or a troubadour's voice in one of the cafés that reminded her of their days together. By then she had relegated Nestor's presence to a few dozen nearly weightless letters, half as many photographs, and her bodily recollections of him. With nearly five years having passed since they spent their last afternoon in that *solar* by the harbor, beautiful María hardly believed it possible that anyone could remain so loyal, or recall her as vividly as he seemed to. (One of his letters, which had arrived around Christmas 1954, not only still professed his undying love for her but, as best as she could comprehend, was of a very filthy nature, the sort of letter that would have caused Ignacio's wormy forehead vein to burst with anger:

> . . . oh, but María, I almost die at the memory of your taking me into your mouth and kissing me until I spilled my milk onto your precious tongue. . . . Do you remember how I lived to trace every bit of you with my saliva, how much I cherished kissing your fabulous *chocha* . . . and how I loved even your *culo*, María— even that tasted like a flower to me. And if you remember, María, that you loved it when you felt me reaching beyond your *tetas* to your mouth, and how you just loved the sight of it and my happy

face and how I could just come because of the look in your eyes, María—whatever you do, don't forget that—and think of me now, remembering your lips and that expression you got on your face as you moved on top of me, and how your head fell back and your eyes closed as if you had just died, and you couldn't help but take me out, and lick *con tu lengua* just a few of those remaining drops, which you passed back to me in the form of a kiss . . .

Those letters, smelling faintly of musk cologne, which kept on arriving, though with less frequency, were always filled with his declarations of unending love. She had become so used to them, had so accustomed herself to thinking about Nestor as a poor *soltero*, a lonely bachelor, whose existence remained dedicated only to her, that María hardly ever imagined that, in those years, Nestor Castillo had begun to find himself a life that she had no inkling about. She knew that he and his older brother Cesar Castillo, the brash one, had formed a band in New York, a group which they called los Reyes del Mambo—the Mambo Kings. Occasionally he'd mail her one of their 78s, recorded with an outfit called Orchestra Records, ditties that consisted of lively dance numbers, along with boleros and songs of love. Receiving their latest, she always expected that his promised song, a monument "to my devotion for you," would be among them, but, as of the winter of 1954, "Beautiful María of My Soul" did not yet exist, except in Nestor's forlorn heart.

NOW AND THEN, HOWEVER, WHEN SOME MUSICIANS, DOWN FROM New York, had come by the club to catch the show or moonlight with the house band, she couldn't help but ask if they happened to know Nestor Castillo. Some did, some didn't, and what the ones who did usually had to say about Nestor—"Oh yeah, a nice fellow, he's doing fine" or "A hell of a musician"—was just enough to assuage María's guilt about the way things had ended between them. But then one night, when a trumpet player with the Mario Bauzá orchestra had come by the Lantern to drop off a package from Nestor and María, pretending to be sheepishly surprised at its arrival, happened to ask about him, this musician, a fellow named Alberto Morales, whom María had never met before, told her: "Oh, Nestor—he's married to a great lady, a *cubana,* as a matter of fact, and he's got two kids, nice children and—"

"You say he's married?"

"Yes, ma'am, for three or four years now. *Está muy feliz,*" he added. "He's very happy." And then, looking at María, he said, "What are you, a cousin of his or something?"

Her face fell, her soul collapsed, her *guajira* pride felt offended. "No," she told him. "I'm just an old *amistad,* that's all."

That night her performance suffered from the revelation; she was surprised by how that little bit of news crushed her. All María wanted to do as she shimmied mambo style across the stage at the center of a row of buxom dancers with half coconut shells covering her breasts was get home by taxi to her and Ignacio's high-rise apartment on Calle 25 and, as was her recent habit, make herself a magnificent drink of fruit juice and dark Santiago *añejo* rum from the great mix of bottles that Ignacio, liking his drinks, kept in plentiful supply in a mirrored art deco bar in a sunny corner of their living room overlooking the sea. Her second thought, as she missed one of her marks and scrambled back to shake her hips when several male dancers were about to hoist her up in a watered down parody of a ritual to the thunder god Changó, was to make her way over to la Cucaracha, where she could take refuge with *la señora* Matilda and the whores whose high heels clicked along those stairways and halls as they went off with their twenty-minute consorts. Surely Violeta, who sometimes sat by *la señora* in the reception area, would take María into her arms and console her with advice: "Whatever ails you," she had once told María, "just remember, men are swine and want only one thing, even the decent ones. But if you want to cheer yourself up, my love, just fuck one of them and leave him so quickly he will be desolate." *(Violeta had laughed, and María shrugged.)* Her third thought: wishing to God that she were somehow back in Pinar del Río, starting all over

170

again: back in that *campo*, with her sister, Teresa, by her side—Teresa so alive!—and joining their *papito* on one of his excursions, guitar slung over his back, to a nearby farm. To be back there would have made her happy—at least she knew what each day would bring: the braying animals, the farmers in the fields, that wonderful waterfall, before her sister drowned . . . And then there was Nestor, disembodied by then, and reduced to two elements: his handsome, poetic face, and, she was ashamed to admit, his enormous *pinga*, sturdy as a branch.

Ay, mi amor, she thought over and over again, in a way she had not before, barely making her way through that evening's show, entitled for the tourists A Night in Havana.

But how quickly things can change. On that same morning, after the finale of her last show, at about 4 a.m., while María was still feeling shocked about Nestor's marriage, a tall and dapper Havana advertising executive, one Vincente Torres, the fellow who had hired her for the Pan American "Fly to Cuba" poster a few years before, made his way backstage to see her. Taking out a group of his American counterparts from New York to see her dance—they all worked for the same agency, Y & R—he had always admired María's solemn beauty. Now and then when he'd come by the club, he'd ask her to join him for dinner, but she had never accepted, not even in the days when she had become a Y & R model. Still, his offers had always tempted her. He was handsome, like a Cuban Cary Grant, and though he wore a wedding band, there was something so mirthful and beguiling about his expressions that she found him intriguing. That night he never failed to take his eyes off María and stood up several times to applaud her, even when her performance had been lackadaisical; otherwise he just stared and stared and smiled, winking occasionally in such a jovial manner that María, having sunk into a depth of sadness she had not experienced since her *papito* died, enjoyed his attentions. In fact, when he went backstage after the show and found her sitting before her mirror, wiping away her running mascara, and asked María, for the hundredth time, if she wouldn't mind joining him for a drink, she finally agreed; Ignacio was away.

So at four thirty in the morning they went by taxi to the Hotel Nacional, just in time to catch the final song by that evening's cabaret performer. María, distracted, hardly heard anything that Vincente said to her. Accustomed to compliments, she could think only about Nestor's deceitfulness: if she was his only love, why had he gotten married? Unsettled, and grateful to be in the company of a gentleman courteous in every way, María found it a natural thing, since she couldn't have given a damn at that point about Nestor, to take an elevator upstairs and follow Vincente into his suite, whose windows overlooked the diamond-filled harbor. He had a stocked bar. He was charming.

After a few daiquiris, María, so estranged from her humble roots and sincerely taken by Vincente, his scent redolent of a lavender cologne, simply nodded when he, after praising her beauty, begged her to take off her clothes. And María, a little stunned but remembering what the whores of la Cucaracha had told her, first removed a pearl necklace that Ignacio in his largesse had given her (but left Nestor's crucifix on). Then, after slipping off her dress and standing before the lucky Vincente in her brassiere and underpants, she put her hair up in a flourish over her head, and, as the whores had once taught her, she reached down and dipped her index finger inside herself and rubbed it over her mouth and behind her ears, and then, as Vincente, the brain behind the poster, out of his mind by then after one of her adamant kisses—a "Nestor kiss," she would think of it—lay back on a bed, undid his trousers, and took out his enraged *cubano* penis, María attended to his ardor, grasping and suckling him until, with a shout—*Mammee!*—he doubled over with pleasure. That night María made this dapper fellow's eyes roll up into his head over and over again. In addition to her captivating beauty and ravishing behavior, there were other ingredients: marijuana, morphine tablets, and cocaine, none of which María indulged in herself, but she did not mind when Vincente did, for they made him a ferocious lover.

Of course, afterwards, she felt low—like *una tramposa* to use one of her mother's terms for the loose women of the countryside, a cheap tramp—but did she really care at that point? Not at all. In fact, there would be others to come along and help ease her pain in those days when she had become foolhardy and confused.

(What neither Ignacio nor even Nestor knew were the most hidden reasons María could be indifferent to the feelings of men. It came down to the way her beloved papito *sometimes treated her. Not the beatings, or even the other extremes of pure affection, but that strange middle ground that, years later, left María feeling sickly inside, as if a miasma, or an infection, invaded her memories. Only once did she confide this to her daughter, during one of her late afternoon mojito/margarita-fueled chats; as if her educated daughter, by then a medical doctor, could come up with an explanation for her mother's occasional improper behavior when she was a girl. You see, before her sister, Teresita, fell ill and they were verging on adolescence, she and María used to take naps with their* papito *on a hammock, the three entangled so peacefully that María easily drifted off to sleep, especially during an* aguacero, *a rain shower that drenched the forests and fields and sent the lizards scattering and cooled the air, which smelled of the most sweet and bitter scents—of rot and fecundity. . . . And sometimes she laid her head against his chest and listened to his powerful heartbeat while he shifted himself around and his palm rested upon her back or along the curves of her hips; and sometimes—maybe it was a dream—his hand massaged her belly, sometimes ambling downwards so that his knuckles dozed and the weight of his hand pressed against the coarse fabric of her dress, and then nothing more.*

*But once she had started undergoing her bodily changes and began to smell different to men, and things got crazy because of what had happened to Teresita—*la pobrecita—*there came that time when her* papi *asked her to share his hammock and she, feeling reluctant and physically cumbersome, obeyed but found that she couldn't fall off to sleep the way she used to, after all he was pressing up against her back, and something fleshy and solid seemed to crawl up along the knobs of her spine. And maybe she imagined that his hand had wandered down below, his dense fingers parting the lips of her "special and most delicate flower," María squirming, her* papito *asking "¿Qué tenemos aquí?"— "What have we here?" At the same time, her* papito's *breath smelled awful, of* *tobacco and* aguardiente *and beer, and, like a dream of her own future, she withdrew into herself while his fingers kept on touching her in places where they shouldn't have, until María, feeling sick inside and sensing that something was very wrong, would finally tear herself away, a terrible shame following her. . . . It didn't end there. Living in a place where the mothers regularly fondled the privates of their male children to ensure their virility, María couldn't help but wonder if her* papito *was doing the same kind of thing with her, or maybe he was just curious. But after a while even she, an ignorant* guajira, *knew that it didn't seem right for a* papito, *no matter how much he loved his daughter, to be doing that—and so, before it could get worse, she started to avoid him, refusing to join him on the hammock and feeling nervous whenever he had been drinking and called her to his side, a puzzled and sad expression upon his face when she refused, as if she had broken his heart. . . .)*

Chapter

TWENTY-EIGHT

One Tuesday evening in 1955, the year that Fulgencio Batista granted Fidel Castro amnesty and the rebel leader, fleeing to Mexico, began to undertake the planning of his revolution; at an hour when Havana's nightlife was just getting under way and María sat backstage preparing for her first show as usual, some two thousand miles north, snow was softly falling in New York City. It was just past nine, and the Castillo brothers, along with several of their musicians, had come down from La Salle Street to mount the stage at a club called the Mambo Nine on West Fifty-eighth in Manhattan. Among the numbers they had rehearsed for their showcase performance was a bolero that Nestor Castillo had been working on, to his older brother's exasperation, from the first days they had set foot in that city: some pain in the neck love song called "Beautiful María of My Soul."

As of that night, Nestor had written so many versions of it that Cesar, getting fed up with hearing every new one, had told him, "Either perform it or let the damned thing go." He said this in the same tone of voice he used when telling Nestor to wake up and forget about María, beautiful and luscious though she might have been. "No woman is worth the agony," he'd say, and Nestor would nod, agreeing, but he'd still mess with even more variations of it, until, after six years in that country, even he began to wonder if he'd lost his mind.

On the stage of the Mambo Nine, as Nestor set some sheet music down before their sometime pianist, Gordito, whose exuberant swaying and tremendous weight sometimes broke the benches during their up-tempo mambos, he still winced from his memories of María. They followed him

175

like a dream, as if he were roving again through the streets of Havana, with its dense, bustling confluences of decay, grandeur, and thriving humanity, her high heels tapping on the cobblestones beneath her, and the aroma of fresh-baked bread and crackers from a bakery filling the air, María beaming at him with affection, their bodies, so used to each other by then that, no matter what else he remembered—sitting on a bench in a deserted church plaza, at an early hour of the morning, holding hands with María, or stopping to buy something from an old mustached *guajiro* standing sadly on a corner with his panniers of bananas and plantains to sell, or the black maids emerging from the doorways with baskets of laundry balanced upon their heads, smiling happily at them—they were in love after all—all such memories, of his times with María in Havana, its windows like sad, drooping eyes, always circled those moments of intimacy that, even those years later, he could still not get out of his head.

Trumpet in hand, his longish fingers testing its valves, he remembered her body and dampened skin, the sight of her opened legs, her knees trembling as she spread them so wide. A stream of notes, fluttering like blackbirds through the room, a slightly pained expression on Nestor's noble face, the memory of how María's womb had always felt like damp blossoms, her skin tasting of the salty and sun-swept sea . . . It gave him an air of distraction sometimes, for behind such recollections a kind of cruel weave curled and twisted through Nestor's Havana. And not the Havana of travel brochures, or of the seedy and glamorous establishments that reeked of gangsters and molls, and down-on-their-luck gamblers, or displaced American socialites in search of a night out with some handsome Cuban gigolos, but the city where she had thrown him off.

Then the devil, perching like a little bird on his shoulder, asked Nestor, "Who had the finest *culo* in Cuba?" and he answered, María, of course, as if he could feel her plump and superb *nalgitas* quivering and nearly slapping his fingers with their sweat again, her rump's pubic hair brushing juicily against his knuckles. All this even while he reached to bum one of Cesar's Lucky Strikes and, on his way, almost tripped over a microphone stand.

Lordy, what a pain: his memories of María still nagged at Nestor even when he had a wife, whom he deeply loved, the studious and pretty and sturdy Delores Fuentes, the mother of their two children, Eugenio and Leticia.

Nestor just couldn't help it. Already away from his beloved Cuba (and María) for too long, he remained divided within himself, the sort of man who believed he could love two women at once and keep it a secret. Too bad he wasn't very good at that whole business, at least when it came to his wife, Delores. Take his songwriting: for all the boleros with their love-drenched lyrics that Nestor had composed during his years in New York, he had yet to write one especially for her. Even if he often told Delores that every flower, star, and sunset, radiant cardinal, and dulcet nightingale on the wing in his songs was really about her, *que ella fue la primavera extravagante, y olía dulce del mar*—that she embodied the extravagance of spring, and smelled sweetly of the sea—how could she have believed that this was entirely true? When she'd see Nestor brooding by their living room window and he seemed to be staring out over the rooftops at the moon's waning crest—his entire body a sigh—she wondered if he really loved her at all. He knew that he sometimes gave her good reason for such doubts, hating himself for those days when, consumed by some inescapable grief and longing, he could hardly say a word to anyone, his own little children mystified by the pain they saw in his eyes. No villain, he really didn't want to seem so sad, and always found ways to make up for the unhappiness he brought into their home: gifts of candy and toys for his children, flowers and books for Delores, which he'd deliver with sincerity and doting affection.

And then, once again, he became lost to the world.

At least he had music and family to console him. Up on the bandstand, and thinking about them, Nestor made a sign of the cross quickly and kissed the little golden crucifix that, weighing no more than a quarter, hung from his neck, thanking God—or whatever made people dewy eyed when they looked up at the skies—for what he, despite his romantic stupidities, had been given.

Though he had written María dozens of letters over the years and kept his marriage a secret from her, he sincerely worshiped Delores. If Nestor lived in a kind of purgatory in those days because of María, without Delores he would have been in hell, and he thanked God for her good nature, her patience, strength, and the loveliness of her spirit. Passion was a large part of it too. During their courtship, which began one afternoon in 1950 when he met Delores as she, startlingly pretty and buxom in a maid's dress, sat at a bus stop on Madison Avenue with a bundle of schoolbooks in her arms, he could never have enough of her. At first, a mutual timidity and propriety informed their polite encounters. They went to the movies and to church, fed pigeons and squirrels in the park, ate ice cream and apple pie at the Schrafft's on Broadway, and attended the local basement church bazaars. Everywhere they went seemed a happy place. Once they crossed a certain line, a naughty delirium took over, and he almost forgot María. They kissed on the rooftops, groped each other in tenement stairwells, and fought frantically in the living room of his and Cesar's instrument-filled apartment, Nestor trying to lure her to bed. One afternoon, while her older sister and occasional chaperone Ana María was away and Cesar was holed up somewhere in the Bronx with a hatcheck girl he'd met in a ballroom, Delores gave in, and Nestor, drowning in her skin, fell in love again. That ardor lasted for a long time, but after a while, when that radiant period of seemingly insatiable desire passed and they had married and were a family, it came down to this: when he laid his head against his pillow at night and dreamed, for all his wishes not to, he still dreamed of María.

It disturbed him, it rankled his heart, and it made Nestor gloomy in moments when he should have been happy. That emotion of feeling free from the burdens of life came to him only through music, when he and his brother were on a stage performing and he would lose himself in the nameless bliss of harmonies and sonorous trumpet solos. Or else when he was writing songs. Not the crazed mambos that his brash *jamoncito* of an older brother Cesar relished but those pensive ballads and sad boleros into which Nestor poured his life and soul. These compositions were so heartfelt as to move even the more jaded musicians in their band, the Mambo Kings. Struggling fellows, who'd been around the block many times over, they were touched by the composer's guileless sincerity. In fact, the band members had a joke amongst themselves, that if he were a king of Spain in the sixteenth century, his name would have been Nestor the Good. (Or with some, "Nestor *el Bobón*, Nestor the Dopey One.")

Languishing plaintively over his tunes on a living room couch in their La Salle Street apartment, a guitar by his side, Nestor approached his songwriting with reverence, as if he were stepping into a confessional. Sometimes the emotions such songs engendered in him were so powerful that Nestor secretly wept; fortunately Cesar, the final judge of his lyrics—he never had any problems with the melodies—was on hand to exorcise the more maudlin of their sentiments.

"Little brother," he would say, Nestor's pad, dense with his neat, diminutive scribbles, open on his lap, "to be truthful, this line—about the world flooding with tears—stinks, it reeks of self-pity. So get rid of it! You hear me?"

And Nestor, loving and trusting his brother, always went along with his advice. Why wouldn't he? Cesar, so unreliable in other circumstances, had pretty good judgment about music, particularly when it came to Nestor's compositions. Despite his preference for earthly rather than spiritual pleasures and his bluntness of character, Cesar, a musician down to his molecules, knew what he was doing. In the end, his arrangements of even his brother's most soporific and sentimental songs always brought out the best. Songs that might just have made one sigh he enhanced by writing swooning countermelodies, usually for violins or voice, during the choruses and turnarounds, and then those songs, so ably ornamented, made their listeners either weep or fall in love.

Thus from Nestor gushed fine and plaintive tunes such as *"¿Porqué*

me dejaste?"—"Why Did You Leave Me?" and *"Sonrisas de amor"*—
"Smiles of Love," and a favorite with the crowds of the Bronx and Brooklyn ballrooms their band performed at for peanuts was a bolero called *"La vida sin felicidad"*—"Life without Happiness." That last bolero was so good that onstage, Nestor, looking out over the crowds and smiling, would take much pleasure in watching many a rum-happy couple begin to neck and kiss when its sonorous melodies rose into a crescendo. That kind of reaction, more than the scant money the Mambo Kings were making, kept him—and Cesar—going.

And so, in that way, Nestor came to write many a commendable bolero, some of them recorded in a cramped studio on 125th Street off Lenox Avenue, the black and brittle 78s lacquer-covered pressings of those songs mostly selling in the market-day stalls and bodegas of Spanish Harlem. At best, a few hundred of them sold every month, and at royalties of two cents a copy, he and Cesar weren't making much money at all. In fact, little had changed with the band after four years or so of performing; they remained as obscure and underappreciated as always. Occasional glamour boys by night, the brothers still spent their days nestled under the shadows of the West Side Highway overpass, just north of 125th Street, in the long, frigid vaults of a waterside meatpacking plant, hauling sides of beef to and fro, their long white frocks washed over with blood. The palms of their hands sported not only the calluses that come to guitar, trumpet, and conga players but also the freezer burns and bone-splinter cuts, nicks, and bruises common to men hoisting one-hundred-pound-plus flanks of fat-marbled beef onto their sore, chafed shoulders. It was hard work, but at least they had regular salaries to show for it, and all the pork chops and sirloin steaks they could stash under their musty coats and shirts for home.

They'd performed at the Mambo Nine before, without much fanfare or expectation, their dream, as nobodies from Cuba, to be discovered by some big-time recording executive or talent scout. It had yet to happen. But that evening, a certain couple, causing a stir, walked into the club. A tall, statuesque lady with a great head of red hair and flickering blue eyes so pretty that Cesar noticed them from the stage, and by her side, a dapperly dressed man in a blue serge suit—Desi Arnaz and his wife, Lucille Ball. They'd dropped by because Esmeralda Lopez, the owner of the club, an old friend of Desi's from Cuba, had told him about two Cuban brothers, fairly new to the States from Havana, who could do it all: They sang like angels, played half a dozen instruments from piano to congas and trumpet, and danced up a storm. Drop-dead handsome, they could also write beautiful songs, particularly the younger brother, Nestor Castillo.

She pointed them out on the stage: Cesar was the strapping, broad-shouldered fellow in the velvet jacket with black lapels and the frilly shirt, a cigarette clenched between his lips, his dark wavy hair, a pompadour at its crest, gleaming with brilliantine. And Nestor, the one holding a trumpet, though a little shorter and far thinner than the majestic Cesar Castillo, had the air of a handsome priest, so good looking that he hardly bothered with the flamboyant grooming and rings that his older brother considered vital to his public image. The show began around ten, and on that night, after Cesar and Nestor and their musicians—Gordito at the piano, Andy on the bass, and Pito on the drums—had knocked themselves out trying to entertain the crowd with several uplifting mambos to little applause, a pissed off Cesar had looked over the room. About twenty people were in the club at that early hour, mainly big-spending corporate types, swilling twenty-dollar bottles of champagne, out to end the night in bed with their secretaries. Tapping his brother on the shoulder and looking out over the room, Cesar said, "What the hell, let's play that 'María' song and see what happens, huh?" Shortly, Gordito, reading off a penciled chart, began improvising a florid introduction. Then the bass came in and the drums. It was written in the key of A minor—*la menor*—Nestor's favorite, and like a malagueña, its opening chords descended flamenco style into a major resolve and chorus.

Now from the moment that Cesar, with his cigarette-ruined yet soulful baritone, stood before the microphone and intoned that song's first words, "Oh, love's sadness, Why did you come to me?" and with Nestor, so apprehensive at first, joining in during the chorus, their harmonizing lovely to the ear, and playing his trumpet like a man possessed by love, even that booze-soaked and jaded audience had started nodding in appreciation of its haunted melody. Sitting beside Esmeralda, Desi Arnaz, smoking a Havana *puro,* felt greatly touched by that song. It was so filled with longing that it seemed to be as much about missing Cuba as about missing a former love, a sentiment that Desi, having lived out in California for so long, must surely have shared. He certainly seemed to, for at the song's conclusion, he stood up and applauded the Castillo brothers enthusiastically.

After the rest of their set, not a bad set at all, when the brothers had come offstage to relax and made their way through the room, they went over to Esmeralda's table, where she made their introductions.

Lacking the luxury of a television set, the brothers didn't know anything about his show, but they had heard Desi's name around and knew he was the most famous *cubano* in America. In fact, Cesar had some kind of vague recollection of meeting Arnaz, as a very young man, many years before in some hilltop club in Santiago when they were both starting out and working that circuit as singers. Still, they were immediately friendly, shaking hands, rapping each other's backs, and almost getting teary eyed—with Cubans, that wasn't an unusual thing. Arnaz was dark featured, handsome, and charismatic in a matinee idol way, and his wife, delicately sipping a mango punch through a straw, was a strikingly lovely woman who hardly blinked through the ensuing conversation. The heart of what they talked about, beyond the niceties of where they had both come from—Oriente, the most easterly province in Cuba—and after they had clicked champagne glasses? It came down to this: Known for employing *cubanos* and helping many an aspiring musician out, Arnaz asked them if they would ever consider flying out to California to perform that "beautiful María" song for a taping of his TV show.

"It's called *I Love Lucy,*" he said.

"Oh yes, of course, *I Love Lucy.*"

Cesar scratched the back of his head at the offer. They weren't actors but could surely use a real break, for after years of working second-tier clubs and ballrooms, and playing Catskills gigs, their band, the Mambo Kings, deserving better, hadn't really gotten anywhere at all. (This was practically Cesar's fault—he didn't like the gangsters who ran the best places and had gotten a reputation among them as a difficult and arrogant two-bit singer, way too big for his britches. It didn't help that he refused to sign any shifty contracts or that he'd bedded down many of their most luscious molls.) Looking over at Nestor, his dark eyebrows raised, Cesar asked: "What do you think, Brother?"

And Nestor, with Esmeralda gently caressing his back as if he was a favorite son, nodded his timid consent. It wasn't easy. Deep down, the very thought that his lingering pain over and devotion to María—the woman whom Cesar called "a hard-on's dream"—would be aired before the entire country troubled him. What would Delores think? But his brother was his brother, and there was very little that Nestor wouldn't do for Cesar.

Smiling, Cesar told Arnaz that nothing would please them more.

"Great! Our show is number one in the country," Arnaz told them. "When you perform that song, maybe it'll become a number one tune!" He lit another cigar. Then, slipping into Spanish, he explained that his wife wanted to get back to their hotel, the Plaza, and that they'd had a tiring day, though, confidentially, he wouldn't mind at all just sitting with them and catching the floor shows, but, oh, his was a demanding schedule, which his wife, Lucille, always tapping upon the tiny face of her diamond-movement watch, kept him to.

As Arnaz was about to leave—Lucille Ball was already by the coat check gathering their garments—he said to the brothers, "I guarantee that you'll have a good time in Los Angeles. But if you have any problems with the music, my good friend Marco Rizo, my arranger, and pianist on the show, lives right here in town. Give him a call, huh?" He scribbled out a number on a card and dropped it on the table. With that, Arnaz, a broad smile on his face, joined his wife; Cesar followed after them, standing on the curbside without a topcoat, a filterless cigarette in hand, his body shivering in the chill, but still waving at the famous couple as they drove away in their limousine through the falling snow.

LATER, AFTER SEVERAL HOURS OF SITTING UP DRINKING WITH his brother, and driving him crazy with all his doubts—"Was that *canción* really any good?" ("Yes, Brother, how many times do I have to tell you!")—Nestor lay beside his wife, Delores, absently fondling her breasts but thinking about María. If he loved her enough to write that song, why did performing it for the first time in public leave him so low? And why was he filled with such utter misery when, for the first time, he and Cesar finally had a chance at some success? And then he slipped back again into that period of darkness in Havana, when María had thrown him off, and remembered what Cesar had later told him again and again: "Why be stupid about that María when you have such a wonderful woman as Delores in your life?" Ah, but Delores. He'd always told her that "Beautiful María of My Soul" was just a song he'd been fooling with, and there he was, after six years in the States, lying beside Delores and wishing he were back in Havana with María. And he hated himself for that thought, for Delores certainly deserved better. "*Te amo,* Delores," he whispered to her again and again. But why was that hole in his heart, like a pin shoved through a photograph from one's happier youth—as if real happiness was never really possible? Why was he wasting his affections on a woman who had turned into air? He didn't know, he was just a citified *campesino* at heart, after all, didn't know anything about the way real Cuban men treated women. "*No soy honesto,*" he told himself that night. "*No soy decente*"—"I'm neither honest or decent." And he hated himself even more. But thank God that his body, in times of such gloom, always faithfully took over. Kept awake by the clanking of steam pipes, he found himself lifting up the hem of Delores's nightgown and, feeling the heat of her bottom, drew back her underwear and entered her from behind, Delores, half asleep, sighing at first and then pushing back in a grinding motion and gasping, but not too loudly because she didn't want the children to hear at the far end of the hall, Nestor, in those same moments, still thinking about María. Then he came after several powerful thrusts, and once he floated back down to earth, he hated himself anew for having that name, that face, that body still lingering stubbornly in his dreams—ah yes, *y coño!*—María, angel of the heavens, delicious as the balmy dawn off the Malecón and, as women are in many a bolero, an unforgettable apparition of love.*

---

* At any rate, that's basically what happened that night, even as hearsay and the passage of time would embellish that story somewhat differently. According to one of the neighborhood kids, a friend of Nestor's son, a plump, myopic, and curious fellow who in later years often sat with Cesar Castillo to hear him talk about his glorious dance hall past, that night unfolded differently. Instead of heading straightaway to their hotel on that snowy evening, Desi and his wife decided to visit Nestor's walk-up apartment on La Salle Street for a midnight meal. Mind you, all those years later, Cesar Castillo was fairly plastered and torn up about all kinds of things in the telling, but even so, with his eyes getting almost teary, he was quite convincing. As Cesar put it, Desi—"a helluva good fellow"—couldn't have been more gracious, and it wasn't long before he was sitting in their little kitchen, making himself at home. After savoring a big platter of *arroz con pollo* and some lemon and garlic and salt–drowned fried *tostones*, which Delores had prepared in a cloud of sizzling oil and smoke, he strummed Nestor's guitar and sang a few Cuban songs—"Mama Inéz" and "Guantanamera"— for his new friends. Cesar would swear that Desi himself grew teary eyed over the warmth of their Cuban hospitality and indeed felt perfectly at home, despite the flecking ceiling and hissing steam pipes and half crumpled linoleum floor. Cesar told that story so many times that, in some quarters, it became the official version. In fact, the plump kid went so far as to eventually put it in a book that he would write about the brothers, even if it didn't get everything right. Whether Desi actually made it there or not, one thing was certain: that wintry night in 1955, the brothers had indeed made Arnaz's acquaintance at the Mambo Nine club and were promised a chance to appear on his show, where, indeed, as walk-on characters playing Ricky Ricardo's singing cousins from Cuba, they were to immortalize Nestor's tormented *canción de amor* "Beautiful María of My Soul," a song which his former *amante* was to hear soon enough on the streets of Havana.

ome five months later, María happened to be walking along Obispo in the aftermath of a terrible argument with Ignacio. Lately, he had started to accuse her of becoming sexually indifferent to him, while she in turn, without actually coming out and saying so, suspected that he wasn't virile enough to give her a child, despite the fact that he claimed to have once fathered a daughter that he lost. And even that loss she had come to doubt—he seemed to spend too much time away in Florida, and more than once she had come across letters tucked away in the soft inner pockets of his *maletas,* his suitcases, letters that she did not have the gumption to read but that seemed on the evidence of the handwriting on the envelopes to have been scripted by a woman; and so, she had come to believe that Ignacio, like so many other Cuban men of a certain age who had taken up with a younger woman, had a family hidden away somewhere. Nevertheless, just to talk about that supposed loss brought out his soft side, though it wasn't much in evidence those days. With a life that had become more difficult because of what his *Hoy* horoscope described as the "mounting influence of unseen contrary forces," his business, once booming in the provinces, had gone into a decline on account of what the government had classified as lapses of security, given that rebels far east in Oriente regularly came down from the hills to loot his trucks as they were en route to the cities and small towns of that province. Nor had that store, El Emporio, proved to be anything but a siphon on his income, though Ignacio did enjoy the air of respectability it gave him. Other matters disturbed Ignacio as well. His chest hair had turned white overnight, and his ticker began to ache. Visiting a clinic, not for anti-impotency and venereal disease treatments, or to experience the wonder cures of *acupunctura* as advertised in the *directorio telefónico de la Habana,* he began seeing a certain Doctor Cintron, who found Ignacio, with that wormy vein on his forehead, one of the more tense patients he had ever encountered, his blood pressure in a range that defied his bulb-pumped *esfigmomanómetro*'s capability to measure.

The doctor's advice? "Calm down, or you'll drop dead one day."

But at this, he often failed. While he still liked to blaze through the crowds of Havana with beautiful María on his arm, Ignacio had started to notice how he couldn't lord it over her the way he used to. More than once he'd seen her looking over his Spanish editions of Shakespeare and had noted her own growing collection of books—frivolous novels written in simple language for women of a certain frame of mind, but books nevertheless: so that *negrito* Lázaro was worth something after all! And her sweetness had begun to fall away, for he found that it did not take too much for him to perturb her, that María often complained about being cooped up in that apartment, that she sometimes wished she'd never left Pinar del Río, that she lived a life no better than her snippy parrots in their cages. And even that would have been fine except for the fact that Ignacio had begun to suspect that María had someone else. This, as it happened, was true.

That fellow from Y & R had been the first—their little trysts taking place in his fancy suite at the Nacional every so often. He certainly was as handsome as Nestor, though he lacked that soulfulness, which she missed, among other things, and he was so good to her that María might have taken up with Vincente openly were it not for the fact that Ignacio would probably have killed him (and her), and, in any case, she knew he had his own nice family in New York City, just like Nestor, that *cabrón.* And once María had learned to conceal her feelings, she also took up with a young teller at the bank where she kept her savings, another handsome fellow whose curly hair, soothing eyes, and fortunate endowment reminded her (almost) of Nestor, their liaisons taking place between seven and eight in the evening out in a house on one of the hills overlooking

Havana, not far from the university, where this young man's deaf aunt lived, hardly aware of the raucously loud acts that made her hounds bark. A third lover, a so-called Spanish count—*el conde*—whom María had met at the Lantern and slept with in his modestly appointed room at the Ambos Mundos Hotel, with its view of the cathedral (of which she had been quite aware and actually enjoyed, as if God lingered somewhere in the distance, though not as close to her as He used to). She did so with her legs spread wide, then closing them tightly as he approached, taunting him, simply because María enjoyed the idea that a former *guajira*, whose *papito* shat with the outhouse door open, could make so lofty and pretentious a personage beg to kiss her fine and shapely rump. Those were just a few, with more to follow in her remaining years in Havana— Violeta's influence and her own suspicion that goodness wasn't worth much of anything had a lot to do with the way she now moved through her days (or nights); or, to put it differently, María, as the line of a bolero might go, had lately been stripped of her illusions. Having traded love, if that's what it was, for comfort, she had hardened inside, and Dios, the savior of mankind, does not thrive in such hearts, not even that of a rather beautiful woman; rather He slowly dies.

And what could Ignacio make of María when she kept grinding her hips in the air, moaning as she slept? Who was she dreaming about? He had her followed, just as he once did with Nestor, by one of his more dissolute and shifty cronies, a fellow named Paco, with a crooked spine and a tendency to drink his way, affably, through half the bars and cafés of Havana. He'd take off behind María when she slipped out of the club or left the apartment building and, in the manner of bad 1940s detective movies, spy on her from the shadows as she entered certain doorways or happened to meet one of those fellows on a street corner or in an arcade. Fortunately for María, the disorder of Paco's mind left him with only the vaguest of memories of her doings. Nevertheless, the very suspicion deeply wounded Ignacio. Over the past year, in one of the more unfortunate turnarounds in his life, he had, while feeling his age—he was somewhere in his late forties by then—actually convinced himself that he had finally and truthfully fallen in love with her, or with her youth and beauty. He made this recent discovery while carousing with other women— among them his shop clerks, market girls, and prostitutes; no matter how voluptuous their bodies, or lovely their faces, or free spirited and unrestrained their voraciousness in bed (or no matter their fear of him), Ignacio found himself thinking about María ruefully, in the same way that she, in the midst of her fleeting love affairs, could not keep herself from wishing that, truth be told, she hadn't looked down on Nestor, in whom, perhaps, she sometimes saw her own *papito*.

By then María would often withdraw into a shell of silence, refusing to as much as look him in the eye and never answering Ignacio when he demanded to know why she couldn't show him love the way she used to; and she simply shrugged when he'd accuse her of being obviously enamored of someone else. Denying everything, once her patience had worn thin, she'd behave as a man would, shoving her indifference into his possessive face, her response coming down to a few words: "And if I did, *¿Y qué?*"—"So what?"

Over the past few months, frightened by the prospect of his own mortality, he'd proposed to María a half dozen times, and on each occasion she told him that she'd marry Ignacio only if she carried his baby. To say the least, in that department, he had been failing lately, his enervating maladies affecting his potency in such a manner that, when he visited his whores, he had to be content with the kind of languorous, time-wasting bouts of love that would have driven him crazy with impatience as a younger man. In other words, he now found it a chore getting it up.

"Who are you, Ignacio, to tell me anything when you can't even satisfy me?" she'd asked him that afternoon.

It was very sad, and her coldness alone half tempted Ignacio to forget about María altogether, maybe even teach her a lesson (but he wasn't that cruel, not anywhere as mean-spirited as some of his acquaintances, fellow businessmen of a rough demeanor who might have slashed her face just to spite her). He just couldn't. In her beauty, and in his memories of what she once had been, and because of his unsteady health—even then as they walked in the arcade, his heart had begun aching and he had felt his loins constricting, along with his gut—he was willing to forgive her everything. María, that delicious beauty, so well dressed in the clothes he had bought her in stores like El Encanto; María, a former hick from a backwards, nothing *valle,* who had become a modest star of second-tier nightclubs, may have turned into something of a spoiled and temperamental bitch, but he had come to cherish her anyway. Her insults, her stillness, the embarrassment of putting up with passersby, who, seeing her face, on the verge of tears and contorting with pain as they crossed the street, judged him harshly—"Hey you, mind your own business!" he would call out—Ignacio thought best to forget. That afternoon, in the interest of preserving his health and dignity, Ignacio, his breathing labored, decided that it would be a waste of his time to argue with her, and in the face-saving manner of *cubano machos,* who may or may not have been petty gangsters, he managed to pull her close and, with a firm tug of her body against his own, his hand grasping her right buttock through her dress, kissed her neck and said: "I will see you later, huh?" And with that he went off and left María to go about her business.

MARÍA WAS ON HER WAY TO SEE LÁZARO ON HER OLD STREET, THE market teeming as usual (how she still loved strolling about its stalls), when she happened to pass by a certain Flor de Saturno's barbershop, opened to the narrow pavement, its tile floors covered with clumps of hair trembling ever so slightly in the fan air of the room, that shop's interior redolent of musk and lilac scents and cigars, the barber snipping away with his scissors and whistling. Just then, from its cream-colored radio, in all its glory, came the unmistakable voices of Cesar and Nestor Castillo, their tremulous baritone harmonies, stopping María in her tracks. It was the first time she'd ever heard one of their records being played over the air. The melody seemed vaguely familiar, like something she'd listened to before, though surely different, like a cousin of one of those sad yet impassioned songs of love that Nestor, in happier times, had serenaded into her window, hummed into her ears, sang between his kisses from nipple to nipple and quivering tendon to tendon, and in those moments of joy when, declaring that nothing in life made him happier than to look into her eyes, he had whispered, then sung some bit of poetry before jamming himself more deeply into her. But could it really be him? As she stood by that doorway, the barber and his customers all bade her to come in. But María remained outside, catching a verse that went:

Qué dolor delicioso
El amor me ha traído
En la forma de una mujer . . .
Mi tormento y mi éxtasis . . .
Bella María de mi Alma . . .
María, mi vida
(Or in English:
What delicious pain
Love had brought to me
In the form of a woman.
My torment and ecstasy,
Beautiful María of my soul . . .
María, my life . . .)

Just as she was about to lean in and ask the barbershop fellows if they happened to know whose recording was playing on the radio, an announcer came on and dispelled all of her doubts: "You've just heard Cesar Castillo *y* los Reyes del Mambo, an orchestra out of Nueva York, performing *'La bella María de mi alma!'*" And that threw María into such a state of distraction that, when she finally sat with Lázaro, who had not been feeling well lately, she could hardly pay attention to her lesson.

"What is it with you today?" he asked her, his voice raspy from a cough that had been plaguing him for months. María had kept looking off, as if she expected Nestor Castillo to come walking down the street.

"I'm sorry," she said. "Do you remember that *músico* I once knew?"

"The nice fellow? Sure, what about him?"

"He was always promising to write a song about me, but I never believed it would come to anything. But, just now I heard him on the radio, over CMQ, singing a bolero called *'La bella María de mi alma.'*"

"And you're sure it's by him?"

"Yes. It's his voice," she said.

"But that should make you happy, huh?" he said, rapping his knee. "Why the long face then, *mi vida?*"

"Because of the lyrics, Lázaro," she said, shaking her head. "He calls me his 'torment and ecstasy'—and cruel, as if I had ever wanted to break his heart."

Lázaro just smiled, shaking his head. "Oh, youth," he began. "Don't you know that most boleros are that way? There's always heartbreak in them, been that way since the tradition started, way back when. I'm sure that fellow— What was his name?"

"Nestor Castillo," she said.

"I'm sure that he's just following that tradition, that's all. I wouldn't take it too hard. Unless, of course, you are still harboring feelings for him." He smiled. "Are you?"

"Some," she finally admitted. "But, Lázaro, I never wanted to hurt that man, the way he says in that bolero."

"Ah, you should just feel flattered anyway," he told her. "However things turned out between you two, he wouldn't have written that song to spite you. No, no, no," he said, shaking his head. "I haven't heard it, but I'm sure he did it out of love—you know those *músicos* are just that way." Then, deciding that to continue their lesson was pointless, Lázaro, with a blood-and-spittle-dampened handkerchief dangling from his trouser pocket, held out his hand to María so that she could help him up and into the courtyard and the hovel in which he humbly lived.

That, in any event, is what took place at about three thirty in the afternoon, in the spring of 1956.

FOR THE NEXT FEW MONTHS, MARÍA HEARD THAT SONG EVERYwhere. It played out of the windows and doorways of buildings, echoed in the courtyards, blared from car radios and bodega entrances, and from speakers over the doors of record shops all over Havana. Out at *la playita* with some dancer friends, where she enjoyed being free from the company of men, a sidewalk band had added *"La bella María de mi alma"* to its repertoire, and soon enough she heard "Beautiful María" being performed by arcade musicians and lounge pianists in the palm courts of hotels all over the city. Suddenly, *"el exito nuevo de los fabulosos Reyes del Mambo"*—or the "newest hit by the fabulous Mambo Kings," as the radio announcers were calling it—was inescapable. Its melody drifted, in disembodied harmonies, into the Havana night from the prows of casino and cruise ships as they crossed the horizon; and even at the Lantern, the house band had worked up a rendition. Soon enough she got to the point that she'd hear its chorus in the whistle calls that followed her as she'd stroll down the street, in the chirping of sparrows along the Prado, and even in the tremulous clarion of church bells. Altogether she heard "Beautiful María of My Soul" so often in those days that she sometimes thought herself inside a crazy dream.

FOR HIS PART, NESTOR SENT HER A COPY OF THE NEWLY PRESSED long-playing 33⅓ rpm album, *The Mambo Kings Play Songs of Love,* on which that bolero was included. The cover was nothing special—done up in the style of 1950s jackets out of New York, Nestor playing a trumpet while Cesar banged on a conga drum, the two of them, she had to admit as she sat before her dressing room mirror, looking handsome and dapper in their white silk suits as they stood posing against the backdrop of some art director's abstracted notion of a New York skyline, a flurry of quarter notes raining down around them. He'd also included a glossy head shot of himself, sort of like the ones María had made up of herself to promote her act, Nestor appearing, much like a star, hair and eyes and teeth gleaming with vitality, a smile on his face and a halo of light emanating from his head (in the same way that photographers showed that rebel leader Castro off in the mountains of Oriente at the time in magazines). Having never sent her such a self-promoting photograph before, nor looking so gloriously handsome, he might have seemed to have lost his humility were it not for the carefully rendered and rather self-effacing nature of his inscription, which said: *"Para la bella María de mi alma . . . mi inspiración. . . . Te debo todo, con todo mi amor, Nestor Castillo."*

". . . To my inspiration. . . . I owe you everything, with all my love . . ."

María's thoughts in those moments at the club? Pleased that she could now read without too much of a struggle—if he only knew!—and amazed to think that Nestor, *ese pobre,* really seemed to be making something of himself in America. Suddenly, she couldn't keep herself from coming to the conclusion that Nestor Castillo, whose letters had been fewer and farther between, had become a success after all, instead of just another lost musician soul. And the song itself? The more she heard its sad but moving melody, the more María believed that Nestor still loved her. The letters he had written her were one thing, but this *canción,* no matter how cruelly its *letras* portrayed María, was nothing less than a public declaration of his undying love for her.

She imagined him in far-off Nueva York, with money in his pockets, pining away for her. She imagined that this recording was selling like crazy, a feeling that grew stronger when a musician friend, who often traveled to the States, told María that the song had been introduced to the vast American public on a very popular television show there, a program that, in fact, was broadcast in English, but with Spanish subtitles, on the CBS affiliate in Havana, *Yo Amo A Lucy,* whose star happened to be Cuban, a real success, by the name of Desiderio Arnaz, a fellow originally from Santiago. Even if the show-business people of María's acquaintance didn't watch it, the fact remained that her sweet country boy and former *amante,* with all his dreams and illusions, had no doubt become famous in his new *país.*

With the record he had sent along a letter "written with tears of regret," professing that, no matter how his life might change, he still couldn't forget how much he had loved her. She was, after all, the sum of his happiest memories of Havana, and perhaps of Cuba itself. Not a day had passed, he confessed, when he didn't think about the life they might have had in Cuba had things not turned out so differently, the sadness of that song something he had carried in his heart from the day she left him. She must have gone over that letter a half dozen times, and with each careful reading, María came to the same conclusion: Nestor still loved her, and she, María García y Cifuentes, in her own unhappiness, owed it to herself—and certainly to Nestor, for the sake of their future and of "destiny," as he might have put it—to make things right, to do what she— persuaded that what she had always felt for Nestor was love—never had had the inclination to carry out before. This, María decided as she got ready to go onstage that night, would involve a journey to New York.

THIRTY

It was the kind of decision that, decades later and in the midst of a new life in Miami, would make María shake her head in puzzlement. At least she had asked for her friends' *consejo*—advice. And not just the ladies over at la Cucaracha, Violeta among them, who saw such a trip as a golden opportunity for María to find a happier situation—"Follow your heart, and, if he really loves you, you'll come out with something to show for it to boot!"—but also her dear old teacher, Lázaro, about the only man she really trusted in Havana. She approached him at the marketplace one afternoon with reverence, and great caution. For María did not want Lázaro to think poorly of her.

"There's something I must ask you," she said. "I need your advice."

"About?" Lázaro asked.

"It's a matter of love."

He scratched his chin. "Who is the fellow?"

"The one you knew—the musician."

"Oh, yes, the one who wrote that song?"

"Yes."

"I see," he said, wiping his mouth with his sleeve. "So what's happened with him?" A squeaking noise came from his throat. "Didn't you tell me that he got married?"

She had, one of those afternoons, when Nestor's matrimony had seemed a betrayal.

"Yes, but I don't think he's really happy."

"Aha," he said, knowing her well enough to wonder what she was really up to. "And so, what are you asking me about?"

"I have been thinking about going to see him in New York."

196

"New York? That's a long way. But why now?"

And she grew excited, sitting down beside him. "Hearing his *canción*, I realized just how much he's still in love with me." Then, touching her heart, she said, "All I know is that I want to see him again, to see for myself if that love is true."

"After all these years? And with a married man?" He just kept shaking his head. "If I were you, girl, I'd forget about it. All that trouble will just bring you more trouble, can't you see that?"

"I've dreamed that he needs me."

"A dream?" He sucked in his lower lip. "No, no, no," he told her. "If I were you, I just wouldn't go."

Disappointed, María looked off, forlorn. "Really, I just wanted your blessing, that's all," she told him.

"Nope," he said. "I won't abide by that kind of foolishness. It always ends up badly for someone."

"I'm going anyway," she told him. "It's what my heart tells me to do."

He started to get up, rather unsteadily, and without offering his knobby-boned hand to her the way he usually did.

"New York? . . . I don't have a good feeling about that."

"But will you give me your blessing, please, Lázaro, for good luck?"

"Okay, okay," he finally said, seeing that some tears had gathered in her eyes, and as he leaned towards her, he began fluttering his hands over her head and reciting some African incantations. It made her feel better. "You have my best wishes," he said, "but I still think you're being foolish." And then, seized by a spasm of coughing, he leaned up against the doorway and closed his eyes.

ABOUT A WEEK LATER, WHEN MARÍA HAPPENED TO MENTION TO Ignacio that several nightclub people in New York City were interested in having her travel there to audition for their shows, she wasn't concealing any truths. In fact, her friend at Y & R, Vincente Torres, who would have liked to keep María as his mistress in that city, had connections with the owners of the club Marseilles and the Latin Quarter, but, until recently, María had never even considered taking him up on it. The idea of staying in that city, which she mainly knew from Nestor's letters and from the movies, didn't hold the least bit of appeal to her. Not just because such a place of concrete and steel and forlorn winters seemed impossible to a girl born in the Cuban countryside but also because the very notion of having to learn English, which she knew a few words of from the clubs, at a time when she was just becoming *más o menos comodita* with the demands of writing and reading her own language, simply didn't interest her. It would have been too much. And for other reasons that most sensible people would have found irrational, María, with her superstitious beliefs and hating the very notion of traveling so far away, couldn't have been dragged off to New York.

And yet, she had suddenly changed her mind.

"Okay, okay," Ignacio told her one day, when she had asked him for his permission. "You want me to go with you?"

"No, Ignacio, I'm going with my friend Gladys. She has relatives up there, in a place called the Bronx. *Ella habla inglés*. She speaks English."

Ignacio probably knew that she had something up her sleeve, but he didn't object, even though she wouldn't even accompany him to Miami before that—when he'd say, "Now the Fontainebleau is the sort of high-class place you should be dancing in. . . ." Lately, Ignacio had been treating her more kindly, and though María hadn't the slightest inkling why, he, like any man connected to her, had come to feel intimations of his mortality. By medical necessity Ignacio had become a calmer man; any aggravation speeding his heartbeat led to dull pains up and down his arms and, with them, a gnarly sensation of misery like worms chewing around inside his chest. "Do as you want," he told her. "But if you need any help, I know people up there." And so it was Ignacio, making a few telephone calls, who arranged for María's passport, even though she had only a cabaret workers' card, and Ignacio who, in a show of largesse, promised to give María several hundred dollars for her trip. He had the numbers of acquaintances in New York she could look up if she became lonely. Altogether, in his blunt and manly wariness, Ignacio couldn't have been more kindly—again and again she would say in the future, "He was good to me, even if I behaved like the devil sometimes."

AND THE BROTHERS? WITH THE SUCCESS OF "BEAUTIFUL MARÍA OF My Soul," a top ten hit on the easy listening charts, the Mambo Kings orchestra was suddenly in demand. In the spring of 1956 they had embarked on a tour, traveling from coast to coast in a refurbished school bus which they'd had painted a flamingo pink, and for two of the most glorious months of their professional lives they performed nightly in the social clubs and ballrooms of both small towns and major cities. Fresh off his turn as a walk-on character on the *Lucy* show and comporting himself like a movie star, the older brother, Cesar, relished every moment onstage, hamming it up for crowds from rural Pennsylvania to California, and satisfying a lot of women along the way. But Nestor? Never having easily adjusted to America, he had slipped into a monumental state of gloom. Under the lights and standing beside the ever vibrant Cesar, and always invigorated by the band's music, Nestor found his moments of joy, but once they returned to their motel rooms, or traveled overnight to their next destination by bus—the stars hanging in the sky just like in Cuba—a profound sadness involving his wife, his children, and María, as well as so many other unattainable longings, overwhelmed him. How could it not, for with every performance there came that moment when the brothers, standing side by side, launched into their touching rendition of "Beautiful María of My Soul." Each time they came to the line "How can I hate you if I love you so?" countless nights, both before and after he had married the wonderful Delores Fuentes, when, for reasons beyond his reckoning, he could only think about María, came back to him.

How could it be that he still felt the same way after so much time? And did María love him at all? He'd thank God that he hadn't abandoned Delores, or flown down to Havana to make a fool of himself anew; thank

199

God that he had his family to go home to after the tour. He'd buy the kids presents and with money in his pockets knew there were so many things that he and Delores could look forward to. And yet, each time they performed that bolero, which he'd truly come to hate in his way, Nestor's heart festered with even greater longing for María. (Cesar, seeing this in his brother's eyes, had to fight off an urge to rap him in the back of his head.) Why the glorious pain? The memories of her, Nestor's own soul suffering through every note, every verse, every ascending trumpet solo: but why?

So imagine Nestor's state of mind when, after years of not hearing as much as a single word from her, he arrived home from the tour to find a letter from María waiting for him. It had taken her two hours to compose, her handwriting, in pencil, erased any number of times but carefully rendered—as was Nestor's, it was almost like the script of a child—and her spelling and sentences, for all her efforts to be correct, occasionally faltering, as they no doubt would, he thought, with a *guajira* from the countryside.

It went, in the English equivalent:

My dear Nestor,

Forgive me for my silents: all the years that did go pass, I had to forget you because I did not know what my *hombre* would have done to me, even if he is not so much a bad man. *Pero él es muy macho, sabes?* If I not had answer your letters, it was because I have feel very bad for my *manera* to write, which as you can see is not so very good. But I could not even put two sententcents together, if not because for my friend, *un buen negro, que se llama Lázaro*—he taught me what I know, even if it is not so good; because of him I had been able to read better your letters to me, but I did not want you to know soo much of my ignorance and stupid *mente*: and then I found out from your friend Miguel that you was married and then I became angered with you.

But now I have gotten older and know love only comes maybe

once in a lifetime, like you have always say. Not long ago, you had send me the song, *muy muy bonito,* "Bella María," of me, and I heard it many times on the radio and it has made me think to write you. Listen to it and I know that you must still love me very very much and it has made me think about how much I have love you too: I mean to say Nestor that I also haven't forgotten what a delicious romance we had. I know you are married, but then I think that you would not have written a song so beautiful or too many *cartas tan afeccionadas,* did you not really have unhappiness? And because, *mi amor,* I really don't have anyone to love me like you, I want to see you again. Even if for a day. I don't want no more, just I am tired of not seeing you for so long and have thought to come to New York just to be there with you. Is that possible? I would come only for a little while. Would you let me know if you want me to, and I will let you know everything of how and when I would have arrived.

Te quiero mucho Nestor, mucho mucho. With all my heart.

María

He had been sitting in the park, a few blocks from the apartment building where they lived on La Salle, boats passing on the Hudson River, the first summery breezes coming off the water, reminding him of his dalliances with María, *la bella María,* along the balmy Malecón. Memories of necking passionately with María as she sat on that seawall, Nestor with his hand up her dress, if only for a moment—María had her dignity after all; memories of looking up in bed and seeing María above him, her thick siren's hair covering her beautiful face, her voice a litany of moans. Just the pain of that memory alone tore Nestor into pieces, and that's why he, at first, after reading it over, had crumpled the letter up and tossed it into a garbage can in despair. María coming to New York? For all his desires for María, he just couldn't see himself being unfaithful to Delores. But, no sooner had he started to walk away than Nestor, swatting away a whirl of hornets circling the melted remains of a Popsicle, decide to retrieve the letter. Flattening it out on his lap, he read it again, forgiving her *guajira* mistakes, read it over until his stomach went into knots, wishing that María had written him such a letter years ago.

He headed off to a local Irish bar, the Shamrock, where the fellows found his quiet manner amusing. Never a hard drinker, he threw back a few rye whiskeys, his heart aching. Then he went home. He must have been a little tipsy when he sat down to write María, telling her that his decision was "yes, come to New York." They'd have to be very careful, no one was to be told—not even his older brother, or especially his older brother. ("She must have had some kind of *papáya*, to make you so crazy," Cesar used to say.) Here was his plan: Knowing that he'd have some free time away from the band the last week of the month of July 1956, when their musicians, by mutual consent, decided to take a vacation break—to hell with the McAlpin ballroom, which had become their usual Sunday afternoon gig—he agreed to meet with María that weekend, but only for an afternoon. (Even that made him nervous.) Planning carefully for the occasion, Nestor gave her the telephone number of the corner pharmacy where for years, before business demanded they get their own phone, the Castillo brothers had received their most important calls—the pharmacist sending a kid up the street to their apartment to fetch them. Treating the situation as if they were spies, he wrote: "When you telephone, María, just say that you have a message from Omar in Havana and leave me the number where you are staying." Then he'd wait, without knowing if María was really going to keep her word. That's what killed him— skulking around the apartment, he spent the next three weeks waiting for the day when the kid from the pharmacy would come knocking on his door, and in all that time, while conjuring all kinds of visions of what might happen, he couldn't look Delores in the eye.

I ndeed, beautiful María had planned to make that journey with one of the other dancers in her troupe, Gladys. With but a single piece of *equipaje* each, they left Havana aboard a P & O steamship for Miami on a midmorning in late June. Only a single photograph of María on that particular day survives: in a florid dress and a Saturn-looking sunhat and dark glasses, she leaned over the railing of an upper deck waving a dainty kerchief at her friend below. When the ladies exchanged places and María tottered carefully down the metal stairs in her white high heels (to break an ankle from slipping anywhere—onstage, in a hallway, or on a church staircase—remained any dancer's greatest fear) to snap Gladys's picture with that Brownie, she captured in her friend, with her newly dyed blond hair, a Cuban look-alike of Kim Novak, whom the two dancers had recently seen in the movie *Picnic*. Gladys wore a lipstick so livid it read from even a distance as a darkish patina, and her eyes were also overly adorned, with fake eyelashes and mascara; her sundress, its fabric of peacock colors, was so short that, as Gladys posed, gentlemen made it a point to congregate by that section of the lower deck, newspapers or cigars in hand, and, as if by coincidence, managed many a long glance upwards at the tent formed by her pleated skirt, and at her spider-lace panties. *(It just so happened that, despite Gladys's tackiness, she and María were to remain friends for many years, until they had been living in Miami for decades, and, as they'd tell María's daughter, Doctor Teresita, during their occasional get-togethers, that journey, despite its later consequence for María, was something of a* relajo *for them—a great amusement—and bonded them for good.)* In fact, men followed them everywhere, even into the casino rooms, where they had gone simply to escape the midday sun, the dancers sitting on

203

banquettes smoking and sipping the drinks that strangers kept sending over to them. Also onboard was a contingent of Catholic priests and nuns from the diocese of Havana, along with some thirty of their young charges, sickly (sadly) Cuban children, most suffering from tuberculosis but a few from nervous disorders (María sighed, recognizing in some the same faint trembling of the hands that her own late sister sometimes exhibited, even with medicine). These unfortunates were on their way, the dancers imagined, to better hospitals in the USA. And among the Cubans onboard, some of whom, they'd learned by eavesdropping, were heading home to different cities along the Eastern Seaboard or to attend to businesses (like Ignacio), there happened to be at least two celebrities. The first was the dapper actor Cesar Romero, said to be José Martí's grandson, who held forth in a corner before some colleagues, and the second, hard as she found it to believe, seemed to be María herself. For several *cubanos*, having recognized her unmistakably alluring face from posters and newspaper ads in Havana, approached, seeking not only her autograph (nightly she practiced writing her name) but a simple nod of congenial acknowledgment and a few words as well. On the other hand, the American tourists onboard, in their seersucker suits, loving to play the slot machines or else to sit quietly about reading issues of *Life* and *National Geographic*, didn't seem to notice anything special about her save her spectacular looks. (Somehow that depressed María.)

That leg of the journey lasted some seven hours, and at about four in the afternoon, after clearing customs in Miami, the ladies, following an initial bout of apprehension and confusion, managed, through the kindness of several Tampa-born *cubanos* whom they had met along the docks, to find inexpensive but clean accommodations near the central rail terminal for the night. The next morning María and Gladys set out on the Silver Star, which left at 9 a.m. for New York City.

IN JUST SHORT OF TWENTY-SIX HOURS, WITH STOPS IN THIRTY-five cities or towns along the way, among them Jacksonville, Savannah,

Charleston, Wilmington, Norfolk, and the capital, Washington, D.C., María and Gladys went north. Riding coach class with occasional (and intimidating) strolls along the platforms during the stopovers—*Will that train leave without me?*—and endless visits to the cramped toilet compartment at the end of their car, along with frequent sojourns in the coach-class passengers' bar and lounge, María had watched, through "grand panoramic" windows, the sleepy marshlands, swamps, forests, and plantations, with their Negroes in the fields, that constituted the terrain of the American South. Eventually, the greenery gave way to bustling, trestle-bridged cities—the sight of Baltimore, with row after row of soot-faced brick tenement buildings, in its bleakness, halted María's heart.

Halfway to New York, she succumbed to brief bouts of nostalgia, not only for the maze-ridden streets of Havana, which she had gotten to know so well, but for the sweet birdsongs of Pinar del Río—how Nestor must have suffered himself, for, as she recalled from one of his letters, the Castillo brothers had made a similar trip to New York by train back in 1949, except they had arrived in the winter. On María's train rode a group of Cuban musicians from Havana, black instrument cases by their sides, playing games of whist and canasta or dominoes for hours on end and drinking away in the lounge. Among them were some first-timers, staring out the windows with the same expression as María, of both hopefulness and dread. It wasn't as if they were entering into the jaws of a lion, but somehow that whole journey, twisting María's gut, felt that way, and more than once she wanted to confide in Gladys about just why she had suddenly decided to visit New York—not for show-business reasons at all but to see just what she still felt for that *músico*, if anything at all. (*Bueno*, to be entirely truthful, she also believed that he would just fall into her arms at the sight of her.) Each time she fantasized about that, her stomach went into cramps, as if her own selfish thoughts were catching up with her. And off to the bathroom she would go, the mirror's image of her beautiful face jostling in the serrating yellow light of that urine-smelling compartment seeming, as María looked at herself, to have taken on a deceitful cast she had never seen before. Oh yes, apparently she had a conscience that bothered her, but she didn't want to let on to anyone that she did. Before leaving that toilet, she'd arrange her hair as nicely as possible—wearing it clipped to the side like a proper schoolgirl with a barrette—touch up the little makeup she put on, and spritz her neck and behind her ears with a spray of Surrender lilac perfume, always smiling sweetly at anyone who happened to catch that beautiful *cubana*'s gaze, as if nothing out of the ordinary were happening within her.

Passing through the car, María noticed that some of the passengers who'd sailed on the *Florida* out of Havana just the day before had also boarded that train—grandmothers, *abuelitas,* with their grandchildren, some of those American tourists, but as well another Cuban, a bulbous-headed, middle-aged fellow with a slip of a mustache, in a lacquered Panama and white cotton suit, whose occasional staring, as he looked up from the handful of magazines and newspapers he kept on his lap, unnerved her. He'd tip down the brim of his hat and nod any time he caught her eye, and that further tangled her gut. She wouldn't have put it past her grand *machón* Ignacio, so apparently magnanimous about her sudden desire to travel, to have hired someone to follow her, if not out of suspicion to make sure that she would be all right.

Nevertheless, by the time they made it into New York City's Pennsylvania Station, whose interior was vaster than anything she had ever seen before, after an endless descent through what seemed like the bowels of the earth—so much like a purgatory, but one that smelled of cinders and acrid electric wires—and they had deboarded the train, María, as the crowds and porters thronged around them, had been relieved that Glady's sister Mireya and her husband, along with a few of their kids, were on the platform waiting. Of course they overwhelmed Gladys with kisses, for they had not seen her for years, and María took such wonderful sentiments in with both joy and envy—to have a family of her own, and people to care about her hit her as another of her reasons for journeying to that strange and distant city.

In other words, she wanted to bear Nestor's child.

ltogether, though the northeast Bronx was not exactly Havana, María found it a pleasant thing to be living with a family again, no matter that the apartment was a fifth-floor railroad walk-up off Allerton Avenue with scarcely any privacy, even if they had given María one of their five kids' bedrooms. Treated as a special guest by Gladys's sister, María had no reason to complain about anything, and though she spoke no more than a few words of English, when they were taken around the neighborhood—*de los italianos* —to their churches, markets, and butcher shops, she was delighted to find that she could speak Spanish and still be understood. María liked that. She spent an afternoon at the Bronx Zoo, which was not far away, and another in the company of Mireya down in the heart of Manhattan, with strolls through Central Park, so much vaster and labyrinthine than any park in Havana; there were excursions to see Macy's department store and the Empires [*sic*] State Building—tense and trying to make a joke, María asked: "So where is King Kong?"—and a quick visit to the clothing factory off Seventh Avenue and Thirty-eighth where Mireya's husband worked as an English-Spanish-speaking floor manager and the owner, a Jewish fellow, laying eyes on María, instantly offered her a job as a foundation garment model. Even after a stroll one night through a neon-lit Times Square, where they had dined for nickels in a Horn & Hardart (whose lemon meringue pie–dispensing machines fascinated her), María had found the city barely tolerable, and not anyplace she could imagine living, with or without Nestor. The noisy and unsettling subway rides from the Bronx alone seemed tedious, and more than once, though María tried to keep to herself, her guarded ways still hadn't prevented some of those men from reaching out to grasp her *nalgitas* or to press up against her. And downtown, as it had been in Havana, she experienced the same, men stopping everywhere to stare at her, and while no one treated her badly, María tired quickly of the city—the mad traffic, the teeming sidewalks, the endless buzz of hearing not just English but half a dozen other languages as she walked along, sashaying from corner to corner, her head raised, gawking at the skyscrapers and, often enough, longing for the quieter and more quaint arcades of Havana, the blueness of the Cuban sky.

In that time, she did make an effort to contact a few club managers. Indeed an agent, an affable Cuban transplant named Johnny Tamayo, had taken María around one afternoon, and she had auditioned, in her most lustrous costume, for a possible future engagement as one of the "sexquisite" dancers at the Latin Quarter, where the actress Mae West, supported by a cast of oiled up musclemen, happened to be the featured star of a somewhat bawdy revue that month. María also turned up at La Conga and the Copacabana, but in each instance, because she was so ill equipped to navigate her way through the intricacies of the English language and feeling out of her element, her performances were so halfhearted that María came off as if she didn't really care if they hired her or not. This, in fact, happened to be the truth.

One late afternoon, however, on her fifth day in the city, when she couldn't take waiting anymore, María went down to the first-floor lobby, where a pay phone had been installed for the poorer tenants of the building and, dropping a nickel in, dialed the number that Nestor had given her. Three rings, and someone picked up: "Claremont's Pharmacy." And because she could hardly speak English, it didn't take long before the red-haired Irish fellow who'd answered the call put her on the phone with the Puerto Rican cook working behind their soda fountain counter, and it was he, Fernando, who later sent a kid up the street to Nestor Castillo's apartment with a message from "Omar of Havana" along with that number in the Bronx.

. . .

THEY FINALLY SPOKE A FEW HOURS LATER, WHEN NESTOR, SLIP-ping out of his apartment on the pretext of buying a pack of cigarettes, had walked over to the Shamrock, a block away, to use their pay phone. For her part, while awaiting Nestor's call, María had sat restlessly with Gladys's family in their living room, listening to the Guy Lombardo and His Royal Canadians hour on the radio. As it happened, just as their landlord's teenage boy came knocking on the door of Apartment 22 with a message that someone had called the building asking to speak to the lady staying with the Delgados, Mr. Lombardo, his selections depending on the latest trends, led his orchestra into a lavish rendition of a certain newly popular song. Since everyone in that building, mostly Italians, listened to that radio program at the same time, the hallways and court-yard echoed, and mockingly so—*te juro*—with the melody of that current hit "Beautiful María of My Soul."

The kid had left the telephone receiver dangling.

"*Sí?*"

"*Hola, María . . . ?*"

"Nestor?"

It had been so long since she last heard his voice that she was surprised.

"Is it you, María?"

"But you know it is, *mi amor*. Are you well?"

"I am . . . well enough, *pero*, María . . ."

"Tell me everything, *mi corazón*. . . . Have you thought about me?"

"Every day since I have been in this country . . ."

She heard a puzzling sound behind her—two little girls bouncing a ball back and forth at the far end of the hallway, playing just like she and her dead sister, Teresita, used to. María shushed them. Just as distracting was the manner in which their voices, separated by a sea of seven years, though familiar, seemed to belong to strangers: Nestor's had grown deeper, and though he still had an affectionate tone, he spoke slowly, and not as gushingly as he used to, as if he were guarding something. And María's—she knew it herself—was devoid of the absolute sweetness that had once informed every syllable she uttered; that voice, formerly so angelic, now had the edge of a more world-weary woman of twenty-six.

"It was the same for me, Nestor. . . . I've missed you," she told him. And when he didn't answer right away, she added: "I've missed you so much that my heart has aches to think about it."

She heard him sigh, heard the murmurs of voices, the click-clacking of a game of pool, and, from the upper recesses of the building, the strains of that song again. That's when he asked her: "How long will you be here in New York?"

"I don't know, maybe a week. I haven't bought any tickets back yet. I don't really know anything, right now, but, Nestor, I came here to see you. You remember that, don't you?" Then: "Please don't tell me I've come all this way for nothing."

"No, no, María, you haven't, I promise you that. It's just that things are not so easy for me as when you and I were together. It's that—"

But before he could continue, she told him: "Just tell me where and when we can meet, my love."

He gave it some thought, and perhaps because he didn't think it a good idea to meet with María anyplace uptown, where they might be seen, he suggested a place reminiscent of where they sometimes went on Sundays back in Havana, not to the bedroom of a friend's *solar*, or to one of those couples' retreats rented by the hours, but to a sanctimonious place that somehow always made them both feel good: a church.

"Please don't think me crazy, María," he said after a few moments. "But have you heard of a very special *iglesia*, downtown—it's called St. Patrick's—on Fifty and Fifth?"

"Yes, I have," she told him. Gladys's sister had pointed it out to her from a bus.

"Good," he said. "It's a very nice church. We can meet there, by the entranceway, yes?"

"But when, Nestor?"

"How is the day after tomorrow? At two o'clock. *¿Está bien?*"

"Yes."

"Then we can stroll around for a bit, but mainly we will get the chance to talk, okay?"

"Yes, Nestor," she said. "On Wednesday, *a las dos de la tarde*."

"So I will see you then. Now, forgive me, María, but I have to go."

They said their good-byes, and then that was all. María headed up the stairs to rejoin the family.

Chapter

THIRTY-THREE

Two days later, at the appointed time, María, in a delicate blouse with mother-of-pearl buttons, a floridly embroidered vest, and a tight pair of toreador pants, stood waiting inside the entryway of the cathedral. After having given herself plenty of time for the nerve-racking train ride from the Bronx and the negotiation of the streets, she'd arrived early, and by two thirty, having watched people coming and going through those doors without any sign of him, she had been on the verge of feeling abandoned, when breathlessly Nestor Castillo came bounding up the steps, his face contorted, dabbing the sweat off his handsome brow with a handkerchief. She had been looking inside, and had thought that she might sit for a while taking in the solemn comforts of the nave, but then she heard his voice— "María!" It surprised her to see how he had changed—his face had filled out somewhat, she supposed from all those home-cooked meals, *and yes*, he seemed prosperous. He wore a fine watch, a gold bracelet, and, she also noticed, a simple wedding band. Dressed casually enough for a mildly warm day in late June, he had turned up in a crisp white guayabera, a pair of pleated *pantalones*, and laceless shoes of Spanish leather, the sort he had favored in Havana. With his hand clasped over his chest, for he had practically run over from the West Side, he poured forth an explanation about a stalled subway, begging her forgiveness. Somehow, as María smiled meekly at the glorious sight of him, they hadn't even managed a salutatory kiss on the cheek, but stood facing one another, briefly taking hold of each other's hands.

"Oh, but María," he said. "It's so good to see you."

212

Soon enough they were inside the cathedral. Maybe a nostalgia had informed Nestor's choice, or perhaps he had thought to set a restrained tone for their reunion, but it wasn't long before they were a few pews back from the altar, kneeling in prayer, like they used to back in Havana before they'd go off to ravish each other like the sinners they became. He had put on enough cologne for her to notice, despite the smell of burning candles and incense that floated in clouds through the nave; and though he seemed intent on his incantations to El Señor, which he whispered with his eyes closed, now and then he'd turn to look at her and smile. After a few minutes, he moved a little closer. Then, in the manner of their earlier times together, Nestor, in the sight of God and his saints and all the angels of heaven, couldn't help but reach down, while in the midst of his prayers, to feel her leg, his hand moving from above her knee towards where her thigh wouldn't give way anymore, murmuring, "Oh, but *mi* María."

With just his touch she felt her undergarment dampening, God forgive her. And some scent must have risen off her skin, a distinctly female aroma, somewhere between burning sugar and raw meat. His nostrils flared—and they both knew what was bound to happen sooner or later that afternoon. Nestor turned to her and said, "Some things no man can ever forget," and then he kissed her, and with that they made the sign of the cross and he took hold of her hand, and they went off together.

HE MADE NO MENTION OF HIS WIFE AND TWO CHILDREN, THOUGH she knew that, when he fell into a silence, that's who he was really thinking about; but he told her much about the fortunes of the Castillo brothers' orchestra, the Mambo Kings—"I wish you could hear us. We're sounding fantastic and get crowds everywhere we play." There was some talk about that television show and how nicely his fellow *cubano* Desi Arnaz had treated the brothers in California, first class all the way: some real good breaks had come about because of that song—"The one I wrote about you, and only you, María . . ." Walking downtown towards Macy's, where she had thought to buy some gifts for *la señora* Matilda in Havana and her hostess in the Bronx—it was just an excuse, a way of passing time—María was tempted to ask him if he really thought she had treated him cruelly. But she knew the answer. In fact, as they were crossing Sixth Avenue, María being María, which is to say still a poor *guajira* at heart, no matter how well she now dressed and comported herself, she couldn't help but ask Nestor: "With such a successful song, you must be making money, yes?"

She meant to pry; or perhaps didn't mean to, but whatever the case, he laughed and, in a slip, told her: "Some money, María, but I've been putting it all away for my kids," the only time he brought them up. And that inspired a period of glacial silence, which María broke with a simple question.

He turned, trying to pull her towards him, even as she backed off.

"So you have a family now, *verdad?*"

"Yes, good children and a wife."

"I'm so happy for you, Nestor," she told him, looking off, to nowhere.

Changing the subject, she talked about her dancer's career; nothing about the fact that she was still with Ignacio, or about wanting a child of her own, or of the men she sometimes went off with—for fun, or to forget herself, or to be cruel, María didn't know why. Occasionally, she'd think about something the older women at the clubs had always told her: "It's fine to have the memory of a love, but it's a fairy tale to think that one can ever go back there again." She ignored that, of course, enjoying the way that Nestor, even for all the *miércoles* of their small talk, looked at her, so sadly, so priestly, so filled with desire. She loved it when he squeezed her hand and smiled. She loved to think, for that afternoon at least, they could both pretend no one else existed in the world, though he soon shattered that impression. "I am enjoying seeing you again," he told her, "but one thing. I have an obligation, *una cita,* this evening, and I must be leaving you by six."

That offended her, but María smiled anyway.

They went to Macy's. She bought an Italian silk scarf for Gladys's sister, a few other items for the rest of that family, a half dozen packages of nylons for *la señora* Matilda. Afterwards, just past four, Nestor suggested that they might go somewhere for a sandwich and a drink, and that's how they ended up in the bar of the New Yorker Hotel, just across from the Eighth Avenue subway on Thirty-fourth Street. As a musician, Nestor knew just about every hotel manager, concierge, and bartender in the city, the Cubans among them at least, and so, when they walked in, they were treated royally and seated at a corner table. They ordered two grilled steak sandwiches on toast (though she only picked at hers) and a bottle of red wine, but before that arrived, Nestor asked for a glass of rum, and so did María, mainly to calm their nerves, because they both knew what was bound to happen. Outside the bar doorway, the floor was covered by a red carpet that led to an elevator, a conveyance, which, with the press of a button, could take them to any number of rooms. In one of them, both María and Nestor knew, there would be a bed which destiny had surely intended for them. Neither said as much, at first, but after a few rums, they started holding hands again, gazing deeply into each other's eyes, and whispering endearments. That's when Nestor, like some fellow out of a bolero, reached over and, touching her face, said: "You must know, María, how much I still love you."

And María told him the same, though she wasn't sure she believed it herself. Nevertheless, after a while, it seemed inevitable that Nestor would have a certain conversation with the barroom manager, who, after going off, came back from a lobby office with a small black tray on which he had set a bill, presumably for their meal and drinks. On the bill he had written, *"habitación 223. Buen provecho,"* and under it, he had left a room key.

UPSTAIRS, ON THE TWENTY-SECOND FLOOR OF THAT HOTEL, IN A drably adorned, though comfortably enough appointed room, Nestor's and María's last memories of each other unfolded. Through the reflections

215

of a closet mirror, María watched herself embracing and kissing Nestor, his hands inside her blouse, his fingers down the front of her toreador pants, a few buttons breaking, Nestor's own appendage bursting out into the world the moment María, kneeling before him, as if facing an altar, undid his trousers—glory be to God in the highest! It sprang out with such force as to tear the seams of his boxers and nearly sideswiped her face. She suckled him then, and he shot his pearly honey halfway across the room, leaving the wallpaper, of a faded art deco design, speckled with dripping stains, his face like that of a crucified Jesus, wincing with pleasure. No sooner had María removed the barrette from her hair, shaking her head like an animal, than Nestor came around again (with a full and dense erection, in the parlance of her scientific daughter, some *forty centimeters* long). But this time, María pulled him onto the bed, and sucked him once more until the bell-shaped head of his sex had turned so livid and large that she couldn't fit him into her mouth without her jaw aching just below her earlobes, so thick she couldn't close her hand around him. María, her panties by the ankle of her right leg and still wearing her blouse, which had bunched up above her breasts, spread her legs wider, and, slipping her own saliva onto her palm, wet herself further. Looking to see what she could glimpse in that same mirror, María, sinning herself to hell, waited for Nestor, the most virile man she had ever known, to fill her up, bit by bit, all the time thinking, *Give me a child, Nestor Castillo, dámelo fuerte!*

She screamed with pleasure and shook with his every exertion, the thin crucifix that hung around her neck singeing her with the heat of their bodies pressing together, poor Jesus surely seeing more than most saintly apparitions ever should. Each time Nestor found his release inside her, María, entering paradise of a more earthly sort, and remembering what the whores of la Cucaracha had taught her, employed new ways to arouse him, performing the kinds of acts no daughter would ever want to hear about. An hour went by, then two, and Nestor had come inside her so many times that María thought that, if ever she were to become pregnant, it would have taken place that very afternoon.

So that's what it was really about, wasn't it, María?

Afterwards, he sighed, he contorted his body mournfully in that bed and pulled the sheets over himself in shame. And when María, caressing his head, leaned close, and in such a way that her nipples dangled across his earlobes and then brushed slowly across the handsome plains of his face to his mouth, Nestor called out: "Please, María, stop, you're torturing me."

"But how, Nestor?"

"You know how," he said, sitting up. *"Tú sabes."*

A funny thing. Even a very decent woman like María, who could have had most any man she wanted and who, at heart, remained the *guajira* she had once been—the country girl who had loved and lost everyone in her family and had been raised to believe that goodness made a difference—found herself welcoming another way of thinking.

"Oh yes, and so I'm torturing you. *¿Cómo?* How?" she asked. And when Nestor turned away and, reaching over to a side table, got his watch, María straddled the small of his back; her burning *papáya*, like an open and succulent mouth, searing the base of his spine.

"So tell me, Nestor," she demanded as she ground her hips against him.

"What?" he muttered.

"Me amas, sí? You love me, don't you?"

"I love and hate you at the same time, María. I love you because you're *mi cubanita.* I hate you because of what you have done to my heart."

She laughed. *"¡Ah, sí, lo mismo que tu bolero!"* "Just like your bolero!" Then, while smothering him further with the heat and bristled dampness of her wide-open womb, she said, "Tell me who you love most in this world."

"Don't ask me that, María, please. . . ."

"Tell me, *mi amor.* Tell me."

His neck strained as he turned to her, his ears burning red. "What do you think? That I'm crazy?" he asked her, sitting up. "It's my family

I love the most, María. My wife . . . *y mi hijos*. It can't be any other way."

And then, unable to help herself, María slapped his face, demanding to know, "Then why, *por Dios*, did you just *cingar* me, over and over again?"

With that, even the noble Nestor shook his head, his opal eyes suddenly growing cold. Pushing María away, he got out of bed and began to gather his clothes; and then a whole other thing happened, María and Nestor flailing at each other, María naked and Nestor with just his torn *calzoncillos* on, pushing her onto the bed . . . and soon enough, out of that violence, when they both hated each other, arrived a contrary feeling, of the purest animal love, Nestor spreading wide María's legs again, and María, her head thrown back over the bed like a Salome awaiting the decapitated John the Baptist, wanting more and more; Nestor going at her until, exhaustedly, he laid his face against her breasts and descended into the purgatorial depths of his soul.

Remembering what he had told her about having to leave by six, María noticed that it was half past seven. Nestor, whose body lay sprawled across the bed half asleep, his member still loping in a shapely curve over his belly button, seemed dead to the world. Licking his eyelids open with the tip of her tongue, María awakened him. *"Amorcito, amorcito, Nestorito,"* she whispered tenderly, but when he opened his eyes and looked around, Nestor, for all his pent-up dreams about María, about having her again, became mournfully sad. By then, in the heart's sleight of hand, María had decided that no man could make love to a woman in such a way unless he truly loved her—forget about any bolero—and that no woman could soften so after such a physical onslaught of maleness unless she loved him in turn. It was the kind of thinking that would have made the whores laugh—it was only sex, after all—but for María, in those moments, it was everything. But what did Nestor do next?

Even if they had just been carrying on as if they were the bawdiest newlyweds on earth, that didn't stop him from recognizing the inevitable: "You know, María, that, after today, we'll never see each other like this again, don't you?" he said, getting up. "It's the only way. Do you understand?"

"But why, *mi amor?*" she asked. "It isn't fair. And besides, I don't believe you."

Then she began to cry for the first time since her *papito* had died—or at least she pretended to—and that really tore up Nestor's heart too. "Please, María, please don't be so sad," he kept on saying. But the more he pleaded, the more María became unreachable, as if she had become deaf, dumb, and mute at the same moment. Not once did she say a word to Nestor as they dressed, no matter how much Nestor, trying to explain himself, pleaded for her understanding. *Yes, he has a wife and children, while I have none.* She remained so indifferent to Nestor that when they had left the hotel and were saying their somnambulist farewells while standing on the southeast corner of Thirty-fourth and Eighth, just outside the subway, María's face did not show the least bit of emotion, and this seemed to torment Nestor even more.

"Well, maybe we'll see each other in Cuba sometime, huh?" he asked her, as if they had just bumped into each other in the park. "My brother is always talking about taking our orchestra down there. That would be nice, wouldn't it?"

He tried to kiss her then, but she pulled away. Passersby, throngs of them, must have wondered why the beautiful woman, with the exotic south-of-the-border looks, seemed to be both wounded and scowling at the same time. Finally, she managed to squeeze out a few words: "*Cuídate, mi amor.* Take care of yourself, my love, and think about me when you are with your wife," she told him. (*"Yes, I was a little cruel to that man, as he was with me," she once told her daughter.*) And then, just like that, she disappeared into the station, soon losing herself in the crowds and not once turning back to see if Nestor had been watching her.

Chapter

THIRTY-FOUR

She had taken some satisfaction in her memory of Nestor's penitential look as she left him, his features twisted into the expression of a tormented saint. But once that had turned into air, María, wishing that things had played out differently between them, passed her last evenings in New York hoping beyond hope that the first-floor telephone would ring and that she would be called down to answer it. When María didn't receive any such message, she decided, on an impulse, to telephone her sometime lover in Havana, Vincente Torres of the Y & R company—she had his card. One afternoon when she had met him in the lobby of the plush St. Moritz Hotel for a drink and retired to a suite with him for a few hours of harried lovemaking, it was really Nestor whom María thought about. In the well-appointed strangeness of that room, a small crystal chandelier hanging directly over the bed and an ornate French Empire mirror on the opposite wall, María would have loved to open her eyes and find herself walking across a field in Pinar del Río with Nestor. In the midst of that little dream, she forgot the crudeness of her former *guajira* life, the toiletless shacks, without electricity or running water, that scent of dung and mangled earth and blood constant in the air; nor did she recall the complete ignorance that had once possessed her as an *analfabeta,* or the shame of thinking, deep down, that not her *mamá* or her *papito,* or the *guajiros* they knew, were really worth much of anything at all as far as the outside world was concerned. What she remembered instead was *la tranquilidad* of her *valle,* its peacefulness and little moments of simple happiness. That's what she used to see in Nestor Castillo's eyes, and, well—wouldn't you know it—in the trail of such a

220

sentiment, María realized that she, despite her lately hardened ways, had actually fallen in love with him.

His glorious physical attributes, his handsomeness, even the fame and fortune María imagined that he had meant nothing next to the heart and soul of the man. The thought that a life with him would never come to be was brutal, and in those moments, beautiful María became lost in a different kind of valley, not of natural gardens and of streams and dense forests, but of regrets.

Later, when Vincente, off to catch a train to a place called New Rochelle, had put her into a taxi for the Bronx, María fell into a period of sustained silence. For days she could hardly say a word to anyone—not even on the night the family threw them a farewell party, a rather pleasant affair during which neighbors came over to partake of their food, music, and hospitality. That evening, despite her pain, María danced many a cha-cha-cha and mambo—she was Cuban after all—and at a certain hour, just when her heart had been lightened somewhat by all the friendliness and music and she was on the verge of enjoying herself, from the family radio ushered forth the opening strains of "Beautiful María of My Soul."

Hearing Nestor sing "How can I love you if I hate you so?" María swore to herself that it would be well and good with her if she were to never hear that bolero again.

Of course she did, again and again in Havana, nearly every time she walked down the street, or passed by one of those open-air cafés with musicians performing on the sidewalks; and as it happened, she was to hear it for many years afterwards, no matter how María would have liked to forget Nestor, her one true love.

STILL, SHE'D NEVER FORGET THAT LAST AFTERNOON WITH NESTOR, and for a month or so after beautiful María had returned to Havana in poor spirits, she waited to discover if so virile a man had produced in her the beginnings of a child. But her monthlies returned with their usual punctuality. (At such times, she used Lotus de Luxe tampons, the dancers' preferred choice, to stay her flow.) For his part, whatever Nestor Castillo may have really been feeling, he felt bad enough about the way they had parted to write María a half dozen letters in as many months. When such letters arrived at the club, she refused to open them, all the better to put him from her mind, and he might have slipped away from her for good were it not for that infernal song, and the fact that Nestor Castillo, it seemed, had decided to journey to Havana, after all.

A year later—in December 1957—at about four in the morning, during a fierce downpour, as María left the Club Lantern and had been hurrying through an arcade towards the taxis parked in a row by that busy strip off Neptuno, she saw, or thought she saw through the shimmering cascades of that *aguacero,* which went rolling like misting walls or apparitions, Nestor, resplendent in a white silk suit, leaning up against a wall, smoking a cigarette. On his chest, radiantly glowing, the crucifix he always wore. But Nestor? How could that be? And yet there he stood, smiling sadly. Then it hit her: perhaps he had left his wife and children and had come to Havana to find her, or perhaps he'd come for professional reasons. It crossed her mind that he might have journeyed there to perform with his brother in one of the upscale venues like the Tropicana or the Sans Souci, but, in any case, he'd already broken her heart, bruised her ego, and sent her packing. And so when he waved, she got into a taxi, thinking, *Que te vaya pa' demonio!*—May you go to the devil! and as he started slowly towards her, indifferent to the rain, she tapped the shoulder of the driver, who knew her from around, and told him: "Hurry, let's go. *¿Me oyes?*" As they tore down the streets, in winds that rolled cans and bottles and rags along the cobblestones, María was both relieved and regretful that she hadn't stopped to talk to Nestor—how hard-hearted she had become! But then, as they turned onto the Malecón Drive, waves flooding the causeway, and just as she was softening—what would a few moments of her time have cost her?—María swore that she saw Nestor Castillo standing by the seawall with his trumpet raised, impervious to the drenching rain, and not a few minutes later, blocks away, María saw him again on the corner of Calle 20, holding his hands out towards her, imploringly, an even sadder expression on his face. Naturally she had to ask the driver, "You see that fellow?" but it seemed he couldn't hear her too clearly, for it had started thundering.

Later, upstairs in their harbor-side *solar,* as gales pummeled the windows, María got into bed beside Ignacio, who, under the influence of Rock Hudson, had taken to wearing silken pajamas. But she couldn't sleep at first, not until she'd swallowed a few tablets of a medicine that many of the dancers, wired from their nights of performance, used to calm themselves, and these tablets, cousins of phenobarbital (which is to say barbiturates), when mixed with a glass of rum, could knock out an elephant, as they used to say. And so she eventually closed her eyes, but, no sooner had she done so than she smelled in that bedroom burning wires and rubber and gasoline, some part of a strange dream. When she buried herself in her pillows, she began to feel someone gently kissing her brow, her eyelids, and then her neck. And she heard a voice: *María, María, why didn't you forgive me?* And with that, María just knew, in the way that superstitious people sometimes do, that Nestor Castillo, in the manner of the spirits of the *campo,* had come to visit her in Havana from the lands of the dead.

IT WAS SUCH A STRANGE THING THAT MARÍA, IN THE LIGHT OF day, hardly believed it had really happened—perhaps that whole ride back from the club had been a dream—but within a few days, in Havana, amongst the musicians who had known the brothers, it became common knowledge that Nestor Castillo, the writer of that famous song, had, on that very night, perished in a highway accident up there in the north near New York. He had been driving a car back from a job during a snowfall, and, somewhere along those icy roads, he'd lost control and collided headlong into a tree, may God bless his soul. She almost lost her mind hearing that news—"please don't tell me that's the truth," María cried on Gladys's lap. But it was true. A few Havana newspapers had even carried a notice about him, and for weeks afterwards, when that bolero he wrote about her played over the radio, more than one broadcaster solemnly noted the loss of so young a talent, a fellow who knew his way with a song, and played the trumpet as if he were an angel.

Beside herself with that news, María finally opened the letters he had sent her; each breathed with Nestor's soul. *"If I could divide myself into two, I would be with you in Havana,"* one of them said. *"I know I hurt you, María, but don't forget, it was you who hurt me first."* And, in another, he confessed that, as much as he loved María, he would never, never leave his wife, Delores. *"She's the mother of mis hijos, as beautiful as you, in her own way, and very kind to me, so please, María, don't think badly of me."* And in each, he asked her forgiveness, just as his ghost had. Each mirrored the others. The last one he sent kept imploring her to write him. *"I know you take pains to write a letter—but please, just write me a few words. It would make me feel less sad—and lonely. Can't you, María?"* It took her hours to go through the letters, to understand what some of his sentences meant, and in the end, it finally hit her that Nestor was gone from this world for good. And so, one night, she purged herself—vomiting often but also contorting on her bed—in misery over Nestor's loss. What was it about life? How was it that the death of her first love, whom she never really took seriously when it counted, could affect her so? She didn't know, but the fact that Nestor was gone from this world for good left her so unsettled that María, who rarely missed a night at the club, stayed home, weeping and weeping until she ran out of tears.

Thank God, as she would tell her daughter, that when Nestor died beautiful María had the consoling (false) distractions of her professional life and, for all his faults, a man like Ignacio to look after her. He'd even forgiven her for taking off to New York the way she abruptly did. (But why, he must have wondered, did she return in such a solemn mood?) In the year that María's romantic dreams about Nestor ended, Ignacio, with his newly humbled manners and worming aches in his chest, had begun to bear the further physical indignities of discovering that, while the rest of him had slowly thickened, his wonderful head of hair, with its sea of crests and waves, had started to thin, to the point that he hated taking off his Panama hat in public and disliked it when María, with the slightest curl of a smile at the edge of her mouth, stared at him in a certain way.

Each evening, just as María headed out to the club, he'd attend to his special treatments, applying a *botánica*-bought remedy of ground bull testicles, dried donkey dung, and paraffin to his scalp. Afterwards he'd wear a hairnet night after night, until he couldn't take that pomade's barnyard odors anymore. On some evenings, when a few of his cronies came over to play cards or dominoes, he'd forgo that process until a very early hour of the morning, or not do it at all. Occasionally, however, in the throes of his own kind of vanity, when he was alone, he'd turn up the radio and spend an hour or so massaging his forehead and temples with some other miracle cure, turning from side to side to examine his profile and imagining his receding hairline, in his slightly shady businessman's way, as proof of some distant affinity to Julius Caesar. (Or, in a moment of patriotic musings, José Martí, poet and father of Cuban independence in long gone days, another great man with a receding hairline, though of decidedly thinner bodily proportions.)

Finding the whole business rather amusing, María, feeling more magnanimously inclined, actually grew fonder of Ignacio and became more playful with him, especially in bed. Like a man who demanded his steak and *tostones* twice a week, Ignacio expected to romp with María, and on those occasions she took to treating that widening patch, hairless as a Chihuahua's belly and reminiscent of a baby's head, with a tenderness that even the bluntly disposed Ignacio found disarming. She played a game with him, pressing her breasts against his crown, her nipples always hardening, and loved to grind her luscious center against that dome until an even stranger thing happened: María, despite her loss of Nestor forever and forever, amen (except in her dreams), had started to come more easily with Ignacio, though some other memories—of clutching Nestor's full head of hair as he lost himself while devouring her *papáya*, of his sweet *pinga*, may God rest his soul—often helped her along. In that regard, their relations improved, even while María still pursued her other acquaintances.

Ignacio himself, in addition to trying to reverse the processes of nature (eventually giving in, he'd settle for a pompadour wig which almost matched the color of his natural hair), wanting to improve things with María—so much a joy to his eyes that he just about abandoned his own wandering ways—decided to seek a further improvement to their life in bed and started subjecting himself to virility treatments at one of the sex clinics in Havana. These consisted of B_{12} infusions, administered intravenously, and injections of distilled water into the membranes of his penis, which revolutionized his amplitude in a manner he had never thought possible before. María, remembering the admonitions of the whores of la Cucaracha, on the occasion of the unveiling of his grander stature, gasped and shook her head incredulously, as if he were that fellow Superman from that bawdy show in one of the cocktail rooms of a bordello near the Shanghai which Ignacio had once taken her to with the mistaken notion of inspiring her lustfulness. To the contrary, Superman had nothing on her past love Nestor Castillo, may he rest in peace, one of those surprising facts that expressed itself in a recurring dream. (Set in the jungles of Africa, it was no doubt inspired by her memories of the Tarzan movies she and her sister used to take in at the Chaplin in San Jacinto. In this dream, she'd hear Tarzan's yodeling cry from the distance, and since she always took on the role of Jane, María would find herself in a tattered leopard-skin dress, standing at the edge of a vast ravine, which she could cross only by sidling along the trunk of a massive fallen acacia tree, and every time she did, the valleys and rivers below would start rushing past her, and she'd have to get down on her belly, straddling that trunk, and slowly inch her way from one end to the other; somehow, that always made her think about Nestor.)

For her part, with a maternal yearning, María never let slip the ruinous notion that, for all her beauty, for all the life in the traffic-stopping bounce of her hips and *nalgitas*, she, at the ripening age of twenty-seven, might never have a child to love. Looking back, she'd think it foolish to have expected a pregnancy after a single final afternoon's romp with the late Nestor, but what could account for the disappointment of her bouts with Ignacio, who, in those days, only wanted to make her happy? Not just mourning Nestor and what might have been between them, María managed to comport herself stoically, though, more and more, as she'd finish her last shows at the club, removing her makeup and, while gazing into the mirror, wondering *Who am I?* she'd almost dread the repetitiousness of her days. Yes, she enjoyed the occasional company of her fellow dancers, her visits with *la señora* Matilda and the whores of la Cucaracha, with whom she drank beer in the late afternoon even while supposedly watching her figure. During her jaunts with El caballero de París, who, murmuring his poetry as they walked about in Central Havana, noticed the somberness of her moods, she couldn't help but withdraw into the darkness of her regrets. Her yearly journeys with Ignacio out to Pinar del Río didn't help much either. She'd ask him to drive her into her beloved countryside, always on a Sunday, so that she might visit the simple graves of her family—which was hard enough to bear, their wooden markers seeming more rotted and overrun with vines each year, as if that fecund earth would one day swallow them up into obscurity for good. But then, despite her joy in breathing the unchanging air of that *valle*, in seeing again the kindly *guajiros* she had been raised with, so many of the other Marías and Juanitas and Isabels she had played with as a girl, poor and uneducated as they remained, had their own broods of children. Some, only four or five years older than herself, were already grandmothers.

They'd spend half the day going from shack to shack—she'd always bring along gifts, loving to show off her new prosperity. One of those new families was that of a sometime cane chopper who'd once looked her over with the sincerest longing at dances at the *cervecería*. He had married a woman named Amalia, and they, with their five children, had taken over the thatch-roofed house where María had once lived, that glorified shack, just a modest *bohío* with dirt floors, whose doorway exhaled the memories of her own irretrievable past. She had no quarrel with them—in fact, that family had her blessing to stay. Just taking a look inside from the doorway, not steps from where her *papito* used to sit with his *cervezas* and strum his guitar, and, quickly glancing through the room at the perpetual half-light in which she had been raised and the corners where, one by one, the two brothers she had never known, her *mamá* and Teresa and her *papito* had died, left María so breathless with melancholy that she suddenly understood the sadness she once saw in Nestor's eyes.

By then, the continent of her religiosity had shrunk to the point that it sometimes carried no more weight than a butterfly's, and yet, each time she visited the graves, saw the house, or went wandering along the trail into the forest, to *la cueva*, with its cascades, where she and Teresita used to go, María couldn't keep herself from making the sign of the cross and kissing the palm of her hand, which she would then set down on each of the family markers, by the doorway of that house, and even on the trunk of the liana-wrapped, star-blossom-entangled trees, as if to seal the fact that she, in from Havana, had visited. And sometimes she'd take in the fields and forest, with its prosperity of birds, insects, and crawling lizards, those flowers that burst out in clusters everywhere, and wonder just what she had done to deserve such a lack of fecundity herself. They'd always stop at *la cervecería*, to say hello to the owner's son, his *papito* having since died, but Ignacio never liked to stay for long, lest María fall into an even more solemn mood. It always took an effort to drag her away, and while they drove back, María, tending towards silence, fell into the anguish of having heard one person after the next inquiring as to whether she had some *niños* at home in Havana. Such visits always left her with the feeling that leaving her *valle* in the first place had not been such a good thing, and as they came closer to Havana and saw their first stretches of slums and municipal dumps, she'd half believe that it was that city itself, with its clubs and casinos, whorehouses and dirty-minded men, that had somehow affected her. Ignacio knew better than to get into an argument about that.

Even some of the girls at the club got pregnant despite taking precautions with the thickest of condoms, and that killed her too. Apparently her feelings of disgrace and disappointment, as if she had somehow betrayed her *guajira* roots, were so transparent that one of the powder room attendants at the club, yet another former flapper beauty or once-known dancer, advised María to put her trust in a well-known Havana diviner, a certain Mayita Dominguez, who ran a mystic *santera*'s parlor on Virtudes, and to go there when she was having her monthlies. There María submitted herself to the cures of San Lázaro, the healer and savior from death, and as a precaution she knelt before the diviner, who said special prayers to exorcise any curses. As Mayita put it, "A *muchachita* as beautiful as you must be wished ill by jealous women every day." That visit left María feeling more hopeful than before, but for further assistance she went to church, reciting just-in-case prayers daily before the altar of the cathedral, where the spirit of her namesake, the Holy Mother, and that of Her Son and those of all the saints breathed and every porphyry, marble, and limestone surface exuded the promises of salvation. In the midst of such religious trappings—*eternal life? why not?*—María begged God to forgive her for any of her chicanery when it came to Nestor Castillo, to absolve her of the sins of vanity and of selfishness: therefore, with her newly pure soul, perhaps he would grant her wish to have a child.

"Mi hija," *she once told her daughter. "You have no notion of what a church can be. Back where I came from, in my* valle, *ours was just a little shack of pine-plank walls at the edge of a field with floors of pounded down dirt, and an altar that was nothing more than a lacquered pine table with a cross, a few feet high. There were no pews—we had to kneel on that dusty floor, or else just stand during the Mass. But you know what? It was a glorious thing for us to believe we were in the consecrated presence of the Lord. And even when I saw much nicer churches in Havana, every time I knelt down to pray, I always thought that the best church I had ever entered was the one I knew as a girl."*

It may have been a coincidence, but not a month after taking such measures, María missed her menses and, after a visit to an obstetrician, learned that God had indeed answered her prayers early in the new year of 1958.

THINGS ARE GIVEN, THINGS ARE TAKEN AWAY. JOYFUL THAT SHE carried within her the baby who would become her daughter, María had, at a certain hour of the day, gone to find her old friend Lázaro, seated as usual by his doorway. The last time she had visited him, about a month before, and not to resume her lessons with him but simply to see how he was faring, he'd refused María's offer to take him to a doctor. Remaining in his courtyard abode, he had resigned himself to the slow and languishing waning of some old animal of the forest—"Just leave me alone and let me go with dignity," he used to tell anyone who tried to help him. He treated María no differently, and though she could see fear in his eyes—which were wise and innocent in their way—he spoke, almost cheerfully, of the world to come: "I'm really not afraid. I just hope, if there's reincarnation, that I come back as a cat—they get everything. That would make me happy!" he joked, slapping his knee before convulsing suddenly with a cough that made him lean his weary shoulder against the wall.

"Wherever I go," Lázaro told her, recovering, "I hope you will think of me, María. . . . Think of old Lázaro every time you open a book and see what the words mean."

"*Maestro,*" she tried one last time. "Why won't you let me take you to the hospital?"

He just shook his head. "When you are my age, you'll understand," he told her. "When your dreams are nothing more than memories of earlier days, you'll know what I am feeling." Then he stretched out his bony hand so that María might help him get to his feet, and she followed him down the cooler hallway to the back door, which opened to the courtyard, to his little home, the place where he somehow had managed to sleep for years on nothing more than a blanket-covered mat. Whatever his malady, Lázaro couldn't let her go without some heartening words. As she left him asking, "I will see you again soon, yes?" he nodded, smiled, and, surely suppressing another cough, told her, "Oh, you will, my dear girl, but I know one thing. Your life is going to be fine, with or without me."

And that was all. She'd intended to return the next day, or the day after, until a week had gone by and that week had turned into the month of her happiness. Finally, with such good news to share with Lázaro, beautiful María had gone to see him again, but he was nowhere about. It was the bookseller who told her. "We just found him back there one day, sleeping for good."

"*Ay, por Dios,*" she cried out, the misery of losing one of her finest friends in Havana, as if one more wonderful part of Cuba had vanished, in her voice.

"But he left something for you," the bookseller told her, pulling from a carton the kinds of items that would soften anyone's heart, even María's. Two books of Cuban poetry, Lázaro's own copies of the verses of the poets Plácido and José Martí. In one of them, he had scribbled: *"To my favorite pupil, María, perhaps now I will finally see you dance!"*

NOTHING COULD BE SAID OR DONE ABOUT LÁZARO, *EL POBRE*. HIS death was inevitable; she had that touch, after all. Still, María enjoyed her felicitous state, despite its encumbrances, though she knew that, within a few months, once she started to show, she'd have to leave her dancing behind. But could María complain? After years of working here and there, she was tiring of that business: the hours, the ogling patrons, the late-night worries that someone somewhere would drag her into an alley and take advantage (at least two of the dancers at the Lantern carried straight razors in their purses because of what had once happened to them). The sore feet, the pulled tendons, the rehearsals, the pinches on the ass, and especially the dietary restrictions. Because she was still a *guajira* at heart, her mouth watered in the way she made men's mouths water at the sight of her, but only over the sights and aromas of a crispy-skinned helping of suckling pork, with sides of sweet *plátanos* and rice and black beans. Now, at least, despite all the calories María burned nightly during the shows, she'd be free to eat whatever she liked: those delicious whipped-cream-topped lemon- and mango-flavored pastries with the maraschino cherries that always made her lick her lips when she passed the festive windows of De Leon's bakery, three- and four-scoop bowls of ice cream at the Louvre parlor, and no end of the chocolate bonbons which club patrons were always sending her backstage, the sorts of sweets which she always reluctantly passed off to the other dancers for their kids. And now? She'd be free to fill her belly to her heart's content, appreciating all the maternity ads she saw in the newspapers about *comiendo por dos*—eating for two. So what if María put on a few pounds?

The manner with which Ignacio looked at her had become more tender. It wouldn't matter, at least for a while, if she stopped resembling a sex kitten à la a *cubana* Marilyn Monroe, whom half of the bombshell American lounge singers and dancers in Havana tried to emulate (when not mimicking Ava Gardner). Soon enough, she'd become a burgeoning *mamacita* with even more succulent breasts, her nipples distended and swollen. Lately, he had actually become more delicate about making love to her (now that Ignacio considered himself so much larger, thanks to his treatments, he entered her only from behind) and treated her tenderly, as if María, in her *embarazada* state, had become the most fragile creature in the world. That suited her fine. She lasted two months before the management at the Lantern started to notice her pregnancy, and, in any case, though María could have kept working as an assistant choreographer, after so much time spent under the lights, she welcomed the idea of becoming a *señora* of leisure, like the fine ladies at the department stores, with their maids following behind them, or the ones she used to see heading up the Malecón in their sedans to the yacht club (unfortunately, for all her beauty, her skin was of a color unacceptable to its members). And she would have time to further improve herself, to take up, as she had always wanted to, a pen in order to record, even with her lapses in spelling, some of the thoughts that came to her, in the spirit of what the *décima* singers and versifiers wrote (and that made her vaguely ache, thinking about her *papito*, Lázaro, and, yes, Nestor, the one she'd let get away).

As for that bolero? Nearly a year and a half after it had first reached Cuba, "Beautiful María of My Soul" still occasionally played over the radio, and it had become a minor standard of sorts, a part of street musicians' repertoires. But now when she heard it, María no longer felt the melancholy that had come over her strongly in the months just after Nestor died. Hearing it made her feel somewhat proud for having been the inspiration behind that lovely tune. At the same time, it still provoked her to think about Nestor, something that, with a baby coming, she thought best to avoid. Besides, she had no room left for tears. With all the leisure hours she spent either strolling in the Parque Central or sunning herself at the *playas* where they used to romp, or alone in her high-rise apartment—yet not quite so alone, the little being forming inside of her keeping her company—María came up with what she considered a most generous notion. She'd write a letter of condolence to Nestor's older brother Cesar Castillo. María knew his address—the brothers had lived in the same building on La Salle Street.

And so, in the same labored and careful manner in which she composed any note, María penned a respectful *carta* in her much practiced handwriting, conveying her immense sadness at having heard about Nestor's passing—for she had loved him very much.

Believe me, Cesar, I wish it had turned out differently, but I am still so happy that at least Nestor and me were something for a time: and I am proud that he thought to compose that *canción* about me.

She described her state of impending motherhood and, while not lingering on it, ended on what María hoped would be a high note: *"To you and Nestor's family, I send my affection."*

It took her a few days to mail that *carta* off. She felt so confident about having done the right thing that, a few weeks later, when Cesar's response arrived, María truly lamented her ability to read. Once she got around to deciphering its wild handwriting—so bad it was nearly illegible—this is what (she thought) it said:

Dear María—

With all due respect, fuck you and fuck everything about you for throwing my brother into hell—and fuck yourself for even thinking that I can give a shit about your feelings, if you ever really had any for Nestor. Now that he's dead, I want you to know that he suffered a lot of grief thinking about you. And don't think he didn't tell me about how you came up to New York to take him away from his wife and kids. Shame on you, woman! The poor innocent actually felt bad about sending you off to wherever whores like you go. . . . I know it because I had to live with him, and though I can't prove it, something *muy jodido* got worse inside him after he saw you. He just wasn't the same after that, and I have this feeling that, if it weren't for you, he'd probably still be walking around now, taking care of his wife—a real lady, in case you didn't know—and his fine kids, who I'll have to look after now. As for your baby—*felicitaciones!*—I hope you give birth to a blind crocodile, because that's what you deserve.

Sincerely yours,
Cesar Castillo

PART IV

Another Life

Chapter

THIRTY-SEVEN

Though she'd long since torn up Cesar Castillo's letter, a dozen others, from Nestor himself, were among the items that María chose to take along with her some three years later, in early 1961, when she'd leave Havana for Florida with her little daughter, Teresita. Not that she hated Fidel Castro as much as some of the Cuban exiles she'd meet there over the coming decades—she thought he was doing some good things for the people, especially the *guajiros,* particularly when it came to his literacy campaign and sending doctors into the sticks; and she supposed that anyone would have been better than Batista, whom everybody knew was some kind of crook. Caught up in the initial jubilation, she had been among the crowds lining the streets of Havana as Fidel and his followers made their triumphant procession on captured tanks and jeeps and trucks through the city in the second week of 1959, after they'd routed Batista's forces in the wake of their successful guerrilla war. She'd hoisted up her daughter—not even a year old yet—so that the heroic leader might see her as he passed, but it wasn't long before she, like so many others, as in a fiery romance, started taking a second look.

At first, though, María had liked him and what he seemed to stand for. She could even lay claim to having met Fidel, however briefly. Five months after María had given birth to Teresita, in a sixteen-hour labor passed in the maternity ward of the Calixto García Hospital, she had returned to work as a fill-in dancer and assistant to the choreographer at the cabaret in the newly constructed Havana Hilton hotel, a spectacular, fully air-conditioned high-rise out in Vedado, its façade boasting of a mosaic mural by the artist Amelia Peláez (for most of that year, 1958, she

239

and Ignacio had watched the construction cranes and their crews at work from their terrace). That's where Castro established his headquarters, the rebel leader taking a suite on an upper floor. The dancers in the cabaret, María among them, got used to seeing him strolling through the lobby on his way to the hotel diner, where he ate his meals. On one of those evenings, Castro and some of his men took in one of their shows; afterwards he made a point of going backstage and shaking hands with each of the performers and musicians.

"I have to confess," she would tell her ever-patient daughter one day, "that it was a thrill. He was tall and broad shouldered, muy bien macho *with a handsome enough face, and the way he looked at me, I knew what he was secretly thinking. In fact, even after I had given birth to you, Teresita, I hadn't lost any of my beauty or my figure—a lot of my friends told me that I looked even better than before. I had added a little to my* pecho"—*she would pat at her breasts—* "and my happiness at having you, even when you don't think I was happy, made my face even more lovely than before. Of course, I felt flattered by the way he had looked at me, but that was all. I had no interest in him, and I wasn't imagining things, by the way,* hijita. . . . *Later on, when one of his guards approached me to say that the* comandante's *door was open to me any time I wanted to speak to him, I had to say to myself, 'About what?' He was a man, after all, and so I kept my distance, though I swore that, if I went up there, like some of the other girls—I mean if I was forced to—I would use that old trick I had up my sleeve, you know, the one I told you about with the shaking that I remembered from my beloved sister, but,* gracias a Dios, *that never came to pass. . . ."*

There had been the summary executions of a number of former Batista henchmen, members of his police force and secret service—their trials were broadcast on the radio and shown on television. And in that atmosphere of quick justice and reform, in which Castro had pledged to rid Havana of its criminal elements, when the casinos were closed and the whores and their pimps rounded up, Ignacio, Teresita's father, if not by marriage by fact, was arrested after his warehouse in the harbor had been raided and found to contain stolen goods. Or, to put it differently, at the tail end of a happy year as a doting *papito* to Teresita and a caring enough companion to María, Ignacio went out one morning and did not come home. During a trial, which María could not attend because she simply did not know what had happened to him, Ignacio, whom she considered a good provider and an essentially honest man, however he had made his living, was sentenced to serve ten years at a prison on the Isle of Pines.

She never saw him again, *el pobre. (But how could it have turned out well for Ignacio, when anyone María cared for seemed destined to a miserable fate?)*

Along the way, the clubs, cabarets, and casinos, and every *maison de joie,* as the bordellos had been sometimes called, were closed down, then reopened, then closed down again. Tourism died, and when María managed to scrounge up work as a dancer, she usually performed to half empty houses. Not all was misery, however: she had been moonlighting at the Parisien cabaret, in the Hotel Nacional, when the dressing rooms began to buzz with excitement over the American celebrity, of Cuban descent, who had come by to catch the heart-wrenching vocalizations of the Mexican singer, the one and only Pedro Vargas—you know, the star of that show, famous in America, the Cuban she'd see again and again on reruns in the future: Desi Arnaz. The performers sort of knew who he happened to be, but before any doubts could set in, their emcee introduced him to the crowd and asked Mr. Arnaz to stand up and take a bow. She could see why he was well known; handsome as hell and with a wonderful smile, he emanated warmth and kindness. At the same time, María happened to notice that, as with Nestor, as with perhaps many a Cuban man of a certain bent of emotion, he seemed a little sad—perhaps he sensed what was to come. In any event, Arnaz had a friend in the house band's pianist, a fellow named Pepe, and it was he who later told the troupe about why Desi Arnaz had come to Havana just then, in the wake of the Cuban revolution: to gather up orchestrations by his arranger,

Marco Rizo, who had kept a backlog of charts in his Vedado apartment—in fact, it would be the last time that the most famous Cuban before Fidel Castro stepped on Cuban soil.

EVENTUALLY, ONCE THE REVOLUTION CHANGED EVERYTHING, beautiful María started to consider something that had been unthinkable to her before: and that was to leave Cuba for the United States. Not to stay in Miami necessarily, but perhaps to go to a place called Las Vegas, which she'd been told was like a Havana in the desert of the American West. She knew this from a magician named Fausto Morales, who used to work the la Rampa circuit and had, like so many other male performers, a fondness for María. The last time she had seen him at the Lantern, in early 1957, he'd told her about his plans to move there, mainly to perform in the big-time nightclubs, where acts like Frank Sinatra and Perry Como were the attractions, but also to open a school for magicians, who were always in demand. *(Years later, her daughter, Teresita, would read somewhere that David Copperfield was one of Fausto's pupils.)* He'd left her with an open invitation—any time María wanted a change of scenery, and a good livelihood as well, Las Vegas was an option. Perhaps, she thought, one day she would take him up on his offer.

In the spring of 1961, when María finally left for Miami aboard a Pan Am Clipper with her little daughter, she took nothing more for herself than a few dresses and some other essentials; everything else—the furnishings of her apartment in Vedado, the money in her bank account (some $2,237)—was confiscated. (She managed to bury several pieces of jewelry in a metal box under the base of an acacia tree out in Pinar del Río, the rest, from earrings to silver and gold chains, save the one that Nestor had given her and a precious Timex, a gift from Ignacio, she gave away.) Without any close family in Cuba, beautiful María stashed what remained of her past in that suitcase: those photographs of her *mamá* and her *papito*, of Nestor Castillo and herself taken in the good times; and photos of María in her dancer's glory, and dressing room shots posed with the comedians, actors, and radio and television performers who used to frequent the places she worked—she brought their pictures as well. And it was not as if she would forget Ignacio. But aside from those items, a crucifix, a handful of precious letters, and one of those notebooks she had filled up for Lázaro were all she managed to bring with her, all that remained of her world. Of course she'd filled an entire suitcase for Teresita, who, not quite four but brainy and alert, if not as pretty as her mother would have wanted—the poor girl taking more after Ignacio—managed to understand that many of the adults on that half-hour flight were very sad. . . .

Even her mother, beautiful María, when not telling Teresita to stop chewing on her fingers and to sit up straight like a proper girl, seemed apprehensive, looking out the airplane window as if she wanted to lose herself in the silver-bottomed clouds. After landing at Miami International Airport, at the end of a trip that had passed in the snap of a finger, the passengers conversing quietly among themselves—the words *"¡Qué lástima!"*—"What a pity!" repeated again and again—María showed hardly any emotion at all. Far from behaving like a bewildered *guajira* of the countryside, she strolled towards passport control, her daughter's hand in her own, with incredible dignity, the same face, now past thirty, that had graced the billboards and beer trays of Havana, and had provoked a thousand dreams as she walked in the streets of her city, seemingly transformed. American flags, U.S. immigration officials moving about, a framed portrait of the president, John F. Kennedy. Only once did María nearly lose it, as they had passed into the arrivals lounge and not a single person among the hundreds of Cubans—from Tampa, from Miami itself, and from other towns and cities around the state—had been on hand to welcome them with the hugs, embraces, and kisses that made it such an emotional moment for so many others. Looking about, with only twenty dollars to her name and not a clue as to how to proceed, María took a deep breath and squeezed her daughter's hand tightly, as if she were never going to let it go. Fortunately, a nun of Cuban descent, accompanied by an American priest who happened to speak a pretty passable

Spanish, had picked María and her daughter out from the crowd, simply because they seemed so alone, without family to look after them. But while that disorientation and the very strangeness of that new setting may have made a less hardened sort cry a little, that was not María at all.

"Put on your prettiest smile, *mi vida*," beautiful María told her daughter.

In fact, if anything, she couldn't help but laugh, a half mad look in her eyes. For as they were making their way towards the exit doors, to the curbside where a Catholic Relief Services van waited to take them to a motel, little Teresita, hopping daintily along as if to a picnic, as graceful as María had been in the countryside, there trumpeted through the terminal a piece of Muzak which, to her bemusement, happened to be that song of love, as performed by the Lawrence Welk Orchestra. "Beautiful María of My Soul"—as if Nestor, watching her from afar, couldn't help but say: *"I'm still here, my love. Whether you want me or not, I'm still here."*

After nearly three decades in this country, María's daughter, Dr. Teresa García, at thirty-two, had but the scantest memories of Cuba. She could remember something of the views from her mother's terrace in Vedado, of looking up and seeing a sheer plate of endless blue, which was the sky, of looking down and seeing mists and the wakes of boats and ferries curling on the horizon, the crest of the city's shoreline receding until it vanished into a plain of light, the roofs of countless buildings glowing in the sunsets like so many jewels. Of rain and mercurially changing, bottom-heavy clouds appearing suddenly. And always some business about the sweet bent-over *viejita* scrubbing the tile floors of their lobby, with its small, somewhat gaudy Rococo fountain (distinctly, a cherub riding a dolphin, water shooting docilely from its spout), that same nice old lady getting up whenever they came out of the elevator and, noisily complaining about her hips and knees (no doubt arthritic), handing Teresita a few hard candies, the most delicious things in the world, a daily ritual. Something too about waiting along the street for a bus, men tipping their hats or winking at her mother, and street vendors nearly demanding that they taste some fresh-scooped coconut or one of their ices dripping with fruit syrups, and marveling over her shiny black patent leather shoes and how those pavestones kept coming as they made their way under the arcades, and more friendly people popping out of the shadows—people she seemed to love now, simply because they were a part of that pleasant sunlit memory, even if she could not attach a single name to any of them.

Sometimes, however, Teresita would make a connection: a framed picture, cut from an old magazine, of El Caballero de París, a famous Havana street personality, a homeless man and itinerant who slept on park benches, and whom her mother had known, hung on their hallway wall, and just looking at it, the doctor would slip back through time and remember some goatish looking fellow bending forward, his bony hands covered with knobs, to pinch her cheeks and say (most kindly, because she wasn't that way at all), *"¡Qué preciosa, la niña!"* Otherwise, a generic sort of *cubano* face, usually male—could be *mulatto,* could be *negrito,* could be one of those lighter-skinned *gallegos*—swirled about inside her head without any true definition. She had no memories of Ignacio, and if it weren't for a few photographs that María had shown her, of the three of them out at a kiddies' amusement park somewhere in Havana, Teresita wouldn't have had the vaguest notion of what her *papito* looked like: of medium height, pock faced, heavy browed, not particularly handsome but manly looking, which was, in its way, attractive, that man's genes were responsible for one of her least favorite pictures—of herself at about the age of three, no doubt taken in Havana, about six months before they'd left.

It was a black-and-white photograph beautiful María kept framed on a table in their living room, and misery passed over Teresa each time she sat down to watch TV with her *mamá*—whom she truly loved—because she couldn't miss it. Until Teresita had turned ten, there had been a squatness to the shape of her skull, her liquid eyes were too set apart, her arched eyebrows so pronounced and close together that she seemed perpetually apprehensive about something. Even her hair, jet-black, seemed awfully thin, and while María had gone to the trouble of dolling her up in a lovely satin dress, with a crinoline underskirt, for that photograph, she had bunched Teresita's hair into a central flourish, like a haystack, and tied it with a bow; and although she had meant well, Teresa resembled, to herself at any rate, one of those rubber shrunken heads or that of a smiling troll such as they sold at a carnival. Needless to say, María herself blamed Ignacio for these imperfections and took to regarding Teresita as she invariably would, with both affection and pity. When she said, *"¿Sabes que eres muy linda, no?"*—"You know that you're lovely, don't you?"—her mother's eyes always conveyed something else, the unspoken *"¡Qué feita!*—How plain!"

Better to remember sweeter things: as when beautiful María had finally brought Teresa out to Pinar del Río, so that the *guajiro* community could see that she had come through with her own little child, and some farmer had taken her around the fields on a horse, her face smothered in its mane, this *guajiro,* with the bluest eyes and toothless gums, just smiling, smiling. Otherwise, what she could recall of that place came down to hens and roosters and pigs—a few goats as well—in the yards, hounds sniffing everywhere, bats flitting through the trees, butterflies the size of her mother's sunhat; and in the forest she had seen the cascades that María always talked about in later years—a little piece of paradise and apparently a place of death, for her mother had told her the story, years later, of her namesake's demise. . . . There wasn't much else to remember—how could she, when she was only three at the time? Nevertheless, Teresita would swear that she'd seen the *mogotes,* those limestone camel-mound hills, out in Viñales. "That's possible," her mother once told her. "Maybe we did go there." And perhaps they had gone to the flooded subterranean caves nearby, exploring those caverns in a motorboat . . . or perhaps that was a dream, just like the idea of Cuba itself.

Nevertheless, in the middle of the day those thoughts comforted her: on the wall of her office in the oncology wing of the Miami Children's Hospital, near Coral Gables, Teresita kept a professional photograph of Viñales valley, the greenness of the rolling countryside with its majestic royal palms going on forever, and, as well, a charming little painting of a burningly red *flamboyán* tree, shady and inviting, beside a rustic *bohío* (to which she sometimes wished she could retreat)—an item she'd bought at a street fair in South Beach. Raised by María, who rarely went to church in those days but who told her countless times, *"Creo en Dios"*—"I believe in God," Teresita kept a small bronze crucifix, whose Jesus seemed particularly anguished, on the wall over her desk, just above a picture of María herself, at about the age of twenty, looking glamorous as hell, taken on the stage of some flashy Havana club. Her mother was so enticingly sexy, like a movie starlet, that every so often someone, a male nurse or social worker, peeking in, made a point of whistling and saying things like *"¡Chévere!"* or "That's your *mamá? Qué guapita!"* Why Teresita kept it there even when she, not as elegant, long limbed, voluptuous, or pretty as María, suffered by the comparison, came down to a simple fact: as much as Teresa sometimes found it exasperating, her mother's beauty had always been a source of pride, though she'd never tell María as much.

They were only keepsakes, but they cheered Teresa up on those mornings when she'd notice a nurse pulling taut the corners of a freshly dressed bed in the terminal ward, yet another of those poor children, none older than twelve, taken by leukemia or osteosarcoma or some other unstoppable disease in the middle of the night. That work was so heartbreaking that Teresita often thought about resigning her position, but each time she got into that frame of mind, it took only one look into the eyes of a stricken child, teary with longing for just a little affection and care, to change her mind. And while Teresita had helped cure many of them, it was the children who didn't make it, Cubans and non-Cubans alike, from all over south Florida, sweet, uncomplaining, and trusting to the end, for whom she inevitably felt the most.

Chapter

THIRTY-NINE

I t sometimes got to her, no matter how professionally she tried to comport herself, for in a way Teresa loved each of those children without even really knowing them. With an oversize purse that often held caramels, gummy bears, and little plastic Spider-Mans, she'd leave the ward with its fairy-tale-creature and funny-animal decorated hallways around eight most evenings, don a white helmet, and get on her motor scooter, which she preferred to her Toyota because on it she could zip through that traffic when it had stalled along Key Biscayne Boulevard, then make her way home to Northwest Terrace, a neighborhood which, for better or worse, had lately seen an influx of newly arrived Haitians. (Cocks crowed there in the early mornings just like in the countryside of Cuba.) Occasionally, at the end of the week, when she most wanted to forget about work, she'd step out to some trendy bar with some of her single girlfriends, and while they'd carry on happily about love and sex without much prompting at all, Teresa took in, at some distance, their gossiping about boyfriends, fiancés, the dating scene in Miami, the pros and cons of certain kinds of men (the Jews, it was agreed, were the kindest and most generous to their women, Italians were genteel and smooth, but watch out! As for the *cubanos,* in their finest and most gentlemanly incarnations, nothing could top them, but *ten' cuidado,* some were hardheaded and *muy machista,* and only wanted you know what, which was fine with some of them). She'd always seem the oldest, even when a few others had five or ten years on her, at least in terms of her bottled-up behavior, but Teresa just couldn't help it—she'd always been overly serious.

To be beautiful María's daughter wasn't always easy, a fact that hit Dr. Teresa García every time she looked in a mirror. As she and María would stroll along in Miami, strangers were always hard put to imagine that she, with her slightly plump figure and somewhat pretty but very serious face, had come from her mother's fabulous cubana *womb. As beautiful María's only child, vintage 1958, she had missed the boat when it came to inheriting the overwhelming gorgeousness, which, as she had heard over and over again, used to stop traffic in Havana, a city that had never lacked attractive women. Among her vague recollections of the revolution, she'd remember standing on a street corner and, as she held her mother's hand, seeing the bearded Fidelistas, patrolling the streets in their jeeps, with their rifles held up in the air, beeping at her mother, their green caps raised in homage to María as one of the glories of Cuba. And when the Russians, solemn and somewhat stiff, started turning up in Havana, even they couldn't keep themselves from offering María small gifts—bottles of Yugoslavian perfume, pints of vodka, and rides in their Ladas (she always turned them down). Later on, growing up in Miami, Teresa, even while knowing that she was a very pleasant enough looking young* cubana, *couldn't begin to touch her mother in her prime.*

She was not at all homely—fixed up and with a few pounds off, the doctor seemed just perfect for the right sort (conservative, not too wild nor demanding) of man. Attractive enough, with long dark hair, pretty almond eyes, and a compactly promising figure, she had just never bothered with men, not even having a real *novio* in high school, and in college, aside from one fellow, who almost broke her heart, she had been too possessed by her studies to pay attention to such things. More on the quiet side (as pensive as a Nestor Castillo perhaps), Teresita tended to be the first to get up and leave once the conversation started to sound a little too repetitive for her taste—she always had the excuse of work awaiting her at home. (She carried a shoulder bag stuffed with folders to prove it.) Nevertheless, given a few drinks and the right kind of music, she could let loose with the moves she'd learned growing up around the dancers in her mother's Learn to Mambo and Cha-cha the Cuban Way studio near Calle Ocho, though hip-hop and Latin fusion threw her.

"Pero, chica," *she would hear her mother telling her, as she worked out on the dance floor with a basic Latin three-step, "it's all the same—remember to move your hips and shake your* culo *like it's on fire, that's all you have to do!"*

Even so, Teresita must have had wallflower written all over her face, and after a while she'd get tired of dancing with just ladies. As well as she shimmied, men would just check her out from the bar, their chins on their fists, trying to figure out if it would be worth approaching her, and usually, so Teresita imagined, thinking *No way*. She just looked too much like *serious business*. Besides, they wanted women practically half her age— with their toned bodies, smooth, bared navels, and sun-seasoned breasts plump in push-up bras. Miami was full of them. After a while she'd give up the good fight, head home, and pass the night on a couch beside her mother, sipping glasses of red wine or Scotch on the rocks and watching beautiful María's favorite Spanish-language *telenovelas* and variety shows on their color TV, the sort of glowing apparition that would have surely dazzled the *guajiros* of Pinar del Río.

"BUT, *MI VIDA*," MARÍA TOLD HER ONE NIGHT. "THE PROBLEM WITH you is that you don't do anything right. You don't put on the proper makeup—when you do, you look like a *payaso!* A clown. And you don't care about dressing sexy at all. What's wrong with turning a few heads? I certainly did in my time, and you can too!"

"Come on, Mama," Teresa told her, looking up from a book. "You know I love you, but you're wrong. Most men want a certain type, and I'm not that way at all. But it doesn't bother me, okay? Just leave me alone about that business! *Déjame tranquilo*, okay?"

"Okay, okay," María told her, lighting a Virginia Slims cigarette, which always offended her daughter's medical sensibilities. "But I'll only say one more thing."

"What?"

"At your age, *no eres una pollita*—you're no longer a young chick—so you should try everything to find someone, because otherwise you will end up alone. You know I won't always be around, and then you'll really be lonely. I'll come and visit you—don't worry about that—but do you want to spend the rest of your life with a spirit as opposed to a real flesh-and-blood person? And remember, I have you—but who will be there when you're getting on?" Then, the coup de grâce: "And don't forget, *no tenemos familia*. We don't have any family."

That made her doctor's composure unravel.

"*Ay, Mamá*, but don't you know you're hurting me with all that talk? Can't you stop sometimes?"

"All right, *hija*, I'm just trying to be helpful," María said. A few minutes of silence. And then beautiful María would add: "But listen to me, I'll only say one more thing. Even if I think you deserve the best, even an ugly man with one leg would be better than none; then at least you can have children! And then you'll be happy, instead of putting up with that miserable brain of yours that thinks too much!"

"Okay, Mama, I appreciate it, but enough, all right? I'm tired from working and—"

"Hey, *chiquita*, I've got an idea! Why don't you go to one of those singles nights at the Biltmore, over in Coral Gables? Yes, it's the 'Black Bean Society'—they have one every month—I have a friend who went there and met some nice fellow, and maybe, if you fix yourself up the right way, you'll have a little luck too and—"

That's when Teresita leaned over and gave her mother a kiss to quiet her down. She owed María too much to stay angry at her for long, but God, when she'd start up with all the nagging about the loveless state of her only daughter's romantic life, Teresita could only take it for so long. She'd want to drown her sorrows in the worst things possible: pizza, fried *plátanos*, *lechón* sandwiches, and dark chocolate truffles (which tasted great with red wine). On many a night, filled with cravings, she'd drive off to some diner and eat her heart out just because she felt like it. (Then a week of weighing herself, of shaking her head.) More often than not, however, if Teresita didn't head her off at the conversational pass, María might well slip back into the re-recitation of her own history as a poor country girl who'd come to Havana with nothing, and how she had learned her life's lessons the hard way . . . and, always, always, just how humble and beautiful she had been in her prime, and the loves of her life. In fact, if she'd had enough to drink, María would go on and on about that *muy, muy* handsome *músico* named Nestor Castillo, who'd once written a song about her: "the man who could have been your *papito!*" she'd say.

(Yes, Mama, the one who wrote you those dirty letters that you don't know I read.)

That led to a discourse about her other companions who followed over the years—not just Ignacio, whose blood flowed through Teresita's veins, but the rest, those men she'd grown up regarding as her temporary *papitos*. She didn't need to hear more. But she always did. ("Even now, at my age, it's nearly impossible for a woman like me to stay alone for long.")

Teresita always made a point of kissing her mother again, and chiding her if she lit another Virginia Slim, which always followed the kiss, and then it was as if nothing hurtful had been said, their life, on such nights, to repeat itself again and again—both being creatures of habit—María taking in her shows, content (and occasionally saddened) in her memories, and Teresita, or Dr. G as some of the orderlies called her, passing into her bedroom along a corridor of solitude and haunted not by love but by the notion that some in this world, no matter how good-hearted, are more or less destined to be alone.

Chapter

FORTY

When it came to romance, Teresita's mother, as opposed to herself, had seemed to lead a charmed life. At least when it came to finding one man or another to pass the time with. Other things, however, did not come so easily. Back in '61, when they'd first come to Miami, for three of the dreariest months of María's life they had stayed in a motel near the turnpike that they'd found barely tolerable (two cots, a sputtering black-and-white television, a sometimes running toilet, no air-conditioning, but a fan that, on humid days, barely did the job). The sort of run-down end-of-the-road establishment one used to find in pre–civil rights Miami—in which the motel walkway water fountains and its public restrooms were marked WHITES ONLY, most of the residents were on the seedy side and somewhat, it seemed to María without her even knowing why, bitterly disposed. (Just a year later, there would be signs up in certain shop windows: HELP WANTED, NO CUBANS PLEASE.) Whenever she and Teresita crossed the street and waited for a bus to take them downtown, there was always someone to stare at María, and not for the old "hey beautiful" reasons she had known in Havana. Until Miami became used to seeing thousands of others like her, María, despite her beauty and light *mulatta* skin, was sometimes regarded as good—or bad—as black. Which was why some folks gave her and Teresita dirty looks or frosty up and downs when they'd stop to drink from those water fountains, and it was no joy to ask or rather beg in broken English for the use of a toilet in a downtown diner when María's stomach had gone bad from anxiety, the owners grudgingly handing over a key. Teresita accompanied her everywhere rather mutely (what was that strange language people were speaking?), and always did as her mother told her.

254

But not all was so bad. To cover their immediate bills, while the re-settlement people at the Catholic Relief Services figured out what to do with the beautiful *cubana* who had no apparent skills beyond dancing, they'd get a hundred dollars monthly from a Cuban exile fund, and they had been promised another several hundred apiece for relocating once a sponsor could be found. María could have stayed in Miami—she'd been told about a job stitching canvases for a Cuban-American-owned sailboat company in Fort Lauderdale, but she hadn't forgotten about her friend Fausto Morales the magician, in Las Vegas. And so when María sat down with one of the agency's counselors, an affable fellow named Gustavo, they'd spend their sessions trying to locate the man. A somewhat hound-jowled and heavyset Cuban of middle age, the counselor bore a slight resemblance to an American character actor, Ernest Borgnine, and though a few months went by before he finally located the magician at a residence in the Lawton district of Las Vegas, María hadn't minded that at all. He himself had first arrived in Miami from Cienfuegos a few decades before, had often gone back to Cuba until most recently. An orphan raised by priests and nuns, he had once almost taken the orders, he told María, but, in the end, it just wasn't for him. No children, no wife, no family. By then, Gustavo, a forlorn but sensibly self-accepting bachelor somewhere in his forties, of few resentments, who spent half his days making telephone calls on behalf of his clients, had taken such a liking to María and her *chiquita* that, having helped them in their travel and document arrangements for their journey to that desert city, he seemed wistful about their departure. And so did María. When Gustavo wished them all the best of good fortune, he, with regret in his eyes, had added: "Please, if you should ever come back here, don't forget to look me up."

LAS VEGAS ITSELF: THE DESERT, THE SCORCHING HEAT OF THE summer months, the Arctic temperatures of every indoor enclosure, the glaring strip at night, and yet another motel, near the McCarran Airport.

Among the surprises awaiting María? Aside from finding the dry Nevada landscape forebodingly endless, she learned that Fausto had married a showgirl who performed in a troupe at a hotel called the Sands, and, as it turned out, his promises to help María find work were impeded by his own busy schedule, her age, and the fact that she could speak only a handful of words in English. Though there was a contingent of former Havana show-business professionals in Las Vegas, among them a fairly well known choreographer famous for the sumptuous spectaculars he had staged during the glory days of the Tropicana in Havana, María could land only two jobs, as a dancer in a side room of a casino and as an occasional cigarette girl—no doubt about it, she still looked good but just wasn't young or tall enough to suit the local tastes. And when beautiful María managed to get onstage again with a troupe of second-rung dancers in a succession of shows that began in the midafternoon and lasted until two in the morning, she usually left with sore feet, a headache, and a depression so severe that Teresita, just a child but a sensitive one for her age, having her first taste of backstage life—for María always brought her along with a few toys and coloring books to wait and sleep and wait and sleep while the shows went on—could see that her *mamá* wasn't happy at all. Fausto himself was sensitive to this, and when he had time off from his school and his nightly act, in which he, a sleight of hand genius and fine illusionist, could seem to levitate, bisect, and make vanish his assistants, and turn footstools into animals, he took them out, usually on Sundays, with his bored wife, who seemed to subsist on chewing gum and rum and Cokes, to eat in one of the better places in town.

A massive fellow, with a great bearded head of flame red hair and blue Celtic eyes, Fausto, who did not look particularly Cuban, regularly charmed María by ingratiating himself with her little daughter. He had a way of pulling *caramelos* from behind Teresita's ears and could throw his voice so that he could hold a purring alley cat on his lap and make it seem to speak, and in a Mickey Mouse manner that always left little Teresita squealing with delight. For his show, which they went to see, he dressed in the outlandish manner of stage magicians, in high boots and with a velvet cape draped over his shoulders and pirates' jangles in his ears. On their outings, he wore a simple guayabera and linen slacks and, in the midst of their meals, occasionally glanced at María in a certain way. Looking back at those months, while recalling a few of those Sundays when María paid the motel owner's daughter to look after her—wonderful afternoons that she spent in a swimming pool, grasping the arms of a dragon float and watching cartoons on the *color* television!—Teresita wondered if María had ever bedded Fausto down. *(She would never say, and why should she?)* But she'd remember her mother's incessant chain-smoking and the way María would stand by their motel room window in the mornings, muttering *"Por Dios, esto es un carajo!"*—"But Lordy, this is a living hell!"—over and over again. This Teresita distinctly recalled, but little else, except that, come another day, they found themselves on yet another airplane, headed back to Miami.

FORTY-ONE

pon their return, when María ended up at the Catholic Relief Services office again, Gustavo couldn't have been happier to see her, and while he, in his professional capacity, attended to her dutifully, helping to find her temporary lodgings—again in a low-end motel—he began to take María and her daughter around the city on the weekends. It wasn't long before these informal outings turned into something else. One evening, as they were eating dinner in a Chinese restaurant, Gustavo, a quiet sort of man who never minced words, took hold of María's hand from across the table and said, "I've been thinking about something, María. And I will say it in front of your daughter. I've grown very attached to you both, and, well, how can I put it? Even if we've only known each other for a short time, I'm very certain that I could make you and your daughter happy." He took a deep breath. "I mean to say that I would be honored to have you as my wife."

Of course, María was taken aback: Gustavo was not the sort of man María had ever thought she'd end up with—she hadn't even shared a kiss with him—but, in those moments, though he was not a particularly attractive fellow, it was the kindness in his eyes and his doting manner towards her and Teresita that did her in. Though there were quite a number of more handsome men in Miami—more and more Cubans were pouring into the city in those days—María, considering her daughter's welfare, made up her mind right then and there that the most important thing was to provide Teresita with a proper home.

This was how they ended up in their house on Northwest Terrace, where Gustavo lived, a stucco-walled ranch-style tile-roofed affair of late 1920s vintage, surrounded by wildly overgrown bushes and trees, among them a massive acacia that loomed over the front patio and seemed hundreds of years old, a tree that covered the ground with greenish red pods every time there was a storm. After Gustavo and María were married in the church of St. Jude, in 1962, with mostly his friends from the agency in attendance and, it must be said, spent a three-day honeymoon in a nice air-conditioned suite in a hotel along Miami Beach, during which, to her pleasant surprise, she learned that the piously inclined Gustavo, while needing to be broken in, happily abandoned his formality in their bedroom—like the others before him, he could not get enough of her—Teresita and María began their life in their new home.

It should be added that the decor of Gustavo's house lacked the female touch. Its furnishings, reeking of past lives, consisted of charity warehouse and Salvation Army castoffs, which Gustavo, a volunteer for such organizations, had acquired cheaply over the years. The best of them was a bed with an art deco headboard, and this María decided to keep, despite the sadness it emanated, for it had been sold to Gustavo by an old Cuban couple at the end of their lives. But the rest eventually had to go. And so for the first few years of their marriage, with Gustavo reluctantly watching a lifetime's worth of savings vanish, María set out to furnish that house in a manner befitting a newlywed couple. Favoring brightly colored fabrics for her chairs and couch, tables with animal feet, and the most modern of appliances—a new refrigerator and stove, and even a color television, bought on time plans—she also covered one living room wall, over a couch, with mirror tiles, to reflect the natural garden beyond their windows. She filled the house with an abundance of plastic plants and vases, usually of a Chinese motif, in which she arranged silk flowers, and put up on most every wall the brightest paintings of the sea that they could find. And, in memory of her mother, Concha, interspersed here and there, between all kinds of bric-a-brac and the photographs from her Havana career, went portraits of Jesus and the Holy Mother, purchased in the religious shops of Miami.

Once they were settled, there followed a decade of reasonably unglamorous domestic tranquillity. Gustavo, Teresita would always re-call, had never been less than kindly, and in deference to his devoutness, María took up churchgoing again though, as she would remark to Teresita, mainly to "say hello to God." Working part-time in a laundry, as a counter lady in a Cuban-owned bakery, and then as an occasional dancing instructor at an Arthur Murray studio near the then dilapidated neighborhood of South Beach, María became one of those Cuban ladies whose greatest pride had nothing to do with the song of love that had been written about her but came down to the duties and joys of raising her daughter, Teresita.

Once she entered school and began to overcome the shock of learning a new language, English, in classrooms filled with other Cuban exile children, who were just as frightened and bewildered as she, Teresita, so capable and bright, flourished, devouring books and skipping grades easily. Her progress was akin to the ravishing changes that were overtaking the formerly maudlin city of Miami. In the early 1960s, as the Cubans began to move there by the thousands, entire neighborhoods, sleepy and long neglected, came back to life, new businesses and restaurants and societies sprouting up everywhere. Their neighborhood's houses, which had been filled with aging Jewish retirees, with Negroes who tended to stare fiercely at the newcomers, and with longtime residents of working-class roots, now became the cheaply purchased homes of the newly arrived. It was María's habit to stroll the quiet streets of that neighborhood with her husband, Teresita by their side, in the kind of *paseo* that families took back in Havana at dusk. In time, beautiful María found her own coterie of friends, ladies of her generation, in their thirties, with their own families, with whom she occasionally played games of canasta and whose conversations at dusk, whether held in the middle of the pavement or at gatherings on someone's front patio (she'd always say to Teresita that it reminded her of the way neighbors gathered in her *valle* in Pinar del Río) always tended towards speculation about just how and when the Communist government of Fidel Castro would finally collapse, and the resumption of the lives they once had in Cuba.

María, however, never had much of that longing or nostalgia: her days as a professional dancer behind her, when she dreamed at all, it was not of Havana but of the sweetness of her former life in her *valle,* which, with the passage of time, she missed all the more. It was something she always talked about to Teresita, especially after she'd hear a particular song on the radio or happened to bump into someone from her province. But even María knew that it was nothing more than a passing fancy: would she ever live in a *bohío* again? Not in a million years. What she missed was her family, who sometimes visited her in her sleep, just presences, borne by memory, who were somehow "nearby" in her bedroom. (More than once, she would wake from the most vivid dream, of seeing her *papito,* Manolo, standing in the corner of the room, his guitar by his side, a look of confusion on his face.) Sometimes she'd get up in the middle of the night, step out into the darkness, smoke a cigarette, and just stand there, for no good reason at all. Teresita always knew: she'd hear her footsteps outside her door but dared not disturb María's moments of reflection, and it would keep her awake until Gustavo, getting home from his part-time night job, brought her mother back inside. What María thought about out there, when there wasn't much to look at except for a few houses across the street, with televisions glowing in the windows, and some stars up in the sky, Teresita never knew. It was just her mother's way.

(The truth be told, María seemed far removed from her life in America. She had little interest in the war in Vietnam, the space program, the civil rights movement. These were subjects that only occasionally touched her, as when one of their Cuban neighbors from down the street lost their son, a Marine, to the jungles. Gustavo, on the other hand, was more entrenched in American culture. He always spoke sadly of the death of JFK, whom some speculated had been murdered by anti-Castro Cubans as retribution for his bungling of the Bay of Pigs invasion and his promise to the Russians that, if they pulled their missiles out, America would never invade Cuba. But Gustavo still had a soft spot for Kennedy, a Catholic, who had once visited the relief center, hence the photograph of Gustavo and Kennedy shaking hands on their hallway wall.)

She had other mild eccentricities. In those days, beautiful María couldn't care less about mastering English, as if it were an unthinkable imposition on her soul. Besides, most of the people she knew in Miami, especially her local acquaintances, in the same boat, hardly spoke anything but Spanish. Nevertheless, both Gustavo and Teresita did their best to help María out. But because Gustavo, with his job at the relief center by day and as a part-time watchman by night (he'd dress up in a gray Armstrong Securities uniform and go off after dinner, toting a club—the relief service never paid well—and come back about three in the morning), wasn't around as much as he would have liked, Teresita, excelling in school, became beautiful María's second, female Lázaro: her teacher. A half an hour now and then was all they, seated around their Formica table in the kitchen, could manage—or, to put it differently, it was all that María could take. She preferred to perfect her reading and writing in Spanish, and it seemed incredibly unfair that, in America, she had become an *analfabeta* all over again. Nevertheless, for all her resistance to that notion, after five or so years of such lessons, even María could begin to understand her daughter when she'd lapse from Spanish into the heavier and coarser intonations of English, a language that always sounded ugly to María's ears.

But on those evenings when Gustavo happened to be home and they watched television, María didn't mind taking in certain popular English-language programs, especially the ones that featured dancing and singing, like *The Jackie Gleason Show*, which was, in fact, broadcast out of Miami in those days. Knowing the work that went into the ensemble routines, María enjoyed pointing out the difficulties of certain high kicks and turnarounds (on such evenings she'd regret that she hadn't become a choreographer), and she'd get up from their Castro Convertible sofa and, taking hold of Teresita's hand, show her a few of those dancers' steps. Movies amused her as well, and if María had a favorite, Teresita would remember, it was *My Fair Lady,* with Rex Harrison and Audrey Hepburn playing the roles of Professor Higgins (pronounced by María *"eeeeegens"*) and Eliza Doolittle, as broadcast in the Spanish version, their voices and singing overdubbed. She particularly liked that story, about the crude but beautiful Eliza's transformation from street waif and flower seller into a quite proper lady who could read, write, and speak, and comport herself as elegantly as any aristocrat, María always smiling at its happy ending, as if Eliza's story had some connection to her own.

And sometimes they'd settle for reruns of the older programs—one of them being *I Love Lucy*, which both Gustavo and Teresita especially liked because Desi was Cuban and quite a funny man. As for María? She'd hardly ever paid much attention to that show until one of those evenings, in 1968 or so, when she happened into the living room just as that episode about Ricky Ricardo's singing cousins—played by Cesar and Nestor Castillo—came on. Knocks on the Ricardos' door, Lucy letting them in, and all at once, Nestor himself, back from the dead in all his winsome *cubano* earnestness, standing beside his brother, a Panama hat in hand and black instrument case by his side.

At first, María didn't say a word but just stood by the living room doorway taking in, as if anew, the glorious black-and-white handsomeness of her former love. (*"Ay, el pobre, Nestor."*) Only later, when the Castillo brothers, in character as Manny and Alfonso Reyes, came out on the stage of Ricky's Tropicana nightclub in white silk suits to perform "Beautiful María of My Soul" and Nestor began to sing, did she say, in a most casual manner, "Both of you should know that the song that fellow's singing was written about me."

"That song?" Gustavo asked. "I've heard it a million times before. Are you kidding me?"

"No," she said. *"Soy la bella María de esa canción.* That beautiful María is me."

Gustavo replied good-naturedly, incredulously: "If that's so, my love, how come you've never mentioned it before?"

"Why? It's because I'm a humble woman. *Soy una mujer humilde,"* she said. "That's all."

Then, as Gustavo raised his eyebrows at Teresita, who gave a little shrug, it hit María that just because she said such a thing people would not necessarily believe her. And though María hadn't particularly dwelled on that *canción* in a long time—for she didn't hear it as often as before—after all she had gone through and all the nights she had dreamed sweetly, erotically, and angrily about what could have been between herself and Nestor, it hurt her pride to think that not even her husband and daughter took what she'd just told them as the truth.

She left that room offended just as the *I Love Lucy* theme, that happy homage to pre-Castro Cubans in America, sounded merrily through the halls and rooms of their house.

LATER, HOWEVER, SHE CALLED TERESITA INTO HER BEDROOM, where she pulled a small lacquered cane suitcase from her closet; it was the same one she had brought with her when they left Cuba, but María now used it for keepsakes and documents. "I'm going to show you something," she said. And from it she took out a large manila envelope that held, among other things, the letters Nestor had written her, and her beloved photographs, of family, of friends, of Nestor—all that she had left of her past in Cuba. The first she showed to Teresita was the glossy studio portrait that Nestor had once sent her, with an inscription to María scribbled out in his neat and careful hand in black ink.

"Recognize him? It's the *guapito* from that show, isn't it?"

"*Sí, mamá.*"

"Well, he's the one who wrote that song about me." Then: "Now, look at another."

It was of María and Nestor holding hands with rapturous expressions on their faces, no doubt madly in love, as they came charging out of the Cuban sea—taken out at *la playita* back in '49.

"That's him and me," she said. "We were lovers, you know." Teresita, just a young girl at the time, nodded as if those words held meaning for her. "He is the one who should have been your father."

And she went on, showing her daughter the others, photographs of herself and Nestor taken here and there in Havana, Teresita just listening, in her pensive way.

"So I hope you will believe me when I tell you something in the future, okay?"

"*Sí, mamá.*"

"Good! Now give your *mamá* a little kiss."

FORTY-TWO

As the years passed, the settled life of that household turned into something else, for after a decade of a reasonably happy marriage, during which time Gustavo, working on behalf of the incoming Cubans and doing much good for that ever-growing community, discovered that God, or fate, does not always reward such deeds. María, loving this man, or loving him as much as she could, and never saying a bad word about Gustavo to anyone, sometimes seemed rather bored with their conjugal arrangements. It's possible that this pious and quiet man, whose worst sin was to say that he felt perfectly fine when he didn't, or that he wasn't tired when exhaustion most weighed on him, had, in María, the first woman he had ever possessed. Whatever went on in their bedroom had, over time, begun to fix upon María's still lovely features a look of amorous resignation.

She never said as much, but Teresita, with her little bedroom just down the hall from theirs, while quietly making her way to the toilet, sometimes heard through their door beautiful María's utterances: *"Qué te pasa, hombre?"*—"What's going on with you?" and "My God, man, there's only so much I can do!" and "What am I to make of a husband who shows no interest in a woman like me?" One night, without daring to make a sound herself, Teresita overheard this: "In Cuba, the men wanted me, as if there were no other woman in the world . . . wanted me so much, Gustavo, that I sometimes went mad, and here we are, Gustavo, and *tú haces nada conmigo*—you do nothing with me like a real man would. . . . So tell me, *amorcito*, what am I to do with you?"

Teresita would hear his sighs and occasionally, but not very often at all, their bed frame knocking against the walls and María's voice, guttural

266

as a cat's, urging him on: *"Dámelo fuerte, hombre,"* and "More!" and "Just a little longer, please! Give me more, and strongly, *carajo!*" Suppressed female cries, the sucking in of air, as if inhaling fire, the bed rocking more loudly, and then all such noises abruptly ceasing, Gustavo, portly by then, falling back or rolling to his side and gasping with exhaustion.

Then nothing more, until the next morning, when the three would share breakfast before Gustavo and María went off to their jobs, and Teresita, an honors student at Miami Northwestern High, awaited her bus. A solemn silence, Gustavo good-naturedly cooking up the eggs with chorizo, María, a bandanna wrapped about her hair, smoking her Virginia Slims, the lady's preferred cigarette, one after another, and barely eating more than a few bites of her food. Then a voice from a Spanish-language station, WCMQ in Hialeah, chattering away about traffic patterns before introducing yet another old classic Cuban *canción* while María, straightening out the buttons of Gustavo's crisp blue shirt, asked him tenderly, "More coffee, my love?" but with her mascara eyes saying something else. Some old Benny Moré heartbreaker, or perhaps a *danzón* by the Orquesta Aragón, but occasionally, as well, another of those songs from that epoch when "Cuba was Cuba," sonorous with violins, a flowing piano, and a beatific baritone, Nestor's own, in his rendition of "Beautiful María of My Soul." Just then, Gustavo, hearing those strains, rapped the tabletop and, dabbing his mouth, announced, "Well, I've got to go." Kisses for his stepdaughter, a kiss on María's cheek, the door opening, and the dense humidity of a Miami morning wafting into the air-conditioning of that kitchen like a mist. *"Cuídate, amorcito,"* María, running hot and cold, would call after him. The door closing, she would stub out a cigarette, click off the radio with a sigh, as if one memory too many had been provoked by that song.

The discord saddened Teresita. She'd grown close to that man. He may not have been the most dynamic stepfather a girl could have, but he was good to her. And he may have disappointed María lately in some ways, but with Teresita, he never went wrong. She loved their tranquil promenades along the streets at

267

dusk, on their way to get ice cream from a truck that always showed up on a certain corner at seven in the evening. He liked to take her places on his days off, and if some book in a shop window caught her eye, he never hesitated to buy it for her. He smelled nice, never raised his voice against her, and not once, in all those years, had he ever laid a hand on her. Best of all, on his days off, he'd sometimes have his friends over from the Relief Services center and cook up a feast, Cuban style. And when it came to celebrating her birthday, he always made that a fiesta too, going to the trouble of getting her a birthday cake, with candles, the kinds of niceties that María, who grew up without such simple rituals, would probably have never bothered with. She was just that way.

But whatever María and Gustavo lacked, as Teresita would speculate years later, it hardly affected the image they presented during those dance nights sponsored by the Gallego Society or the Cienfuegos Club. Held in the ballrooms of Miami beach hotels, these were merry affairs, packed with people, live bands, and more Cuban food than any such crowd could possibly consume. (Having too much food, as opposed to the paucity of such things back in Cuba, was the point.) Teresita loved to see them out on the floor, most elegantly dressed, dancing to boleros amongst other couples of every possible age, from *los ancianos* to *los nenes;* enjoyed observing that ritual of stance and attitude in which, with their faces pressed gently together and heads tilted slightly upwards, both of them smiled, as if seeing something magnificent in the sparkling globes revolving below the ceiling. A good enough dancer, Gustavo never stepped on anybody's toes, and he even had a certain grace.

Teresita knew this because, seeing her sitting alone, he'd pull her out into the crowd, that dear and sweet man, who always had something nice to say to her—"If those fellows only knew what they're missing" and "Don't be shy, you're as pretty as your mother," which she knew was a lie but appreciated anyway. Though she would have preferred to stay home and study, or chat with her friends on the telephone, or simply watch some TV—in those days she really didn't care about "boys" one way or the other—Teresita, having no choice about the matter, did her best to enjoy herself, mainly by overdoing it with the food, crispy *tostones* and the rinds of suckling pig—*lechón*—cooked up in the proper Cuban manner with tons of garlic, salt, and lemon juice, along with a nice heaping plate of rice with black beans, and maybe a little fried *yuca*. It was food that, as some of her Jewish friends at school would say, was "to die for." Sucking in her stomach, whenever Teresita felt that someone's eyes were on her, her greatest downfall came by way of the pastry tables, which were stacked with sweets, the diabolical napoleons being her favorites.

On one of those nights, Teresita had been sitting off to the side, gingerly nursing each scrumptious bite of one, when she noticed Gustavo coming off the dance floor with a pronounced limp, and when he sat down, María off somewhere in a frenzy, showing off with some young caballero during an upbeat mambo, he kept rubbing his shin and ankle, as if to get something working again. Back home, later that night, he took off his black patent leather shoes to find that both his feet were swollen and lividly purple; the more he rubbed them, the more he groaned in pain. A local doctor, who couldn't have been very thorough, Teresita would think years later, diagnosed him with gout, but it turned out to be the boiling point of a diabetes-induced heart-related malady that, undiagnosed, only worsened in the following months and culminated in a stroke, which befell him as Gustavo sat in his office, helping a newly arrived exile couple with the paperwork for the government-subsidized purchase of a house.

That was God's reward for all his good deeds, María kept thinking. *"Gracias pa' nada, Dios"*—"Thanks for nothing, Lord"—she snapped at the sky after the priest had finished leading them in a final benediction and the cemetery workers, hoisting down ropes, lowered his coffin into the ground. Grasping her mother's hand, Teresita, only fourteen at the time, was in tears. She had been crying for days. From the strange moment when María, late one afternoon, found her reading a book in her bedroom and told her, almost nonchalantly, that her step-*papito* was no more. And through the three days of his "showing" at the Gomez Brothers funeral home—"formerly located in Havana"—Teresita had been mystified by María's indifference. For her mother showed hardly any emotion. He may have been only her step-*papito,* but she missed him.

The house already seemed emptier without Gustavo, and on one of those evenings after they'd gotten home from his three-day wake, just the sound of the ice cream truck's chimes at dusk brought her to tears, and every time she worked up the nerve to touch something that had belonged to him, like the plump brown wallet he had in his back pocket the day he died, which the police had returned to them in a plastic bag along with a rosary and comb, it broke her up too. But María? She had hardly shed a tear.

"Oh, but don't you understand, *mi hijita,*" she said to Teresita, "that Gustavo's passing was God's will? There is nothing to be done when someone's time comes—believe me, I know." And when Teresita, feeling as if that was not enough of an answer, asked her: "But tell me, Mama, did you love him?" María said, "Of course, I cared very much for him, but was it a deep and burning love? No. . . . If I chose him when I could have looked around for someone else, it was because he was a decent man, and I wanted *you* to benefit from his decency." Then: "Did I want him to die? No. Did I want to deprive you of him? No. That was in El Señor's plans, and nothing changes that. *Es el destino*—It's destiny."

"But, Mama, why is it that you haven't even cried?"

"Why?" María said, getting up to refill a glass with red wine. "Because it doesn't change a thing. Believe me, I've wept enough to last me two lifetimes—just to think of my own mother's passing makes me cry deep inside at night. But by now—and you will understand this when you are older—I've learned that in this world you have to develop a hard skin. I learned this the hard way, and, believe me, you should too."

Oh, but the hard skin? Even years later Dr. Teresita wondered if she herself had become muy durita, durita, *as her mother used to say, without really intending to.*

That same morning, when Gustavo was laid to rest, to join the others in María's life who had once meant so much to her—her *papito,* her mother, her sister and two brothers, old Lázaro, and Nestor Castillo, and likely Ignacio too—and many in that crowd, among them more than a few of the reverent *cubanos* Gustavo had helped in the darkest days of their early exile, wept unabashedly, only beautiful María, dressed appropriately in black and under a veil, remained curiously unmoved, and that, sharp as a snapshot, was something Teresita would never forget. The ceremony ended, and as the crowd began dispersing, María, perhaps feeling robbed or relieved—it was impossible to tell—tossed a rose onto his coffin, peered down for a few moments, made a sign of the cross, and then, as if it were the most ordinary late Saturday morning, asked her daughter, "What would you like for lunch?" And when Teresita, taken aback by the casualness of that remark, shot her a disquieting glance— Teresita's large eyes, dark as coals, flaring—María shrugged and just started walking off to a waiting Town Car. Later, on their journey back home, María, always content to watch the world go by, glanced over at her daughter only once, and when she did, she said, *"¿Y qué?"*—"And what? Tell me, what am I supposed to do?"

FORTY-THREE

f course, there was soon someone else to fill the void left by Gustavo in that household, a dapper *cubano* of the old school, with a thin mustache, and gleaming (dyed black) hair, whom beautiful María met about a year later at a *quinces* celebration for one of Teresita's *amigitas* from school. He happened to be the honoree's uncle. They struck up a conversation because he had kept staring at María from another table, as if trying to place her. When he finally walked over, he said: "Haven't I seen you somewhere, maybe in Havana?" And then: "Of course, at one of those clubs. Say, didn't you dance at the Lantern?"

"Yes, I did," María answered, with neither pride nor shame. "It was my profession in those days."

Nodding happily, he sat beside her, sipped his drink, lit a cigarette. He was a well put together, tautly built fellow, maybe fifty, clouds of some overpowering cologne floating off his skin. He wore a well-fitted light blue suit, a Cuban flag pin on his lapel, with a crisp open-collared shirt, a rush of silvered hair flowing upwards from his chest and just a distinguishing touch of gray at his temples; his eyes were remarkably penetrating. And yes, he was handsome.

"Well, believe it or not, I caught a couple of your shows, back when; in one of them you were dressed up like an Egyptian—like Cleopatra—is that right?"

"Yes, that revue was popular for a while."

He slapped his knee. "Lordy, I knew it. God, I remember thinking, *Now that is one hell of a good-looking woman!* And if I didn't approach you,

272

well, it's because I didn't think I had a chance in heaven." He did not mince words. "Tell me, are you married?"

"*No, soy viuda*"—"I'm a widow," María said in such a downcast way that Teresita, sitting beside her, half rolled her eyes up into her head. "My husband died last year—a good man, you understand. *Un santo*," she told him, looking off sadly.

"Well, here's what I think," he said, shifting his chair towards her. "Life is too short to throw it away by feeling bad about things. What do you say about you and me going out somewhere one night—anywhere you want!" He touched his heart. "It would honor me." Then, as a waiter brought him another drink, he made a big show of pulling out a thick wad of bills, the way Ignacio used to back in Havana, peeling off a ten, and stuffing it into the waiter's frock pocket with a wink.

"My name's Rafael Murillo," he told her and, like a gallant, withdrew from his jacket pocket a card: "*A sus órdenes.*"

When María extended her hand, he turned it palm up, like a reader, examining her lines closely; then he went into all this ecstatic *miércoles* about her youthful appearance and beauty, as if he had just bumped into her on a street in Havana twenty years before. Teresita just listened, knowing that for her mother's age—past forty, well, forty-three by then— everything he said was true. After all, beautiful María could have passed for a fine-looking woman somewhere in her luscious mid thirties, for she had kept her figure and had the complexion of a lady who, aside from her slowly aging *mulatta* genes, still rubbed palm oil and honey on her face each morning. How good did she look? When mother and daughter went for strolls in South Beach, or along the consoling sidewalks and shops of Little Havana, it was beautiful María, in tight pink or canary yellow slacks, with an unforgettable walk, who drew all the stares.

Once their introductions had been made, she and Rafael danced a few cha-cha-chas and mambos, but mainly they drank, chain-smoked, and shared stories about Cuba, as it used to be. Eventually, he got around to trying out his charms on Teresita. "Looking at you I can see that the apple doesn't fall far from the tree," he told her exuberantly at one point, and while Teresita, a sweet girl at heart, smiled at the compliment, she hardly believed him, thinking herself, as she always would, only ordinary looking at best, even if that was far from the truth. (Years later, in her doctorly guise, it would always surprise Teresa when one of the hospital orderlies whistled good-naturedly at her figure.) Later, when they had stepped out from the Holiday Inn by the harbor, into one of those languid, perfume-filled Miami nights, the sort reminiscent of a delicious Havana evening, her mother's new acquaintance offered to drive them home in his fancy 1972 DeVille. After he'd handed three dollars to the valet, with the windows rolled down, his elbow out the window as he steered with a single hand, María beside him, Teresita in the back, they drove through the velvet night.

Along the way, he spoke about the two restaurants he owned: "One is called El Malecón, up in Coral Gables, have you heard of it?"

"Of course," María answered. "That's yours?"

"Yes, indeed, my brother and me opened it about six months after we came to Miami, in '64," he began. "It started out as a hole-in-the-wall, we did hardly any business at all at first, but, you know, with things improving in the city, business picked up. We advertise in all the hotels with brochures, and, thanks to taking care of the concierges, we've done pretty well. Good enough to open a second place along Key Biscayne Boulevard—that's my favorite. It's the Siboney, after Lecuona's song, and even if it's not as fancy as the other, which is more upscale, *para la gente con más dinero, sabes,* I love it the most because we've done it up like the old seaside *friterías* outside Havana, and I just like its views of the ocean."

"So you've succeeded," María said. "I'm happy for you."

"Yes, thank our lucky stars," he said, tapping the dashboard top. "But, even as good as we're doing, I still look forward to getting back to Havana one day, you know, after that shit is overthrown." He shook his head, his suave and happy-go-lucky manner dissipating in that moment. "It's something I don't like to think about too much—you know, I put a

lot of faith and hope in that man, and I didn't want to leave Cuba, but—"
And he went on about what happened to him and his family in the same way that so many of the exiles did in those days, things turned upside down, the stomach-churning Russians coming in, the businesses nationalized, the food shortages, the government's snoops and spies, the assaults on liberty that he and his family just couldn't take anymore.

"Surely, you understand what I'm saying, huh?"

"¿Cómo no?" María answered. "Even my daughter, Teresita—even she knows that we Cubans didn't want to leave. But we had to, right, hija?"

By then, he'd turned up Twenty-sixth. "Our house is the fourth one on the right, over there under the big tree," she told him. And when he had pulled up, he asked them to wait, and, like a gentleman, this Rafael Murillo got out and walked over to the passenger side of the car, opening the door for each of them.

"Your carriage has arrived, mi condesa," he said to Teresita, bowing. Then to María, "I will see you soon, next week. I'll bring you both to the restaurant—we have a little band that performs there on Friday nights—okay?"

And with that Rafael Murillo, winking at them both in a pleasant way, got into his car and drove off into the balminess of the evening.

A FEW THINGS ABOUT THIS RAFAEL: HE HAD A PLACE UP IN FORT Lauderdale, a condominium, to which he would sometimes take María for a weekend afternoon. He was separated from his second wife, whom María, finding him so handsome and genteel, thought must surely have something wrong in la cabeza, for he would sadly say that he missed his kids on a daily basis, and that it wasn't his idea at all. He belonged to an anti-Castro organization which met in a downtown hall twice monthly. He wore a gold bracelet on his right wrist, inscribed with the words "Liberty or death. Viva Cuba Libre!" and was furious about the American cowards of the Kennedy administration who had betrayed the Cuban

275

cause during the failed Bay of Pigs invasion, even if it had taken place over a decade before. He regularly telephoned María at night from his restaurants, calls that she took only in her bedroom. He was generous, and never came to visit their house without some gifts for María and Teresita. ("Tell me what you need, and it will be yours," he said.) Finding it unusual that María did not own a car and depended on slow public transportation or rides with friends to get where she needed to go, he offered to buy her a car so that he wouldn't always have to pick her up for their *citas*. Learning that she didn't know how to drive, he promised to pay for lessons, but she refused, having a phobia about cars, not only because she had grown up among horses and donkeys, and had always regarded automobiles with wonderment, as if the driving of such machines was intended only for men, but because they made her think about Nestor Castillo's death.

He tended to come by the house very late at night, after his restaurants had closed—usually with packages of food, aluminum-foil-wrapped platters of fried *chuletas* and steaks and of paella, which would feed them for the next three or four days. When he'd arrive, Teresita knew; their voices were always hushed, and she could also tell from the faint aroma of the coronas he smoked that wafted into her room, and then by the whisperings that came from María's bedroom down the hall. At first, he never stayed the night, but after a few months, on some mornings Teresita would find him sitting by their kitchen table, in Gustavo's former chair, María always smoking her Virginia Slims and attending to him dutifully. As Teresita waited for the school bus, he'd always inquire about what she was studying, her chemistry and biology and French textbooks beyond him. He'd say things like "I can tell that your daughter is going to go far."

On the weekends, when he happened to drop by and Teresita, having examinations, would have preferred to stay home and study—she did her best thinking in her pink-decorated bedroom—he'd give her a twenty-dollar bill so that she might take some of her friends off to the movie theater in the sprawling mall, across a wide boulevard a few sweltering avenues away. Sometimes she went to the movies, but, just as often, she sat in a McDonald's eating juicy hamburgers and studying. She always waited until past four thirty, when Rafael had taken off for work, before finally heading back. But one afternoon, when she came home and saw the DeVille still parked by the curb, she made the mistake of going inside anyway. That's when she heard them through the door: beautiful María, in her ferocious widowed way, screaming in pleasure, the bed frame slamming against the wall, and Rafael moaning and crying out, *"Así, así, así!"* as if the world were about to end. It was so disquieting that Teresita, without daring to make any noise herself, slipped back outside, took a walk down the street to where some of the kids were playing a game of dodgeball, and let an hour pass before she finally made her way to their door again, fearful that they would still be going at it. That it had gone on in kindly Gustavo's bed seemed awfully wrong, and the notion put Teresita in a rather solemn frame of mind, as if something sacred had been violated; he had been her mother's husband and the only *papito* she had really known, after all. But Teresita dared not say a word, and later, as she sat out waiting on the patio, when Rafael finally left, she just smiled when he pinched her on the cheek.

FOR A TIME, MARÍA, IT SHOULD BE SAID, SEEMED HAPPY, OR AS happy as a woman like her could be, at least when it came to the physical act of love. Amorously speaking, Rafael was a most enthusiastic partner, who, in possessing María, seemed to be playing out some dream. She was his *cubanita caliente,* his *cubanita de la noche,* his *cubana* with a *chocha muy fabulosa.* The man kissed every inch of her body, and every curvaceous dip and valley of her flesh, fucked her so adamantly that it was as if, with his wildly glaring pupils, he were making love to Cuba itself. (Well, he had reinforced the notion by showing her a piece of arcane Cuban currency with an image of the goddess Athena to which she seemed to bear a close resemblance.) For her part, she ran with this new breath of passion, buying the most scandalous of transparent undergarments from a boutique called Los Dainties. He just loved her sexiness. At a costume ball held at carnival time, he asked María to dress up as a showgirl, with plumed headdress and a rented outfit so diaphanous and scanty that her arrival set all the older women, *las ancianas,* who in some other age would have been chaperones, grumbling, every male head turning, perhaps enviously, their wives fuming. But did they care? They came home laughing, throwing each other around, drunkenly happy, and the racket that María and Rafael made later that night—"I'm going to devour you!"—not only woke Teresita up but provoked the neighborhood hounds to bark.

But as the year went by, even María, lacking any relatives of her own—a very sad thing for Teresita more than for herself—began to wonder why Rafael, with two brothers and a sister, each with their own large family, and birthday and holiday parties to attend, never once invited them to any of their gatherings; that did not sit well with her at all. "You know I don't want to just be your little *pajarita,* that you hide away," she told him. "If you don't think of me as anyone special to you, then don't expect anything special from me."

Growing aloof and withholding from him the favors of her perfectly ripened body, and that luscious *papayún* that had driven Nestor Castillo crazy, María finally got Rafael to concede that perhaps he had been keeping her too much a secret. (That is to say, María, strong willed by then, harangued Rafael into admitting it.) And so, one delightful Sunday afternoon, in a somewhat guarded mood, Rafael brought María and Teresita along with him to his brother Miguel's house, out in Fort Lauderdale, where his kin and their in-laws had gathered to celebrate one of his *tías'* seventieth birthday. It seemed, at first, yet another cheerful, jammed-with-kids-and-older-folks affair typical of extended Cuban families in Miami. And while he had taken María around, sheepishly introducing her as "a friend" to various relatives, from the very start they regarded her as if she were a leper.

It didn't matter that she had dressed conservatively, in just an ankle-length skirt and a blouse with some frilly workings, and had worn around her neck both a delicate pearl necklace and a crucifix. She still cut swaths through the coterie of his siblings' and cousins' more ordinarily pretty wives with her gorgeousness, all but a few of their expressions asking, *Is this the latest cheap* tramposa *for whom Rafael left his saintly wife and children?* Of course, some, his brothers particularly, were civil enough with María, and the more the other men drank beer and daiquiris, the more María glowed before them. (Translation: "If you're going to mess around, that's the sort you do it with.") But, as had often happened in her life, the women, the younger wives especially, seemed outraged by her presence, none of them saying a word to María when she'd smile at them, their eyes squinting, daggers in their pupils.

What, then, could María do but have a few drinks, when, at a certain point in the afternoon, Rafael made himself scarce? She had watched him huddling with one of his older sons, a good-looking college-age fellow; her eyes had followed Rafael as he later disappeared into the house to have some words with another woman, a petite brunette, seemingly suppressing tears of both anger and righteous indignation, who, as it turned out, happened to be his wife.

"*Por Dios,* I'm bored," María said to Teresita as she sat down beside her mother in the yard, her expression telling her all.

It was an hour before he finally came out, and when he did, Rafael curtly told her: "We should go." As they drove back, María did not say a word, trying her best to maintain her dignity, even if she was a little drunk. For his part, Rafael, no doubt burdened by his violation of familial decorum, said to her, "Well, it was what you wanted, wasn't it?" Once they got back to their house on Northwest Terrace, Teresita locked herself in her room and, for several hours, took in another kind of disturbance: not of two people making love but of Rafael's shouted recriminations: "What we had was perfectly fine before you had to stick your nose into my family life! Why I allowed this, I don't know, but I wouldn't have, if it weren't for you!" Then he went on and on before storming out, not an iota of tenderness in his voice.

A month went by. One evening, at dusk, Teresita looked out her window and saw them sitting inside his DeVille. He was gesticulating wildly, while María, her arms folded across her lap, didn't move at all. Until she slapped him in the face and, as María later put it to Teresita, told him to shove his own fingers up his ass. Shortly, as María stepped onto the pavement, he drove off, tossing into the street a bouquet of flowers, which María didn't bother to pick up.

And that was the last of Rafael.

IT HARDLY RUFFLED MARÍA'S FEATHERS, HOWEVER. THAT SAME evening, after dinner, she sat by their kitchen table pouring herself a cup of red Spanish wine. Sitting across from her, Teresita put aside a school notebook she had been writing in. "Mama, can I ask you something?"

"Of course, *mi vida.*"

"That man, Rafael—did you even really care about him?"

María laughed. "Are you kidding me? I liked him all right, but did I fall in love with him, is that what you're asking me? No, *por Dios,* no! And even if I did, what difference would that make? What is love between a man and a woman anyway, *pero un vapor?* Something that comes and goes like the air."

Snubbing out her cigarette, María held out her arms to her daughter. "Come here, *querida,*" she said, and Teresita went to her side. That's when María smothered her with kisses, repeating, as she stroked Teresita's hair: "It's you I love—*mi Teresita, mi buena*—and no one else. Never, never forget that, *hija.* The hell with everyone else!"

Chapter
FORTY-FOUR

But to say that love was air and to really believe it, deep down, were two different things. For, in the quietude of her bedroom, beautiful María had more than her share of wistful moments, even if there had been others who had come along: The manager of a movie house. A much younger dance instructor she'd met at the Biltmore in Coral Gables, where she sometimes gave group lessons to the tourists. An accountant, missing two front teeth, his jackets flecked with dandruff, had helped her sort through the chaos of her dance studio receipts and was a very nice fellow indeed, but too attached to his overbearing mother and therefore too controlled and timid for her taste. *("That one, Félix," she told her daughter, "wanted me to be just like his mamá.")* A construction contractor, who did some work on the house and, without children, left her because she was not of that fecund age anymore. And there were others. Cubans all, they came and went as momentary diversions; a few she took to bed, most often in obscure motels, but never with any expectation of receiving the affections she had known during her *juventud* in Cuba. *(Oh, but papí, y Nestor, y Ignacio—yes, even Ignacio!)* In the end, they meant very little to her, and since Teresita, sizing them up, rarely seemed pleased when she brought any of those men home, beautiful María hardly cared about their value as potential step-*papitos*. Occasionally, she considered remarrying—a few had proposed—but since she was more or less *comodita*—most comfortably disposed—in the house that Gustavo had left her, and could not really see herself making room for someone else, despite her loneliness, the notion somehow held out no appeal for her.

. . .

BY HER FIFTIES, MARÍA HAD STARTED TO FEEL HER YEARS. SHE still turned heads, but more so, as time went on, from a distance. Men continued to check her out, surely, but not as often as before; nor did men stare as long as they used to; the sensation that their eyes followed her all the way down the street vanished—a woman like María just knew. And, though she still looked very well preserved, even beautiful, María found herself feeling stunned by how much younger more and more people, both male and female, seemed to her.

Keeping her figure from the days of her youth largely intact by giving dance lessons from ten to five at the studio she had opened downtown and, swallowing her pride, the hour she spent twice weekly sweating away in a pink outfit on a treadmill at a nearby YWCA—where all the local Cuban women gathered in Jacuzzis afterwards to boast about their children and grandchildren—could not compensate for the inevitable and subtle changes of her features: not wrinkles but a general slackening of her skin, which so perturbed María that she took to dwelling more and more on newspaper ads for face tucks, and her cabinet filled with youth-restoring creams, rich with all kinds of so-called miracle enzymes, that she'd heard about on the radio. Yet as wonderful as María looked for her age, there was no concealing the passage of time, which could be read in her eyes, the future, and all its hopes and promises, having ceased to be the endless thing that had once shimmered so brightly in her pupils. Stripped of her illusions about what her romantic life would hold, María, like a character out of a bolero, began to think more and more about the past—how lovely it had been, no matter the difficulties she had endured. And once she did, the more she returned to her memories of that *músico* Nestor Castillo.

NOW AND THEN, ESPECIALLY DURING THE YEARS WHEN HER BRIL-liant daughter had left Miami to study medicine in New York and she would come from work and indulge in a few five-thirty cocktails, María, feeling lonely, not for men but for her Teresita's companionship, would turn on their living room phonograph, an RCA console, and play the somewhat weathered Mambo Kings album she had happily found one afternoon at a neighborhood flea market for twenty-five cents. As if putting on a zarzuela or a symphony, she'd listen to each selection in order, from their raucously freewheeling, drum-and-horn-section-driven *descargas* to their songs of love, and always with the greatest sentimentality each time she heard Nestor's sweet baritone voice, the climax, of course, reached with the last offering of Side A, "Beautiful María of My Soul." Some evenings it gave her such a thrill that she'd put it on over and over again, the distance of time having made its melody seem even lovelier than before, and, despite her dislike of certain of its lyrics, she'd feel glorified, as if their love had been immortalized forever and forever, amen. But when she'd had too much to drink, and Nestor's ghost filled the room, and the particulars of that irretrievable romance came back to her in such a way as to provoke the saddest of emotions, she'd cut it off, lest she begin to wallow in the kinds of sentiments that María still found painful.

(In that sort of mood, she'd recall the accusatory letter that Cesar Castillo had sent her. That her impulsive journey to New York in 1956 could have contributed, in any way, to Nestor's passing was the sort of notion that sometimes made her jump up in her sleep, her heart beating rapidly, just like he used to make it. Then that guilt would sting her like a wasp, pains she would feel for days, until that too eventually faded.)

So María had to be careful, because even she, with her somewhat hardened shell, could find herself adrift on a sea of regrets. On such nights, she'd go through her cache of keepsakes—what were they but ordinary photographs, most of them fading, of her *mamá* and *papito*, of herself as a young beauty, and yes, of Nestor Castillo, that *joven*, whom she came to believe had been the love of her life: that which she had thrown away? In such a mood, she'd read his letters over again, and not just the tender ones but also those letters that overheated her skin with reminiscences of their lovemaking.

(If she could have seen Teresita's expression one evening when she, home from Florida International University, had, out of curiosity, dug them out of her closet and read each and every one. My God! *is what she had thought.)*

Then months would go by without her once playing that song. And while María, at a certain hour, tuned in to Miami's Channel Five to see if that particular episode of *I Love Lucy* in which Nestor and his brother had appeared happened to be showing, for the most part she kept her little secret to herself. Teresita knew about it, and so did her former dancing colleague from the Lantern Club, Gladys, who, since moving to Miami from Havana, had become an occasional close companion. (They had spotted each other in a mall, around 1980, in the days just before Miami had gotten a little crazy over the influx of the Marielitos. It had been a happy reunion, and, yes, Gladys believed her when it came to that song—María had told her about Nestor.) But the few times María had mentioned this to anyone else, like her neighbors, her claim was met with more than a little skepticism. Because to call yourself the inspiration behind what Cubans of a certain generation had come to regard as something of a minor classic fell into a category of self-aggrandizement that only invited ridicule and, in María's opinion, unspoken accusations of vanity and silliness.

Nevertheless, beautiful María sometimes wished that everyone knew. What was she, after all, but just another exile lady, a former dancer from the glory days of Havana, whom no one would ever remember, save perhaps for her daughter?

During those long months in the 1980s while Teresita lived away, María had her routines. She and her old friend Gladys, married with her own grown children, met occasionally on the weekends, usually Sundays, to make forays to the restaurants and shopping centers of the city. María would join Gladys on excursions to the beach, where, baking in the sun and sipping drinks of rum and pineapple juice, she passed those pleasant hours under an umbrella, taking in the escapades of frolicking youth on the white sands. Gladys, it should be said, though a few years younger than María, had ballooned appreciably while living the good life, becoming one of those immense *cubanas* who, however portly, still sashayed with a former dancer's sexy pride. They'd sit and look out over the water—and inevitably the horizon's oceanic murmurings, soporific in effect, whispered that to the south, just a few hundred miles away, lay Havana, portal to Cuba itself. But it may as well have been China—oceans off—for neither of them knew of any Cubans who had gone back. ("Remember when those cruise boats would leave Havana at six in the morning and come back late at night from Miami, loaded up with the tourists?" María would say. "Remember the trip we made?")

Miami had changed since the days María first arrived. It was all fancied up, prospering in ways that the first exiles could not have imagined. If there had been any blot on the mark the Cubans left on the city, it came down to the scattering of criminals and asylum inmates that *ese loco* Fidel had unleashed on Florida when he allowed the Mariel boat lifts. Though most weren't criminals—Gladys's husband, Ramón, had been on one of those boats in the Florida-bound flotilla, returning with six of his relatives—there had been a spike in crime; one had to be more careful at night in certain neighborhoods. But over all, as María and Gladys warmed their bottoms, enjoying their spiked *refrescos*, they were accepting enough of their life in that city. Miami wasn't Havana, at least the one they knew, and, for María, it seemed a million miles away from Pinar del Río—just thinking about that, and the great internal distances she had traveled from that tranquil *valle*, sometimes left her so quietly disposed that she wouldn't say much at all.

Though she had enjoyed those outings—Ramón always dropped her off at the house in Northwest Terrace—the hardest thing for María was to come home to an empty house: on with the radio in the kitchen, on with the television in her living room. A glass of rum with diet Coke usually smoothed her over, and gloriously so, as she showered—*didn't that bring her closer to God?* Then, having gotten the sand off, she'd attend to her only companion, the little black cat with the white paws María had found mewing inside a garbage can down the street, Omar, the name that had popped into her head. She felt so much affection for the creature she sometimes wondered why she had bothered with men at all, and this Omar seemed to know, for he followed her around wherever she went, curled up next to her on the couch when she watched TV and smoked, and jumped into bed with her, the way men had once always wanted to, at night.

And sometimes, settled on the kitchen table, just purring away, and with an Oriental wisdom burning in his eyes, Omar watched María as she would sit writing what she called her *versitos*. It was a vocation that she, a former *analfabeta*, had only dabbled in over the years but, to which, with Teresita away in school, she had lately devoted herself. Her interest was helped by a poetry-writing course that she had enrolled in at an adult education center at Dade Community College. Meeting on Wednesday evenings at eight o'clock and lasting for two hours, it had become the high point of her week. Conducted in Spanish by an Ichabod Crane–looking fellow named Luis Castellano, a former native of Holguín, the class consisted of a dozen Cuban women, mostly well into their fifties if not older, no men, and the poems were shared aloud, often to laughter and sometimes to tears. For to hear spoken the pure emotions of such ladies in that intimate setting, as expressed in poems with titles like *"Mi Cuba preciosa"*—"My Precious Cuba"—or *"El jardín de mis abuelos"*—"My Grandparents' Garden"—or *"Un domingo por la mañana en Cienfuegos"*—"A Sunday Morning in Cienfuegos"—was to be steeped, as María herself had put it to Teresita in a letter, *"in the honey of our bees."* Plump, aged, still shapely, kindly disposed or enraged by what life had dealt them, each week they held forth, their voices cracking sometimes, their hands trembling. And you know what? Not a one of their poems was bad, or could be bad; their plainspoken utterances, like songs without music, just took everyone back to what they felt and envisioned when remembering, ever so bittersweetly, that which they had lost and wished to recover: the very notion of Cuba, which hung over the room like the branches of a blossom-heavy tree.

They wrote about street life in Havana, with its singing vendors, and of their small towns in the provinces, or some colorful *fulano* they knew, or of a local rake, a first love, or the sea, the siren songs they heard as echoes in conch shells found on a beach, of smelling fresh morning bread from a bakery next door, *muy sabrosito siempre,* of chameleons and roosters running wild in an auntie's living room, of *el campo en Oriente,* with its blossomed air after a rainfall, of the mists rising along the ridged foothills of the Escambray mountains, and the stars that rose, one by one, like diamonds over that horizon; of watching the impeccably dressed, straightbacked planters of Matanzas riding regally by their porches on their silver-spurred white stallions, of singing barbers and lovestruck morticians, of childhood *negrita* nannies; of husbands, and sons, and beautiful daughters; of distant Spanish ancestors from Vigo or Fonsagrada, or Asturias or Barcelona, Madrid and more—all this turned that ordinary classroom into something of a chapel in which everyone prayed to the same heaven.

From María García's writings:

If Cuba were a man
He would be so handsome,
I'd faint in his arms.
He would smell so sweetly of flowers,
And of the rain at three o'clock.
His kisses might taste of tobacco, but I wouldn't mind,
He would be good to me, after all.
He would dance like a rumbero *from Cayo Hueso*
And speak deliciously like a song . . .

María wrote other poems, another side of herself coming out, her own sentimentality, at their writing, surprising her. By her kitchen table, one evening, the Frigidaire humming beside her and the GE radio turned low, just scribbling the words *"Mi papito, Manolo,"* brought him back, and she found herself nearly weeping. Witnessing this sadness, Omar's ears curled, as if he could understand María; and he seemed almost clairvoyant when she began to write about Nestor, Omar getting up and rubbing his bony, purring head against the knuckles of María's hand.

Oh, Nestor, I have something
To tell you,
Even if what we had
Was long ago.
Without knowing it
I loved you,
And love you now,
Wherever you are. . . .
So, believe me when I say
I just didn't know.

SHE WROTE ABOUT HER *VALLE* OFTEN, A FEW DITTIES ABOUT HER dancer's life in Havana, and a poem about learning to read, which she called, simply, "For the Negro, Lazarus." And though she never published those verses anywhere, except in the blue-covered anthologies that their teacher, *el Señor* Castellano, put together on a Xerox machine for that class, beautiful María just enjoyed the time she spent with her little poetic community. On such nights, when, it should be said, she sometimes felt an attraction for the *maestro*, despite his incredible homeliness, María always came home with a feeling of accomplishment, among other emotions, that, indeed, she had come a long way from the days she had been an ignorant *guajira*, unable to read or write a single word.

From another of her verses, which was just a jotting entitled *"Mi amiga Eliza"*:

She wore rags like me
She was forlorn like me
Knew nothing like me
Had little like me
We look so much alike
That when I see her
In my mirror,
And ask, "Eliza, why the long face?"
She tells me, "Oh, cousin, it's because
I know that while I am so happy
You are so sad."

As much solace as beautiful María took in her verses, the source of her greatest pride in those years was Teresita, about whom she bragged to anyone who would listen. ("Oh, but if only your abuelos could have known—and your papito, Ignacio, whose brains flow in your blood—oh, they would be so happy!") Teresita had always been one of those cubanitas who, with an exile's passion, excelled in every subject in school, science being her greatest interest. She was helped by a very high IQ—a measurement that meant little to María. That she had decided to study medicine, all on scholarships, had surely to do with the way María had raised her. When it came to matters of health, a day never passed during Teresita's early adolescence that María did not find herself worrying that her daughter might come down with the same symptoms of epilepsy that had taken her tía, at so young an age, from this world. Teresita had grown up hearing her mother, at the public health clinics, asking the doctors who examined her if there were special tests for that disease. Nothing came of them— she was always a healthy girl—but any time Teresita suffered from a fever and exhibited the slightest trembling, María, taken back to Pinar del Río and the sufferings of her sister, inevitably rushed her off to the nearest hospital. Early on, epilepsia was a word that Teresita had learned through her mother's wistful stories about her aunt, may God bless her soul, just so that she would know something of her own past; and it was the first disease that Teresita, in high school, with a burgeoning interest in the sciences, looked up in the library encyclopedia.

And so, it can perhaps be said that Teresita's interest in pediatric medicine came first to pass because of María.

. . .

OF COURSE, MOTHER AND DAUGHTER SPOKE ON THE TELEPHONE at least a few times a week, whenever Teresita's taxing schedule as an intern in New York, with a specialization in pediatric oncology at the Columbia-Presbyterian Medical Center, allowed her the time.

"Have you met anyone?" María inevitably asked.

"No, I'm too busy, Mama. If you knew my hours, you'd understand."

"But there's no one there you like?"

Teresita sighed. "No, Mama, not yet."

It was something María always asked her, and it always made Teresita want to get off the phone, or say, "Mama, can't you just accept who I am?" But she knew that María would simply have thought, *Oh, but she's just become too americana.* Still, their conversations jostled along pleasantly, and dutifully, Teresita filling her mother in on the routines of the week, and María occasionally reciting her latest verses over the phone, never once failing to let her daughter know how much she missed her. In fact, though Teresita often sighed during their conversations, she felt the same way. María, after all, had been everything to her, the fount of what she thought of as her "little Cuban-centric world."

Always too pensive for her own good, and one of those demure and ever obedient *cubanita* daughters who always seemed to recede into the shadows of the kitchen when María had friends over and things became lively, Teresita, with her 160-something IQ, had, over the years, grown more attached to abstract notions than to the practicalities—and pleasures—of daily existence. In high school, when thrown in with a crowd of rowdy *cubanita* adolescents who mainly talked about one *guapo* boy or another, and fretted about whether their asses were too big or their halter tops were sexy enough, Teresita thought them frivolous. Among those friends she was known as somewhat of a wallflower, and so straitlaced that they would chide her with this taunt: "Hey, loosen up, Teresita! Do you think we're back in the Cuba of our *abuelos?*" She went to high school dances, but never with any man-killing intentions and, to

María's chagrin, never bothering with makeup. A budding feminist, Teresita refused to wear the clinging, short-skirted dresses of her classmates. Competing on her high school swim team well enough to have once won a bronze medal in a regional meet, she always wore an old-fashioned one-piece suit which the coach claimed, aside from her tendency to suddenly put on weight, slowed her up.

And when María, off in her own world, spent the evening playing old Cuban records on their phonograph, often that Mambo Kings tune over and over again, Teresita, having a little cassette player, listened to the kind of music that would have made her friends gag. A high school music appreciation class, run by a progressive fellow, had "turned her on" to both Bach, Mozart, and Beethoven, and jazz. Not that she didn't like Cuban music, but, having been raised on it, she had come to prefer just about anything else. And yes, she had been taught to dance Latin style by her mother, but there was something about the way her mother pushed her—"Be sexier, move your hips more!"—that put her off. Sweating in her leotard, Teresita would tell her, "Come on, Mama, you know that I'm not you!" And María, shaking her head, would say, "Oh, but I'm just trying to help you, *chica.*" Teresita knew this, but María worked her so hard sometimes, she couldn't help but wonder if her mother was trying to put her through the paces of a professional dancer in Havana, 1947. *(Well, she'd heard her mother talking about those days often enough, of a nightclub life, both sleazy and glamorous, to know that it surely wasn't easy for her to have navigated that predatory world. And she'd feel grateful that she had been spared all the difficulties María, as she often reminded her, had endured. Yet, when she'd look at herself in the floor-to-ceiling studio mirror, Teresita, neither as beautiful nor as long-legged as her mother must surely have been at her age, just wanted to run out of that place and head home, to her room and the companionship of books.)*

So she was a solitary sort. Whereas other *cubanitas* of her age would look back at the drudgery of their high school studies and prefer to remember their various *novios*—even Teresita noticed how some of those boys swaggered along the halls with erections bunched up in the fronts of their tight jeans—she, in those years, had only one *sort of* boyfriend, another brainy *cubano exilio*, whom she had met in a chemistry lab. Rolando wasn't bad looking—in fact, at first glance, he was handsome enough, with Elvis sideburns and expressive brows and eyes—but his face was a mess of luridly green, white-topped pimples, which prevented him from thinking he could ever look good. He blamed these outbreaks on the constant pressures that his demanding parents put on him to excel in school. (This she almost envied; María hardly ever bothered to ask Teresita about her studíes.) Nevertheless, it was his general melancholy— shades of María—and his self-effacing ways, that touched Teresita's heart, and while they never became a couple, meeting here and there in the malls, where they'd find a secluded spot to furtively kiss, she owed her first sexual experience to him. This took place in the bedroom of her house one afternoon while María was off at her dance studio: his trembling hands slipping inside her blouse and caressing the plumpness of her breasts, her nipples (shades of María) shooting up and hardening at his touch, and then, as good as losing her virginity, Teresita let him ease his fingers into her panties, where, feeling him fooling around, she came. In kind, to put it in the most unscientific language, in the midst of a longish kiss, she jerked him off. But that was about all. They went out for a while until Rolando, confusing that afternoon's frolic with love, not only took to calling her every day but began to behave so mawkishly around her at school that Teresita, finding him bothersome and too much of a distraction from her studies, just had to cut him loose.

She'd finally had a regular *novio* in college, at least for a time, a premed student of mixed Argentine and Lebanese descent, named Tomás, who, breaking the sacred seal of her virginity, could not get enough of her, his favorite part of Teresita's body lying between her legs, the taste of which he swore intoxicated him. Altogether, their romance seemed to others an instance of cerebral love between two of the best pre-med students in their school. How could it have been otherwise? For Tomás also happened to possess a handsomeness that turned many a female head, and some might have wondered how she, of an ordinary *cubanita* prettiness, had managed to snag him. (She wondered as well.)

One evening, after they'd been together for about five months, Teresita brought Tomás home to María, on whom his striking looks and intelligence made a wonderful impression. So wonderful that for weeks afterwards, María pestered her daughter about having Tomás in again for dinner. On that second occasion, it startled Teresita to find that María had abandoned her usual blouse and tight evening slacks for an even tighter hip-swallowing red dress with a slit skirt, of such décolletage, that Tomás, during the course of their meal of *arroz con pollo,* could not avoid taking in the alluring shapeliness of María's breasts. And she embarrassed Teresita further with her constant compliments of him. "Oh, but how it makes me happy to see my daughter with a fellow as nice looking as you!" and, "Surely, if you don't want to become a doctor, you can become a movie actor!" Such remarks, abetted by a few cocktails, and María's later insistence that she show him the steps of a dance called the "mozambique" on their living room floor, left Teresita so peeved afterwards that she resolved never to bring him back there again.

It didn't matter. A few months later, for reasons Teresita could not comprehend, Tomás began to make himself scarce. Perhaps someone else had entered the picture—she didn't know—but, in any event, Tomás gradually disappeared from her life. And while Teresita never once mentioned her disappointment to anyone, she began to think that María, whose questions about that "wonderful boy" began to drop away, already knew. If so, María, being María, kept it under her hat—perhaps out of fear of saying the wrong thing to her daughter. And while Teresita, for all her pride, would have loved to have lain her head on María's lap and cry her eyes out, she never did; and not from any animosity, but simply because, when it came to such moments, they just weren't that way with each other at all.

And now, an image of Teresita, having taken a shower and drying herself off with a towel in the bedroom mirror of her lowly Fort Washington flat, on

West 188th, in a neighborhood of Hasidic Jews, Holocaust survivors, and junkies. What did she see? A young woman, of thirty or so, and about five feet two in height, with cinnamon skin, sometimes a little too chubby in places—she kept her belly sucked in—but nice, a great mane of dark hair falling over her shoulders, a woman with shapely hips and pendulous breasts, their nipples like berries, and a flourish of curling black pubic hair in the shape of a spade between her legs. And her face? Stepping closer to the mirror, in her ordinary prettiness, she could see that her almond eyes were her best feature; but when she tilted her head up at a certain angle, and her cheekbones glowed and the slope of her face elongated, she thought that she looked just like her mother, María.

Actually, in those days when Teresita lived in New York and her mother kept asking, "Is there someone?" there had been an American fellow, a certain Derek Harrison, whom Teresita had met at the hospital during her second year as an intern. They'd had an affair that lasted about six months, their passions enflamed, in part, by their exposure to patients who were dying. It was as if one atmosphere fed the other. With AIDS just coming to light, when Teresita and Derek, a fellow intern, stole some moments between rounds, they'd slip into a vacant operating room to ravish each other at three in the morning, and once—the sort of thing that made even Teresita smile—standing up in a janitors' closet, she had hitched her skirt over her belly, her panties down, her body writhing, her *papaya* damp and hungrily drawing him in.

It was wonderful and exciting while it lasted, but Teresa, in her naïveté, confused this fellow's desire to escape the more funereal side of their profession with affection. She'd almost told María about it as a blossoming kind of love, but before she could, he had started to grow more distant, detached, in fact, and while they had continued to fool around for a while, the boiling heat of their mutual infatuation reduced to a simmer and then cooled to a tepid broth. By then, while doing what he could to avoid her, this *sinverguenza* Derek finally confessed that he, from a very good WASP family in Philadelphia, happened to be engaged. If there had been any time when Teresita wished a man to hell, it was then.

But, as with Tomás, she never told María about her broken heart. What would her mother have said to console her anyway?

INDEED, ONCE TERESITA RETURNED TO MIAMI, IN '87, TO BEGIN her post at the children's hospital, a decision which made María very happy, they resumed a life as mother and daughter (along with Omar, the cat) that, compared with many another Cuban household in Miami, bubbling over with aunts and cousins, uncles and *abuelos*, was *muy callado*—quiet. Teresita's position at the hospital took up a lot of her time; she'd come home exhausted, often finishing up patient reports in her bedroom before joining her mother in the living room. On the weekends, however, María and her daughter were nearly inseparable. They liked to eat lunch at one of those outdoor cafés along South Beach—now jammed with tourists and hustling young people. Amazed by how much things had changed—for the worse in some ways, with all the noise, traffic, and tacky souvenir shops—even she, no prude, never quite got used to seeing, as they'd stroll along the beach, the European women who wore only bikini bottoms playing volleyball or dancing to rap music from boom boxes in the sand. (Yes, Miami was a long way from Havana, 1949.) Sometimes they'd go to an art fair, or church bazaar, or to an afternoon outdoor concert with some friends, but mainly they kept to themselves. And while she was ever grateful for the fact that they had each other, with each passing week María became more distressed to see her only daughter staying at home on Saturday nights when most unmarried women her age were at least trying to find a *novio* if not a husband.

(Oh, but María's lectures, while the poor young woman was just trying to mind her own business: lectures about broken hearts and the loneliness of solitude, the stupidity of today's juventud, *squandering their opportunities for life and love, especially the ones who got too many American* cucarachas *in their heads!)*

To please María, Teresa dipped into the crowded, overwrought Miami club scene, singles nights at different venues, and while she occasionally went out on the dates that her mother had cajoled from friends, Teresita had yet to meet anyone, Cuban or not, she thought compatible. ("So what was wrong with that one?" María inevitably asked.) Her mother's continual urgings, it should be said, occasionally got on Teresita's nerves, becoming, at a certain point, something Teresita just didn't want to hear about.

But they had their good times: paid well, living cheaply, Teresita was able to take beautiful María to Italy on a vacation. To Rome, to Florence and Venice, then Naples and Sorrento and back. Her mother loved not only the way Italian men regarded women but the gruff yet kindly vendors in the markets with whom, as during her stay in the Bronx, she could speak Spanish and always be understood. She dissolved in the sunsets, daydreamed in the wisteria-rich gardens, and, touring the ruins of Pompeii, wondered why people bothered to preserve such old things. Roma, in particular, with its self-contained and lively neighborhoods, so reminded María of Havana that she felt completely at home. And she liked the way men gave her daughter the most interested looks, following her every move down the street. "You see," she'd say, "they know how to appreciate you," Teresita simply nodding.

What most surprised María, however, was how she felt after that two-week sojourn when they arrived back in Miami. She couldn't wait to get home, not just to Omar, whom she had left with her next-door neighbor Annabella, but to the city itself, and the familiarity of her neighborhood and house. She'd feel the same when they made their other trips, now and then: to a medical convention in Los Angeles, to a seaside resort along the coast of South Carolina, and to Washington, D.C., where that elegant lady and her daughter acted like happy tourists.

Then back, as always, to the usual routines of their days.

PART V

Oh Yes, That Book

One morning, in the autumn of 1989, while Teresita sat in their kitchen reading *The Miami Herald,* as she always did before heading to the hospital, Omar the cat purring away on her lap, she came across a book review whose subject matter not only caught her attention but made the fine hairs on the back of her neck bristle, as if a ghost had entered the room. The review was of a recently published novel about two Cuban musicians, Cesar and Nestor Castillo, who, as it happened, travel to New York City from Havana in 1949 and end up as walk-on characters on the *I Love Lucy* show, where, by yet another coincidence, they perform a romantic bolero, "Beautiful María of My Soul."

> With exuberant and often erotic detail, *The Mambo Kings Play Songs of Love* serves up enough sex, music, and excitement to keep the pages turning effortlessly. . . . And when it comes to its descriptions of passion, watch out! Just the scenes between Nestor Castillo and his love in Havana, María, left this reviewer reeling . . .

Of course, there was more to that rather euphoric review, but it was to that reference that Teresita kept returning. The familiarity of its story so startled Teresita that she was tempted to tell María, off in the living room performing calisthenics to some morning exercise program. But not wanting to agitate her—would María be happy? Or outraged? Or would she care at all?—she finished that review and, taking note of the fact, listed below the piece, that its author, a certain Oscar Hijuelos (a strange enough name, even for a "Cuban-American who makes his home in New York"), was to appear that next Friday evening at a bookstore in Coral Gables, Teresita decided to go.

For the next few days, while attending to her duties, Teresita remained surprised by her annoyance over the fact that, however it may have happened, her mother's story had, from what she could tell, somehow been co-opted for the sake of a novel. Feeling proprietarily disposed, as most Cubans are about their legacy, she was determined to ascertain by what right the author had to publicize even a "fictional" version of her mother's life, without first seeking permission. It just made Teresita feel as if her mother's privacy had been violated, and while she had gone through any number of machinations about the possibilities of pursuing a lawsuit—even calling up an attorney that someone had once recommended over another matter—once she arrived that evening, having rushed to make it by seven, she found the atmosphere in that bookstore, jammed with hundreds of curious people, Cubans and non-Cubans alike, so reverential and kindly disposed towards this Hijuelos that it somewhat calmed her down.

The author himself seemed rather self-effacing—in fact, a little overwhelmed by the crowd—and why wouldn't he? A balding fellow, more Fred Mertz than Desi Arnaz, of a somewhat stocky build, in glasses and, to judge from his fair skin, blond hair, and vaguely Irish or Semitic face, not very Cuban looking at all, he read aloud from his book *The Mambo Kings Play Songs of Love*, the title of which he had surely taken from the very same LP María put on the phonograph from time to time (driving Teresita crazy). Stopping to make some aside, he attested to the verisimilitude of the novel, which he said he had written out of a pride and love for the unsung generation of pre-Castro Cubans, the sorts of fellows that he, growing up in New York City, had known.

She couldn't judge the quality of the prose, which sounded rather colloquial to her ear—Teresita tended to read the vampire novels of Anne Rice—but the thickly packed audience seemed to appreciate the author's guileless presentation. One section had to do with this drunken musician

Cesar Castillo, known as the Mambo King, holed up in a hotel room in Harlem at the end of his life and dreaming about better times, and the next was a longish recitation of how this character's brother Nestor Castillo had met his wife, a Cuban lady named Delores, in New York in 1950 while nursing all these longings for the love of his life, left back in Cuba, the beautiful María of his soul, for whom he had tormentedly written a song. It was enough to make Teresita tap her low-heeled shoes impatiently on the floor (she was standing in the back), her skin heating up over what she did not know. She experienced not anger, or righteous indignation—he seemed a harmless enough fellow—but she felt annoyed over the intrusion of it all, just the same.

At the conclusion of his reading, the author took questions from the audience, and while some of them were asked in Spanish, usually by the older folks—nicely dressed Cuban ladies, or their husbands—he'd answer in English, which seemed just fine with everyone.

"Why that particular story?" someone asked. "You mentioned earlier something about the two brothers, the Castillos, going on the *I Love Lucy* show. How is that?"

"Well," he began, "growing up, that's a show we all liked in my home; for us, it was Desi Arnaz, and not Lucille Ball, who was the star." There was laughter, nods of approval from the audience. "You've got to remember that it was the only program on television that featured a Cuban in those days. . . . But, on top of that, I was always wondering about those guys who'd turn up on the show—you know, those walk-on characters who'd always just arrived from Cuba; they reminded me of what we used to go through at home in New York; that's what got me started."

"But did you know of any Cubans who were on that show?" the same person, who seemed to be a journalist of some kind, asked, following up.

"Yeah, sort of. I mean, I heard some stories about that kind of thing from time to time . . . and, well, what can I say, I just ran with it . . ."

Someone else raised a hand: the question, having nothing to do with the novel, concerned the author's opinion of Fidel Castro and the Cuban revolution, "which, as you know, Señor Hijuelos, has been a tragedy for us all."

"What happened seems unfair and unjust," he answered gingerly. "We all know that. I have a lot of cousins who left and stayed with us in our apartment—so I know, that, yeah, it was a tragedy," he concluded, in his New Yorker's way, quickly pointing to another hand. It was Teresita's.

"I understand you have this song that you mention in the book, 'La bella María de mi alma.' Are you aware that it was a very well known bolero back in the 1950s?"

"Yeah, I did know that, but there are so many boleros from that epoch I could have chosen. I mean to say that it was one of those songs I heard growing up, and it just never got out of my head."

"But surely you must know that your story, with that song performed on the *Lucy* show, the *real Lucy* show, which I have seen many times, by the way, sounds suspiciously like it was taken from real life. Is that correct?"

"That's a complicated question," the writer answered, his face turning rather red as he went into some high-sounding *miércoles* about literary technique, and the kind of pastiche he employed, mixing up reality and fantasies—"which is what any novel is really about."

Listening patiently, Teresita nodded. "So I take it that you must have heard from somebody about the Castillo brothers, yes?"

"Yeah, stories—they lived in my neighborhood, in fact."

"But did you hear about any María? Was she a real person in your mind?"

"Only in the way that I imagined her from hearing that song."

"Oh, I see," Teresita said. "I thank you for your answering me."

"Well, thank you, and, by the way, what do you do for a living here in Miami?" This was a question he sometimes asked of members of the audience.

"Soy doctora," Teresita told him with tremendous dignity, many in

the room nodding with appreciation of the fact that she was yet another *cubana* who had done well for herself.

A few others inquired about the music in the book, and a few just thanked the author for having made the Cubans proud (such compliments were always his greatest pleasure). Soon enough, the store's owner went to the podium and announced that Mr. Hijuelos would be signing his novel in the back of the store. It took Teresita about twenty minutes, a copy of that book in hand, to make her way to his table because so many people, Cubans in particular, were asking for inscriptions, often in Spanish. "Make it out this way: *'Para la bella Tía María,'* please," or for a cousin or a niece, so many Marías being around. Teresita had to admit that, despite his harried manner, he seemed not to mind taking the time to get each one right, and he seemed friendly enough: "How wonderful, my mother was from Holguín, like yours!" he would say. Or "Yeah, I spent time in Cuba, out in Oriente, when I was a kid, before Fidel of course." Accumulating business cards from many, he took pains to sign each book carefully.

Finally, Teresita found herself handing her copy over to him.

"And who should I make this out to?" he asked.

She smiled. "My name is Teresa, but please make it out to *la Señora María García,* okay?"

"Sure."

"I haven't had the chance to read your book, but you should know something," she went on, leaning over him as he wrote.

"Uh-huh?"

"My mother is the María of that song, the one you put in your story. She was very close to Nestor Castillo."

He looked up, blushing. "Seriously?"

"Yes," she said. "And I will let you know what I think once I've read it, okay?"

"Sure, why not?" he said affably enough, though his expression was not happy.

"Have you a card, so that I can be in touch with you?" she then asked.

"Not really, but here," he replied, and he scribbled out an address on a piece of paper and gave it to Teresita.

She looked it over. "This is your publisher's address, I see. Wouldn't it be better if I had one for your home?"

He wrote that down, then stood up to shake her hand, which she appreciated, and with that Dr. Teresa García gave him her card and, thanking him again, added: "As I said, I will let you know what I think." With that she went off, but not before picking up a few books for the sick kids on her ward, and then she got into her Toyota and drove over to Northwest Terrace, where she spent half the night reading that novel most carefully.

And the author? Satisfied by the evening's turnout, and gratified to have met so many nice Cubans, while standing outside the bookstore having a smoke, he felt more than a little rattled by what Teresita had told him about the "real" María. He'd already been sued by a female bandleader who claimed her moral reputation had been damaged by the book, just because of a scene in which Cesar Castillo ravaged one of her musicians on a potato sack in a basement hallway of a Catskill resort where the Mambo Kings had been playing. And, though he'd made the whole thing up, he truly regretted the fact that he, for the sake of realism, had carelessly used the real bandleader's name. The lawsuit had come and gone quickly, dismissed by a judge as a frivolous claim, but it had caused him enough distress that he didn't want to go through something like it again, and surely not over the María of his book, whose sex scenes with Nestor Castillo, if the truth be told, were decidedly raunchy, though, he thought, presented with a redeeming romantic touch.

FORTY-EIGHT

That night, after coming home with her heavy bag of hospital folders, and after sitting with María and watching television for an hour while sipping whiskey, Teresita, leaving her mother on the couch and kissing her good night, slipped back into her room, past a hallway filled with photographs from the epoch of her mother's glory, and finally collapsed into bed with that book, *The Mambo Kings Play Songs of Love*. She actually liked aspects of the story at first, even enjoyed reading about the brash circumstances that brought the Castillo brothers to New York; enjoyed, in fact, and curiously so, the prologue, which involved the fictional character of Eugenio Castillo, Nestor's son, from whom, it seemed, much of the story seemed to emanate. (His voice seemed so earnest, she wondered if this Eugenio, in fact, was a real person.)

Of course, she was most anxious to peruse the sections recounting the romance of Nestor and beautiful María, and coming to them after some one hundred pages, she found herself somewhat pleased and repulsed by what she read: One evening, Nestor, so sensitive, so noble, so tormented by his feelings about the sadness of life, encounters beautiful María on a Havana street in the aftermath of an argument she has had with her overbearing, indignantly disposed *novio*—not Ignacio, of course, but someone like him, and Teresita wondered how the author might have ascertained such a premise. She did not mind the portrayal of a ravishing beautiful María at that point, and, even as she felt a humming annoyance in her gut, she somewhat liked the idea of seeing her mother's life, however altered, being told in so attentive and mythical a manner; that is, until she began reading a section, tucked away in the thick

307

texture of prose (*"too many words!" was her opinion*) that began with the sentence "She liked it every which way: from behind, in her mouth, between her breasts, and in her tight bottom." (These words she underlined.)

From there the text went on to detail, in a rather heated manner, the kinds of sexual caprices between Nestor and María that, whether true or not, were not rightfully meant for the world to share. Able to take only so much of such high-blown hyperbole about Nestor's "agonizingly long and plump" *pinga*, with which the author seemed obsessed, Teresita, to put it bluntly, could barely bring herself to read on. The book to that point had already lingered too much on the supposed sexual grandeur of the Mambo Kings; in fact, the filthy-minded author seemed to dwell excessively on scenes in which a woman's mere presence could provoke the grandest of erections in its characters. And because María, with a few drinks in her, and with a candidness for which *cubanas* are famous, used to tell Teresita, as she got older, that Nestor was as long and as wide as "any innocent woman could ever take," Teresita could not help wondering about how some distant New York City author had tapped into such apparently truthful and intimate information and had, on top of it, the nerve to put it all in a book.

IT TOOK TERESITA A FEW NIGHTS TO GET THROUGH THAT NOVEL; she still preferred those vampire stories, of course, and yet, whether that book was good or bad, her annoyance had, in any case, so tainted the experience of reading it that she could hardly find anything redeeming about its story. Altogether, with her sad duties at the hospital and with her own loneliness—about Cuban men, she didn't have a clue as to what "it" would be like—this book's sudden existence amounted to one hell of a shameful headache: her mother's life, after all, was being aired like dirty laundry. Spending the next few weeks mulling over her options, and not breathing a word to María, her daughter kept thinking of one thing: to sue that presumptuous *hijo de puta*. She even left the hospital at lunchtime one afternoon to visit with the attorney, a certain Alfredo Zabalas, whom she had spoken to before. But she did this reluctantly, for Teresita wondered if, by doing so, she would be opening a quite public can of worms. The lawyer, on the other hand, hearing her tale and seeing it as a clear case of defamation, seemed very interested, almost indignant on María's behalf.

"The truth remains that, whether it's fiction or not, an unkind reader might read that book and interpret the character of your mother as something of a whore," he said. Then he wrote down some notes. "You might make a nice amount of money over this matter," he said. And that held some appeal for Teresita. Her mother didn't have a retirement fund, and she always worried about what might happen to María if, for whatever reason, Teresita fell out of the picture. *Being around dying children will do that to you.*

Nevertheless, as this gentleman began to detail the process of filing such a claim, and all the paperwork and fees and processes involved— among them the eventual deposition of both the author and her mother—Dr. Teresa, a most private sort herself, began to have second thoughts. It just seemed so tawdry and soul destroying, and, in any event, just to sit for an hour in that office depressed her. And so she left it with Mr. Zabalas that she would have to think it over, as much for her own sake as to spare her mother from the inconveniences of a long, protracted hassle, *un lío,* as they say in *español.*

Then, after a while, Teresita cooled down a bit. The book was already out there, and, besides, it occurred to her that hardly anyone knew her mother was beautiful María. Who on earth would equate the sexually voracious María of that novel with the real beautiful María, who wore curlers in her hair each morning as she went out to discard the trash and get her newspapers in Northwest Terrace? Who in their neighborhood read "literary" novels anyway, or ever stopped to consider the book pages of *El Nuevo Herald?* Not Annabella, their next-door neighbor, or Beatriz of Havana from down the street, or Esmeralda, baker of chicken pies, her mother's canasta partner. Such books just floated above them like birds, without ever landing. The Cubans they knew just weren't into that kind of thing, and so, Teresita pondered, even if some of her friends might remember her mother's claim to have been the inspiration of that song, it was still absolutely possible that the novel would come and go without anyone from their little world even noticing. That notion calmed her somewhat.

And the author himself, she remembered, hadn't seemed a bad sort. He was a little uptight perhaps, but apparently he took the deepest pride in his Cuban roots, and, in Teresita's mind, that was almost enough to outweigh the incredible transgression. Yet, no matter how much she circled around the notion that the author hadn't really meant any harm, that his María was an invention, she wanted to hear an apology from this Hijuelos himself. So, as the weeks went by, she started to call his New York city telephone number, leaving a half dozen messages without once hearing any response. And that was nearly enough for her to reconsider the legal approach once again. But then, one Saturday afternoon, while María was off somewhere with her friend Gladys, Teresita, considering it a nagging duty, dialed him again.

He picked up this time. There was loud mambo music playing in the background, which he turned down.

"*Señor* Hijuelos?"

"Yes?"

"I don't know if you remember me, but I am Dr. García, the daughter of María—we met a few months ago in Coral Gables."

"Oh yes, of course. How are you?"

"I'm fine. But do you know that you're a very hard fellow to get ahold of? Did you receive my messages?"

"Yes, I did. But I've been away. I meant to get back to you."

"Okay, but the reason I'm calling you is to discuss your book. I will tell you, I was not too happy about your depiction of my mother."

He sighed or lit a cigarette—she could not tell which.

"Look, Dr. García, as I told everybody . . . as I tell everybody, the book is mostly just invented. Sure there are some things I took from life, but I promise you that the character of María, for example, just came into my head from hearing that song."

"I see, and have you ever considered what someone like my mother, the real beautiful María, would feel if she read your book when you have her doing so many things that are improper?"

"Look, I never even thought the book would get published, and, well, her character was really about the song."

"But the sex? Why did you have to put so much in? Did you even consider that someone real might be on the other end?"

"To be honest," he said, after a moment's silence, "if I ever thought that it would offend someone, maybe I would have done some things differently. But it is a fiction, after all."

"Come on," she said. "We both know that you must have gotten some parts of my mother's love affair with Nestor Castillo from somewhere. Isn't that the case?"

"Okay, okay. All I knew is what I was told, just bare bones, by one of the guys in the book, Cesar Castillo," he finally admitted. "He was the superintendent of my building, and, well, he liked to tell stories, that's all. The sex was just intended as a kind of music, like saxophones playing during a recording. You know, an effect."

There was a momentary silence, during which Teresita coiled the telephone cord in her hand.

"Whatever you call it, you should know that such things can hurt people's feelings. Do you understand that?"

"Yeah," he said. "But what do you want me to do?"

"Well, I will tell you this, Mr. Hijuelos. I was very close to making this a legal matter, but I am not that way. No, what I want from you is to make an apology to my mother one day, like any decent *cubano* would. The next time you come to Miami, I want you to see for yourself that there is someone on the other end, and not just some anonymous *fulana* whose reputation you can disparage. Will you do that, for me?"

"If that would make you happy, yes."

"Good, I expect you to honor this request, do you hear me?"

"Of course."

"*Hasta luego* then," Teresita said, hanging up.

Somewhat relieved—for in the interim yet another lawsuit, involving his book's cover artwork, had been mounted against him—he felt nothing less than pure gratitude that Dr. Teresa García, though obviously (and perhaps rightly) peeved, had taken what he considered the high road. She was surely sparing him—and them both—a lot of grief. As for Teresita? Satisfied that she had made a statement in defense of her mother's honor, Teresita, who had been trying to drop some weight lately, got dressed in a blue jogging outfit and took off for a half an hour's amble along her neighborhood's humid, sweat-inducing, tree-rich streets.

And that was the last of it, for a long time.

FORTY-NINE

For her part, María remained blissfully unaware that such a book existed. Teresita kept her copy hidden away, with certain pages clipped together, and did not say a word about it to her mother. But it was only a matter of time before María inevitably heard about its existence. Her former writing teacher, *el Señor* Luis Castellano, with whom María dined from time to time, had, while keeping up with the latest literary trends, particularly works by Cuban Americans, read the novel himself and, knowing a little about María's connection to that song, went to the trouble of buying her not the novel itself but the audiocassette tapes of that book, as read by the actor E. G. Marshall, in English, of course. (Even Teresita had to scratch her head over that one.) Fortunately, when María finally got around to playing those cassettes one Saturday afternoon, her first impressions were very good: just to hear Nestor Castillo's name spoken aloud made her gasp, and that book's early mentions of the song Nestor had written for her, "Beautiful María of My Soul," naturally piqued her interest. But altogether, though her English had improved out of necessity, as some of her pupils at the dance studio didn't speak much Spanish, just to listen to its prose was rough going.

She could follow enough of it to get a general sense of a story, but with the book's endless references to postwar American popular culture and (for María) its arcane nods at writers like Edgar Allan Poe—*"For me, my father's gentle rapping on Ricky Ricardo's door has always been a call from the beyond, as in Dracula films, or films of the walking dead, in which spirits ooze out from behind tombstones and through the cracked windows and rotted floors of gloomy antique halls . . ."*—it may as well have been rendered in Mandarin Chinese as far as she was concerned. And when she pushed the fast-forward button and came across these lines about Cesar Castillo's enormous *pinga,* which *"flourished upwards like the spreading top branches of a tree, or, he once thought while looking at a map of the United States, like the course of the Mississippi River and its tributaries,"* María, while finding that just as opaque, understood enough to ascertain that she was not hearing a recitation of the Bible. Nevertheless, she stuck with it for several hours, mostly skipping through it and searching for mentions of herself—*"Now he remembers and sighs: the long approach to the farm along the riverbank and forest—"* (skip, fast-forward)—*"They had their picture taken in front of a movie poster advertising the Betty Grable film* Moon over Miami—*"* (skip, fast-forward)—*"The night of the dance, Delores was thinking about what her sister—"* (skip, fast-forward)—until, at long last, she stumbled upon the line that went *"My name is María—"* And with that she made herself a drink, settled on the couch, and did her best to slip into the hearing of a story that she never thought would be told.

A few hours later, when Teresita had come home after catching up on some work at the hospital and she saw María's puzzled, dreamy expression, the first thing she said was *"Pero, Mamá,* didn't I tell you not to listen to those tapes!"

"But, *mi vida,"* María said, "from what I could tell, it's not so bad a story. *Es que no entiendo inglés muy bien.* It's just that I can't understand English that well. It's a pity, yes?"

"Yes, Mama, but you have your ways," Teresita said. The truth be told, in those moments, at least, she was grateful for the fact that María had never bothered to go to school to improve her English.

"Have you read that book?" María asked.

"Well," Teresita said, and she nodded. "Yes, I have."

"It's a little dirty—*es un poquito sucio*—yes?" she asked with all sincerity.

"Only now and then, but, Mama, you shouldn't trouble yourself about it." Then, seeing that her mother seemed a little low, she added, sitting beside her, "Besides, the María in that book isn't really like you."

"But isn't she beautiful?"

"Oh, yes, very beautiful."

And that made María, who had struggled through that maze of English, smile. The bawdiness of its sex and the details of the story may have passed over her head, but not the notion that it was about her, and in a most flattering way. Now that she was almost sixty, if anything, her vanity spiked, María felt rather proud about the matter, and if she had any regrets at all, it was that so few people knew that she was the María both of that song and now—oh, how proud Lázaro would have been—of a book.

While the Miami newspapers sometimes wrote about its author, who had lately won some kind of big-deal prize (which made the Cubans jubilant with pride), the more important thing in María's life came down to her mounting involvement with that scarecrow Luis, with whom she not only occasionally dined but also went off now and then for the afternoon to an undisclosed location where, Teresita assumed, they had what she liked to gingerly think of as "relations."

Thin as a starving *guajiro* and with a mortally wounded air, he must surely have been overwhelmed by the voluptuousness of María's ripened body, and yet during his visits to the household, when he would sit quietly with them in the evenings as María watched her favorite shows, Teresita remained amazed by her mother's serene attentiveness to the man, as if, indeed, he had given her something to be extremely grateful for: affection. Homely as any Cuban man could be (Luis, in one of his running jokes, referred to himself and María as "Beauty and the Beast"), he must have been doing something right, for, if Teresita was not mistaken, María had taken to doting on Luis and with the kind of tenderness she had usually reserved for Omar, their cat. Was it some autumnal rush of love? Or just the companionable dalliance of two poetic souls finding ways to amuse one another? Whatever the case, despite Teresita's own loneliness, beautiful María, doused with perfume and floating through life in clouds of smoke, seemed happy enough in those days.

. . .

EVENTUALLY, TERESITA GOT TO MEET THE AUTHOR AGAIN, WHEN he returned to Miami the following autumn to promote a paperback edition of that work, and this time, at the same venue in Coral Gables, she could not help but notice that this Hijuelos, in the blush of his apparent success, seemed far more world-weary and solemn than she remembered. Somewhat sheepish about facing yet another crowd, and spotting Dr. Teresita with beautiful María by her side in the audience, he made a last-minute change and chose to read a few selections that, while mentioning María in passing, were sweetly clean—spick-and-span, in fact. In one, he told of the Castillo brothers' meeting with Desi Arnaz and Lucy on the night, in 1955, when they first performed Nestor's song of love, and then he read from selections that were like sound poems. Once again, the evening followed form—a Q & A, a signing, and afterwards, as he had agreed with Teresita, the author finally met the still startlingly good looking and well preserved María, who, in addition to an ebony comb in her pulled-back hair, wore a dark felt-buttoned, hip-hugging dress of considerable décolletage. Once Teresita made their introductions, María, looking the jittery author over, said, "So you are the one?" And, as an aside, whispered, as she tugged at his arm, *"Sabes, joven, que me debes mucho"*—"You know that you owe me a lot."

Shortly they went over to a Spanish restaurant a block or two away, where, as it happened, the affable media personality Don Francisco of the popular *Sábado Gigante* television show, which María often watched, had turned up with a small entourage. Walking in, they saw him, formidably tall and broad shouldered in a blue serge suit, standing by the piano bar, crooning, a drink in hand, an old Cuban bolero, *"Siempre en mi corazón,"* into a microphone. That very fact, along with the decorum and stolid Spaniard's gilded ambience of the restaurant, and with the way that Don Francisco, a consummate showman, bowed, winking at them as they passed inside, impressed the hell out of María and, most fortunately, put her into a good frame of mind. She may have been a *guajira* in her former life, but as she made her way to their table, María exuded nothing less than an amber dignity. This is what happened: After they ordered the house specialty paella, and a few bottles of good champagne, the evening unfolded agreeably enough. Having recently flown to Sacramento, California, for a deposition regarding the aforementioned second lawsuit, the author had been quiet at first, a certain formality and carefulness attending his every word. But once it became clear that neither Teresita nor María bore him any animosity, and as the champagne lightened spirits, the conversation, mediated by Teresa, who switched from English to Spanish, veered quickly to matters that for María, after so many years, had weighed on her heart.

"*Mira, chico,* so did you know *los hermanos* Castillo?" she asked him at a certain point.

"Yes, ma'am," he answered. "I knew Nestor when I was very little, but Cesar much more."

"*Y Cesar, ¿está vivo?*"

"No, *señora,* he passed away about ten years ago. In a hotel room in Harlem."

Yes, of course, thought Teresita, *just like in his book.*

"A pity," María said. "They were both very handsome men—and wonderful musicians." Then: "And Nestor's family? What can you tell me about them? He had children, yes?"

"Yes." He nodded. "A boy and a girl—they're now grown. His daughter's name is Leticia—she's married now with three daughters of her own."

"And the son? What do you know of him?"

"Eugenio Castillo? I still see him. He was my best friend, growing up. We were at his *papi*'s funeral together, way back when. He's a public high school teacher now."

"And does he have a family?"

"No, he never married. *Es soltero.*"

"And you? *¿Estás casado?*"

"No, I'm not," he told her, looking down.

And that made María glance over at Teresa; then she whispered into her daughter's ear, Teresita smiling. (Later, as they left, when he asked her what that was about, Teresita told him: "She said it was too bad you're so bald.")

As María kept staring at this Hijuelos, he could read in her eyes what he read in many Cuban eyes: "a strange fellow." His New York manner was so pronounced, and his body language so unfluid and earthbound, that, no matter how much Spanish he used, the waiters continued to address him in English. Teresita, somewhat of an outsider herself, reading his weariness, started feeling an empathy for him. And, at one point, she made a toast: *"Para nosotros cubanos!"*

Then a lull came over the conversation, the three munching away.

"Bueno," María began, finally breaking the silence. "You—*Señor* Hijuelos—are probably wondering what I think about your book"— *"librito"* she called it—*"verdad?"* He nodded, and she sipped from a glass of champagne. "If you must know, I found it *muy, muy interesante."* She laughed. "And *muy sucio* sometimes! Very filthy! But, I will tell you this, my real story was very different from what you wrote. I came from *el campo del* Pinar del Río, really from nothing. I was the daughter of *guajiros, una analfabeta,* in fact, and whatever I have now, I came by through the grace of God and the sweat of my brow. But my greatest blessing is this one here, *mi chiquita,* a doctor," she said, and she kissed her daughter's hand. "Even if her *abuelo* couldn't read a word of anything, she became a doctor, and in a country where she didn't know at first *ni un pío de inglés!* Not even one bit of English. Can you imagine that? Forget all the sex, which is only air, that's what you should put in a book someday, *sabes?"*

He nodded again.

"As for that *buenmoso* Nestor Castillo, I will tell you this: I don't regret that I knew him, and if I regret anything—"

"Mami," she heard her daughter interjecting.

"—it's that we didn't stay together. But it was my fault, understand. I was too worried about comforts. And if you are alert and a real thinker, which you seem to be, you will also know that certain Cubans of my generation were destined to be *muy jodido*—fucked—anyway because of the revolution. . . . Even if Nestor had stayed with me in Cuba and we had made a home for ourselves and had a family, we would have ended up in the States, leaving everything behind." She paused to sip some champagne. "And sometimes I wonder if he would still be alive if I'd married him those years ago and come with him to Miami or New York. Either way, it would have been our destiny to live away from our *patria*—*Cuba*. Does that, *Señor* Hijuelos, mean anything to you?"

"Of course it does," he said.

"Then you know that it brings a sadness of its own."

She became subdued, staring off into a corner of the room, where a chandelier glowed and music emanated from an electric piano. By then Don Francisco had long since left, and few patrons remained. That's when beautiful María caught herself speaking, as she would put it, *miércoles*.

"Can you tell me something, *chico*?" she asked. "Do you remember Nestor as a happy or a sad man?"

"He seemed nice enough, a quiet fellow, used to sit outside the stoop of my building with his brother, handing out quarters to us kids."

"But did he ever say anything to you about Cuba?"

"No, *señora*, he kept that to himself."

"I see. And nothing about me?"

"No, I was just a kid—why would he?" he said, shrugging, and though María was about to say "But you know that I never wanted to hurt him in any way," she thought better of that and kept it to herself.

The end of the dinner proceeded, with scorched flan desserts served and *tacitas* of espresso. For his part, the author, so wary of legal matters, was happy that they, as a trio, seemed to have become rather friendly. He'd almost forgotten about his conversation with Teresita the year before when, as a waiter cleared the table, she steered him toward the fulfillment of a certain promise, saying, while María was away using the bathroom, "Isn't there something you'd like to say to my mother?"

"About?"

"An apology."

319

"Of course."

And then, when she had returned, without looking María directly in the eye, he said, "There's something I have to tell you, *señora*."

"Tell me."

"If there's anything in my book that offended you in any way, for whatever reason, for all of that I sincerely apologize, *señora. Con todo mi corazón.*"

María was a little surprised by this; it was nothing she had required or expected. "*Ay,* but why say that? All such things, after all, even books, are soon forgotten. *La vida es sueño,* after all, okay? But if it will make you feel better, I will accept your apologies. I promise you."

With that, María reached across the table and took hold of his wrists. "But you must promise not to forget me. You are as good as family now, and as family"—she made the sign of the cross over him—"you must be loyal, understand?" And with that she surprised Teresita, slapping the author's right cheek. "Don't forget it, okay?"

"I won't," he said, feeling rather startled himself.

Then they parted: Mr. Hijuelos, who had paid the bill, heading back to his hotel by taxi, and beautiful María driving home with her daughter in their Toyota.

FIFTY

María's opinion of the author was that, though too "Americanized," he was a decent enough fellow: he helped that notion by sending her a gift basket of chocolates and dried fruits the next Christmas, but beyond that he had become but a recent memory and his book some odd artifact that they'd nearly forgotten. That is, until the waning months of 1991, when they heard that a film called *The Mambo Kings* had been shot in Hollywood and was slated to open the Miami International Film Festival that coming February. This, of course, sent up red flags with Teresita, who, having read about it in the newspapers, called him in New York to request, at the very least, that he provide three tickets for the premiere—for her mother, herself, and Luis. Though most of her calls were swallowed up by the netherworld of his answering machine, someone from the film's promotion company eventually forwarded, by overnight mail, an envelope with their tickets for the opening (though without any for the afterparty, it should be noted).

And so it was that beautiful María, Teresita, and Luis, he in a nice dark suit and looking very dapper indeed, arrived at the premiere that February evening, the seventh, navigating through the crowds of press and onlookers onto a red-carpeted walkway unnoticed, not a single camera flashing at their approach. The flashbulbs were reserved for the stars, among them the queen of Cuban song, Celia Cruz, who drew the greatest applause from her devoted fans behind the barricades as she got out of her white stretch limousine, a blinding flood of lights exploding around her. They had paused in the lobby as the other stars came in, but then, discouraged from lingering by some charmless security officers, were rushed inside to take their seats, the audience around them quite nicely turned out, and, as the papers would later put it, an air of anticipation buzzing through the hall.

Then the houselights dimmed. A musical prelude, a shot of Havana, a sonorous trumpet playing, and boom—the interior of a Havana nightclub, with a mambo troupe gyrating onstage and then the outraged Cesar Castillo, played by the handsome actor Armand Assante, charging through a dressing room and approaching, rather roughly, a dancer, beautiful María, portrayed by the gorgeous Talisa Soto, whom he accuses of being a whore for the way she had thrown off his younger brother Nestor. Her gangster *novio* and his cronies intercede, and Cesar ends up with his throat cut in an alley, wherein a bereft, perhaps guilt-ridden beautiful María kneels before him. While he should be bleeding to death, despite a kerchief wrapped around his neck, it was Dr. Teresa's opinion that, in real life, he wouldn't have long to live, and María's opinion that no such thing had ever happened, though she enjoyed the fact that she was being played by so dazzling a woman. Tenderly the film's beautiful María begs Cesar Castillo to take Nestor away to America, and so the plot's mechanism begins, for the next scenes are of a well recovered Cesar Castillo, looking sharp in a sporty shirt and shades, dancing the mambo down the narrow aisle of a bus headed north to New York, a charming moment, with a solemn, forlorn, tightly wound Nestor, played by Antonio Banderas, no doubt thinking gloomily about María. Later, while settled in New York in the early 1950s, the brothers form their orchestra the Mambo Kings. And along the way, Nestor is shown working on his bolero "Beautiful María of My Soul," which, as eventually performed by the brothers in a nightclub and later on the *I Love Lucy* show, in an episode invented for the film, bore little resemblance to the bolero which María's former love, Nestor Castillo, had written and recorded with his brother Cesar and actually sung on the real *Lucy* show those many years before.

It was both an exhilarating and a nerve-racking experience for María to wait and wait for her character to appear again—she does so as a dreamy, sea-soaked memory of Nestor and herself carousing on a beach (she liked that)—but from then on that other beautiful María hardly turned up again at all, save in some photographs. Two scenes María found particularly painful to watch: Nestor's meeting with his future wife, Delores, at a bus stop while Nestor happens to be working on that *canción*—which Teresita recalled from the book—a bit of rekindled envy passing through María's soul, and the film's depiction of Nestor's death in a car wreck while driving back from a job in New Jersey through a snowstorm, which had been surely taken from the real Nestor's life. It was too much for María to bear, even if she knew they were just actors, and handsome ones at that; she got up to use the ladies' room, where, after urinating, she stood before the mirror to retouch her lipstick.

She liked the film well enough, but she wondered why they couldn't have done something more in the beginning with Nestor and María in Havana, just walking the streets and sitting in the *placitas*, holding hands; or portrayed the way he, with his head in the clouds, used to sing up into her window, and how they'd find musicians in the alleys and courtyards of Havana, Nestor playing his trumpet and making her feel proud; or even a scene of the way they'd race up the stairways to his friend's *solar*, unable to keep their hands off each other—that would have been nice too. Then, thinking about what went on in that bed—nothing that could be shown in a Hollywood movie—she flew headlong into a vision of the life they might have lived had they stayed together in Havana, maybe raising a little brood of children, or maybe living in the States, in a house with a nice backyard, Nestor, a success or not, as her husband, doting on their children and, even in his sixties, ravishing her nightly with love.

She reached into her purse for her cigarettes. As she lit one, distant music throbbed through the walls, a trumpet solo rising above, voices singing; and then, just like that, in the blink of her mascara eyes, as she dabbed her face with a dampened hand towel and sighed, she saw in the mirror's reflection Nestor Castillo himself, as gloriously handsome as he was in his youth in Havana, in a white guayabera and linen slacks, standing some ten feet behind her against the Italian-tiled ladies' room walls.

"¿En qué piensas, Nestor?" she asked him. "Are you happy?" (And behind that, María, unable to forget the love-filled afternoons at the Payret, felt his fingers sinking inside her panties once again.) Nestor just smiled, and rather sadly so, in the way, as María had been taught, lost souls do, envying earthly life. "But the movie, what do you think?" she said to him. "It's about you!" As an apparition trapped in some other world, he could not comment on such tawdry things, and when Nestor finally spoke, with hardly any voice at all, and so softly, he told her: *"¿Pero, no sabes que te quería?"* To which she answered, "And I loved you, *mucho, mucho. . . . "* Just then, however, as Nestor seemed about to step towards her, two women in tight, slinky dresses, talking about how they would die to be fucked by the actor playing Cesar Castillo, strutted in, and with that, in the blink of an eye, Nestor vanished, his sad smile, on that soulful *guapito* face, as beguiling as Maria remembered. (*Ay, pero Nestor.*)

Reeling, she got back to her seat in time to watch a distraught Cesar Castillo, unable to perform anywhere since Nestor's death, milling about the Manhattan club he had opened in his late brother's memory. Nestor's widow, Delores, wanting him to get back to the passion that is in his blood, implores him to go onstage and sing, yes, that song about the other love of Nestor's life, "Beautiful María of My Soul." Once that music starts, with all its flourishes, though the emotional logic of that moment escaped Teresita, and even María thought the wife surely had some *cucarachas* in her head to make such a request, Cesar agrees, and, as he belts out the movie version of Nestor's song of longing for María, in a filmic sleight of hand, Nestor, in a white tuxedo, reappears magically by his brother's side, as if he had indeed been resurrected from the dead.

Maria trembled, then sighed.

Afterwards, the principals were brought onstage and introduced, among them the author himself, who put on a hammy show of blowing kisses out to the audience. *"Por Dios,* who does he think he is, Marlon Brando?" Teresita asked her mother. And once the actors had taken their bows and the theater emptied, Teresita, María, and Luis made their way to the Versailles restaurant to eat a dinner of hearty Cuban fare and discuss the film. Luis's favorite parts featured the character that Celia Cruz played, not just for her performance but because she was the only Cuban who had a major role in it. Teresita was grateful that the film exhibited restraint when it came to the love scenes—it was far less randy than the book—and she thought the sexy actors playing the brothers were exhilarating to watch. As for María? Had she been one of the celebrities interviewed by the press afterwards she would have summarized her reaction with a simple phrase: *"Fue muy bonito"*—"It was very nice." But, the truth be told, there was something about the experience of watching the *Mambo Kings* movie that had left her feeling a little glum. It was if she had been dropped into a dream in which some other version of herself had become nothing more than a watered-down walk-on character in some fantastic show, as if she, the real María, who had just peered into the eyes of Nestor Castillo, had yet to really exist as far as the world was concerned.

FIFTY-ONE

She'd eventually get her just dues, however: not money but a modicum of recognition. After the film had been released in Miami, a Spanish-language radio station out of Hialeah, WCMQ, had queried its listeners about which version of "Beautiful María of My Soul"—the original, from 1955, or the one composed for the movie—was the better. Opinions were divided along generational lines—the older listeners, having their own memories, preferred the song as it had been written, while the younger folks voted, almost universally, for the one performed in the film. Along the way, while discussing the movie itself, the host of a nostalgia show entitled *Cuando Cuba Era Cuba,* in recalling that he had once met the Castillo brothers in Havana, wondered on air if anyone out in the listening audience happened to know anything about the woman for whom the original bolero had been composed. ("By all means," the pitch went, "if you have information, please call in.")

That query brought in responses by the drove; apparently there were more than just a few women out in south Florida's radio land, *cubanas* all, who called the station claiming to be none other than that grand beauty herself. Out in Northwest Terrace one morning, it happened that María, while preparing to head out to her dance studio, heard the following, as she was removing curlers from her hair.

"*Muy buenos días.* My name, of course, is María. I know that everyone is wondering who beautiful María is, and, well, I should tell you, *señores y señoras,* that it is me. I met Nestor Castillo, who in the movie *Los Mambo Kings* was played by that *guapo* Antonio Banderas, when I was a young and veerrrry beautiful woman. Yes, that's true. . . . I was on my

326

way to meet my *papi* at the Gallego Society in Havana, and walking along the Paseo when my heel broke. And while I was bending over to pick it up, I saw Nestor, so handsome, so elegant, crouching down to get it for me. Well, while he handed over that heel and looked at me with his beautiful eyes, I knew that there was no resisting him. And so we became—how should an *abuela* put it?—lovers, hee, hee, hee."

Another call:

"*Señoras y señores, soy la Señora María Pena,* and, *veramente,* I am a woman of late middle age now, but in my time, when I was *una pollita,* I frequented the clubs of Havana. I wasn't one of those young ladies of easy persuasion to whom any man could suggest anything and win her favors—I would never sleep with a man outside of matrimony, do you understand that? But, I will tell you that men were attracted to me like flies to honey, and these two young Mambo Kings, I swear to you, were no different. Well, one night I happened to be in a club called the Eight Ball of Remedios when these two musicians, the Castillo brothers, and their little combo turned up. One of them, the older one—Cesar, I believe he was called—was very handsome but so arrogant and full of himself that he held no interest for me. I will tell you anyway, in all modesty, that he liked me a lot—and kept smiling my way—because I was very beautiful *y tenía una figura fabulosa,* round in all the right places, *un cuerpo* that left men dizzy to look at me. . . . But then his brother Nestor, *mi amorcito,* came out holding a trumpet, and I can tell you it makes me burst with delight to remember *que lindo* he was, like a prince and not just any musician. And so refined and delicate in his movements that I nearly died with desire just looking at him. . . . I watched him all night—and Nestorito certainly, and I mean certainly, noticed me. . . . Afterwards he came over to my table, but so shyly, to tell me that my smiles had made him happy. *Y bueno,* after that he sat down right next to me, and we got to know each other a little; and that very night, after a bit of pleasant conversation, he looked deeply into my eyes, and, like a Valentino, declared that I was the kind of girl he might love. Well, the rest I cannot tell you, as young children might be listening, but

I will only say this: when you hear that *canción, 'La bella María de mi alma,'* that María was me."

That same morning, despite the impossibility of more than one beautiful María existing, still others vied for that role. Bemused, the program host took the calls good-naturedly enough, for there seemed to be no end to the number of late middle-aged *cubanas* who wanted to believe they were truly María. Oh, they met Nestor while strolling along the Malecón, or in the Cementerio de Colón, or out at the dog track; or they bumped into him in an arcade. There were so many claimants that the host began to have fun assigning these Marías numbers: "Here, on the line, we have María *número siete.*"

After a while, María, listening to that program over several mornings, finally lost her patience with that whole business and decided that she just had to come forward with her story. She had, after all, photographs of herself and Nestor to offer as proof, as well as a dozen faded letters he had sent her from New York in those days. And so María, in that atmosphere of hoopla—for everyone in Miami was still talking about that movie—called the station, but somewhat reluctantly, for even those years later the very thought of Nestor and what could have been still passed through her heart as a wistful lament.

A telephone interview with a producer, a nice young *cubana* named Estelle, followed a few days afterwards, and, short of describing Nestor's *pinga* in marvelous detail, María could not have been more persuasive. And so as a lark and a possible amusement for the listeners of that show, for in a realm of so many other Marías she seemed the most credible, they invited her to appear live on the show. Crackpot or not, one Saturday morning she set out with Teresita to go on the air.

En route, María, pouting as she did whenever she contemplated the past, hardly said a word, as if she were saving herself for the interviewer, though she occasionally broke her silence over some landmark along the highway, her only utterances being "Eh" and *"Sí"* and *"Mira, allí."* Once they had pulled into the radio station parking lot, which like so many others lacked charm, María, feeling somewhat delighted, put on a show for the roly-poly entranceway guard. Crossing the lot, she broke out into an impromptu rumba, shaking her shoulders and hips as if she were a young girl again, and as if this fellow could possibly have known just who she happend to be. Her daughter sighed, and the roly-poly attendant broke out into the broadest ain't-that-just-like-my-grandma grin. It was under such circumstances that beautiful María, at the resilient age of sixty-two, *más o menos*, but still nicely put together, walked into the studio's greenroom, where she was to wait beside her daughter for an hour before going on.

The young producer handed her a cup of orange juice, which she gratefully accepted, though, to be honest, María, her nerves on edge, would have preferred a drink of rum. To her medically astute daughter's annoyance, she lit a cigarette *("Pero son Virginia Slims!")* and tapped her feet to the Cuban song the station was playing for its radio audience, *"El manicero,"* or "The Peanut Vendor," as performed by Antonio Machín, lead singer of the Don Azpiazú Havana Casino Orchestra, circa 1932, his emphatic voice blaring amicably through the studio's ceiling speakers. Aside from pointing to a basket of pastries and ordering "Pass me that one," then "No, that one," María had hardly a thing to say to Teresita, for when she felt nervous, María tended to descend into herself, her thoughts lost to the world. She passed the time looking over some *People* magazines while Teresita stayed busy rifling through a stack of hospital folders. A mind-bludgeoning block of advertisements and news stories about world and local events that hardly interested her boomed through the room, and then, finally, when she was nearly at the end of her patience, the producer escorted María into the broadcast booth.

There she took a seat before a foam-padded microphone, which, in its phallic bulk and the way it seemed to stare at her, she found both familiar and obtrusive. After a few more commercials, she waited for the host, this goateed fellow named Emilio Santos, to make his introduction.

As the segment began, he cued up a tape: it began with Marco Rizo's stirring theme for the *I Love Lucy* show and then slipped into Desi's introduction of the Castillo brothers as they had appeared on the mock stage of the program's Club Tropicana in the spring of 1956 to perform "Beautiful María of My Soul." With its violins, piano, and the uplifting harmonies of Nestor and Cesar Castillo, that bolero played in its entirety—some three minutes. María listened carefully and, hardly moving at all—she was just staring at her daughter seated in a corner—emanated both dignity and a sense of justly earned entitlement. Finally, it seemed, after so many years of obscurity, her moment was about to arrive.

"Compañeros, amigos, damas y caballeros," the host excitedly began. "I hope you are enjoying this lovely morning, and speaking of loveliness, for true beauty is never subject to the castigations of age, with us today is the one and only María Rivera, as she called herself for the stage. . . . If this name does not immediately ring any bells with my younger listeners, please go ask your *abuelos*—your grandfolks—about the 1956 bolero the original 'Beautiful María of My Soul,' a cherished song from *la Cuba que fue*. As my listeners know, we have been up to our necks with other Marías lately—what imaginations some of you ladies have!—but our visitor today, a most elegant and well-preserved woman, surely beautiful, has presented the station with undeniable proof of her claims—mainly letters from Nestor Castillo himself, and some wonderful photos that, well, it breaks one's heart to see, for this couple was obviously in love."

Turning his chair towards her and raising a hand as a cue, he said: *"Señora María García, muy, muy buenos días,* and thank you for coming on this show. So now, we can begin, yes?"

"Sí, señor."

But before she could say anything, he started reading from a sheet.

"A longtime resident of Miami, María García y Cifuentes hailed originally from our beloved province of Pinar del Río and moved to Havana proper during that city's golden age, in the late 1940s. There, she was a popular figure in the Havana club scene as a dancer." (He cleared his throat, seemingly suffering from a cold.) "Performing in some of the best clubs in those heady days before the greatest debacle of Cuban history took place, she also fell passionately in love with the composer of that most famous song. She, the one and only beautiful María herself, is here today to tell us her story."

María did not say a word for a few moments, the host prompting her. And then, for the next seven minutes, until a commercial break, she spoke slowly, serenely about her *valle,* her *papito,* and the little tragedies that led her to Havana even while the program's host, seemingly exasperated at times, kept interjecting, "But tell us, *señora,* about Nestor Castillo!"

She finally did, shrugging. "When I met Nestor, on the street where I lived in Havana, he just reminded me of those pure souls I knew from my childhood, the kind of fellow who would never hurt anyone intentionally—he was a romantic sort, loved to sing to me, loved to dream aloud in my presence." She sipped from a cup of water. "I knew no one else like him. He treated me as if I were made of gold, loved me as if there were no tomorrow—why I let him go to America without me, I cannot say. But he was the one, as the old songs say, who got away."

Then commercials, and the host, fearing that the segment might be dragging, took another approach. "Now that we're back, may I ask you a question about the movie, which I understand you've seen?"

"Of course."

"How did that feel to see yourself depicted on-screen?"

She shrugged. "It was okay. I liked the actress who played me well enough—a lovely *muchacha.* But it wasn't me, you understand. I just wish that someone would one day make a real story about us Cubans, by Cubans, for this country to see, *entiendes?*"

And that was all. Thanking María, the program's host, disappointed in his hope for a saucy story or two, bade her well and reminded his audience that they had just been listening to the real beautiful María, and to please refrain from further calls about the matter of her identity. As a concession to her appearance, he plugged her dance studio in Miami and made sure that she and Teresita left with two coffee mugs, emblazoned with the station's logo. On the drive back, María did not have much to say about the experience, except that she felt as if she had been trapped in a jar or, more graphically, that someone had shoved a *dedo*—a finger—up her *fundillo*—her ass.

"But, Mama, it was you who wanted to go on that show."

"I know," María told Teresita. "I was angry that so many women were claiming to be me. But you know what? Even as I sat there talking to that very nice man, I got the feeling I was wasting my time. None of us can go back. All those memories are what? Just little dreams."

Nevertheless, from that single radio interview, a lot of people became interested in the real María. *El Nuevo Herald,* stoking the nostalgic embers of its Cuban audience, did a feature article about her for its Sunday Arts supplement. A photograph of a much younger María, her shapely body posed upon a couch-size magenta seashell in one of those glittering showgirl's outfits, with a ridiculously high plumed fake-gem-studded hat piece balanced precariously atop her head, appeared on the front page. And, while they had provided a brief, more or less accurate biography of her life, along with some quotations, to María's greater satisfaction, they had ended the piece with one of the verses she had written in Luis's class: "If Cuba Were a Man." Cristina Saralegui, who had a very popular talk show on the Univision network, invited María on her program, and while María was most flattered by her interest, she felt too intimidated about appearing on camera and (possibly) shattering her image as an eternal beauty, so she reluctantly refused. Even Don Francisco, of *Sábado Gigante,* had someone on his staff call María to ask if she would be willing to attend a filming of his program out of Miami, just so he could introduce her from the audience. This she almost did but changed her mind at the last minute, suffering from a terrible headache, or so she claimed. But she agreed to appear alongside the actress Talisa Soto in a print advertisement for Europa perfume, shot in South Beach for a promotion about the "Two Marías, eternally graceful and fragrant." (The actress was very nice, and María liked the fact that Ms. Soto had brought along her charming Puerto Rican mother, and the fact that she, doted over and dressed up in a wonderful gown, did not come off badly in the photographs and was paid a two-thousand-dollar fee for her troubles.)

And in her neighborhood? From just that smattering of publicity, she became a most notable figure; a lot of folks along her street who never used to, suddenly invited María and Teresita in for Sunday dinners. (These she did not mind.) If there occurred any alarming incidents, they had to do with jealousy, when some women, recognizing her in downtown Miami, glanced at María enviously, as some used to back in Havana, and her notoriety induced more men, usually much older ones, to stare at her hopefully, though rarely with lust. (She had even been approached for autographs again!) This lasted for about six months, and in that time as a local celebrity, a silly period as far as Teresita was concerned, beautiful María rarely ventured from her home without putting on a pair of large black sunglasses, even at night, as if she were a movie star, and she had taken to wearing an enormous sunhat by day, with a florid silk scarf tied around its brim, its length trailing unmistakably behind her as if it were the tail of a kite.

But for all of that, and despite the fact that at least people now recognized her as the María of that song, María made the discovery that she simply didn't care about being better known. Her past life with Nestor, despite that song, that novel, that movie, was most splendidly preserved in the realm of her own memories.

What mattered to her the most? Her daughter, and her motherly concerns over Teresita's tepid and unromantic existence. While Teresa hardly paid attention to that notion, her workweeks proceeding routinely as before, María's own love life hadn't turned out too badly. Once she got used to the idea of Luis, despite his plainness, his bony body, his pocked, unsymmetrical face—those eyes that always seemed to be rheumy behind wire-rimmed glasses—she fell in love with another side of him. In fact, after a while, as in a fairy tale, the more beautiful María looked at Luis, the more his homeliness began to fall away. Though he seemed hardly anything like the handsome Nestor Castillo, with his liquid,

333

soulful eyes, María, after so many years of general indifference to men and of few expectations, came to think of that Ichabod Crane–looking Cuban as somewhat handsome. And, in time, given the little comforts she extracted from his presence, María ached more for his company.

For what it's worth, even Omar the cat, with his Oriental prescience, took a strong liking to that man, perhaps for his poetic soul. On many a night, as María slept in her bed with the homely Luis snoring occasionally by her side, that *gato* would slumber beside her, purring sweetly and approvingly, the pads of his soft paws set gently upon her face, no matter what María happened to be dreaming.

Two years later, on an April evening in 1994, something sad happened to Dr. Teresa: this nice kid, the son of Cubans, only twelve years old, had died on her ward, and Teresita, who had had the highest hopes for him—he'd lingered for three months, and whenever she could Teresita read to him from children's books and could not help but caress his brow whenever he gasped from pain—left the hospital feeling as if her life was sometimes intolerable. Even though she knew that, for all her successes, there was bound to be a heart-wrenching tragedy, all she wanted to do was get drunk that night. Riding her motorcycle, she had stopped off in a bar along the bay, the Sunset Cove, and after downing three double whiskeys, she began to wonder how her life might have turned out had she been born sixty years before, in Pinar del Río, like her mother. She decided that she would have ended up, in all likelihood, an ignorant, maybe happy *guajira*. Without worries, without such heavy responsibilities, and without having to look into the eyes of a child who was dying—what killed her the most was the fading sweetness she read in his pupils. She had a boss who, seeing the hard way she took such "episodes," suggested that Teresita consider general practice as an internist, but she, for the life of her, couldn't. Every now and then, as she told those kids they would be all right and felt the ebbing pulse of their soft hands in her own, their eyes, so hopeful and longing, she wanted to believe that all would be well. And at such moments of grief, Teresita daydreamed of another life, of being so good looking and shapely a *cubana* that she could see herself on the stage of a Havana nightclub, circa 1947, performing, for all her mother's complaints, in so seductive a fashion as to keep an audience of horny men enthralled. But that hadn't been her fate at all.

During her fourth whiskey, she had to laugh: over the club's jukebox had come a version of the movie's "Beautiful María of My Soul," as performed by a group called Los Lobos. And that was enough for Teresita to finish her drink and leave: not because she hadn't found it more or less pleasant but because it had nothing to do with the version she, with her Cuban pride, had grown up with. Wobbly enough, she left a five-dollar bill on the bar and then, heading out, even while in some corners of that flashy bar couples were fondling and kissing one another, mocking her solitary state, Dr. Teresita, beautiful María's daughter, her helmet on, raced home, almost wiping out on the highway.

MARÍA WAS SITTING BEFORE THEIR GLORIOUS THIRTY-TWO-INCH RCA color TV watching a *telenovela* when, as Teresita walked in, she said the following: "Tell me, *chica,* what's with you? Don't you remember that we're leaving for New York tomorrow?"

It was then that Teresita, with so many other things on her mind, recalled that she was due the next afternoon, a Saturday, in Manhattan at an oncological conference, the two of them to stay at the Grand Hyatt hotel by Grand Central Terminal. "Of course," she said to her mother.

"So you should pack a suitcase tonight, yes?"

"I know."

María, in the glow of the television's screen, added, "And bring a nice dress. We're going to a party after all."

"A party, what's that about?"

"*Por Dios,* don't you remember that *yo no sé qué cubano,* that fellow Hijuelos, who wrote that book?"

"*Sí, mamá.*"

"Well, I called him, and when I told him we were coming to *Nueva York,* he invited us to a fiesta, that's all. *Una fiesta de cubanos.*"

. . .

THEY FLEW UP TO NEW YORK ON A 7 A.M. FLIGHT, ARRIVING AT LA Guardia about ten thirty, then checking in to the Hyatt. Later, as María strolled north on Fifth Avenue to Central Park, shopping along the way (she had her daughter's credit card), Teresita spent her time in an auditorium on West Fifty-seventh Street, attending a series of lectures about the neurological terrors and cancers that could, out of the blue, blight children. A cocktail party took place at four. When she came back, exhausted, to their hotel room at about six thirty, the last thing Teresita wanted to do was to head out again. But María insisted; after all, she said, "The author himself has invited us."

IT WAS A FEW HOURS LATER THAT MARÍA AND HER DAUGHTER made their way uptown by taxi—the subways were not for María—to a building in the West Eighties and a rambling first-floor affair of some seven rooms, the domicile of none other than Chico O'Farrill, famed composer of Afro-Cuban jazz, whose songs María had often heard in the clubs back in Havana. He was standing by the front door and could not have been friendlier—in fact, he told María that she seemed awfully familiar to him somehow. Had she ever been to Mexico City? Or Havana? And for a few minutes they got to talking about Cuba, and the Havana club scene before Fidel—"I was a dancer back when," she told him. And he snapped his fingers—it seemed that he was about to place her—but then, before they could go on with this chitchat, so many other folks came streaming in through the front door that, with Teresita feeling a little tired, they just went inside, entering an immense living room jammed with people, their numbers exaggerated by their reflections in the mirror-tiled walls.

So what happened?

Lingering by a buffet table, after moving through a crowd that included many a mambo luminary of the day, beautiful María, Teresita by her side, happened to spot, across the room, Hijuelos, long ago adopted by the O'Farrill clan as one of their own, walking in with a friend, a tall and handsome fellow whose intensely dark eyes and melancholy expression so reminded María of Nestor Castillo that for a moment she could hardly get her breath. What else could María do but wave to get the author's attention? Not long after he had come over to greet them—"I'm so happy you could make it," he said—María, beside herself with curiosity, just had to ask, "And who is that *caballero* standing over there in the corner?"

"Well," he said. "Guess I should introduce you."

So, with María waving her over, Teresita made her way across that bustling room, and shortly found herself standing before that rather self-effacing fellow, who had just been contentedly taking things in.

"This lady here is *la Señora* María García—the one I told you about, who knew your *papi* long ago," Hijuelos said to his friend. "And this is her daughter, Teresa."

He just smiled and nodded meekly.

"In any event, this is my childhood pal, *un amigo de hace tiempo*, Eugenio Castillo."

"*Encantada,*" said María, smiling as if she were seeing Nestor again.

"*Encantada,*" said Teresita.

Like a gentleman, he shook their hands, told each in a soft voice, "*Con mucho gusto,*" without being so bold as to engage their eyes directly.

With that, he had to put up with María's onslaught of compliments: "But, my God, you look like your father! But taller and, I think, even better looking, if that's possible!" Then, as Eugenio Castillo sipped from his drink and simply nodded, as if such words were meaningless, beautiful María turned around to find their hostess, Lupe O'Farrill, standing by her side. Once their acquaintance had been made, she led María away to introduce her around, and Hijuelos went off to get some *lechón*, leaving his friend Eugenio Castillo to converse alone with Teresa.

And what did they talk about? It was not as if each was unaware of their parents' importance to one another: Eugenio had grown up with that song about beautiful María incessantly in his ears, and along the way he had occasionally heard his mother, long since remarried, wistfully lamenting just how much that song, about another woman, had bugged her. But his *papi*'s death had taken place so long ago that his mother's anguish seemed overblown to him, in a Cuban manner. ("Oh, she gets hysterical sometimes.")

"When my best friend wrote that novel and put me in it, as the narrator, I was pissed off," he said bluntly. "But you know what? I figured he meant well, and what the hell, he brought my *papito* back to life. But at first, it was rough." He wiped a fleck of dust from his nose. "And for you?"

"It was very weird. *Muy extraño*," she told him. "But, you know, my mother, María, doesn't seem to mind that she was put in a book, even when she thinks the author got rich."

He nodded, smiling, and shifted his lanky frame, perhaps feeling that in Teresa he had found a kindred spirit.

AN HOUR LATER, AFTER MARÍA HAD MEANDERED THROUGH THAT apartment, chatting with folks and recognizing, vaguely, as she passed from one hallway into another, Tito Puente, and Ray Barretto, and the American character actor Matt Dillon, a mambo fanatic, holding forth in a cramped vestibule, she plumped down on a leather couch to listen, entirely surrounded by mirrors, to a Cuban-style salon, her face reflecting back at her a hundred times over. With the very dapper and gentlemanly Marco Rizo, Desi Arnaz's former arranger, sitting before an upright piano playing the melodies of Ernesto Lecuona, Cuba's Gershwin, if such a comparison can be made, none other than Celia Cruz herself, a most down-to-earth lady, slipped out of the crowd and began to sing, her lovely voice filling the room.

As María felt comfortable, almost to the point of slumber against the couch's soft leather cushions, she had looked around to see if Eugenio Castillo and her daughter were still conversing. Fortunately—as she hoped—they were, that gallant, his head bowed low as if in reverence to

Teresita, whispering tenderly to her and smiling, as if he had stepped out of a dream.

FOR THE RECORD, EUGENIO CASTILLO AND TERESA GARCÍA, HAV-ing met at that party, maintained contact over the next few years. Now and then, when the telephone rang at around nine thirty at night and María answered, with a melodious *"Aquí!"* it was that schoolteacher Eugenio Castillo, asking, in his measured voice, if he might speak to her daughter. Every so often, on the weekends, Teresita would feel the sudden compulsion to go off to New York, where that *buenmozo's* companionability and, perhaps, his affections awaited her. (*"Por Dios*, if he's anything like his *papi!"*) And María? Oh, she still ached over her memories of that *músico* from Havana—and for so many other things. It was as if her heart would never allow her mind to forget. But as Nestor Castillo himself, may God preserve his soul, might have put it, even those *delicious pains* began to slowly fade. For in the course of María's ordinary days, so unnoticed by the world, she and Luis became as close as any sacrosanct couple, fornicating occasionally, and, in the wake of such intimacy, mostly listening to each other's verses, which, as it turned out, were nothing more than songs of love.